XENATION:

DRAW THE LINE

By

Lazette Gifford

Copyright 2015 Lazette Gifford

An ACOA Publication

www.aconspiracyofauthors.com

When humans found the abandoned -- and ancient -- space station, they moved in to study the place they called Xeno-Station, and then shortened to Xenation. Following them came three other races, all intent on learning secrets. Only now one of the humans has a dangerous link to the heart and controls of this alien place, and he's learning there are secrets and dangers no one imagined.

Xenation: Draw the Line
A Conspiracy of Authors Publication
www.aconspiracyofauthors.com
Copyright 2015, Lazette Gifford
ISBN: 978-1-936507-56-6
Cover Art Design Copyright 2015, Lazette Gifford
Cover Art: Ron's Space Brushes, available at DAZ3D.com

First Print Edition, August 2015

For C. J. Cherryh and Jane Fancher who have been wonderful inspirations and role models.

Thank you to the people in chat at Forward Motion who cheer every writer on, knowing how difficult the job can be even when we love it.

And for Russ, who has always been wonderful and supportive of my special insanity.

There hath gone up a cry from earth, a groaning for the fall

Of things of old renown and shapes majestical

Prometheus Bound, Aeschylus

CHAPTER ONE

Morgan Michael Doreet had prepared himself *not* to be impressed with the station, despite his appointment as the head of the science team stationed there. He'd read everything he could about the place from the first reports (when most of the news teams dismissed the find as an elaborate hoax) to the last reports sent a couple months ago by the science team based on the station. The surprise of finding an abandoned alien space station had given way to annoyed frustration. The station remained, for the most part, closed to the science teams. Everyone lived in the only area accessible, a small band along the edge, while the station kept its secrets behind impenetrable walls.

Oh, there were still interesting *things* to be found on the station anyway. If nothing else, the unusual company proved odd enough. In the narrow habitable area, the station accommodated humans, Norishi, Ksa and even a few Click, bringing together four alien races who normally wouldn't live in such close proximity although they shared an affinity in habitats. That they had all taken up residence to study the station seemed far more noteworthy than the scanty reports on the makeup of the station's structure.

Soft bells chimed to draw attention as the captain announced they were coming off the slide path and into real space. Morgan leaned forward, waiting for the first glimpse of his new home . . . this place at another edge of exploration where humans went to see what they could find, because curiosity was their worst -- and best -- trait.

The *Blue Star* came out of slide, slipping nicely from the path of dull red and bright yellow lines and into the cold darkness of real space again. The pilot had a good touch without any of the sudden drop-and-lurch back to reality that he'd felt on the last craft. They arrived relatively close to the station, there not being much of a gravity well to worry about here. Morgan stood on the View Deck and blinked as real space came into focus.

The station looked blocky, which was not the shape a space station should be by human standards. He caught a hint of grayish-green color from the glowing surface, created by self-rejuvenating phosphorescent bacteria in the walls; he had read those reports. Altogether, the station appeared dull and unpretentious despite its unusual origins.

Then he began to realize the *size*. Not just know the abstract numbers in a report but to actually comprehend what those numbers meant. The small glowing bubbles he barely saw at this distance were grow-domes tethered to the larger station. Each one held one hundred acres of land but they looked like tiny peas set against the edge of the station.

While Morgan tried to accept what he saw, he noticed a movement off to the left. While he watched, a huge dark block of the station rose, narrowed, turned and rebuilt itself near the area where humans, Norishi, Ksa and Click lived.

Seeing the station -- truly comprehending the size, power and *alien-ness* -- finally took his breath away. Xeno Station, or Xenation as the people stationed here called the place, turned out to be far more impressive than he had expected. Frighteningly so for the man who came to take over the science section. People at the Inner Worlds Council back on Mars expected him to find answers.

One of the *Blue Star* crew, her grey and blue uniform neat, stepped up beside him. She stared for a moment, and then shook her head. Yellow and blue curls bounced up and down and her dark face creased with a look of trepidation.

"There's been a lot of changes since the last time we were here half a year ago," she said. "More blocks out here towards the edge. Maybe that means the station is going to open new areas?"

"Maybe," he agreed, and wondered if he should hope so. New areas would be an important coup when he took over from Samplin, who had resigned to go back home. Samplin would be leaving with the *Blue Star* in a couple days. This was going to be a quick changeover, but that didn't worry Morgan. "Have you seen the station make this kind of change before?"

"This is the second time I've seen it happen." She frowned, leaning closer to the screen, her thin arms resting on the bar that ran across this side of the long, narrow room. This wasn't really a window but they did a damned good job of making it look like one. "I've made six trips in the last four years. I don't know. Just looks like the place has been more active since the last time. A lot more bulges, a lot more blocks. I don't know if I like it."

She gave one last shake of her head and headed away. He tried not to let her attitude worry him.

Morgan remained to watch through the rest of the approach. The ship headed inwards on a slight curve and didn't noticeably slow until they reached the grow domes: bubble-topped and crowned with solar panels capturing ambient light from the distant bright blue star that claimed this system. The domes stayed tethered to the bulk of the station by long filaments of bonding cords which snaked their way through the dark, glittering with the trace lights to keep the few craft from snaring them. They made a pretty spider web of tiny stars. Part of the dome had a clear covering allowing for the capture of even more of the ambient energy and making the enclosures into self-sustaining eco-systems. As the *Blue Star* went by, he had a close view of what looked like a wheat field, the stalks waving slightly in an artificially created wind. A little farther on workers swarmed over an infrastructure, putting together another dome to help support the expanding human population. So far, the other three races seemed content to have their food imported, but humans liked to be self-sufficient wherever they went.

Morgan saw movement to the right and caught a glimpse of a greenish Click ship leaping out from the station like a small round ball tossed aside by a giant. In the next breath the craft darted into slide drive so quickly his breath caught, expecting an explosion and disaster. Instead he only saw a little flash of red as the ship disappeared onto the slide path.

Another thing he'd read about but never actually seen.

Almost immediately he spotted a long thin Norishi ship pulling out from a dock to the left and lower down. He watched as the craft moved past; jet-black, arrow-shape, and without a show of any of the weapons for which the Norishi were so well known. He wished the Norishi hadn't made a base at Xenation, but the aliens appeared determined to make certain of their presence wherever humans and Ksa settled.

Which, from all he could tell, was very odd since the Norishi apparently hated all races except their own. The Norishi had secrets, too. In all the contacts, both friendly and unfriendly, not a single male had been spotted, even though the females appeared to be very close to human females in appearance and in physiology. At least that was the rumor but since no one admitted to doing a real examination of one of the dead, he couldn't be certain. Such an admission could start an interstellar war, and the Norishi were trouble enough already.

Morgan would much rather not have them around. They complicated matters in an already unstable situation. Everyone here dealt with far too much politics, which he generally detested, whether alien or human.

"Five minutes to docking. Please go to the nearest seating."

Morgan gave one last glance to the screen and crossed to the seats where he still had a good view of the station as they moved closer. The other passengers were apparently holed up in their suites but he'd wanted more than the small computer screen view when he arrived. This would be home though he couldn't say for how long.

Morgan felt the maneuvering jets fire and saw the ship's angle change slightly as they ran with their side to the ship, leaving him with a view along the edge, staring out at a far distant star and the faint trail of a comet, barely visible to the eye. Debris of all sorts littered the area around the station, giving rise to speculation about a planetary system that might have been here once. Some suggested a very old and devastating war but no one had found signs of any sort of battle.

Who knew what secrets Xenation still held?

Morgan saw a slight ripple of movement along the station wall, followed by a slight bump before they stopped. He had expected something far more violent since they were not matching speed to a spinning station like they would have with anything human. Instead, the station itself caught and held them, somehow bleeding off acceleration from one heartbeat to the next. The ship came to a gentle stop.

Damn, if they could get their hands on any of the technology that ran this station --

Which, of course, was a big part of his job. People back at the Inner Worlds Council wanted at least some of the power represented by this station though they were getting wise enough to know they couldn't walk in and grab a few things. Samplin had come in with that attitude and two years later gladly let the position go to someone else.

Nearly everyone who came to Xenation expected to make their name and fortune here. In some ways, Morgan felt the same way. He wanted to believe he would be the one to break open the secrets, explore farther into the station, and come out again with the answers.

However, he admitted he also took the position because this was an unusual place and far from the crowds on the Inner Worlds and the continual oversight of politically-connected supervisors who wanted findings to coincide with whatever pet theory they wanted to promote. Despite the local politics of four different species, Xenation would give him peace to study the station itself and maybe time to work on other projects as well.

He didn't need to worry about the human politics here. He had known Station Master Neva NiGwen for years before Neva and Ashur, her late husband, came in the first wave of humans to settle and explore the station. Morgan knew he could work with her. He tried not to worry about the Norishi and Ksa. The Click were just there; people worked around them.

The captain announced they had docked and people could leave the ship. Morgan had been staring at the side of the station where swirls of bacteria brightened and faded. He reluctantly left the view and went back to his room where he gathered up his personal bag. His few other crates would be sent out by the crew. There were only a dozen other passengers on the ship and he was the only one stopping here permanently. He had only met a few of others in passing because he'd tied himself to a computer and studied every Xenation report he'd grabbed back on Earth before being shipped here. This wasn't where he had expected to be going and he hadn't been prepared.

Two months in transit had helped. He'd read everything four times over. He could have written a book on Xenation by now, without ever setting foot on it.

However. . . .

The more he read of the reports, the more he had felt as though *something* was missing. The reports seemed to lack the enthusiasm he would have expected in an endeavor of this kind, even given some of the frustrations. He'd worked on newly settled colonies a few times and he saw none of the same reactions here.

He appeared to be the last of the passengers heading out, the others to spend a few hours wandering the strange station. The captain, a short pleasant man, stood by the door as everyone left, a nice service, not often seen on the smaller craft running out on the edge of humanity's turf. The double doors of the airlock stood open, but he could see little except a distant wall beyond. There was already a difference in the air on the ship as it took in the atmosphere from Xenation.

"Welcome to your new home, Etech Doreet. I assume you are not trying to carry a powered weapon of any sort onto the station?"

"No, I'm not. I know better." He noted the scanner that blinked green on the wall by the door. "Do people still try?"

"Just removed two laser pistols from the group ahead of you," Captain Ness said with a nod towards the open airlock doors. "I didn't expect you to be that stupid, but I'm required to ask."

"Have you ever had someone get past you?" he asked, pausing even though he was anxious to see the station.

"Not me. Did talk to one Captain a couple years ago who let someone through. He had to stop making the run. The station won't let the ship dock anymore. I don't want to take that chance."

He'd heard of that happening with ships but hadn't been sure he believed it until now. There were enough odd rumors about Xenation that it was hard to tell the real from the imagined. This pointed to the station having considerable intelligence of some sort. He held back a shiver and looked out at the shadowed area beyond the ship.

"Is this a profitable run?" he asked.

"Better than most out here at the edge." He gave a bright smile. "This is the only place a free trader can have direct contact with the Ksa and Click. We don't pick up much, but any little item can bring a profit."

"And the Norishi?"

"We don't deal with the Norishi," he replied with a quick shake of his head. "Or rather, they won't deal with us. We have gotten a couple Norishi things but only through the Ksa. And everything is approved through the Station Master, by the way. They have a great open market here."

Doreet nodded, but his attention had finally turned to the area beyond the airlock. Xenation was already a place steeped in mythology. He was a modern day Shaman, come to see if he could make connection with the powers of the past.

"Good luck with your work, Etech."

"Thank you." He pulled the strap of his bag up over his shoulder, and headed out of the airlock.

The first thing he noticed was what he often did on new worlds: the taste of the air. He had the full feel of it now that he was outside the *Blue Star*. Most stations had a filtered taste, either good or bad depending on how well the system worked. Stepping from this ship to the station brought something entirely unexpected. The air had a slight taste like unripe green apples. Not unpleasant, at least.

Then he noticed that the docks, unlike those on any other station he'd visited, were not bitterly cold. The gravity was no problem, either. The *Blue Star* had been adjusting the gravity to match Xenation's since they left the last port, so he felt comfortable walking here.

Lights hung on tall poles and illuminated the area in intersecting circles on the metal floor but still left the very high ceiling lost in shadows. Spots glowed on the dark walls in both bright and muted colors as though a rainbow had spattered itself across the area. Self-sustaining bacteria, he reminded himself. Some of it glowed in spectrums humans couldn't see.

Just bacteria. Just light. But damn, the pattern looked like art to him; and like many others who had stepped into the station, he felt a whisper of kinship between humans and the long-gone aliens who had built Xenation. The colors made him feel oddly comfortable.

For the most part, the station was built of normal materials, though; the metals had been mined from the system. Humans did the same thing when they built their own stations.

Something squeaked and bounded towards him. Morgan stepped back in haste as a brown, furry ball swept past and another not far behind. He recognized the Click's nuisance pets, which he had read were often loose on the station. These were slightly larger than a beach ball and he could see a couple short, thin limbs as one creature grabbed a nearby pole and rushed upwards. About midway to the top the animal leapt off into the shadows and he couldn't see where it went.

A moment later the pet dropped, perhaps a fall of two floors or more, and landed a few yards from him. Before Morgan could react, the creature scrambled back to his feet and darted away, apparently no worse for the landing.

This was his first encounter with *anything* alien. He watched the pet disappear into an area off to the right, darting between two poles where a sign with red glowing letters saying *Market* hung between them. In a moment, the pet disappeared amid the makeshift booths.

The market had sprung up between the human and Ksa areas since both groups were trading people. The Ksa -- and the Norishi -- looked human enough that he couldn't tell one from the other at this distance and in the poor light, but he still stared for a long moment while his heart pounded a little harder.

Closer at hand and on the left he found something far more familiar and somewhat comforting. The dockside work yard, with various pieces of equipment torn apart and laid out, made the odd port seem normal . . . until one of the Click pets bounded through the area. A woman with wild orange and pink hair dropped a wrench and dived at the animal, catching the creature by the fur and lifting him off the ground.

"Give it back," she said over the clinks and clanks all around them. She gave the creature a little shake. "Give it back *now*."

Limbs appeared and something square dropped into her outstretched hand. She leaned over and set the pet back on the ground and gave the little guy the kind of friendly pat you would give to a not-so-well-trained puppy. The pet gave one slight bounce, spun and started away. The woman watched for a moment as she shoved the stolen box into her pocket and unexpectedly gave three quick claps.

The pet spun and bounded back to her. Now that was *damned* interesting.

"This is for you." She pulled a wrench out of her pocket. The pet quivered with excitement as he stretched upward and she put the wrench into the creature's hands. She clapped once and the creature squeaked and flipped before he darted away.

Odd thing to give to an animal but he could see the others at the work yard looked pleased. One slapped her on the shoulder. "Well done, Felice! Let's see if it turns up in the market!"

She smiled, noticed Morgan for the first time, and gave a little nod before going back to work. He wanted to know what that exchange had been about, but he'd wait until he had some official standing here. They might have simply told him, but he wanted people to understand he wasn't someone passing through.

As a scientist, the entire exchange intrigued him from the initial 'give it back' to the clapping which seemed to have some sort of communicative significance. He felt a chill go up his arms; a feeling he always got when he found something fascinating he didn't quite understand.

The pet had gone and the humans returned to their work, clanging on metal and using small torches to make repairs. He hadn't considered how they would have had to go back to the basics without laser-powered tools, though he did see a few with small power packs. A small tank fueled the torch and he wondered where they got the gas for it. Maybe mined it nearby. This was a rich system for gasses and minerals.

So much to learn. Most people wouldn't understand why the idea made him grin.

His eyes had begun to adjust somewhat. To the right of the market he could see the Ksa and then the Click zones, clearly marked with signs high up on the walls, and written in several languages. Ahead, he could see a signs proclaiming the human zone.

To the left beyond the work yard would be the Norishi Enclave. Two guards stood there in the inevitable grey and brown outfits they all wore. Short haired, medium height -- at a distance they seemed very human. The Norishi were notoriously unfriendly, though.

All but the market and the human area were red zoned to humans. Trying to cross uninvited into an alien area would get a human locked up in the makeshift detention and shipped off with the next transport, whatever it might be. The human area held the same restrictions to the aliens, but the humans tended to be more lavish with invitations.

Between the market and the entrance to the human section stood a makeshift building, put together from bits of colorful plastic crates. Light came from inside and a little laughter. The sign read *Xenobia Bar and Grill.*

Morgan headed towards the welcoming sounds. He wanted a place to sit and take in the feel of Xenation. Besides, he knew better than to rush into the science department and upset the situation when they would only now be hearing about the changeover. Samplin wanted out, so that wouldn't be a problem, but he couldn't be certain how much Samplin had told the others. Best to let the man handle the changeover in his own way. Morgan would have time enough to strut in and flex his muscles.

He heard a commotion behind him just before he reached Xenobia's door. The wild-haired woman jogged past him with a nod and stopped at the opening. "Rafe, you here? We have problems!"

Almost immediately a tall, thin young man with long, dark hair came out the door. Morgan didn't think this could be the infamous Rafael Karim until he saw the metal plate melded to the left side of his face, a graceful curve of silver and blue that arched under his eye, across his cheek and up to the ear, disappearing into the hairline.

Morgan watched him go past thinking Rafael might be as interesting as the station itself. Rafael Karim had survived the only major disaster on Xenation and he had lived because the station saved him, grafted the metal link to his face, and sent him back to work with the others. The link supposedly kept him tied to . . . whatever ran the station. Rafe claimed not to know.

More than two hundred others had died in the accident. Or maybe they hadn't.

Morgan hadn't expected his first look at the Displaced to happen within minutes of stepping on the station. Reports said they rarely showed themselves but he could see the gathering of swirling white and color moving near the dark ceiling and rushing down towards the work yard.

The lights began to dim on the poles and he felt a chill -- a real chill -- in the air. Others came from Xenobia and a few from the market gathered to watch. No one looked happy.

Morgan followed Rafe to the work yard though he kept back at the line with the others who had gathered. Rafael circled the area where waves of color, mostly pale reds and oranges, began to coalesce into sinewy shapes. Morgan could see an odd reflection on the metal plate on his face -- or perhaps the surface glowed. Rafael put a hand to the surface and winced, but he shook his head and finally stepped closer to the colorful show.

The colors began to take on forms and shapes. Morgan thought they didn't look so much like the traditional gauzy description of ghosts but more like holographs with badly tuned lighting.

He looked for the projector and wondered if maybe the Click pet had planted one up towards the ceiling where he couldn't see. Another of the pets had been in the work yard and could have placed a receiver there as well.

He had heard the pets were loose in the bay area, and sometimes even wandered into the Human Enclave. Having them set this up was an easy answer. Unfortunately, he also knew easy answers were rarely the real ones.

A flash of light drew his attention back to the drama before him. Rafael had his hands up and the ghosts swarmed in as they moved closer to him. Not ghosts. The locals called them the Displaced. No one knew quite what the station had done (if the station really did create this illusion), but theory said they had taken those who surely would have died in the one big disaster and pulled them . . . somewhere else, a place which might be slightly out of this reality. They did not find bodies and very little debris, but some of the science department thought everything had been disintegrated by

Xenation to avoid damage.

According to the reports, the Displaced began to appear a few days later. Rafael's link gave him some sort of control over the apparitions -- if you believed the stories.

Some thought this a hoax. Station Master Neva NiGwen didn't believe in the Displaced or Rafael's control and since she had been here at the time of the accident, he tended to agree with her.

This made a good show though, and probably very entertaining for the locals who were stuck out here with very little to do but work. He watched as Rafael lifted a hand again, and wondered how he got the effect that made his hair flow out like a wind blew past him when there was none on the deck.

The lights dimmed more and the area grew decidedly colder. Then a light flashed within the swirl of colors, which had grown richer with blues, greens and lines that seemed almost black though they glowed. The light flashed again with a quick strobe of brilliant white, and Rafael took a sudden step backwards with one hand going to his chest.

"Son of a bitch," the wild-haired woman whispered. He saw her pull up her wrist and hit the commlink she wore. "Yang? This is Felice. Rafe is going to need you. We have some really annoying Displaced down at the work yards again."

The lighting grew dimmer all across the area and added a bluish caste to the scene. Rafael stood in a mass of Displaced, apparently holding them back from something while they grew more persistent. Morgan could *almost* hear words and still looked around for a projector. There had to be sign of one somewhere. Morgan also listened to the nervous whispers from the people who watched. He would have thought, living here, that they'd be used to the show by now.

"I hope he gets them in hand pretty soon," another woman said. "Otherwise we're going to be in for a long cold time before we can regain heat and power. I don't want to go through that again."

People gave nods and grunts of agreement. Morgan didn't remember reading anything about power loss associated with these reports. Perhaps this was a recent development. It would take a lot of manipulation to drop the temp and the lighting in an area this large, though. He found himself intrigued by how anyone managed it.

Golden light flashed as one of the Displaced wrapped itself around a tool with a power cube. The figure brightened and others swept in, as though to suck off the power. Rafael cut between them, and reached into the mass of light as people on the dock made new sounds of worry. He yanked the power cube back away.

Morgan saw Medtech Yang arrive at a run, recognizing him both from his blue uniform and from the face in the files he'd studied. The man came to a breathless stop next to Morgan and stood there, shaking his head.

"Still at it?" he asked, looking worried.

"Still at it," Felice answered. She ran a hand through her orange and pink hair and looked worried. "Let's hope he gets help soon."

"What happens if he loses?" Morgan asked.

"They suck down all the power they can find, ruin equipment and make life miserable," Yang replied. He frowned. "And you are?"

"Morgan Doreet, the new head of the science section."

The introduction drew quick glances of surprise and worry from some of the people, but Yang only nodded.

"Well, we'll have time to talk later," Yang said. "Right now I have to concentrate on my problem child."

Those words brought a sprinkling of laughter, though the sound hinted at worry. Morgan could now see his breath and the lights went almost dead around them as the Displaced grew brighter. He wished he had sensor equipment in hand, though he noticed the Yang did. He would want to see those readings later, after the show.

"Come on, Xenation, baby," Felice whispered. She shoved her hands into her pockets, and scrunched up her shoulders, obviously cold. "We need help here."

The medtech moved closer to Rafael who waved him away. Yang didn't go closer, but he held his place, even when a couple of the Displaced figures began to move his way.

"No," Rafael said quite clearly. "No, it's not him you want."

The words drew them back.

"What would happen if they decided to go to Yang instead?" Morgan asked.

"Hard to say," Felice answered. He could see goose bumps on her arms, and was glad he had on a long-sleeved shirt. "The last guy went into a coma for nearly four days. Then he left Xenation and said he'd never come back. Damn shame. He was a good tech."

So good that he might have found answers Rafe didn't want him to know? Was he chased off?

Morgan was still considering the possibility when he thought he felt a sudden change. A moment later the glowing spots in the wall nearby began to brighten and a slightly warmer breeze blew past him. He looked over his shoulder, trying to figure out where it originated.

"Finally," Felice said. "I thought Xenation had gone to sleep on us."

The faint scent of green apples grew stronger for a moment, mingling with something less identifiable. The air warmed by several degrees which proved to be almost too much at once. Morgan felt the edge of a headache try to take him but he fought the feeling down. He didn't want anything to interfere with his perception of this entire business.

He had expected the Displaced to just disappear, but something far stranger happened. He felt little waves of wind slip past him and as each blast moved inward, something invisible seemed to grab one of the ghostly figures and drag it away from the others. The Displaced fought the movement, but they apparently had less power as individuals rather than a whole. The lights on the poles brightened. People began to nod and move off, looking relieved. Only Felice stayed where she was, watching Rafael and the medtech.

When almost all of the Displaced were gone, Rafael

went down to his knees, his part in the show over. Morgan
wanted to head into Xenobia and do some quick notes on
what he had seen, as well as the incident with the Click pet
leading up to it. He didn't think he would find anything
particularly helpful. He didn't remember seeing anything
about the pets in earlier reports. Had people gotten so used
to seeing them that they didn't even consider their actions
anymore? Not likely in a settlement made almost entirely of
scientists.

He watched as the medtech got Rafael back to his feet.
He looked unsteady, and in the better light, Morgan could
see a line of blood running beneath the edge of the metal
graft. A couple Displaced still hovered nearby and Rafael
reached out towards one, as thought to call it back. Yang
took hold of his arm and pulled it down while saying
something too quiet for Morgan to hear. Rafael bowed his
head this time and Yang had trouble holding him to his feet.
Felice came to help.

Only one displaced still remained, circling and drifting
towards Rafael. The shape turned and started away . . . and
then came to Morgan.

The apparition stopped before him, diaphanous and
undulating with the warm breeze. Morgan looked up . . .
and into the face of an old friend: Ashur, Neva's husband.

The hair stood up on the back of Morgan's neck and his
heart pounded too hard. Unsettling, even the way Ashur
turned his head, nodded in the old way he always had. The
Displaced smiled and then began to drift away and Morgan
had the urge to try and call him back, to try and understand -
-

No.

This could not be real. He looked to where the other
two took Rafael away and reminded himself off all the
reports Neva had sent him. Rafael played tricks. This was
some kind of game, probably cooked up with the help of
some of his alien friends; that was what Neva said.

Morgan would find the real answers, no matter how
hard Rafael tried to hide them. He remembered everything

Neva had written. . . .

But he had looked into the face of an old friend, and Morgan suspected this was not entirely what he had been led to believe.

CHAPTER TWO

H uman capacity limited.
Human population exceeds base.
Dictionary on, language comparison on.
Duplicate, codify.
Language install, preliminary.
Xs+Yz, max z crystal barrier x y.
Autochange.
Complete.
Recheck data.
Rebuild.
Complete.
Begin atmospheric recycle.
Scan.
Recheck.
Complete.
Disturbance.
Rebuild Complete.
Function reset null.
Auto reset.
Instructions.
Await Key.

CHAPTER THREE

Rafael remembered going to his knees on the hard, cold floor by the work yard. The area smelled of plastic, metal and coolant which proved to be an odd, overlaying human sensation. When he briefly closed his eyes, the scents made him think of being somewhere else entirely.

And that made him wish he had never come to this damned station.

Rafe heard whispers and almost words, but pain rose through the side of his head and blocked out everything but the need to be calm and make everything go away. He had pushed the Displaced back from the tools and especially from the power packs, which they would drain. They couldn't afford to lose any more equipment which took months to replace.

The rest of the area around him had gone dark except where he looked into the mass of Displaced.

"No. Not today," he whispered, though even those words had sounded too loud. The Displaced were memories of another time, and they would not get past him today. If he stepped aside, if he let them take what they wanted, then it would be too easy to step aside the next time. The Displaced would win.

Did anyone care what this confrontation cost him?

Maybe not, but he cared for the people who would suffer for his weakness. So he held his ground and tried to convey to Xenation that he really, *seriously* needed help here. And it came, finally, only a few heartbeats before he would have collapsed. He felt the first tingle of warmth and shivered both at the cold it chased away and because the wind came to his call. His face hurt and the sounds in his head grew louder while the echoes on the dock melded into a scream of noise that tried to tear at him apart. He almost lost his hold on the Displaced, but he kept his hands up and warded them away with the power Xenation had given him, little though he understood it.

Faces. People he had known. Ashur, looking at him and giving a little shake of his head as though --

He didn't know what the Displaced wanted. He didn't know what they were except that they had faces of friends long lost and they haunted him. He wanted to give them everything they sought because he had survived and they hadn't.

They disappeared, one at a time, sucked away in little whirlwinds. Each one that left lessened the drain on the systems and on him. The lights began to glow brighter, which was no help for Rafe since it doubled his headache. He welcomed the warmth, though. The walls glowed with splotches of light, and he thought he saw patterns in the darker colors: circles like black ice and a couple squares of a deep rich blue that might mean something, but it hurt to look and to think.

He wanted to rest. He wanted to be someone other than the person who had to come out to deal with the Displaced and to look into the faces of lost friends. Most of the people on the station were new since the accident. They didn't really understand the full depth of what he did here which brought him both pain of the body and the soul.

Ashur, as usual, was the last to leave. He drifted away and paused for a moment to look at someone on the edge of the crowd. Rafael, released from the duty to protect others, went down on both hands and started to lie down and curl up --

Yang arrived.

"Come on. Let's get somewhere I can look you over," Yang said, taking hold of his arm.

"Leave me alone. Let me rest."

"Not here." Yang pulled him upwards. He didn't cooperate, for all the good that would do him. "Come on. You can't rest here. People have to get back to work."

Rafael wondered why he always tried to argue. He never won. Yang pulled him up and Felice moved in to help, carefully putting an arm around his waist. She looked worried so he tried to offer her a smile, but it felt as though half his face -- the part around the metal --didn't work.

He thought Yang would take him to the labs, but instead he headed into Xenobia, which cheered him up a bit. Rafe hated the labs and the equipment there, as well as the constant repetition of test-after-test that never showed anything different.

So he stopped arguing as the two took him across the open space where the warm breeze still blew and into the café. Too loud! He almost collapsed at the sound of the music blaring. Yang said something to Buris who immediately cut the sound system off. People stopped shouting and the noises became a dull and almost pleasant wave of sound that washed over him as Yang got him into a chair. He gave a nod to Felice as she patted him on the shoulder before she left. Rafe was glad he'd helped her out -- but damn the Displaced were getting more difficult to handle.

"Clean up your face." Yang handed him a cloth from the bag he carried. Rafael took the cloth with a shaky hand and wiped at the side of his face, finding blood on the cloth. The entire area round the graft felt warm and painful, and his left eye wouldn't focus yet.

Yang held out a slim tube he'd drawn from his med bag and Rafe nodded, though only a little. Yang put the tube to the side of Rafe's neck and pressed the injection. Numbness spread up through his face and downward into his lungs. He hadn't realized how much breathing hurt until the pain went away. The pounding headache eased back to a dull throb and he could almost stand to hear the voices of others nearby.

Buris lumbered over to the table and brought two beers. The big man nodded and went away again without speaking, knowing how noises bothered Rafe after an encounter with the Displaced. They were a good group, which reminded him of why he did still try to help rather than stepping back and letting the Displaced do whatever they wanted.

"Better," Yang said with a wave of his scanner. The word still made him wince. "Rafe?"

"Yes, better," he agreed, testing out the sound as he spoke softly. He finally dared to look up at Yang. "They are stronger. Or am I weaker?"

Yang frowned and lifted his scanner, running it over Rafe a couple times more, as though the readings would change. "No, you aren't weaker."

"Then they are stronger," he repeated, starting to feel a little more connected with everything and analyzing what had happened. "I don't know what's going on, Yang. And I don't know why Xenation took so long to step in."

"The vids from the grow domes show there was a good amount of reshaping going on not long before the Displaced showed up. Do you think that could have slowed Xenation?"

"Maybe so." He wiped at the side of his face again. The bleeding had stopped, but he still couldn't see clearly out of his eye. He took a sip of the beer; weak stuff, hardly worthy of the name, but still welcome. "But they were stronger and they didn't seem as random as they used to be. Not one or two gathering and creating trouble. Now they come in groups. I rarely find any of them alone."

"You think they have some purpose, some reasoning, don't you?"

Rafael had never said as much to any of the science people who tended to side with Station Master Neva NiGwen. She insisted, even still, that he created the Displaced for his own reasons.

"I don't think they're normal," he said and then looked to where a stranger walked into the café. "And I don't think they're acting normal, even for them."

The man settled at a table not far away and took an active interest in Rafael. He always found that unsettling. Yang saw him look that way and he glanced over and then back.

"New head of science," Yang said softly.

"Is he?" Rafael replied and felt a new wave of worry. Someone new on the station was bound to be a problem, especially someone with power. He gave the man a quick glance, noting the solid build, brown hair and eyes and the inquisitive stare.

Yang sipped at his own beer, a moment of peace. "You know Samplin wanted out. He'll have gotten the word he can leave by now. I don't know if I should be happy to see him go or not. He's not been much help, but he hasn't interfered in much, either."

"True." Rafe tried hard not to look at the new man, but he was too aware of him sitting a few tables away. "I get the feeling this one is going to be trouble."

"You think everything is trouble," Yang accused.

"And when have I been wrong?"

Yang didn't argue. Rafael sipped more of the weak, warm beer and tried not to feel the weight of the new man's stare. Of course he was interested. Rafael was one of the station's ongoing projects, after all. Maybe this would mark a change. Samplin had lost interest in everything over the last year and just wanted out although with his career still intact. He couldn't simply pack up and leave, like many of the workers did who slipped off with whatever berth they could get on an outgoing ship.

Rafael wanted to leave with the rest of them and escape this nightmare. He wanted to forget he had ever spent time on this station. His finger traced the edge of the graft, knowing he couldn't leave until Xenation let him go. He'd tried to go out the grow domes once and they'd had to bring him back before they got more than a kilometer away because the break from Xenation was killing him.

Trapped here. Trapped here forever; him and the Displaced. He wondered why the station didn't let them all die.

"Drink your beer," Yang said, nudging his arm.

He sipped again, trying to dislodge the darker thoughts.

He didn't hate this place, at least. There were aspects of Xenation that he still found fascinating, both in the station and the aliens. He had friends, especially among the Ksa, which no one else could claim.

Not a bad place, except --

One of those exceptions came through the door into Xenobia. Station Master Neva NiGwen paused at the opening, looking around with the light framing her in a brighter glow from outside the little makeshift building. Her golden hair strayed into curls around her face, and her blue eyes narrowed as she looked inside the darker area. Neva didn't come here often, and Rafael did his best not to be anywhere she went, which was inevitably futile in a world as small as theirs. There had been better times, before the accident, but now she blamed him for things he had no control over and wouldn't listen to any reason when it came to him.

He wanted out of the café. He could see her eyes narrow and felt a stab of pain at the look. Then she turned away and scanned the room --

The new guy stood.

"Morgan!" she shouted with obvious delight. She crossed to the table and they embraced.

"I'm screwed," Rafael whispered.

Even Yang looked appalled as the two laughed. Neva glanced towards Rafe, her eyes narrowing with anger, as though she silently accused him of purposely showing up to ruin her reunion with an old friend.

"I have to go," Rafael said. He took a last, long drink of the beer, hoping that helped keep him to his feet from here to the Xenobia door. After that he would crawl off somewhere if he had to. He didn't care. He just wanted to walk away from another nightmare.

"You are in no shape --" Yang said and stopped when Neva laughed again.

The sound felt like salt in a wound and far worse than the pounding of his head. Yang must have seen his reaction; he ferreted around in his bag again, pulling out something.

"Give me your hand. This will help, at least for a bit," he said.

Rafael reached across the table, trying hard not to show how the movement hurt. Yang pressed a small tube against his wrist and before he drew his arm back, he could feel the blocker easing some of the pains. Yang ran the scanner this time, even he looked pleased.

"I wish we could do that more often, Rafe," he admitted with a shake of his head. "But --"

"But I don't want to get addicted," Rafe finished the thought. He took another drink of beer, actually tasting the pale liquid this time. "I have enough problems without purposely creating more for myself. I'm going now."

Yang packed up his bag, obviously intending to walk out with him. Rafe started to argue and changed his mind. He didn't mind having a guard between him and the table he must pass.

One last drink and he stood. He felt steady, though he feared the strength wouldn't last long enough. The blocker steadied him and kept some of the pain at bay, but he could already feel the discomfort starting to make inroads again. He didn't want to waste this gift. He let Yang get to his right and they started away, Rafe giving a nod to the startled Buris who knew how long it usually took him to recover.

"Medtech Yang," Neva said. "Won't you join us? I'd like you to meet the new head of the science section."

She did not, of course, invite Rafael. He gave a quick, unobtrusive tap on Yang's arm and kept going, trying to ignore the petty little action by Neva though it hurt on very many levels. He didn't pause as he headed out the door, leaving Yang behind.

The muscles in his left arm had begun to cramp and his head pounded with each step. He paused a half dozen steps from Xenobia, intending to head into the human sector. However, that would just put him back into Neva's path if she took this man -- Morgan -- to his new office. Rafe was not going to rush anywhere and he would not have stood up well to one of her tirades. Better not to be where she and the new head of science could easily find him.

He took the long walk across the embarkation area for ships and on to the Market. His sight blurred with every step and he had to pause too often, probably looking as though he was dead drunk rather than half dead.

He finally put a hand over his left eye which kept seeing odd colors in the walls, and designs that he suspected no one else noticed. Yang had said the eye structure had shifted slightly, just as part of his brain had shifted slightly after the graft.

Damn the station that changed him and tied him here, trapped in one nightmare after another.

He couldn't leave and Neva wouldn't, which put them in constant conflict. She didn't believe even what Yang told her about what was happening to him. She wanted everything to be a lie and he couldn't understand why. She should have known him better.

She did know him better.

Would things have been different if Ashur had survived? Probably.

Rafe still tried not to be bitter though at least those thoughts, and the surge of anger, had gotten him all the way to the market. He felt better as he stepped through the two poles that marked the opening. He could hide among the booths. He could talk with the people, both human and Ksa. While some of the humans worked low level jobs for science or in admin, they didn't often play by Neva's games when it came to him.

The market fascinated him. He enjoyed watching how the products changed with each incoming ship. The *Blue Star* hadn't been in port long enough for anything to make it to the booths, but a Click ship had swept through two days ago and he saw some of their items. Click tended to trade things with curves and mostly balls, arcs, cylinders. He rarely saw anything box-like come from them and the one time he had, he suspected they'd gotten it from somewhere else.

Click did not actually trade, either. Often they dropped items at different booths and took nothing in return. Rafe had tried to figure out a pattern and he thought they came to booths where people treated them and the pets with a little kindness. He didn't say so because the others would then pretend kindness in order to get the baubles. The Ksa, he knew, were trying to teach the small aliens about trade, but no one could be certain what they understood.

The Ksa took a great deal of pride in their trading abilities, and they often brought Rafe small gifts they knew would fascinate him. He had a collection of small, alien artifacts in his room where he could sit studying them for hours between one disaster and the next.

No one wanted to hire him and Neva wouldn't trust him with any high admin job. Yang paid him for work he could do, which was mostly report scanning and synopsis. It didn't take much to survive on Xenation, which was a damned good thing since he wasn't going anywhere else.

The market had three distinct areas and several edges where the groups merged a little more than was usual. He entered from the human side, but just ahead and to the right sat the Norishi sector with the inevitable guard. No one went into that part of the market without permission. He wondered what the hell they were doing if they didn't want customers.

Show, he supposed. The Norishi were big into show.

Even as he came through the human gate, he saw business starting to pick up along the haphazard aisles lined with booths made of everything from crates glued together to fine woven Ksa tents. The Norishi had several plain, black box-like huts, with the wares laid out on tables at the door. No one ever got inside the large huts which made him wonder why they went to all that trouble of putting them up . . . except, again, for show.

In all, the Ksa sector out did them all, though. They had tents and open-air stands, with everything festooned with ribbons and flags. Rafael had begun to realize the colors and the symbols on the flags were far more than just decorative bits of ornament meant to draw attention. They all meant something to the Ksa and he wanted it all to mean something to him as well.

The Click had no section of their own. They wandered in and out, dropping things here and there at different booths. Click artifacts fascinated everyone and even the Norishi sometimes tried to lure them into their part of the market.

The click pets were less welcome. The little creatures got into *everything*, opening anything closed and sometimes making off with odd items. People rarely got those things back, so they made certain nothing of importance sat out where little pet hands could grab them.

Rafael had come to like the little pests, though. He'd learned a few Click sounds and could clap his hand and click his tongue in an approximation of some simple, Click commands. He could sometimes get the pets to come to him or to stop or sit. He'd taught the sounds to a few others, but he wasn't certain anyone had any luck with it but him. He wanted others to get the same responses so he knew they reacted to the sounds and not merely to him.

He had begun working on an audio file dictionary and so far had five definite words and six maybe ones. Even the Ksa admitted to having trouble understanding the Click, and they'd been in contact with them for over one hundred years.

Rafe, feeling a little better, moved slowly through the human section, visiting with friends and trading a couple Ksa stones for a woven bag he could sling across his shoulder. A few booths later he bought some bread, glad to see Gladys had gotten in supplies to bake again. She'd imported an oven with a small powercell and now she was the darling of just about everyone on the station, including the Ksa and -- because she was a woman -- the Norishi. Rafe suspected she would probably make the kind of money the treasure hunters who came to Xenation only dreamed about.

"The new shirts are done, Rafe," Orin said, waving him over. He pulled out two nice shirts from behind the table, both well-tailored. One was a light blue (the color of the summer sky . . . but he pushed that thought aside in haste) and the other a shimmering silver. Rafe handed over his ID and paid for them with some of his hoarded creds. His old shirts had started getting ratty and Neva would never let him draw on station personnel clothing. In some ways, he decided he didn't mind. This allowed him to be an individual, and wear things that didn't make him look like the others.

He touched the metal at the side of his face. Not that he would look like them anyway.

"Greetings and 'eace vetween us, Rafael."

He turned, giving an automatic bow of greeting to the two Ksa men who had come up behind him. They wore dark suits today, the collars inlaid with a green braid design, and both wore long cloaks which meant they were on some official business.

"Greeting and peace between us Etinon and Saris. Is the market good today?"

Etinon patted the shoulder bag he carried made of some sort of alien leather and intricately detailed -- as was almost everything the Ksa did -- with gold and silver inlay. Rafael had come to realize each design held some significance, but he hadn't figured them out yet. He also didn't know what was proper to ask the Ksa who were open in many things, but not some matters. The Ksa had strict rules of protocol. He tried very hard not to cross over those rules and allowed the Ksa to take charge of most conversations.

"Narket is fine," Etinon said. "Other natters are trouvling, friend. Can you walk with us? You look unsteady."

He was the official business? Rafe suspected this wouldn't be good, but he gave a quick nod and placed the new shirts in his bag.

"Another round with the Displaced," he said, waving his hand back towards the work area. "I can walk with you. Thank you for the invitation."

Orin watched with obvious worry as he walked away with the two. If something bothered the Ksa enough to come to him, this meant real trouble out there somewhere. The Ksa handled their own affairs and they didn't need him for anything trivial.

Rafael asked nothing as they moved along the booths.

He always observed the strictest protocols with the Ksa. While the Norishi were all about show and drawing attention, the Ksa had rituals that were imperative to their species. They forgave others for not knowing the rituals, but they treated those who at least took the time to try to learn with extra respect.

The Ksa stood taller than most humans, though not by much. Humanoid in shape, but slightly different with longer fingers, a thinner, flatter face, and a mouth and lips that could not form the letters b, p, or m. They replaced the Bs with Vs and the Ms with Ns and usually just left out the p sounds entirely. Rafael knew a few Ksa words from the market, but the Ksa he met spoke fluent human basic. They didn't seem to think it important that he learn their language, at least as long as he observed what rituals he knew. The words appeared to be less important, in most respects, than the actions.

They were walking towards the Ksa market, where the gateway hung with ribbons of dark, rich colors. He had come realize this gateway and ribbons created something of a message board, giving notice to other Ksa about matters within their sector. Today he saw far too much black hung in long streamers on both sides and frowned at the sight.

Saris saw where he looked and nodded. "You are wise."

The words sent a chill through him as they neared the gateway and he let the other two go ahead. He paused, clasping his hands together and bowing his head a little lower. "May I, a stranger, be accepted within your realm?"

"Cone within and ve welcone to our 'lace," Saris said, bowing is head.

Something told Rafe this was not where he really wanted to go today. He had the feel of one disaster after another striking, but he bowed his head in return. "Thanks to all within for the welcome."

He stepped inside the gate while giving one last distrustful glance to the black ribbons.

Nothing seemed amiss within the well-kept area of the Ksa market. He saw Ksa and humans doing business at the tents, and heard the usual scrabble of words as they made deals. The Ksa loved deal-making, and they did the trades with the kind of joy and enthusiasm that humans usually attached to sports. When the humans set up their first booths, the Ksa were quick to make their own area. Rafael thought they had been waiting for a sign that it would be permissible.

The market drew the two groups closer together. The Norishi, who seemed to have no idea of what markets and trade meant, had joined in with their exclusive little area, though Rafael thought they did so only to keep an eye on the other two groups.

At the next turn between the tents he saw something unusual -- a Click adult standing by one of the tents and holding what seemed to be a glass tube of swirling colors, perhaps a foot long and four inches in diameter. On the other side of a table stood Asa An, a woman of the Ksa and probably their finest trader, but she didn't seem to be having any luck. The Click -- which stood just chest high to the woman on his back legs, and far shorter on all four -- waved the glass tube towards the new group as they neared, making the series of clicking noises for which the group was named. The language proved very hard to decipher, though Rafael was starting to make progress, mostly with the pets who understood a few commands, much like dogs did back on earth.

The Click resembled the pets in the way that humans resembled the smaller monkeys of home. The Click had longer bodies, more pointed faces seen only occasionally through a cascade of head fur. The fur grew shorter from the shoulders down and formed a long mane around the neck. The facial expressions, through rarely seen, were easier to understand than the language, and from the wide-golden eyes and flared nostrils, Rafael could tell this one was very happy.

When Rafael held back, the Click pressed forward, waving the tube towards him.

Wanted to trade with him? He didn't even think about it; but rather reached into the pouch he carried and drew out the first thing he felt, which turned out to be a loaf of bread. He held that out, and the Click quickly exchanged the items, moving so fast that Rafe almost dropped the glass tube. The Click turned and scurried away on four feet, practically dancing through the line of tents as he headed toward the Click Enclave.

"Well done," Etinon said with a deep bow.

Rafael found the glass fascinating and he turned the object over several times. Something moved within, like bubbles of liquid moving through the air.

"I had not intended to trade within your territory," he apologized and held the object out. "I think, by rights, this belongs to you."

Asa An was the first to shake her head, and it seemed to Rafael that the other two waited for a sign from her.

"You have studied things fron the Click," Etinon said with a nod. "What do you think this is?"

"I have no idea at all," Rafael replied and could barely draw his attention away from the object.

"Ah. Though you night learn," Asa An said. Both Etinon and Saris nodded. "Take this thing. See if you can find a use for it."

"I can't trade --" He frantically tried to think of something he could give in return because he really did want this piece of magic. *Alien.* He couldn't even guess where it might have originated.

"Not trade," she said and waved the item away again. "I hire you. Find out what you can."

Several interesting aspects of the situation came to mind. First was that humans had *never* taken hire with the Ksa for *anything.* He wasn't sure how the human authorities would like it. Oh, he knew what Neva would say, but that had nothing to do with the real situation.

The other problem? The Ksa were trying to hire him to do something he was in no ways certain he could handle. If he failed, now would that affect his relationship with them?

"I don't know if I could learn anything. I don't have the kind of equipment I would need."

"You learn things without equipment," Saris said. "You do so often. We see so."

"I could break it trying to learn anything."

"Then we would learn this is not the way to handle such things," Asa An said. "Take this thing. Tell ne if this does anything nore than nake pretty colors."

He nodded and held it closer. The object felt heavier than he expected and the surface warmer. He peered through the slightly opaque glass mesmerized by the colors. Then he opened his shoulder bag and drew out the blue shirt, wrapping the cloth around the glass and packing it away as safely as he could.

"I will let you know what I learn. It may be that the humans learn of it as well. I have few secrets from them."

She nodded, unconcerned. "You have not asked of pay."

He smiled this time. "I have the glass to study. It fascinates me. That's pay enough."

All three of his companions looked startled and then pleased. Rafe had no idea what little cultural boundary he had just crossed, but apparently he had done so well.

"We nust go," Saris said with a nod down the path. "There is still such we wish you to see."

He'd forgotten they brought him here for another reason. The thought damped his elation at the idea of this new discovery, though perhaps what they had wasn't so bad. He had only seen the ribbons, after all, and everything else seemed normal.

They headed down the aisle towards a tent he knew usually featured human vid equipment which the Ksa had traded for from others. As allies, everyone -- including Neva -- was glad to let them have some of the equipment which might mean better communications with them.

Etinon stopped and nodded to Onay, the proprietor who brought out a portable vid screen and set the small, square device on the table, nodding without a word. Saris pulled a small battered compbox from beneath the table. Human made, but common with the Ksa these days. He connected the box with the viewer.

"There is such that you need to see," Saris said and tapped the screen on with one quick, long-fingered jab.

The screen brightened. Numbers scrolled over the upper right, which made this vid from a human ship. That set a cold chill in him, since the box had fallen into Ksa hands, and not human. He wanted to ask questions about the name of the ship, the location, but remained silent and watched.

He was right. Less than two minutes later, the numbers jumped, and the vid changed and focused on a ship which had plainly just dropped into the area. Long, sleek: Norishi beyond a doubt. The craft spun, even as he watched, darted forward and fired.

The humans didn't have time to raise shields and they didn't fire, which mostly likely meant they didn't expect the attack or that they were a merchant craft with little or no weapons. They didn't survive. Rafe saw pieces of debris blast outward from explosive decompression just before the vid cam went black.

Four minutes of vid and it changed all the peace and lies from the Norishi. He leaned forward, hands on the counter before the screen. His companions said nothing and no one else had come near.

"What was the ship they destroyed?" he finally asked, doing his best to keep his voice calm.

"We do not know." Saris sounded apologetic. "There was little left when our 'eople arrived. They knew enough about hunan technology to sift everything for this record. They found little else. Sone of the con'uter with it, though nothing worked. "

"Where?"

"The Drivesta Systen, close enough to Drivesta 'rine that larger 'ieces of the craft had already veen dragged down into the gravity well and lost."

"Who knows about this?"

"Very few," Etinon replied with a quick bow of his head. "We did not give it over to hunans yet. To you -- you we think should know of this evil act. You did not ask if we know the Norishi craft."

He looked up, startled as his mouth went dry. "You know the ship?"

"She is called *Atta* -- it neans *The First* -- and she is their nost 'owerful warrior craft."

"*Atta?* A warrior craft?" he said and felt a new wave of worry. "But --"

"Vut she 'retends to ve a trader, and is here often," Saris said. "Tell ne that a few of your own hunan ships do not do the sane?"

"We have never seriously tried to hide it," he answered and won nods from his two companions. "I doubt we even fooled Xenation, but as long as the weapons aren't active, she's willing to let them come in. But this--" He waved to the screen, his arm trembling. "This is a problem. What do you expect me to do with the knowledge?"

"What is wise," Saris replied. He lifted the small box from the vid reader and handed it over to Rafael.

"I don't know if I can take this to Neva. She mistrusts --
"

"The Station Naster nistrusts nuch," Etinon said. "In sone, she is wise. You, though, trust everyone. You nake friends on all sides. This is good, vut dangerous for you."

"Whom should I mistrust?" Rafael asked.

Etinon tapped the hand that held the box. "I would start with the Norishi."

CHAPTER FOUR

N eva had been wonderfully happy to see Morgan which had brightened his day and put a great deal of his worry to rest . . . at least for now. He'd had a view of Rafael and the medtech and he had seen the way he looked panicked at the sight of the two of them meeting.

He didn't quite understand the reaction until Neva invited the medtech -- and not Rafael -- to join them. She ignored him completely. Rafael didn't seem in the least bit surprised and headed out of the building, walking far steadier than he should, considering how pale he looked.

Once Rafael disappeared through the door, the three had a pleasant, quick meeting. Neva laughed and joked and she only showed signs of stress again when her commlink beeped.

She looked at the screen and frowned. "I'm sorry. I have to go. The Norishi are asking for a meeting. I'd take you along Morgan, but they'd never put up with a strange male in the group."

"I understand," Morgan said and patted her hand. "I'll be fine."

"I hate to abandon you." Her eyes flickered towards the medtech and Morgan suspected she really feared leaving the two together.

"I'm sure we'll have a chance to catch up again later," Morgan said and smiled.

She stood and gave them one last worried look before she hurried away. Yang, however, didn't take advantage of her absence to speak about Rafael. After a few more sips of beer, Morgan went with Yang into the human sector of Xenation where they walked past doors covered with cloth and finally to a sign that said Science. The human area seemed to be laid out on consecutive curves, which seemed odd given the boxy shape of the station itself.

The walls gave light in all directions, making this a rather shadow-less place. The temperature felt comfortable, and the gravity had been settled in this area to an Earth-norm. He wondered how Xenation managed that one, since many of the people here were not from Earth.

"How did you get these rooms?" he finally asked as they reached the open door to the science section.

"Xenation gave them to us. For the first few months, we lived on the docked ships and spent some time in the bay area. Then one day things *changed*; the opening appeared, and we had quarters within the station itself. It was disconcerting," the man admitted looking around at the walls. "And it took a long time to trust that the rooms wouldn't disappear -- with us trapped in them -- again."

"But you got used to it."

"Yes," he said and laughed. "The air's better than on a ship. And the chance to move around more, and to be in contact with the station itself, won most of us over. The others who came later mostly just take this for granted, at least until they see the first Xenation rebuild. Then they start to get an idea of how wondrous this place is."

"I saw some rebuilding happening on the way in," Morgan said and did give the walls a worried glance. "Any idea why the station rebuilt now?"

"None at all. It happens. She might open some more space for us, which would be nice. Most of the station personnel share rooms -- at least two to a space -- but not the higher ranking people like you. There has to be some perks for drawing top people in. I live at the meduint, though, which isn't very busy, but not always empty either."

"What kind of problems?"

"Fights most often, but sometimes the alienness of Xenation starts to wear on some people. We've had to ship a few workers off because of paranoia, either about the station or one of the other races. We don't need that kind of trouble."

"You haven't shipped Rafael off, though."

"We tried at Neva's orders." He gave Morgan a dark look. "I ordered the ship back. I didn't want him dead."

"You believed leaving would kill him."

"I was with him. It *was* killing him," Yang replied.

Morgan had read the report. He didn't remember seeing the medtech's name anywhere. However, this wasn't the time to get into the discussion, not in the halls and without reports on hand to go over.

"I don't understand the circular layout," he said, waving a hand towards the wall.

Yang seemed to take the hint quickly and even looked relieved. "Ah. We have a theory," he said and tapped the wall beside him. "The only plan that Xenation had to go by for humans came from the ships we came in. Since the corridors there are all circular, we think that's where she got the idea."

He nodded, thinking this made sense if the computer had enough reasoning.

"And the gravity? Was it always Earth Standard?"

"No. I have a theory for that one, too. Gravity used to change a bit at any time. But Rafael is from Earth."

"Ah." Morgan nodded. Then he shook his head, dislodging questions again, mostly about how he thought Rafael communicated with the station. They'd have to wait. "We'll discuss the entire Rafael situation later. I don't see any reason to rush into judgment. There's plenty else here that I need to see first. And I need to get settled in."

Yang nodded and Morgan looked into the science department, which seemed to be one large room and several smaller rooms off the sides. Equipment, most of it powered by individual power cells, sat against the walls. People had been working but as he and Yang came closer he could see the anxious faces of the rest of the science team, another twenty-seven people, who worked at trying to understand anything they could about the station.

Samplin sat on the edge of a desk and smiled so brightly you would have thought he had just been given a reprieve from a death sentence. The smile did not help Morgan's state of mind.

Yang left him and he went inside. The introductions went quickly. He knew the names that went with the faces already since he had taken time on the journey to go over every file and memorize what he could. It would help with the transition if he acted as though he had always been here and knew what they did.

He suspected the biggest problem would be getting some of the people back into a normal routine. He could tell from the later reports he had read that Samplin let them run wild after he lost interest. Morgan's initial plan had been to stop any unauthorized experiments and tests, but after only a couple hours on the station, he changed his mind. This wasn't a 'by the book' situation. He'd review everything, but he realized these people probably had a better idea of what to look for than he did, and there were no books or regulations that would cover studying an abandoned alien station. He glanced at the walls, realizing how easy it was to get used to Xenation. He needed to remember that this *place* was not as simple as it looked.

Morgan began to see relief in the eyes of a few as they discussed experiments. While having no supervision had to present a lot of freedom, it also meant they couldn't request supplies or even get outside reviews. Morgan intended to be open to ideas, but he wanted to control and correlate the work so they could build up an overall view and not a lot of little peaks.

He talked with the people for a while longer, and looked over some of the long-running experiments. For a while, Samplin even sounded enthusiastic and Morgan thought he caught a little hint of regret for a moment or two.

But it passed.

"I'll leave you with the gang, then," Samplin said. "And I'll go give my official resignation to Neva and then pack up my rooms, which you will have as soon as I leave. They're at the end of the hall, so you're always within reach of work. That's good and bad. "

"I imagine so," he said with a quick nod. "Where do I stay until then?"

"At the medunit with me," Yang replied. Morgan hadn't noticed him standing at the door. "I need to do your physical anyway. Besides, we jokingly call it Hospital Hotel. It's where most people stay if they are here for a few days and don't want to remain on the ship for some reason. It's the only place set up to handle people."

"That's your office." Samplin pointed to an archway into another area. "I've already stripped out my belongings, so you can take it over right away. Renita Diaz is the office assistant but she also works lab, so she isn't sitting around all the time. She's out running atmosphere reports at the moment. We do them whenever a new ship comes in. You'll meet her soon. I'll just leave you to get settled in."

He turned and walked away so quickly that Morgan couldn't have asked a question, even if he'd thought of one. The action didn't make him feel any better after taking over, but he nodded for Yang to come with him into the office.

The room stood barren of anything but two file cabinets, a desk with one chair behind it and another in front. The room seemed too large for the few items. Spots of color showed on the walls, at least relieving the area of the sterile and empty feel.

He crossed and sat on the edge of the desk and looked back at the Medtech who settled in the chair; he seemed comfortable there and must have spent some time with Samplin.

"Everything seems pretty much straightforward," Morgan said and moved to the more comfortable chair behind the desk. *My place.*

"Pretty much so. Samplin didn't authorize all the experiments, you know."

Odd thing for the local medtech to know, though he supposed people noticed what others were doing in a place this small. "I think this is the place where we need some innovation, and they took advantage of Samplin's lack of interest in order to branch out in ways that maybe wouldn't have looked proper in reports. I'll let everything go for a while longer, but I'll tell them I expect real reports on the work." He frowned. "No one mentioned any work with Rafael."

"No, of course they didn't. They already heard you are a friend of Neva's. They're going to be very wary of reporting anything that might make her -- or you -- upset. You seem like a nice guy. They don't want to mess up the relationship."

"They think knowing Neva is going to be a problem?" he asked. He tried to quell his own reactions about how she had acted towards Rafael. "I've known Neva -- and I knew Ashur -- since before they were married. In fact, I was best man at the wedding. I was there when Tali was born and if I hadn't been off on a science mission to the fringe, I might have come along when they settled here."

Yang looked worried at the catalogue of links he had with the Station Master.

"Tell me why you think this is a problem," Morgan said.

Yang paused for a breath and another, and then leaned forward as his voice softened. "Because Neva is a problem and I don't think you missed it."

"She has what she thinks is a legitimate complaint against Rafael. I'm not certain where you fit into the problem. I have read the reports --"

"No, you haven't."

"I read everything --"

"You read everything Neva *allowed* out of the station."

Morgan went silent, feeling more of a nagging worry taking hold of him. Neva was an old friend and he desperately didn't want this to be a problem. But Ashur, in the form of one of the Displaced, had looked at him and he couldn't quite make himself believe in some trick set up by Rafael, either.

"I have nearly 200,000 words in reports and less than half of that has been released," Yang said. He looked straight into Morgan's face and must have cast all caution to the wind

-- and threw the future of his career in with it, given what he knew about Morgan and Neva's past. "Neva is a problem, at least where Rafael is concerned. Rafe doesn't need more trouble. He needs someone who is going to help."

"Samplin didn't help?" Morgan asked while still trying to make some sense of this strange situation.

"Samplin gave up very early on," Yang said quietly. Morgan nodded, having seen the reports -- the reports that left this place. He'd noticed when Samplin just simply stopped bothering to write more than a few lines here and there. He saw no reason for this to go beyond the room and he appreciated that Yang was being open . . . unless he was setting things up for Rafael. He didn't know. He couldn't know until he heard all the sides, and seen *all* the reports.

"Did he just give up because of Neva?" Morgan asked. Yang pulled the chair closer to the desk. Someone passed outside the door and glanced in, but the desk sat across the wide room and no one would hear them unless there were aspects of Xenation he didn't know. He supposed he would find out.

"Neva and Rafael were the deciding points, I think," Yang said. "But this wasn't a position Samplin was comfortable with anyway. He had come up through the ranks at the IWC facilities. He was used to doing tests, getting results, reporting them higher up. He was good at the work, in fact. I hope they take him back. He'll be happy there."

The observation reminded Morgan that this man was also the psych, and probably knew what he was talking about when it came to Samplin. Morgan would pass the recommendation for a new position on to someone else. He didn't want Samplin to look like a failure when he left Xenation if for no other reason than he might find himself in the same position a few years down the road. Xenation was no easy egg to crack.

"I'll see what I can do for him," Morgan said and saw a quick smile from Yang. "So, you are saying Rafael had no one but you?"

"Others have done tests in passing but nothing more.

They didn't want to come up against Neva's increasingly unreasonable behavior towards him. I can still help him because she knows she dares not press the matter with me."

"I don't understand the reasoning behind her supposed attitude," Morgan finally admitted, his fingers drumming on the desk. He stopped. It was a bad habit. "She doesn't seem to be showing any other unreasonable reactions? Am I wrong there? I would think if there was some basic break in her personality, you would have had her packed up and out of here. Why haven't you?"

"Because she's damned good at the work here and she isn't broken. She's just being selectively blind and for all her own reasons."

"What reasons?"

"The scout that had the accident, the *Brady* -- did you see the vid on it?"

"There's vid?" he asked, shocked.

"Oh yes. We had cams set up in the bay at all time, recording everything Xenation did. We still do. We're scientists. We want records of *everything*. The vid was part of the original report, but I think Neva cut it out. Some of us have slipped out copies since then but we couldn't do it officially so we've never been certain if they got to the right spots."

He wanted to curse because he really suspected this man might be telling him the truth about the situation. Well, at least some of the truth. Not all of it. He didn't believe Neva had completely and entirely misused her position to purposely ruin someone's life. This made no sense at all.

"What aren't you telling me?"

Yang looked at his hands for a moment before Morgan saw resignation in the man's face. Morgan knew he wasn't going to like this any better than he'd liked anything else so far. Damn.

"Ashur and his team took the scout ship and headed out to make a survey of the debris in this system in hopes of getting a better idea of why the aliens had abandoned this place. Rafael had wanted to go, but Neva vetoed it saying some top personnel from science had to stay behind --"

"He's science?" Morgan said, already startled. "I was under the impression he was. . . ."

"Just some dock worker? Yes, that's how most of the reports seem to read. But he was Ashur's second. Ashur hired him straight out of a very high profile spot in the IWC labs where he'd probably be the head of some department by now."

"That doesn't make sense. That's --"

"Let me get through this part. I think everything will make more sense afterwards and after you've read the full reports," Yang said. He looked determined. "Neva has to know that this discussion is inevitable and that one of us -- and most likely me -- would tell you the full story. I think I saw the look in her face when she left you with me."

Morgan nodded. He had seen the look as well, so now he sat back and curbed all kinds of questions he wanted to ask. "Go ahead."

"Ashur went off on what was going to be at least a six month journey. We had trouble getting reports into the station back then so the sad thing is we don't even know what he found and we haven't done another scout since . . . but that's something else. Here is what happened. Ashur was gone for six months. Neva and Rafael became lovers."

"Oh *hell.*"

He didn't even doubt this truth because Ashur had spoken often enough about how he and Neva had grown apart. Before they left for Xenation, he'd said he doubted the marriage would last and one of them would likely come back without the other. They'd stuck to it mostly for their daughter who needed special care, for all the good it would do them.

Morgan had been blinking, staring at nothing. Yang looked a little surprised, no doubt because he'd taken the news so well. He had probably expected denial from someone who knew the two. However, because he knew them was precisely why he did believe this part of the story.

"There was also a problem right at the end. Rafael had

been reading data on the station. He thought the scout should hold off for a while. Neva decided to bring it in. Rafael went down to the bay to wait. I think he intended to talk to Ashur before Neva had to because he wasn't going to put her in that position. And then . . . everything went bad."

"So Neva has a double bout of guilt," Morgan said. He tapped his fingers on the desk. Dropped straight into a problem here that had nothing to do with the science work. Oh yes, this felt very much like all the other jobs he'd ever had. The IWC often sent him into places that needed straightening out. He had known this was one of them, but he hadn't thought the problem would be Neva herself. "Why haven't you had Neva removed? Don't tell me you couldn't have gotten word out with one of the IWC Captains who come here. They are required to check in with you if they have any medical problems from crew. In the last three years --"

"Yes, yes. I could have sent word with a number of them." He leaned back and looked exceedingly relieved. "But here's the thing: Except for the problem with Rafael, she's been an incredibly good Station Master in a very strange situation. She does as well as anyone can with the Click, she's reasonable with the Ksa, and more than anything, she can deal with the Norishi."

"Ah. Because she's a woman."

"Because she's a damned *smart* woman," he corrected. "The Norishi would tear apart anyone who wasn't up to their standards, woman or not. We *need* her. We just need her to stop fixating on Rafael and to stop believing he's doing this to her on purpose."

"I want to see the reports," Morgan said. "I want to see the vid and read the reports before I make any decision."

"Absolutely. You can't take my word on this. For all you know, I am working some scam with Rafael specifically to get her out of here. Samplin has all the copies of the reports on his comp. If you have any trouble accessing them, or if you have questions, I'll be over in medunit. When you're done today, come by there and I'll show you where you're staying for a night or two. I suspect you'll be having dinner with Neva. I will not go along even if I am invited. You need time with her, too."

Good plan to give him the time alone with her. Yang stood. Morgan did as well and reached over to shake hands, but his mind was a long ways from the polite exchange of words as the man left.

He sat at the desk and keyed on the computer, taking out his master chit. He put in his own codes, which truly and officially put him in charge of the science department here. Items lighted across the desk, showing him the work on various projects in real time reports. Interesting that Samplin, who had lost interest in most everything, still apparently kept his eyes on things. Good.

He found the Rafael files and began reading. The sooner he got through this, the better.

He did not watch the vid attached. Not yet.

CHAPTER FIVE

Neva stared at Tican and ignored the others who came with the Norishi woman. She was in just enough of a bad mood to be the kind of bitch the Norishi appreciated. She was even less than normally human-polite to Tican, putting the Norishi woman at a disadvantage since it relegated the Norishi leader to a lesser role as well, though higher than the guards Neva ignored.

She and Tican sat at the table in the conference room. The other two stood by the doorway. Neva couldn't decide if she wanted to drag this out so they went back aching from the higher human gravity or push through and be done with them.

Get it over with. She had far more important things to worry about than the usual No-No complaint. The nickname suited the Norishi since if you asked the Norishi for anything, their first answer would always be no. Automatic. It hardly mattered what you might suggest or ask. *No.*

She had stopped asking the Norishi for anything helpful quite a while back. She wondered if they'd noticed.

"Why have you come to my office today?" she demanded, putting the onus on Tican to get to the point. She belayed her sense of urgency by leaning back in the chair and looking relaxed, if not bored.

Tican Canta moved her hand with the slightest show of distress. She rarely got a reaction from the Norishi Ice-Bitches, and she told herself that as the Station Master she shouldn't feel that little glow of pleasure . . . but there it was, the best part of her day so far.

Not true. She'd been delighted to see Morgan's name on the *Blue Star's* manifest, to find his credentials and the order for him to take over science in the comp transfer. She'd been elated to see him in person and talk with him.

She'd been less happy to leave him alone with Medtech Yang, but that would happen sooner or later. Let Yang get everything out of the way so she could talk with Morgan later.

Tican had not yet spoken. Neva waited, one eyebrow raised.

"We have a proposal for a trade agreement with you," Tican finally said.

Well that banished all the other thoughts as she sat up straighter again. Her mind ran through a dozen thoughts, the most prominent being that Tican had said 'you' and not 'with the humans.' She knew the implications immediately: *you* meant her specifically as the head of an important human station. They would not have brought this deal to a man if he had been in charge.

Stupid, blind misandrist society. But she could use this and she didn't have to pretend not to be interested now. Anyone would have been.

"You have the proposal with you?"

Tican reached into the pocket of her jacket and pulled out a small chit. Human-made. Neva had no doubt the chit would work in their computers, though she wasn't stupid enough to drop it straight into one. She would *never* trust the Norishi that well. Even the Click had some human-made computers although no one could quite figure out what they did with them.

"As you will see, there will be increased Norishi ship traffic to Xenation soon. This is no small trade agreement and we trust you will find the terms lucrative and work with your people to make this a satisfactory endeavor on both sides."

"I will go over this matter." Neva felt as though a poisonous spider had dropped onto her palm. She fought not to drop the chit immediately on the desk. "Thank you for bringing this to me."

Tican nodded with the little smirk that passed for a polite smile from the Norishi.

"Is there any other matter?"

"There is a new head of human science," Tican said.

Not a question but that wasn't a surprise. Word always spread quickly in Xenation.

"Yes. Morgan Michael Doreet. He --" Do not say he's an old friend! Not of a male! "-- worked with me in other projects."

"Then perhaps you will finally get the Rafael matter in hand."

That statement threw her, though she did her best to control the reaction. What the hell did Rafael mean to them? They had no Displaced. They hadn't been here then, just humans and a few Ksa.

"Perhaps," she said and no more. She thought she had given too much away even in the single word, which admitted Rafael was a problem. But then they would know she had a problem with him anyway. Damn small station. "Is there anything more?"

"No," Tican said and stood, unfolding her tall, too thin body from the chair. Norishi never looked comfortable in human chairs which was another point of pleasure for Neva.

She stood as well, a little more slowly and gave a gracious nod. "Thank you for bringing this to me. I shall speak with you again tomorrow at this time."

The Norishi liked precise times and places. Tican nodded, turned and walked away with her people. She hoped someone warned Morgan --

He wouldn't need the warning. He would have read reports and knew enough to stay clear when Norishi were here on business.

Neva sat back down and looked at the chit, turning the gift over in her hands and wondering what this little piece of tech really held. There was no way in hell she was going to slip the chit straight into the computer, of course. Not before security went over it --

And just on cue, Ardi walked in shaking his head and looking as worried as she no doubt felt, at least about this little problem. Tall, fit, and with skin a natural tan color -- he perpetually looked as though he had just gotten back from vacation on some exotic world. She tossed the chit to him and he caught it and held the small square between two fingers as though he expected poison, so much like her own reaction that she smiled.

"You caught everything?" she asked as she keyed monitoring back off on her computer. She didn't think the Norishi realized yet that humans let other humans, especially security, listen in on private conferences.

"I caught it." He dropped into the chair where Tican had been seated and put the chit on the table, still staring. "I can't say I trust this much."

"Oh, you and me both!" She nodded emphatically finally letting the worry she'd hidden from the Norishi slip through. "There are three pieces here we need to look at, I think. First is the idea of trade at all. Maybe this is legit and we can't dismiss the possibility just because we think the Norishi are crafty sons of bitches -- *daughters* of bitches. Sorry -- I wouldn't want to insult them, after all."

Ardi gave a little laugh as he pulled up his pocket comp. This one was a special security build with a number of refinements mostly made because of contact with the Norishi and the Ksa. She trusted that whatever happened, a problem with it would not hook back into the main system.

He dropped the chit into place and let it run through several scans while they talked. "The second thing?" he asked -- quizzing her, she knew.

"The mention of more ships coming to Xenation and trying to make me think they were related to the possibility of trade," she answered and shook her head with more worry. "That's the bothersome one, you know. What are they really going to be doing with more ships here?"

"Perhaps a few more settlers are coming in on their side, but I don't trust that much at all," Ardi admitted. He glanced at the screen of his pocketcomp and frowned. "Nothing yet.

I'm running it on deep scan, though, so this will take a while. We can't be too careful."

Neva agreed. He looked up from the comp again and quirked one eyebrow, saying nothing. She knew what he waited for though.

"Yes, the third thing." She frowned. "The reference to Rafael. What the hell does Rafael matter to them? They don't have any Displaced. He's my -- he's our problem. Strictly a human-related disaster."

And she wondered if she meant Rafael was a disaster or if she meant the disaster that created the Displaced. Sometimes everything ran together in her mind. She wanted the memory to go away. Really wanted it to disappear and give her peace.

"There is more to Rafael than the Displaced," Ardi said. He put the comp down and didn't watch as the scan continued. She didn't often give him a chance to discuss the Rafael and he plainly meant to take advantage of the moment. She clamped her mouth closed and sat with her arms folded over her chest, determined to hear him out even if she didn't like what he said.

Rafael was trouble. The Norishi must have realized it too --

No. She didn't trust that part. She just didn't trust their reference to Rafael and that made her slightly more interested in what Ardi had to say this time. He must have seen the change in her attitude. He gave one of those little nods that could annoy the hell out of her sometimes, knowing he was reading her so well. However, it was his job to be able to tell moods at a glance, and to read danger signals in humans. Even in her.

"Rafael has been making a lot of friends out in the market," he said. "Especially among the Ksa. I suspect our friends don't trust that kind of unregulated contact."

"I'm not sure I like it," she admitted.

"Because it's Rafael."

"No --" She started then stopped, considered the situation. "I would rather it was someone like Yang or even

Morgan --"

"The new head of science, whom you have known for a long time."

She did flash a quick smile this time and felt a small bubble of laughter start to erupt. Ardi looked very serious and very worried. "You don't trust me," she said and saw him get uncomfortable at the words, which finally did get a laugh from her. "I don't trust Rafael. I don't trust him much at all."

He looked up into her face. "Really."

She started to snap back an answer but held those words within as she'd learned to do over the last few years. He finally leaned forward, looking Neva in the face. She held back the urge to tell him not to lecture her.

"You know about the Ksa messenger packs, right?"

Rafael, who spent a lot of time in the bays, in the market -- anywhere that would keep him busy -- had noticed some cultural aspects of the Ksa and the Norishi. The messenger packs were specific pouches they carried when they were on official business. She nodded.

"Etinon and Saris --" Important names in the Ksa Enclave "-- came out with such a pouch today. They took Rafael back with them and through a gate strung with dark ribbons."

She felt a little chill this time. "Damn. Rafael? Where did they take him?"

"We don't think they took him into the Enclave, just back into their own market area. He hasn't come back out yet."

"I don't like this at all," she admitted and ran a hand through the curls at the edge of her face, trying to push them back. Everything had begun to annoy her now.

"I didn't think you would. We can grab Rafael when he comes back out."

"No. Not yet. Let's see what he does. We don't want to upset the Ksa."

Ardi nodded agreement. He trusted Rafael which made her want to mistrust him. She shook that feeling off and tried to look at the rest of this situation as a whole but that wasn't any better.

"The Norishi and the Ksa, both moving in odd ways at the same time, and both of them with something about Rafael," she said. "That can't be good, can it?"

The pocketcomp beeped and kicked the chit back out. Clean scan, then. He handed the chit over to her, and she held it in the palm of her hand still thinking it looked like a spider, ready to leap out and bite her in the ass.

"What the hell am I supposed to do?"

"No one expects any decisions today," Ardi said. "Not even the Norishi."

She grinned and wrapped the chit in her hand. "Humans have a reputation for being careful when it comes to reports and numbers. I think the Norishi are about to find out how anal retentive we can be. My office will be going over these reports, and writing reports and analyzing the numbers until I have at least tripled the amount of data already here. I'll send updates to the Norishi every morning."

"And in the meantime?"

"Start correlating everything you can on the Norishi from the last three months."

"More reports," he said with a little laugh.

"And keep an eye on Rafael."

"Oh, I do that. I *always* do that."

He left and she sat there, stunned by those last words and wondering what he meant. If he worried so much about Rafael, why was he always giving her so much trouble?

Maybe . . . maybe he worried for Rafael's safety, out there with the aliens, with no official back up and with no real standing. The thought started to worry her --

But she shoved that worry away and stood, chit in hand, intending to go start work on the *real* problem.

CHAPTER SIX

Rafael wanted to rush back to the Human Enclave and hand over the compbox, but he knew better than to do anything so obvious. He didn't dare draw attention to what he carried so he buried the box below the Click tube and started working his way out of the Ksa Market and stopping at some of his regular booths. He even parted with a couple creds when he found Lorfa had brought out a new batch of odds. The name suited the strange, twisting growth. The plant had a remarkably pleasant taste to both humans and Ksa and like nothing in human seasonings. Dried and grated, odds could be sprinkled on the often bland food that came in a low cred job, making a nice change in otherwise boring meals. He'd heard they'd started to use odds up in the Admin kitchen as well.

Etinon and Saris stayed with him, which wasn't unusual as long as no one paid attention to the messenger pouch once they left the Ksa market area. Rafael didn't think anyone had really listened to him about what he thought the pouches meant anyway. His two Ksa friends knew the worth of not rushing off like madmen with something this important.

He'd get the box to Ardi. The head of the human security team would know what to do and he trusted Ardi would take this seriously even if the box did come from him. Ardi could get the information on to Neva without telling her more than the box came from the Ksa. She could be reasonable as long as his name stayed out of situation.

That thought still felt like a knife in his gut but he'd

gotten used to pain. Rafe did his best to work around her. Sometimes, he wished for was a new Station Master and to never see Neva again. On a purely professional level, she had done an exceptional job here and even gotten some of the Norishi to trust her. That hadn't been easy since she had males working with her.

Rafe wanted to know more about the Norishi and their males. If the rumors were true, the Norishi women were not dramatically different from human women. So where were the males? Why did they mistrust males so much?

So many damned unanswered questions about the station and about the beings who had settled here. The Click -- damn, he still wanted to see the inside of a Click ship because no one had any clue how they worked.

But he never would. He wouldn't do anything but walk the outer edge of Xenation and play whatever games the station wanted to play with him. He had no choice. He'd tried to kill himself once, just after *The Accident*. He could think about that moment now with nothing more than a little whisper of distress. He'd had the knife --

Xenation had stopped him. Paralyzed him. He'd feared she would never let him move again and the fear had driven the other pains away for a while. He'd tried again in another way when Neva ordered him off the station and he knew going would kill him. Rafe had told Yang to give him something to knock him out or else Xenation would never let the ship leave if she could sense him there. He'd known what would happen.

The memory of the pain when he awoke, only a short distance from the station, still made him ill. He had wanted to die but the pain went on and on, and he couldn't tell if Xenation did that on purpose or if it just happened.

Yang had brought him back. Even Neva hadn't seriously suggested he leave again.

Rafe tried to make life interesting here. He tried to make a science out of studying not only his unique connection to Xenation but also the dynamics of the market, the interaction of the different aliens, and the changes in objects brought for trade.

He wished the Click would set something up. They were getting the idea of trade. Rafe thought he might understand more about them if he could see what else they brought out and what they took back with them.

He and his companions had wandered out into the human area and headed slowly towards the exit. Rafael found a booth with some sea shells which seemed odd things to bring in and damned expensive. Still, they came all the way from Earth and people felt that draw to something from the home world. For him this was more of nostalgia; he had collected shells on the beaches of home, long ago.

"I thought those might draw some attention." Brody stood behind the counter and tapped the glass case. Her long, dark hair fell forward, and she brushed the strands back, annoyed. He always wondered why she didn't just cut the hair off. "I've had them sitting in quarantine for over a month while Neva got the okay to sell them which just came through. I don't know if I'll sell many, but they've drawn a lot of people to the stand and look in the last two days."

"They're lovely," Rafael said, and tried to keep the sound of longing from his voice.

"What is this?" Etinon asked, leaning down and staring as well.

"They're shells from sea creatures on earth," Rafael explained.

"Yes? Really from aninals of Earth?" Both he and Saris learned closer and were enthralled for their own reasons.

Rafael closed his eyes for a moment and called back things he hadn't thought about in a long time. "They're the exoskeleton the creature secretes, which provides protection and support for the body, since they have no inner skeleton. These here are cowries and this I think is a whelk. Clams, oyster, and mussels there."

"Thank you!" Brody grinned widely. She brought out her pocketcomp and started taking notes. "Anything else you can tell me about these beauties?"

"I'll see if I can remember more but you can look most

of this up in the library files," he said. Etinon and Saris still looked closely at the case. Rafael suspected she was going to get more sales from the Ksa than from the humans.

Seeing the shells made him momentarily melancholy. He would have stayed and looked for a while longer --

"Get the hell out of my way, Rafe. I have work to do."

He turned to look into the face of the stocky, well-muscled man who probably should have been running a bar in some port town rather than head the human bay area on Xenation. The position put Ekhardt in charge of the market, too, which Rafael thought a very bad idea. Ekhardt didn't like aliens of any type and he made that all too plain some days.

"I said --"

There was, of course, plenty of room to walk around. Ekhardt harassed Rafael whenever he got a chance. He especially caused trouble if Neva was around but it had gotten to be a habit with him. There were times when Rafael thought about teaching him some manners. Instead, he gave a polite bow of his head and stepped aside, which enraged Ekhardt most days. Today, Ekhardt's face darkened and his fists balled up but the Ksa moved closer to Rafe and Ekhardt knew better than to cause trouble with them.

He growled something impolite and kept going.

Saris watched Ekhardt stalk past before he turned to Rafael with a look of confusion on his face. Ksa didn't often allow that look in public and Rafe suspected he was about to get involved in the kind of conversation that was better held with a professional trained to deal with aliens.

"I do not understand why he does this," Saris said.

"This?" Rafael asked, his mind already racing ahead, knowing what Saris found confusing.

"He is in'olite to you for a reason," Saris said. "And to some others, vut nostly to you. Why?"

A straightforward answer seemed best. "He thinks that showing his contempt for me will bring him closer to the Station Master."

Everyone knew Neva had problems with him. Saris and Etinon looked bothered though Brody only nodded and looked a bit disgusted. "I do not understand why the Station Naster causes you such 'roblems," Saris admitted.

"That's something I cannot answer for her," Rafe replied and they being Ksa -- a people who had very strict rules of behavior among their own -- both nodded in a quick dismissal of that line of discussion.

"Does this vehavior work for he?" Etinon dared to ask with a wave towards Ekhardt.

"Neva isn't that stupid."

That drew quick smiles from both of the Ksa, but Etinon turned again to where Ekhardt had gone. Rafael could hear the sound of his growling voice somewhere back in the booths, where he obviously found someone else to harass.

"Ekhardt is good enough at working the bays, unloading the ships and the like," Rafe said with a shrug. "He can run crews and get things done. Unfortunately, he's not a diplomat and the larger the market gets, the more trouble he has handling the work."

"Es'ecially with those who are not of his own kind," Saris added.

Rafe turned back to the Ksa with a start. This wasn't news to him because he knew Ekhardt certainly didn't like Ksa, Norishi or Click any better than he liked humans, but he had never considered the man more than a nuisance. "Is this becoming a real problem?"

"Everything Ekhardt does becomes a real problem," Brody mumbled.

"A-e, a-e," Saris replied and gave a little human-like shrug. It had taken a while for Rafael to realize A-e was the Ksa's way of saying 'maybe' and now the shorter version was starting to work its way into human slang. "He is not 'olite with his own so you cannot ex'ect he to ve so with others."

"And the population is starting to get larger in both humans and others," Brody added, leaning forward on her case. "We're reaching a critical mass, I think."

"This neans?" Etinon asked.

"The more people we have, the more possible

interactions between them," Rafael answered. "With humans, that usually means there will be more problems. We tend to be too much of individualists and we want our own way. Working in groups can sometimes be a problem, especially if the group isn't vetted for personality conflicts."

"Vetted?"

"A professional looks over the makeup of the group and searches for obvious problem spots. This can be especially important on ships where they are going to spend a lot of time together in small spaces."

"Though free trader captains seem to have a knack for picking up good crew even without professional vetting," Brody said. "And professionals don't always find the real troublemakers on military ships."

Etinon and Saris looked perplexed.

"Is there something about Ekhardt that we should be aware of?" Rafael asked.

"He should not insult Ksa nerchants," Saris said, which was uncommonly straightforward and worried Rafael for that reason alone. "They have an s'ecial 'lace in our society and to insult they is a natter of grave consequence. You do not want this to go on."

"You could have come to me before this," Rafael said. His head still pounded and he thought maybe everything had gone crazy today.

"We are uncertain what is 'ernited," Etinon replied with a slight shrug.

"You can bring any problem to me," Rafael said. "Or to Ardi if I'm not around. Any time a human is a problem, let us know. We don't want trouble."

"No? Then why do you so often look for it, Rafael?" Etinon asked.

Brody laughed and Rafael found himself grinning. The two Ksa looked even more confused now but that wasn't surprising. It happened just about every time he and his friends had a discussion about human motivations.

"Let's just call it a character flaw that is more prominent in some people than in others," Rafael offered.

"A flaw you share with Ekhardt?" Etinon asked, looking back where Ekhardt cursed again. "I should not like to think you were like that nan."

"The same results from different reasons. Ekhardt goes to start trouble to make himself important. I find myself in the midst of trouble because I try to stop it."

"Ah. Yes." They both nodded this time.

He wanted away from the subject and looked back at the stand and the shells. "You should see if you can get a few small rocks, Brody. Not gems or anything that pricey. Even if you could afford them, no one here could make enough to pay for them. But some small, river-worn pebbles would be nice. I've heard some people put them into settings and wear them as good luck pieces. A half-pound of little pebbles could go a long ways."

Brody nodded with a look of calculation in her eyes. "My cousin back on earth is helping me out with this. She already has the contacts she made when she sent me the shells, so she can go to the authorities and ask what's permitted. Not a bad idea, Rafael."

He nodded, gave one more glance at the pretty shells, and moved on. He didn't doubt he'd be back to look again but it was never a good idea for him to stand wistfully over something. It did his state of mind no good and pointed out an obvious weakness to others.

He touched the metal on the side of his face. He had weaknesses enough.

"Ekhardt is creating trouvle," Saris said, as though echoing what Rafael had stated. Then he realized Saris was telling him something. He nodded to go on. "There are things in the narket that we know were not neant to ve there. Dangerous things -- sonetines infornation, other tines forvidden things."

"Drugs?"

"Sone."

No news to him. He'd heard from Yang that a black market in drugs had started up on the station and he knew Neva was doing her best to track down the source which they knew was in the market but hadn't found yet.

"Ekhardt," he suddenly said, putting together what his companion said. "He has the access to ships when he works the bays and the market when he works here."

"He is careful of hunans watching. He is not as careful of Ksa." Etinon said with a smirk.

That sounded like the stupid SOB. He had such a distain for aliens that he probably never considered they could see him doing something wrong. Ekhardt was just plain stupid. The man needed to be moved out of the position in the market. Even if he wasn't part of a black market situation, he still didn't have the personality for delicate work that included aliens.

At least Rafe could no longer hear him cursing, though by now Rafael's head ached almost to distraction. Too many things to consider and that on top of a bad round with the Displaced. How had he ever gotten into a position like this? He should have been working in the labs, buried in comp simulations and reports.

Though sometimes he thought the others made a mistake, sequestering themselves in their room with the equipment. He made Xenation itself his lab. Some of the problems were wider than he could see, and some were introduced by outside forces (like Ekhardt), he though he still had a better feel for the station than the others did. He experienced more of Xenation even without the link.

Today, though --

"I need rest," he said when his legs started to get weak and his arms shaky. Yang's shot had worn off and the adrenaline of what the Ksa gave him had held him up longer than he expected. "I'm going back to Xenobia and just sit for a while."

The two nodded and continued on with him. Pride almost made him tell them to go away and that he didn't need their help or their protection, but he couldn't be certain either was true. The vid in his case worried him. He said nothing as they started out of the market and back into the open bay.

The dock team were back to work on the repairs they'd been occupied with before the Displaced arrived. Felice gave a wave, wrench in hand. He hoped Xenation kept the Displaced in line for at least another day or two . . . if the station had control over them at all. He had never really been certain.

A group came out of the shadowed archway to the Human Enclave, just beyond Xenobia. Rafael feared seeing Neva and some of her people at first and he didn't know if he felt any better watching Tican and two Norishi companions instead. At least, though, they would be easier to deal with. He simply moved aside and bowed his head in simple politeness.

Tican and her people did something *very* odd. They slowed. Tican bowed her head in return. "Rafael," she said.

A simple greeting, a little politeness.

Tican *never* acknowledged males. Norishi certainly never called them by name.

He watched them go past, panic sending a new surge of adrenaline through his system and nearly making him almost ill this time. He looked at the two Ksa and found them as shocked as he had ever seen them.

He watched the Norishi head to the left and towards their own Enclave.

This couldn't be good.

CHAPTER SEVEN

Morgan spent his first day on Xenation ensconced in work. He hadn't expected to be thrown into the quagmire so quickly, but he didn't mind. He sat in the Spartan office while the others brought him reports and asked questions. Most seemed genuinely pleased to have someone interested in their work, even if they were nervous that he might tell them to stop. So far, though, all the reports looked fascinating. He wasn't going to rush into any decisions.

Between those meetings, he studied the reports about Raphael and the Displaced that Samplin had on his computer. Most of them came from Yang and he suspected the man might be biased. However, the more he read, the less he felt this was a setup. Yang had started out skeptical as well.

Every time he thought this might be a trick, he recalled Ashur's ghostly face and felt a chill. The Displaced might not be what Rafael had said -- whatever that might be, because he hadn't found that reference yet -- but they were certainly *something*.

He didn't want to think about discussing the problem with Neva. He didn't know what she really expected. She knew professionalism would come before friendship in a situation like this. Even so . . . even so, she had been the one who suggested him as a replacement for Samplin.

Ritter came into the office to talk about her work on tracking Xenation transmissions. That had been an official project, but Ritter looked just as nervous as the others. Her study seemed to be one of the more promising. She showed him readouts of sub-radio frequency measurements she'd been taking.

"And this is from today." She pulled up some scans on her pocketcomp. "This was during the new build back behind the human sector. If I'm right, these patterns here should coordinate with the movement or size of whatever Xenation did. And this --" She brought up another screen with a quick jab of her finger. "This is a spike of activity that happened not long afterwards. My guess is we had another Displaced incident. We don't always realize this far back from the bay and they rarely come in here, even though they want power sources for some reason."

"Yes, we did." Morgan looked over the readings and frowned. "I heard the others say Xenation was slow to answer. Weaker after the rebuild? Distracted by doing something somewhere else?"

"I wish I knew." Ritter ran a hand through her short blonde hair. She looked bothered. "I get the feeling there's a lot more we aren't reading yet. I'm looking for the frequency, but it's either outside the range of anything we've discovered or else on such a narrow band that we're just not able to refine fast enough to see it yet."

Morgan found himself intrigued by this information which might give them a direct link to the station or at least a better one than what Rafael might represent.

"I have a lot of graphs and numbers," she said, dropping a chit on the desk. "But not a lot of results. I think there's far more we're just not reading. I would like to set up more stations in other areas of Xenation to try and get a better triangulation on where the transmissions even originate. There's only so much I can get sitting here in the lab."

"And there's a problem getting the equipment?" he asked. They didn't, after all, have an unlimited budget.

"I have most of what I need but I can't get permission to place it. I tried Samplin, but he wasn't interested. I even went to the Station Master, but she was worried about some of the equipment slipping out of human hands especially since this stuff deals directly with human communications."

"Ah." That made sense, though probably an unnecessary precaution. No one doubted the Ksa and Norishi had such equipment already. They still took precautions. "And no way to put equipment out at the proper time to get a reading?"

"There is no proper time," Ritter said with what sounded like years of frustration sitting below the surface. "There is no pattern I can find to when Xenation does anything at all."

"How long have you been at this work?"

"I came with the first team," she said with a snort of amusement. "I've been at this since the moment we docked, over eight years ago. I want a breakthrough, Etech Doreet. I *need* one. I've dedicated far too much of my life to this station to walk away now."

"Someone suggested you go?" he asked.

"Samplin did but I know he based his suggestion on his personal level of frustration. I'm close to some sort of breakthrough. I have started picking up patterns within the transmissions themselves and that's a big step forward. They are recent changes, too. I think this means something is changing within the station itself."

That drew all his attention. "What do you need?"

Ritter sat forward, hands on the desk and looked him straight in the face. "I need more stations set up; nothing else is going to make a difference."

"How big are they?"

"No more than pocketcomp size."

"So they could be hidden if need be."

She nodded. "However, if we go around hiding recording devices, someone is going to notice and who knows what the Ksa and Norishi might think when they figured it out."

"True. How many of these spots would you need?"

"I'd be happy with three more besides the one in the lab." She waved a hand back towards the room where the others still worked. "I have one set up at the farthest corner of the Human Enclave. If I could get more at angles out in the bay area, it would help. I would really like to place one out on the closest agro dome as well but that one isn't as essential as the others."

Morgan thought this would be an interesting problem to solve. He liked puzzles, which he suspected made him a really good choice for Xenation. "I'll see if we can come up with something."

"Thank you!" Her eyes brightened.

"I assume it's about time we close down here?" Morgan asked, looking out at where the others were starting to shut down equipment.

"Yes," Ritter said, glancing back that way. "Some of us keep monitors with us since there's no telling when Xenation might do something. Since the Human Enclave is so small, we can get back here fast enough."

He nodded. "I'll see you tomorrow, then."

Ritter smiled and left. Morgan picked up his chit and filed it into the computer with the others and watched while everyone else left.

Then he went back to the files on the Displaced and Rafael. He couldn't leave the problem alone. It was time he *saw* the truth. He pulled the video up, leaned forward, and let it run.

The bay area looked empty. The cam showed some crates, but no market, a small work yard, and no Xenobia. He also noted there was also less phosphorescence in the walls. He wondered what that might mean.

A couple people worked on some equipment at the right side of the area. He thought one of them looked like the woman who had run into Xenobia looking for Rafael, though not quite as wild looking as she was now.

He almost didn't recognize Rafael at all. Morgan might not have noticed him. Shorter hair. Not quite as thin. He had rushed into the area while looking at a pocketcomp and suddenly waved it in the air and began shouting.

"Back! We have a problem! Get into cover!"

No metal on his face. He looked younger and part of Morgan protested that he was too young for Neva. He wondered how Rafael had known there was a problem --

The others began to rush away and Morgan could clearly see the problem manifest already. The bay wall bulged inward, looking like putty. The nose of the ship came all the way through, and the shock sent the area shaking. Rafael fell and scrambled back to his feet again. He might have been shouting, but the sounds of the ship blocked out everything else.

Rafael took a step backwards. Stopped. Why would the fool stop and watch that ship, unless he knew --

The ships nose cracked and pieces flew outward. One hit Rafael in the head and he went down and then he was rushing back up rushing towards the ship as someone tried to escape from the damaged craft.

Light flared -- the engine must have blown -- and Morgan could see and hear the wind howling through the bay as decompression began to sweep through --

The walls flared brightly. Grid lines of dark blues formed across the bay area. A ball of light grabbed Rafael and held him in place while the ship continued to come apart, pieces flying through the bay, though they disappeared when they reached the grid.

Balls of light, darker than that which held Rafael, swarmed into the ship and out again as parts of the ship dissolved into light. Morgan's mouth went dry while he watched and read, the scans embedded into the vid. He wondered --

The ship exploded and Morgan pulled back from the screen in shock. Pieces tore holes in the outer walls and impacted the inside. The cam fell, but he could still see Rafael, caught in the maelstrom of destruction. Impacts hit the inner walls, but didn't penetrate and even in the tilted vidcam's view, he could see the outer walls already repairing themselves as waves of light rushed up over the holes. All the pieces of the scout ship disappeared.

Xenation repaired Rafael, too. He could see blood flowing from the head wound and how he lay, limp and unresponsive on the floor though still encased in the protective light. Morgan squinted and leaned closer, trying to see what was happening with Rafael. He could see, he thought, how small waves of light moved across Rafael's face, replacing the damaged area with the graft of metal that seemed to appear like magic.

Not long afterwards, people arrived and carried him away. Someone picked up the cam and the scene went dark.

Morgan sat back and forced the tenseness out of his body. He felt as drained as though he had been present at the disaster itself. He felt a new wave of worry because he could not begin to see how Neva could consider Rafael responsible.

Rafael must have done something before he arrived at the bay, though. After all, how had he known something was about to go wrong? He almost reached forward to play the video again. No, not yet. Better to think about it for a while. Better to try and put some distance between himself and the original shock he felt to be able to view the scene as objectively as he could.

He needed to find out how Rafael had known there would be a problem. He wondered if he should ask Yang or if he wouldn't be better going to Rafael himself. Or perhaps he might even ask Neva. She was the one who held the other view of the situation.

Though not tonight. Not right away. He needed to approach this carefully. Neva had problems with Rafael and he feared to make the situation worse by pushing her. She could be stubborn. He remembered that very well.

He still had to wonder why she wanted him for this position. She had to know he wouldn't stand by her for friendship's sake if he found she was in the wrong.

"Morgan?"

He looked up to find Yang back at the door and shaking his head in disbelief.

"Problem?" Morgan asked and worried about things going wrong again already.

"You are working late on the very first day you got here. Tell me you aren't going to be one of those people I have to shepherd around to make certain they take care of themselves. I have enough of those already."

"I was trying to go over the Rafael material," he admitted.

Yang nodded. "That's good . . . but you know, the Rafael material has been there for a long time and it'll be there in the morning. Come on. We're going to dinner so you can meet some of the people outside of your office. They're all wondering about you, you know."

"And they all know about my meeting with Neva at Xenobia."

"Oh yes." He laughed. "We're a small group. I imagine the Click even know about it by now."

"Dinner sounds good. How is the food here?"

"Better than you'd expect. I'll treat you at Xenobia. This should be interesting."

He thought that was probably some kind of warning. Fool that he was, he didn't argue as he went with him.

Xenobia had far more people crowded into the small area then when he first arrived. He was all the way inside with Yang before he realized many of them were Ksa. The two groups mingled on a casual level without trouble, though the humans were more polite to the Ksa than humans were too each other.

Rafael sat at a table in the corner and gave Morgan a quick, nervous glance. Morgan tried not to read guilt into it. After all, he had to be worried about the situation between the new head of science -- someone with a lot of power here -- and Neva.

Yang introduced him to humans and Ksa. Neva arrived later. Rafael remained and spent a lot of time with the Ksa, who seemed to like him. They had an excellent meal and good conversation that rarely ventured into work-related material.

"We'll have an official, welcome dinner after Samplin leaves," Neva said when they were mostly done and the others were leaving.

"You know those kinds of things don't interest me,"

Morgan replied with a shake of his head.

"I know, but the dinner is not for you. It's so we have a reason to break out some of the good food and party."

Even Rafael laughed at that one.

The evening did Morgan good by easing the tension he'd felt. He realized the Rafael situation was not a problem that would blow up and cause a major disruption. Even if it turned out that Rafael was somehow manipulating the situation and creating the scenes, they didn't seem to amount to anything more than an occasional disturbance now and then.

He let the worry slip away for the night and found himself talking to Ksa the same way he spoke with humans; talking to *aliens* face-to-face as though they were no different than his apartment neighbors back on Terra Nova.

Seeds from the same tree. He had heard the term lately, and standing here with the Ksa, sharing food and drink, he thought maybe there might be something to the odd, fringe idea making the rounds. They were far too much alike and the idea that like groups had been seeded on different worlds suddenly seemed a plausible idea to him.

Or maybe he'd had too much of the local beer. Granted, the liquor wasn't especially strong since they couldn't waste much grain, but this still gave a bit of a kick, especially after such a long and stressful day.

The others retired. He saw Yang and Neva having a serious talk so he didn't go to beg one of them to show him to his own bed. Instead, he took a seat at the bar, accepted a quarter glass more of the local brew -- after all, it was only polite -- and looked around the group again. Odd place. Strange people. He liked Xenation already.

He saw the guy who had been introduced as the head of security sit down at the table with Rafael. He wished he could have heard that conversation because Rafael looked a little surprised and then nodded. He reached into the bag hung across his chair and dug around for a moment, and then brought out some small box and handed it over to Ardi. Raphael looked relieved.

He saw two of the Ksa watching as well. He could not read their emotions.

"Ready to go?" Yang asked, coming up beside him.

"Yeah. Long day," he said and slid off the seat. His legs even felt a little wobbly. He couldn't be that tired. "I hope it isn't far."

"Nothing is far in Xenation," Yang replied. He patted Morgan on the shoulder. They made their farewells and he even gave Neva a little hug, but he found himself glad to be out of the close confines of the bar.

He looked out over the bay. The lights had been dimmed since they pretended to day and night here, with a regular planet-bound schedule. He'd heard such things helped people on stations, but he'd never lived on one long enough to care.

The Norishi had a guard at their entrance, watching across the distance with a hand on a weapon which he thought must be sword-like. That was almost as disconcerting as the half dozen Click pets that suddenly bounded through like furry, animate basket balls.

This was going to be a damned interesting place to live.

CHAPTER EIGHT

Rafael had expected trouble from Morgan Doreet, but that didn't happen. Not the first day, the next -- not in the entire week since the man arrived. More days passed and he stopped being nervous every time he saw the new head of the science department. He had heard good things about Doreet from Ritter and Price. Even so, he saw the man watching him sometimes and it made Rafe nervous. Trouble was coming from that direction . . . but not yet. He could deal with later.

They had other problems instead. Ekhardt had made trouble in the market again and more than a few people were upset with him, both Ksa and human. He'd insulted a Ksa merchant out shopping in the human section and the Ksa had all withdrawn into their own sector.

Then they called for a Tribunal, which was a close to a joint law court as they got on Xenation. Ksa had never asked for one before.

Neva and Ardi sat on the Tribunal for the humans, Saris and Onay for the Ksa, and Tican and Eris for the Norishi. The Norishi were never happy to be called out to deal with outsiders, but they never turned down the opportunity, either. The Click had been invited, as best could make them understand, but they only showed up to watch.

Rafael rarely came to the show but he'd passed word on to Ardi that they were having trouble with Ekhardt. The head of security asked him to be close by in case he had questions. Rafael did *not* want to be caught up in trouble with Ekhardt, though it would hardly matter in the long run.

Ekhardt hated him already. He supposed he might as well make the antagonism count for something other than Ekhardt's bad manners.

Mostly he didn't like to be here because people naturally stared at him while Neva purposely did not look his way. It hurt still, sometimes, in ways the others never seemed to understand. Maybe Yang did. He wondered what Morgan thought. He'd been on Xenation for nearly a month now and they'd talked briefly a few times. Rafe could see other questions the man had not yet asked in the etech's face when they talked. If Morgan sided with Neva, at least he did so more politely than Ekhardt.

The table where the Tribunal sat and where the witnesses would speak was set up outside Xenobia on a slightly raised stand. Chairs were mostly scavenged from Xenobia as well, and Buris stood at the doorway, watching the proceedings. They had a good turnout too.

They started with the Ksa merchant. She was an elderly woman named Dra who dealt in spices and whom no one really wanted to annoy. Ekhardt, sitting to the right, glowered at her and everyone, but he'd been told to hold his peace, if not to be polite. The Ksa woman didn't speak basic very well and Saris did some translating.

The discussion went quietly enough as Dra explained how Ekhardt had grabbed things from her booth and shoved her aside when she protested.

"What do you say to this?" Neva asked, looking finally at Ekhardt.

"How do we know what she's really saying?" he asked with a smug glare as he implied that Saris, one of the top Ksa at the station, was lying.

All the Ksa stood and left; a chilling sight to watch the group turn and walk away, including Saris and Eris. Saris had turned Rafael's way briefly with a look that mixed anger and dismay. Rafael doubted the others saw or recognized the emotions in the man's face. No one else spent as much time with the Ksa as he did.

"Well, that doesn't look good," Felice said beside him,

shaking her head.

"It isn't. You don't insult the Ksa," Rafael said with a shake of his head. He had a headache and for once it didn't come from anything directly related to Xenation. "How the hell can they let Ekhardt get away with something like this?"

"I don't think they can. I don't think they will. Neva does *not* look happy," Felice said. She patted him on the shoulder. "I'm going back to work. If they go after Ekhardt then I don't want to be in a position where he comes after me. Better to be working and acting like I have no idea what is going on."

"Yeah," he said. "Good luck."

She looked grim as she left and a few of the dock workers hurried off with her, a very unhappy little group. The Norishi left as well and he thought they looked more pleased than anyone else. Rafael watched the Ksa disappear into the market, and they didn't look back. He didn't know if even he dared to go talk to them after this.

"Rafe!"

He turned and managed not to grimace as Ardi hurried over. He'd never had trouble with the head of security even though the man worked closely with Neva, which made their relationship fraught with possible problems.

"Ardi," Rafe said. He could see rage barely held in check in the man's face and he braced himself. Even though this wasn't his trouble, everything that happened on this station came back to haunt him lately.

"Rafael." Ardi glanced at Neva who had gone to Ekhardt and then back to him. Yang and Morgan came over with Ardi, obviously interested in what the man had to say or else avoiding getting pulled into the tirade with Ekhardt. "Look," the head of security said, sounding flustered. "I'll get straight to it. You know the Ksa better than any of us. What can we do to make this right?"

He hadn't expected the question but he had an answer.

"Here's the problem, Ardi," he said, and decided to be as open despite Morgan being there. This wasn't a situation to dance around. "We know Ksa society is based on a great deal of ritual politeness. We also know they have trouble trusting humans because we aren't often polite to each other, let alone to them."

"So true," he mumbled. "What's the answer?"

"Ekhardt was not only rude, but he accused the Ksa of *lying*. If another Ksa had done so, they probably would have gone to weapons. We're lucky they just walked away."

"The Ksa don't get into fights," Ardi said with a shake of his head.

"The Ksa have a deeply ritualized form of politeness within their society. There's a reason for it, you know. My suspicion -- and this is only based on observations -- is that outside of those bounds of society, they are an extremely aggressive people. They have had to find a way to tame their aggression for the sake of their civilization."

"Hell," Morgan said, stepping closer. "That's an interesting theory. Do you have anything more to back it up?"

"Tales of past wars that some of my friends have eluded to," he said. He was surprised to find Morgan so interested -- or maybe not. Morgan seemed to have a genuine curiosity about everything on the station, which made him a surprisingly good choice for head of the science team despite his ties to Neva. "They haven't told me anything directly and because it's easy to step over the bounds, I haven't asked."

Both Morgan and Ardi nodded. Rafe thought they were both going to start looking closer at the Ksa again. "This doesn't help this situation," Ardi said. "I think this makes the situation more difficult."

"Nothing is easy. You are going to have to get Ekhardt to apologize," Morgan decided.

"That's not going to happen, at least not in a way that will sound like he even halfway means what he says," Rafael replied. "Maybe Neva can apologize for him. She's high enough in stature that her apology should mean something to them. But how often can she cover for him? He's gotten away with this once and he knows he has a button he can push now. He'll create this trouble whenever he can."

"We need to keep him away from the Ksa," Ardi said.

"Can't do that unless the Ksa retreat from the market and we don't want that to happen --"

"Or if Ekhardt retreats," Ardi said and suddenly smiled in a way that Rafael couldn't help but return. "We've wanted him out of there for some time anyway. This is a good reason to remove him. We can move him --" Ardi stopped and looked at Morgan.

"Out into the open. Neva trusts me, remember. I know you suspect of him things far worse than lying."

Ardi nodded and still looked pleased. He turned to make certain Ekhardt couldn't see them. Ekhardt didn't look pleased by the lecture Neva was giving him. He was about to learn the limits he had crossed in whole new ways. This was not going to be his best day. Might be the best fun Rafael had seen in a long time. About time they brought the little bastard down.

"If we can get him out of the market, he'll have to make his connections elsewhere and we'll have a better chance watching him," Ardi said. He glanced towards the market and frowned. "There's too much that can go on under the counter, so to speak."

"The bad thing is that he's going to make life hell on the workers," Rafael said and glanced to where Felice and her crew were back to work already. "I hate to do that to them. It's bad enough working for him already."

Ardi nodded and pursed his lips. "I can't remove him from there but I can make it harder for him to be a pain in the ass. I'm going to add some new patrols to the bay because I'm worried about all this increased trouble, you see. Ekhardt doesn't like to look bad in front authority."

"That should help," Rafael agreed. "But what about the market itself? Can you leave it without supervision? Ekhardt wasn't much help, but he could direct people how to set up booths and he did stop a couple of fights. He even did a little to keep the pets in line."

"Do the Click understand the purpose of the market at all?" Morgan asked.

"They seem to be catching on a bit. It's not really the Click that are so much a problem as the pets. They want to grab everything. People have learned to put things under coverings and keep an eye open for the little furballs."

"What other problems do you see?" Ardi asked, glancing towards the market.

"Fights, mostly among humans. Questions on trade worth; Ekhardt didn't have any kind of head for that part. Keeping people from insulting the Norishi."

"And the Ksa, obviously," Morgan said.

"The Ksa are far harder to insult. This became a problem because we were at a formal gathering and they expected certain rules of conduct. Ekhardt stepped way over the line there and would have been even if this had been a strictly human meeting. I think he's afraid of the Norishi and doesn't cross them. I saw him kick a Click pet once, though. Lucky the little guy thought it was a game."

"Yeah, I remember the report," Ardi said with a frown. "I didn't know it came from you."

"I keep my name off of anything that is going to go through Command."

Ardi frowned but didn't argue the point. "We have a big ship coming in tomorrow or the next day." Ardi glanced at the bay area with a shake of his head. "A lot of supplies and we suspect some things for Ekhardt's black market. Getting him out of the area will help us track him. Unfortunately, there's also going to be an influx of material in general and at least a dozen visiting humans. We can't let them loose in the market without someone watching over them."

"True," Rafael said.

"Good. Then we'll put you in charge of the market," Ardi said with a quick, firm nod.

He couldn't find his voice for a moment though he knew he had started shaking his head the moment Ardi said the words. "No, no. It won't happen. Neva will *never* allow it."

"I am putting you on my payroll. You'll work as full time security. I'll have your ID updated as soon as I get back to the office."

"Ardi, you can't possibly think she will --"

"Neva! Ekhardt! "Ardi shouted and waved them over.

Rafael's immediate reaction was to start backing away and get out of the blast zone before one or the other -- or both -- exploded. He would have left except that Morgan moved up beside him and blocked the way. He thought the man might have done so intentionally . . . or perhaps he put himself beside Rafe to show where he stood in this one. Neva did give her old friend an odd glance as she and Ekhardt arrived.

Rafael gave Ardi one look of despair. He couldn't hide the emotion as he usually did but the head of security plainly didn't care.

Neva kept her face mostly neutral, but there was a little color in her cheeks. He hoped that came from dealing with Ekhardt who was an officious SOB at the best of times -- and this wouldn't be one of those rare good times.

Ekhardt had stalked over, his own face dark red and the pulse pounding in the vein at his throat. They were going to need Yang soon if he didn't calm down. What Ardi was about to tell him wouldn't help.

"Don't start in on me," Ekhardt warned as he glared straight at Ardi. "Neva already had words with me and I don't need to take that bullshit from you, too."

"I'll make what I have to say short and sweet then," Ardi replied and not in the least bit rising to the bait. "Given the current situation, we can't let you deal with Ksa anymore."

"Fine by me. I don't need to talk to the lying bastards."

Rafael felt his arm twitch. He wanted to grab Ekhardt by the throat and beat some sense into the man. He held still and waited for the real bombshell to hit.

"Good, glad you agree," Ardi said. "It means we're banning you from the market."

Ekhardt's mouth opened. His face paled. Neva gave a quick pleased nod Ekhardt didn't see. The man stood before them looking as stunned as Rafael had ever seen him.

"Banned -- out of the Ksa market, you mean," Ekhardt

said as his eyes narrowed and color returned to his face. The
rage would hit any moment now.

"No, I mean the *entire* market. The Ksa are likely to be in
other areas and we are not going to let your presence trigger
more trouble. You've caused enough already."

"You can't -- you don't have the authority --"

"Ardi is the head of security," Neva replied. Her voice
sounded quite calm and pleasant and Rafael had to fight not
to grin at her reaction. The news obviously pleased her
though he suspected she wasn't going to like the next part.
"If he says you are banned from somewhere, I'm not going
to second guess him."

"But --"

"It's done," Ardi said. "However, we do need someone
else to keep watch on things in the area. Given that this has
become such a gathering place for all the groups, I decided to
hire Rafael and put him in there."

Neva's eyes narrowed as she glanced his way; the first
time she had even acknowledged he was in the group. He
braced himself for the next words . . . but she only turned
back to Ardi with a quick nod.

Well hell.

Ekhardt, predictably, took the news badly.

"Son of a bitch!" he shouted, loud enough that everyone
in the area turned and stared. "You can't do that. You can't
put him in there --"

"I can and have," Ardi said and did not raise his voice at
all. "You made your choices, Ted. I told you before that you
were going to have to live with them."

"No way in hell will I stand here and put up with this!"
He stepped forward and swung at Rafael. He didn't think the
man even knew what he was doing as the rage took complete
control of him.

Rafael caught hold of the arm before it connected, and
used his leverage to force the arm up with a painful twist,
putting Ekhardt down on his knees with a rather unmanly
yelp of pain.

They had everyone's attention now, of course. He

couldn't hear sounds anywhere else.

"Don't do that again," Rafael said and let go of the arm. Ekhardt went down on his hands and knees.

Ardi looked surprised before he grinned. "Yes, I think you'll do just fine in security."

Rafe glanced at Neva and even dared to meet her look. She nodded and walked away. Morgan went with her. Ekhardt stood, glared at Rafe, and then went after her. If he thought he was going to change her mind, he plainly didn't know Neva at all.

Rafe looked back at Ardi. "So, what is really going on?" he asked. "What am I *really* looking for in the market?"

"Everything you've already been reporting," he said and sounded serious again as he stepped closer and his voice dropped. "And you're going to try and make amends with the Ksa. I'm sure Neva will do a formal apology, and we might even get Ekhardt to do one --"

"Don't bother. He'd sound insincere and the Ksa can read that quite clearly in humans. Just make sure it's apparent he's out of favor for what he said."

"That won't be hard. For the rest . . . people who have been doing black market sales are probably going to try and get around losing their link. Ekhardt runs the bays so he could walk small items from one area to the other without much notice. We actually don't have a clue who might be involved with him. Yang says there have been illicit drugs turning up in screenings, though. Could be very small. And . . . we think may be other things are moved through the system. Most of it is likely alien in origin and not cleared for distribution into the human holdings."

None of this surprised him, including the trade in alien artifacts. People were fascinated with anything that came from the alien groups and some people had approached him since he had contact with the Ksa. He thought about the tube in his room. He still didn't know if it did more than produce pretty colors. Ardi knew about it already. So did Morgan and he hadn't asked for device which gave him more hope of working with the new head of science.

"I'll do what I can." Rafe touched the edge of the metal along his face. Ardi looked unsettled by the move, as though he hadn't noticed the plate lately. "But there may be a problem if -- *when* the Displaced show up."

"Key me through your ID whenever you have to deal with them. Since you'll be under my jurisdiction now, it'll come straight to me."

He nodded and wondered if he would like having a boss again. Samplin had been one in name, and Morgan never even hinted he should be working for science. He missed working in the field he had loved, analyzing everything, taking readings. He still did so in his own way.

"I can hunt you down a security suit --" Ardi said.

"No. At least not yet. Let me go on as I am. I'll tell everyone I'm taking over for Ekhardt but if we don't go out of our way to make this obvious, people might not really think of me as security."

"Good point," Ardi said. "Very good point. We already have this cleared with Neva, so I don't see any problem. Good luck. And thank you."

Ardi walked away.

He had a new job and better pay than doing occasional odd work for Yang. Maybe he'd save up and buy a couple shells. *Purpose.* He hadn't realized how much of a difference it would make until now.

He headed for the market.

CHAPTER NINE

Morgan walked away with Neva as she headed back through the milling crow. Many people still whispered, shocked by the entire play of events. He waited for her to speak, but she only shook he read now and then as they headed to the admin section. Neva and Morgan looked in the doorway to where people were busy working. Some glanced her way but they were all trying to stay out of the blast field.

Ekhardt caught up to them there by the door, but Neva turned on the man and lifted a hand before he began to speak.

"Don't say anything. *Don't*. You have already created one situation that is going to be hell to try and fix."

"They're lying bastards --" he began his face going red again and his eyes bulging. "You can't --"

"Maybe they are. Maybe they aren't. They are *Ksa*, though, and you just created the kind of incident that could get the Inner World Council itself interested in the mess. The last thing I want is for them to think we need supervision out here and send a squad of Whites to help out."

Those words won a quick, nervous start from the man. Ekhardt didn't want officials here, beyond a doubt. He was so obvious that Morgan found it pathetic to watch the way he backed down, turned and rushed off.

"Loathsome little toad," Neva mumbled. Morgan bowed his head, hiding a grin. "This might be the chance I need to get him off the station. I hope so. Ardi wants to hold on to him so he can tag the man and maybe break the smuggling and black market ring. How can so much be going on with so few people?"

"We are an ingenious race, Neva my friend. And we are most dangerous and creative when we're bored."

"There's a frightening thought." She stopped and leaned against the wall just outside the admin room. The buzz of computers and the soft voices within sounded almost normal. "I wish Ardi hadn't put Rafael in that spot though. Damn."

"You don't trust him," Morgan said, breaching the subject of Rafael for the first time since his arrival.

She looked back at him, her dark eyes narrowing. "No, I don't."

"What happened, Neva?" he asked. He wanted to hear her side and understand. "Just tell me what happened."

He didn't tell her he'd already seen the video. Maybe she knew he had. She probably suspected at any rate.

She shook her head. "The others have told you."

"Why did you ask for me in this position?"

She stopped, caught off guard by that one. Her face changed a little. "This is the perfect spot for you, Morgan. This is the kind of place you've trained for all your life. There are questions everywhere and you *love* questions. You want there to be mysteries. Samplin was good at first because he could set things up. He can look at a set of notes from Pathfinders and decide exactly what kind of equipment should go in to a new world . . . but once he has it set up, he gets bored. He wants to go somewhere else."

That made sense. He'd picked up a lot of that attitude in Samplin's notes. He wanted, at the very least, to set up more positions on Xenation, and it just wasn't possible since they were limited to so small a space. He had put a few comp-run readers out at various spots on the outside of the station, some clear at the far end. They'd been sending back interesting data, but he'd never done anything with the information.

Had that been Rafael's work, to look over the reports that came in? Maybe he'd have to ask.

He nodded to Neva who looked likely to turn and walk away from the original question -- and that probably said a lot of what he needed to know, though none of it good.

"I want to understand what happened."

"We all do," she said. She looked around. They were alone in the hall. "Rafael knew something was going to happen."

"What did he know? How?"

"I don't know," she said, and sounded more frustrated than angry. "He'd been doing some studies on his own. He thought he understood some of the readings from the station and he didn't like what he saw. He showed me, but I couldn't see so and told him. He went to the bay . . . so I called the captain of the scout and said there might be a problem. He didn't see it either. So he came on."

Now that put an entirely different view of things he had thought and eased one persistent knot of worry he'd felt every time he thought about the accident. Neva had never been careless when it came to other people's lives. He could not imagine she had the one time everything went bad and especially with a warning in hand from someone she had still trusted at the time.

"He warned you about what was going to happen. He went to see --"

"Did he?" she said. She looked up into his face and he could see the true distrust and doubt. "Is that why he went down there? Or was it to make certain things went the way he wanted them to?"

Someone appeared at the end of the hall, saw the two of them talking, and went another direction. Morgan would have found it amusing at another time. Maybe they knew enough not to bother Neva when she was in a bad mood and the trouble with Ekhardt and the Ksa had probably been enough for the reaction.

She had glanced down the hall and frowned as well and then started to turn towards the room and work. However, he wasn't going to let her go just yet.

"Do you really think he did something purposely?

Why?"

She looked up. Her cheeks colored a little and her eyes narrowed, though this time with embarrassment.

"You and Rafael were having an affair. I heard about that already," he said and made nothing of it.

"You were Ashur's friend." She was annoyed by his reaction. This was not going to go well.

"Yes, I was. I'm your friend as well and always have been. I'll reserve judgment on Rafael. I know more about you and Ashur than anyone else here. I know you were already talking about splitting up before the chance to take over Xenation came along. I know you both took this post for your careers and not for the chance to stay together. Am I wrong?"

"No. No you aren't. But still --"

"It was only a matter of time, Neva, and I don't mean that as a slam of any sort. If it hadn't been for Tali, you would have split long before you came to this station."

"Tali," she said, with a little whisper of regret that had not been there before. "Yes, and look how well that turned out."

He sighed. They'd gotten a bit off topic, but he didn't try to pull her back yet. At least she was talking and he hoped it would help him understand.

"I still feel guilty about everything," she said. Her voice was soft and her head bowed. "Guilty about abandoning Tali to the hospital. I tried to write to her. You don't want to know the note I got back." Her face reddened and her hands curled into fists. He didn't remember ever seeing that kind of rage from her when talking about Tali and for a moment she couldn't even speak. "I couldn't bring her out here."

"No, you couldn't," he agreed. He had only known Tali as a small child but he'd been there when her parents finally had agreed she needed specialized care. She had no sense of right and wrong. She had no care about whom got hurt. She liked causing pain -- both mental and physical. She had problems and by the time Tali reached her twelfth birthday it had become impossible for her parents to follow her around and keep her out of trouble. Specialized care was the only answer to keep others safe.

"We never should have taken this position, Morgan. We never should have moved out here. Now I've pulled you here as well --"

"I came because I want to be here. So did you and Ashur. Things have happened, Neva. You can't blame that on this station. What about what happened to Ashur? Why do you really think this was Rafael's fault?"

There. He'd asked the question straight out. She stood still for a moment with her fingers still balled into fists but her head tilted a little to the side and her eyes blinking. She was finally going to tell him something, even if this wasn't quite the whole truth.

"We'd talked about Ashur coming back," she said softly. "We'd talked about what we'd tell him. I was . . . I was certain Ashur wouldn't make any trouble about a divorce. You are right; we'd both known we were only together because it was convenient and comfortable. There wasn't any passion left. Rafael, not knowing us all that well, was a little more worried. He liked Ashur. They'd worked well together. Rafe came to see me the morning after we got news the scout team was coming back in. He said not to worry and that he would deal with Ashur."

"And you think he meant more than talk to him?"

"I don't want to believe that. I really don't. But -- but -- he was starting to get the station to do things, Morgan. To make changes that helped us. He told me everything was still experimental and he didn't have any kind of definite control. He could get lights to brighten in the wall and he could get doors into more rooms sometimes. Not always, but sometimes."

"I want to talk to him," Morgan said and found himself suddenly far more interested in Rafael than he had been a few minutes before. The reaction made Neva laugh, which he supposed was good.

"I don't know if I can trust Rafael or myself at this point. The way the station latched onto him afterwards makes me all the more uneasy about dealing with him. I don't want him near anything sensitive."

Surprise made him stop and rethink the situation. "It's not him you mistrust."

She started to say something, then stopped. "You're right in some ways. I don't trust the contact with Xenation. I think the station really does have some control of him."

He couldn't argue the point since he mistrusted the link as well. He was glad Neva admitted at least part of the problem with Rafe. He thought it would make things easier to deal with if he didn't have to worry about stepping carefully around her. Not perfect, but better.

"I looked at the video of what happened," he admitted. "Obviously he knew something was going to happen. Has anyone asked him how he knew?"

"Yang did. He wasn't very coherent at the time, though. I don't know if he's asked again but I trust that if he comes up with something, he'll let me know. I try to stay clear of it, Morgan. I think that's the best thing I can do, because we have enough problems."

"We do?"

She gave a little nod. "I don't know if Ekhardt is part of a bigger problem or just a little pimple of annoyance all his own. His little act today may have cost us the respect of allies whom I think we need. Or the Ksa may be trouble all their own and are just playing us."

"Do we need the military?" he asked and began to worry about safety of the site.

"Ardi is military, just not in uniform," she said. "So is Yang and pretty much all of Ardi's team. Except Rafael. I don't know what prompted him to give Rafael that position."

"Maybe he's better at that work than a military person would be," he said with a shrug. "He's good at dealing with some of the people. Far better than Ekhardt would be."

"Ekhardt needs to go," she said, changing the subject again. He knew he wasn't going to get any more out of her on the subject of Rafael. "I'm going to talk to Ardi about it. I think he's becoming far too much of a liability and especially since we may have trouble with the Norishi already. And if he has screwed things up with the Ksa --"

"Do you really trust the Ksa?" he asked. "I haven't been here long enough to get a feeling for them except that they appear to be friendly. I don't know if I trust that much more than I trust the Norishi's attitude."

"You're right, of course." She ran a hand through her hair as he considered the depth of her problems. "But the Ksa have been helpful in the past; truly helpful when we've had problems, like the time one of the grow domes started to lose the tether to Xenation. They went out and helped get it hooked back in. That counts. We believe they are truthful and friendly and that lying is a major sin for their culture -- which brings us back to Ekhardt, damn him. If they aren't what they pretend we are bound to find out eventually. However, if we automatically distrust the ones who are helping us, we would do better to pack up and leave."

"Yes. You're right." Morgan began to mentally catalogue more things he needed to start looking over, like all the previous long term contacts with the Ksa, both on the station and off. He almost pulled out his pocketcomp.

"There are reasons not to trust Rafael," she said, unexpectedly coming back to the subject. "He does have a lot of links with odd things -- the station, the Ksa and he is even starting to connect with the Click. The rest of us don't have those links. He was an exceptional scientist."

"Still is from what I can tell. You know about the Click toy?"

"Yes." She frowned. "You could ask him for it."

"I could. Rafael is the best person to look the device over. None of my people asked for it and I certainly don't have time, so it stays with him for now. He and Yang did some scans of it at the Medunit and I have copies of those. I know the work he's doing and I think he's probably the best person to play with it and see what he can find out."

"Your choice," she said. It seemed to take a lot for her to agree even that far. "I have to get back to work."

He put a hand on her shoulder. She flinched at the

touch but he held on anyway. "I needed to understand your side. You have some excellent points about Rafael. He has a link with the station. I am going to talk to him, especially after learning he used to have some control over Xenation."

"Why did the station do it?" she asked. "Why did it save *him*?"

"And not the others? I wish we knew the answer. I doubt Rafael knows. I suspect it's something that bothers him, too."

"I have to go. I have to find a way to apologize to the Ksa and hope they don't just pull out. That would leave us with the Norishi, and I don't trust them at all."

"And the Click," Morgan added.

"Oh yes, the Click. They're such a help," she said with a laugh.

"Kind of like the station," Morgan said. "Makes you wonder what they're really doing here."

"I have enough other things to wonder about," she said. "At least they stay out of trouble, which is more than I can say for my own people. I'll talk to you later."

"Good luck," he said.

She gave a languid wave of her hand and headed into admin. He went on to his office. It had been a better conversation than he had expected. What he had learned made him want to go out and drag Rafael into his office and have a nice, long talk . . . but not right now. Rafael clearly had other work and he thought making amends with the Ksa might be more important than his own curiosity.

CHAPTER TEN

R afael considered going to Xenobia and getting a couple drinks to calm himself . . . but that probably wasn't the best way to start out a career in security. So he turned and headed straight for the market.

He saw no sign of the Ksa, which was bad for this time of day but no surprise after the last incident. He didn't know if he could get them back and he'd be sorry if they packed up and left Xenation --

Which would leave the humans alone with the Norishi. He didn't like the idea even if the Norishi were suddenly nominally friendlier towards him. In fact, that was probably a good part of the reason why he didn't trust them. He didn't believe their sudden change in attitude towards him and it hadn't expanded to any other male. Hell, they were not as friendly to many females as they were to him. They nodded to him. They occasionally said hello. Once they moved aside and let him through first.

He shivered remembering it.

Brody gave him a glum nod when he neared. He noticed she had sold a couple shells as he leaned against the case and glanced down at those ephemeral ghosts from home.

"Well, Ekhardt sure made a mess of things, didn't he?" Brody asked and pushed back a strand of her hair. She looked into his face this time; not a lot of people did that any more. "What are the Ksa going to do now?"

"Who knows?" he asked.

"We kind of hoped you do. You've gotten the closest to them."

"I can stand in their shadows and watch them. I have no idea what most things mean . . . except I had warned the others about the need to be extra polite with the Ksa."

"And they still left Ekhardt loose, the guy who isn't polite to anyone."

"He isn't loose anymore. He's been banned from the market."

He had wondered what her reaction would be and found it reassuring to see a quick smile cross her lips. He didn't want to mistrust friends and think they were in the black market with Ekhardt. This wasn't an absolute sign, of course, but better than he had hoped.

"No more Ekhardt bullying us around? Damn, that's good. But they're going to need someone to come in and keep an eye on things. If nothing else, we need someone to pick up the pets now and then and get them out of supplies."

"They've already named someone. Me."

She leaned forward and caught him by the shoulder, surprising him. The grin broke into a short laugh. "Oh damn that's good news! Congratulations, Rafe. "

"I'm not sure this is a job I'm up to," he admitted but didn't go into the personal details. "I'm not ready."

"You can handle it, but don't let yourself get into anything you can't walk away from," she said turning serious. "There are problems, Rafe."

"We suspect there are things going on we need to know about," Rafael replied softly. Odd knowing part of the 'we' included Neva and the rest of admin. He froze for a moment on the thought and then shook his head, focusing again.

"Ekhardt had a rule that you just didn't ask," Brody said as softly. She looked a little worried and glanced towards the entrance to the Human Enclave as though she expected Ekhardt to show up. They were bound to worry until they got him off the station.

"And you said nothing to Ardi or Neva?" he asked.

"Ekhardt suggested it might not be wise to bring things to people who didn't want such matters out in the open."

He looked at her and felt more than a little shocked. She

blushed and looked down at the shells.

"Maybe you couldn't be certain about Ardi but do you really think Neva would ever be part of something illegal on this station?"

"I didn't want to think so," she admitted and glanced back up. Her fingers tapped lightly on the glass, a nervous gesture. "But she never removed Ekhardt even though we all knew he was into things which had to be obvious to admin, too. They didn't do anything, Rafe."

"Until now," he said.

"Until now. But even so, they haven't taken him in and he's been removed for something that has nothing to do with the rest of the trouble."

"That's what it looks like, yes," Rafael said.

She focused on him, startled this time and a little smile played at her lips once more. "Ah. Letting him have a little rope to hang himself?"

"And taking him out of the market so if he does make any moves, it will be in new places and with less cover. I'm trusting you, Brody. I really shouldn't, in the larger scheme of things, except I think, if nothing else, your position here near the opening to the market would make it hard to do anything clandestine even with Ekhardt's help."

"The only thing I'd do with Ekhardt is shove is ass out an airlock. If we had one," she admitted.

He stifled a laugh and stood up straighter. Others would notice him here and he didn't want to look as though he made some sort of deal with Brody before anyone else even realized he was the new security. He had appreciated talking to her, though. She helped to ground him in the larger picture. Her openness reassured him that many of the others wouldn't have a problem with him, which meant some of them might even be willing to give him answers.

He had another situation, though. One that he thought he had better try to address right away.

"I need to find out if the Ksa will even talk to me," he said with a shake of his head. "That might be the worst problem over all. I don't want the Ksa to pull out."

"No," she said. She cast a glance and across to where the Norishi guards stood before their Enclave. "No, I don't want the Ksa gone either. Xenation would be far too frightening without them. They make the place seem . . . less alien, I guess. It sounds odd."

"The Norishi appear to be more like us," Rafael replied as he stood and straightened his shirt. "But I think that makes the other differences all the more obvious. They're unsettling. The Ksa are different enough we accept they aren't going to be exactly like us."

She pursed her lips and nodded. She patted him on the arm. "Go do your work."

"Job," he said with a surprised shake of his head. "I have a job again."

She laughed as he headed away. He trusted Brody would start spreading the word but he had more important matters to handle. He didn't slow as he neared the Ksa gate. Only a single ribbon, long and dark, hung at the entrance. However, a guard stood before the opening and he wore a bladed weapon at his side which was something Rafael had never seen with the Ksa. The guard did not move when Rafael came forward and stopped with his head bowed and his hands held together. He caught a hint of surprise in the guard's face and a little lessening of the tension in the Ksa's shoulders at the show of politeness.

"My apologies for this intrusion," Rafe said. "I have news I wish to impart to Etinon or Saris if either are available."

The guard turned a little and gave a signal with his hand. Someone from one of the booths hurried away. Rafael gave another polite nod and stepped back, waiting with his hands folded, careful not to do anything which might be interpreted as impolite or nervous. Patience, he told himself.

Movement caught Rafe's eye; a half dozen pets charged through the Ksa booths and towards them. They appeared amazed and intrigued by the guard where there had never been one before. They congregated around him, climbed up onto his arms and one tried to get his knife. Repeatedly.

Rafael tried not to laugh. He really did . . . but the Ksa guard finally gave way to a grin and snort. Rafael laughed, drawing some of the pets to himself with a few claps. They were both trying to untangle themselves when Etinon and Saris both arrived.

"Well, this is a sad day for the Ksa," Saris said, though he gave a snorting laugh as well. "We are undone vy the Click 'ets. Our shane will go with us forever. No, no, little one. I do not care to have you in ny hands --"

Rafael didn't know what had brought on this behavior in the pets, but they had helped. He was able, finally, to give a credible bow to his friends even with a pet in hand. "May I speak on serious matters?"

"Can one talk seriously at such a tine?" Etinon asked, taking a pet from Saris. "We are all undone. Vut s'eak freely, Rafael. To you we will always listen."

"Ekhardt has been removed from his position in the market and banned from coming within the area," he said. All three Ksa froze in surprise. "You will have a formal apology from Station Master Neva NiGwen. I could even promise you an apology from Ekhardt, but we would all know it would be insincere and I think that more of an insult than a help."

The three stared at him and he could not begin to decide what had so shocked them. That Ekhardt had been removed? Did they, in fact, think he acted on the approval of the human admin, much like Brody had feared was true? He didn't know what to say and with the Ksa that usually meant best to say nothing at all. He waited for their questions.

Saris made a sign with his hand towards the guard. "Disnissed," he said. "We are again o'en to all."

The guard nodded and took down the black ribbon. Etinon put up a red one and a shorter blue one. Rafael didn't know what the two meant but they appeared far less ominous.

The pets went off with the guard, and Rafe could hear the snorting laughter of Ksa all through the booths. This had gone far better than he could have hoped. He thought his two friends looked relieved as well.

"I have been put I charge of overseeing the market in Ekhardt's place," Rafael explained. He hoped that didn't set them off for some reason. They took the news well and he thought with a little more pleasure.

"It is a good 'osition for you," Etinon said with a bow of his head, added politeness. "You are trusted. This is a good sign of the hunan intentions."

"Ekhardt is a known problem. Humans sometimes appear to be slow to deal with a problem if it is not life-threatening. In this case, it is necessary to take Ekhardt outside of his normal space and see what he does. It may bring more than his wrong-doing to light."

Both Ksa nodded as though they were willing to accept that the humans were, actually, doing something right.

"We are not 'leased with the Tri'unal. This was a grave insult. We shall ve cautious of this natter for a while," Etinon said. His voice had an odd little growl that nearly got a bad reaction from Rafael as though the man he had known had suddenly morphed into a wild predator. The sound won a kind of fight or flight reaction with him.

And the two Ksa had noted his reaction.

"We are not all what we seen to ve," Saris said. He did not growl but the words hardly reassured Rafe.

He didn't need complications right now. He wanted things calm, at least in one quarter, before they went after Ekhardt. They were going to have enough trouble dealing with the humans involved with -- what had Neva used to call him? A toad.

Rafe couldn't ignore what he had heard from Etinon but he could put his reaction aside as a scientific study for later. He would analyze the sounds and compare them to other reactions from the Ksa. Maybe he would even come up with a pattern and a reason, and be able to apply this to his own observations in other matters. Anything . . . anything to make this not be a problem right at this moment.

He took a deep breath and nodded. "I need to speak with others among the humans," he said and bowed his head.

"Thank you for your understanding."

The two Ksa bowed their heads. He felt as though that was at least one disaster averted.

CHAPTER ELEVEN

Morgan didn't think he would ever be bored at Xenation, except possibly with the food. He'd been something of a gourmet in his life and the lack of proper supplies quickly started bothering him. He began looking at importing spices and a few canned items. Fresh would be better but that just wasn't possible until they could free up some spots in the grow domes. He'd already talked to the head of the agro department about the possibility in the future. Canned was better than nothing at all.

He started making up a list of what he could use to make some nice Italian dishes when the screen changed and he found himself looking into Neva's distraught face.

"What's wrong?" His heartbeat had gone up. Neva didn't panic over small things.

"Tali," she said and then took several quick breaths. "Tali is here."

"*Here*?" There must be some mistake.

"The *Shaw*. She's on the *Shaw* and it's about half an hour out from dock. I caught the name on the manifest. What am I going to do?"

"Go meet her at the bay," he said. "I'll be there, too. We'll find out what's going on."

Neva gave a quick nod her face ashen. The idea of meeting her daughter obviously scared the hell out of her. Or maybe it was the thought of having the wild child here on the station. They had a delicate balance on Xenation and Tali had been a problem from the time she could walk. She had always taken the idea of 'no' as a personal challenge. By the time she hit twelve, her parents could no longer control her and several medtechs gave the same suggestion -- special hospitalization and care. Either that or drugs so strong she would need to be watched over constantly anyway. Her parents decided, finally, to give Tali the best life she could have which meant not with them. They hadn't even had an offer for Xenation yet, which had barely been found. Even if they'd stayed on Terra Nova, Tali still would have been in special care.

The decision hadn't been easy for either of them . . . but it had been the right choice.

If Tali turned out to be a problem -- and he couldn't see any reason why she *wouldn't* be -- then Neva would have to send her away. This would be the kind of incident that would likely mean a breach that would never heal. He suspected Tali wouldn't care and Neva would care too much. This was a damn stupid thing to have happen and he wanted to know how she got out of the hospital where they were caring for her and how she managed to travel all the way out here.

Morgan began to clear his desk and push away without really thinking about the work. He didn't want to be there when Tali arrived but he knew Neva would need the support of a friend. Then he thought of another, potentially worse problem, and put a quick call into Ardi.

"Morgan," the man said, looking at him with a frown.

"You know about Tali, right?"

"Yes," he said and still frowned.

"Warn Rafe to stay clear of the area."

"Oh hell. Right. Thanks."

Morgan cleared the link and stood, pushing a hand through his hair and trying to decide how best to handle this situation. He did not want to get involved in a family problems. Unfortunately, trouble with Tali would involve the entire station just as the trouble with Rafael concerned them all. He knew this wasn't going to be good.

CHAPTER TWELVE

Tali brushed a hand over the clean white, long sleeved blouse and grimaced. Stupid, damn suffocating clothing, covering almost every inch of her. She wanted to rip everything off. Norden tapped her on the arm; his signal to stop fidgeting and she nearly snapped at him -- but she held back and only gave a curt nod.

She had to play the role and couldn't let her anger loose now or she would ruin everything. Tali wanted this done, and done properly, otherwise she wouldn't get justice. She wouldn't have her revenge.

They reached the airlock door. Captain Stern said something polite to her and her two companions. She bowed her head in return to the woman, playing the perfectly demure and quiet girl before they walked out into the ugly, dull interior of the station.

Tali hated the place from the first breath and she wonder why anyone would come all the way out here to live in some place so boring. Anger surged once more and she had a hard time fighting the feeling back down as they stepped out into the open. She hated stupid people and the things they did.

People nearby watched her. She knew it; measuring her. Judging her. They didn't have the right.

She couldn't even get a fucking drink. She had to play little Miss Perfect for this show and since she'd have to take a physical to stay for even a few days, she didn't dare have any liquor or drugs in her system.

This was hell. She wanted this charade done and

everything settled --

And there she was. *Mother.*

They looked alike, she thought and shuddered a little though no one would notice. The same hair, though hers was longer. The same shape of the face. Did she have nothing from her father? Was it all from this woman?

If she'd had a weapon on her, Tali would have drawn it and killed the woman who had ruined her life. Instead, she practiced the calming techniques Norden had taught her, which mostly worked. She supposed a little show of emotion wouldn't be unusual. She just had to be sure the others thought the color in her cheeks had to come from anything but the rage she felt.

"Tali," the woman said.   Her voice trembled with weakness.

She stepped forward and carefully put her arms around Neva. She'd practiced the move, the tentative little hug that grew a little more intense when Neva returned it. "I'm so glad to see you," Tali whispered; the first of many, many lies she had rehearsed. Neva responded as she should with a little tightening of the embrace, so easily falling for the act. Oh yes, this would be fun in the end.

Tali looked over her mother's shoulder, judging the reaction of others and saw shock in the faces of quite a few. She spotted an unexpected familiar face close by: Morgan Doreet. She hadn't seen him in years and his presence unsettled her for a moment. He could be a problem. She had never trusted the man.

She did not see the one face she had wanted to mark from the first. Rafael wasn't here. A shame. She *really* wanted to meet him.

"Ma'am," Norden said, all proper. "I'm Caleb Norden. I was hired by the Terra Nova government to accompany your daughter on this journey."

"Why -- why are you here?" Neva finally asked, pushing Tali away and looking into her face. Tali could see the mistrust there and worry.

"I have the comp chit that explains everything," Norden

said with a bright (and entirely false) smile. "The people who treated your daughter for so many years realized she had finally made a breakthrough and keeping her penned up with the others was no longer a good, or wise, choice. We sent info. I assumed you had gotten it."

"No I didn't," she said and still frowned.

"I feared as much. I sent information myself when the case was turned over to me, but there seemed to be some question about where to send the files to get the information to you quickly. I was heading out to the Pavo Fringe and offered to take the side trip with Tali since it gave me an excuse to spend a few days in such a wondrous location. I never thought I would get a chance to see Xenation." He let his eyes glance around, going a little wider -- oh yes, they had both practiced the act for long enough.

"I see," Neva said and gave a little shudder of a breath. "But why -- why did you come here, Tali?"

Show time.

She pulled away keeping her head down and taking several deep breaths as she *tried* to speak. When Neva reached for her, she took another step away. "I had nowhere to go," she said softly, her voice trembling. "No one I knew. They asked me where I should go. I said . . . I said I had a mama still. But if you don't want me -- if you don't --"

Neva stepped forward and took her into her arms again, pulling her tighter.

"You have me," Neva said. "This is just not the best place to be for anyone who isn't working here. There's so little for you to do --"

"I just want quiet for a while," she whispered. "I want to have quiet and peace and a place to rest."

"You'll have that," Neva replied. She even sounded happy. "We'll move Ardi out of the suite next to mine and you can stay there."

"I'll go start packing then," a man said with a bit of a laugh.

Ardi, the head of security. Oh yes, she recognized the tall, dark man. She'd studied everyone she could on the way in, hoping to find the best ways to deal with them for the short time she would be here.

Neva took hold of her hand, leading her like a little child, talking about this place as though she loved it. The rest of the station didn't look any better but she nodded appreciatively at the things the woman pointed out like the pathetic market, the one little bar (where she might steal something worth drinking, if it came to it), and off to the left where the guards to the Norishi area stood.

Just look interested and dazed at the same time, and she'd get through this. Norden, she noted, had started talking with Ardi. Good. They needed to get accepted as quickly as possible. She hadn't watched the others leave the ship, but she caught a glimpse of Wood already at the door to the bar.

There wasn't much else to see out here in the bay except ugly walls with spots of color like someone had vomited on them. Nothing else. People working on things. Her mother nattered on about stuff Tali really didn't give a shit about, but she nodded and pretended interest and just hoped the woman shut up soon.

At least she wouldn't be here long.

And then . . . something changed.

The air grew scary cold and the lights dimmed. Her mother looked frightened and Tali thought they had a breach and they were all going to die --

"Displaced," Ardi said. "There they are."

A moving mass of white fog and dull colors swept down through the bay towards them, swirling through the air like a miniature storm as the lights dimmed more and the area grew colder. Her mother had started to pull her towards the opening to the Human Enclave but Ardi stopped her.

"No. If they follow you in, we could have all kinds of problems with the equipment."

"I have to get Tali somewhere --"

"No. There is nowhere you could take her that they can't follow. If she's the reason they came out, best to handle it now."

"Me?" she said, confused as the two drew her attention

from the Displaced. She looked back and could see faces and shapes now. She shuddered this time. Norden had said the Displaced weren't real, but now --

"Where is Rafael?" Neva asked.

"I told him not to come near when the ship docked," Ardi replied. Tali listened, interested despite not taking her eyes off the flowing mass of shapes before her.

"Get him. Get him here *right now.*"

Ardi said something more but Tali didn't hear.

She looked into the face of her dead father.

For the first time in her life she thought about death and ghosts -- about the people she and Norden had killed at the hospital to cover her escape. News of the explosion there would reach Xenation eventually, but they should be done and gone by then. Still, she didn't want to think about the dead they'd left on Terra Nova and the others they'd killed along the way while they set up this plan.

These ghosts scared the hell out of her.

CHAPTER THIRTEEN

A rdi's orders had been succinct, but then they always were. *Don't go near the bay when the ship comes in. Stay out of sight.*

No problem. He didn't know why, but it seemed like a good plan if Ardi was that insistent. He'd gone to the far end of the market and wandered through the Ksa stands. He had an income with a few credits added to his account every day. He could actually *buy* things. He thought this would give him something to *do*. The others saved the credits for when they went back home. He was never leaving Xenation. He decided to start making the best of it and create a place of his own here --

His commlink beeped, startling him. He still wasn't used to being on-call but he didn't mind. Something else to do --

However, as he brought the link up he realized the problem. He could feel the cold growing in the air.

"Rafe here," he said. "I see them --"

"Displaced. At the entrance to the Human Enclave. We have a problem!"

He started running and people knew to get out of his way. The Displaced were becoming stronger and more directed. They had become physically taxing for him to drive away. It hurt.

This needed to be done and he was the only one who could handle them. This wasn't a purpose he had chosen for himself, but he didn't turn away from the duty.

Rafe had expected to find the Displaced at the work station as usual. This time, however, they massed closer to

Xenobia. He could see Neva who had taken a young woman into her arms as though shielding her. Had they attacked?

He rushed forward, one hand brushing against the plate on his face. *I need your help fast on this one, Xenation!*

He thought he felt a response as a little tingle against his skin beneath the graft. The wind picked up, and he saw lights dancing across the walls, all of it like nothing like he had seen before.

Rafe came to a breathless stop right at the edge of the Displaced. He still couldn't tell what had drawn them here. He could see no sign of a power source, which was the only thing that had brought them out before.

"Keep them away! Keep them away!"

"They won't hurt you Tali!"

Oh damn, damn, damn. *Tali*: Neva and Ashur's daughter. The realization of whom the stranger was threw him off just as he reached up into the Displaced. He lost his concentration.

Chaos.

They swept in around him, all the faces of people he had known before the accident: Marta, Nick, Morton, Cheslyn. Angry faces with mouths open, shouting words he couldn't hear and or understand. Just sounds and cold . . . and an abyss he had kept back from since the Displaced first arrived.

Ashur? He wanted Ashur because he could deal with him. This time the Displaced drove him to his knees, drew the breath from him, and left him cold and aching as he got lost in the mass of white --

Where he should have been anyway. One coherent thought in all the rest of the chaos; he should have been one of the Displaced from the start and not left behind on the bay floor, cut off forever from both sides, living in a greyness --

"Rafe!"

Felicia had leapt into the mass with him and grabbed hold of his arm. He feared for her life far more than he worried about his own.

"What's wrong?" she demanded while her teeth

chattered and her eyes watered. He saw her skin paling in the cold. "What's happened?"

"Lost . . . lost my hold." He could barely get the words out. Everything hurt with an agony that made even breathing hardly worth the effort. "Lost --"

"Neva's girl?" she asked softly at his ear, warm breath against his icy skin.

He nodded. "Took me by surprise. I need -- Felicia, I need a power source."

"Ah. Stay on your knees. Don't fall again!"

He hadn't realized he had fallen at all, but he was on his knees now. She had been holding him there. He put one hand to the floor and lifted another toward the Displaced, trying to pull them into a mass so he had some control over them. *Xenation, Xenation* -- but he didn't know what he wanted from her this time.

He could barely see Neva holding to Tali. The girl looked like her mother. He didn't like the stare she gave to him or the Displaced. He looked away first and tried to find Ashur, and when he did, his heart pounded harder for a new reason. Ashur hovered nearby watching his wife and daughter with an odd and worried look on his face.

The look confirmed what Rafael had believed from the start. The Displaced did have some form of existence still and knew what happened around them. They were trapped somehow, unable to be fully here. While Ashur appeared worried, the others seemed insane. They scared him.

He felt ill and the Displaced started to get away from him again.

"Help me, Ashur. Help me keep them back --"

He had never called on Ashur before. He saw rage in Neva's face which made him cringe and want to crawl away. However, Ashur had heard him or at least understood what was needed. He saw Ashur move, sweeping towards other Displaced and driving them back into the mass of white.

And Neva saw too. Her face paled and she looked faint. He would not have wished this knowledge on her. She couldn't do any more than he did, which was damned little.

His arm started to give way. He could not feel his legs at all and had trouble breathing, each slow inhale drawing ice into his lungs.

He thought about letting go. Maybe he would become one of the Displaced this time. It couldn't be worse that the life he led, already cut off and not trusted by so many. Maybe he could help Ashur. And if not . . . the insanity he had seen in the faces of the others was a draw of its own. He could let go of everything --

A hand dropped onto his shoulder: solid, human. The touch drew him back to here. He gasped for breath, trying to focus as Felice knelt beside him, her hand moving from his shoulder to his arm, maintaining contact as though she knew he needed an anchor to stay in the world.

"Rafe, are you listening?" she demanded. Her voice sounded distant and Rafe could hear a roaring in his ears. Lack of air? He gulped and nodded. "Power pack," she said, pushing the box in front of him. "Do we power it up full force?"

"I --" he said, and coughed, tasting blood. "I. Go."

"No. You'll fall flat on your face."

"Go --"

Felice reached over, opened the box and hit the power amp on.

He didn't have the breath to curse and he didn't have the time to do more than throw himself in front of Felice as the Displaced turned and massed on them. He grabbed the power pack and held it in front of him, which was a dangerous thing to do because the power became unstable. However, this was the best way to keep the Displaced focused on him.

"Rafe -- son of a bitch --" Felice took hold of his arm and held him up as he stood. He could barely see anything with the Displaced so thick around them. He'd never seen them act this way and he feared this had more to do with Tali than some other change.

He held the power box up, forcing his arms to remain steady. He could see the blue glow fluctuating and prayed to whatever alien gods might still be in this place that the supply didn't explode. The Displaced came like the sparrows used to come to the bird feeders when he was a child, pushing at each other aside as they reached for the food.

Did the power source represent food or something far more dangerous? He thought they became stronger. Was that good? Would they be easier to deal with if they became more human?

He looked to Ashur and found him coming closer and worried. Rafe knew that look too well. He did not, however, expect the next move. Ashur reached into the power pack and drew out so much energy that he glowed with power, and the others backed away in haste. Felice, who had been softly cursing, fell silent. Ashur lifted his arms, ephemeral shapes trailing light, and clapped his hands.

They heard the clap like thunder as power discharged and streamers of neon lightning danced through the air. The other Displaced leapt up and swarmed, trying to catch at the power.

Rafael snapped the power pod closed while they were distracted. He saw Ashur give him a nod, but he didn't have time to think about that interplay now. He had to get the Displaced to leave the area.

Neva pulled Tali towards the door of Xenobia, as though just to get her out of sight, which worked for him as well, taking the distraction away. He put his hand to the side of his face, touching the metal. His fingers tingled with the cold and he still couldn't do more than gasp for breath.

Felice trembled and he suspected that came from the cold since the Displaced had never worried her much. The bay had gotten damned dark, too. He feared they were going to be a while recovering from this incursion.

Focus. He had to focus on the Displaced. And the Station. *Get them away. Get them gone.*

A warm breeze brushed against his face.

"Finally, finally," Felice whispered, her voice trembling as well.

The Displaced fought the wind. Rafael feared Xenation

would lose this battle, but in the end, they finally dispersed, each pulled away and disappearing into the darkness overhead. Ashur lingered the longest, staring towards his wife and child before he swept down to look straight into Rafe's face. His lips moved.

"Be careful," Felice said. She worked the dock where they had loud noises and used ear plugs. They often learned to read lips. "He said to be careful."

Rafael nodded. Ashur swept away on the wind with the others. He still didn't know where they went. He wanted --

The warmth hurt and breath still wouldn't come. Yang arrived and even he look more frantic than usual. He shouted something but Rafael couldn't understand the words. He wanted to rest. He felt warmer, at least --

Felice caught him and with Yang's helped him stretched out, his head against her arm. He thought he should be able to breathe better now, but he couldn't. The Medtech pushed something against his neck, and then something else, this time over his chest. His heart pounded too hard. Felice and Yang were speaking, but he had no idea what they were saying. Colors moved in the wall. Sounds echoed through the station.

He could see past Yang to where Neva and Tali stood. Tali looked enraged. Dangerous. (Be careful. . . .) Neva seemed worried as she watched him and that helped a little. Better than usual.

Beyond the two of them he saw movement at the door to Xenobia. Ekhardt stood there, just inside the shadows. He saw another man come closer; small, thin and not a local. They both spoke and moved away together.

And that was the last Rafael saw or felt for a while.

CHAPTER FOURTEEN

Morgan remained with Neva and Tali until they got her squared away in the room that had been Ardi's place. Tali went straight to bed, exhausted. He could see her through the edge of the cloth covering, pulling blankets up around her head and waving her mother away. Neva walked out of the suite with him, shaking her head and looking far too worried. The situation had aged her in ways hadn't seen before.

"This isn't good," she said softly as they headed down the empty hall. No one had followed them.

"Tali?"

"Tali is a problem I'm not ready to face, even if she is better. Hell, ready isn't even the half of it. You saw her reaction to what was going on --"

"I think she had reason to be afraid, Neva. I was scared. Something wasn't right, and even I know it, though I haven't been here all that long."

She said nothing for the next few steps as though parsing those words. Then she sighed. "Hell. I need to go to the office. There's bound to be a lot of worried people. Ardi hasn't contacted me though. There can't be any real trouble."

Morgan wanted to tell her to pack Tali up on the ship when it headed out, but he couldn't. This was going to be hell. He could see the trouble brewing and he had no idea how they could handle her without making some sort of bigger problem.

"Morgan, can you do something for me?" she suddenly asked, a hand on his arm.

"Of course," he said and managed not to wince as he considered the babysitting job he was about to take on.

"Can you check on Rafe?"

Her request surprised him and he fought not to show the shock. "Glad to," he replied and smiled. "I was going to head over there anyway."

She nodded, lips clamped tightly together, and hurried down the hall towards the admin area. There went a woman with far too many emotional conflicts. He watched until she disappeared around a curve, and then he turned back to head toward the medunit.

He could hear the sounds of the medical area before he got there and they didn't sound good. Equipment gave out warning beeps almost overcoming Yang's insistent voice. He couldn't quite make out the words until he had entered the first of the two rooms. The area had a scent of antiseptic and other things medical-related that he couldn't quite name. The light in the rooms were dulled and he could hear uneven beeps of some equipment that he feared should have sounded steadier.

"Come on, boy. You have to pull yourself together," Yang said as he leaned over the diagnostic bed in the second room. Equipment flashed warnings on the wall unit, and Morgan -- who had some medical training -- knew those weren't good readings. Red bars ran across far too many of the lines. Even the heartbeat was fast and irregular still.

"Is that normal?" Morgan asked softly. "Normal for him, after an encounter -- that much hyperactive brain activity."

"Not this much, no," Yang said with a quick glance back. "I'm busy --"

"Sorry. Neva asked me to check in on him."

That produced an odd spike in the readings that neither of them could miss.

"Oh, so you are listening!" Yang sounded amused and relieved. He signaled Morgan closer, though Morgan had no idea what he was supposed to do. "Come on, Rafe. Come back out."

"You think he's holding back on purpose?" Morgan asked, intrigued by the readings despite himself. He glanced at Rafe: the face was too still and the metal plate all the more obvious since Yang had pulled the hair back from his face. And damn, he looked even younger now, which didn't help.

"He's not reacting on a conscious level," Yang replied. He nodded at a little change in the readings. "His subconscious is fighting the idea of coming back. This happened more often at the beginning. It's getting worse again."

"The readings aren't good," Morgan said, his finger tracing over the graphs. "Some of this --"

"There is something alien in his head, Morgan." Yang looked at him with a frown. Rafael heard and the readings jumped in a different way this time. If he had the graphs right, he saw despair in that leap. "It's why I worry about what's going on in there so much. So far, it hasn't altered anything I would consider crucial to personality. Rafael is still who he always was. But we have been seeing subtle shifts in the occipital and parietal lobes, mostly dealing with vision."

"Which means?" Morgan asked, looking over the graph of the brain again.

"He's seeing things the rest of us don't."

"Oh, now that's interesting," Morgan said. A spike again, and not despair. He couldn't decide if he should read that as annoyance or amusement.

"This bout has me worried," Yang admitted. "The Displaced weren't acting in their usual way and they hit Rafe far harder than before. I have the physical damage under control. I'll know better when he wakes up and I can see how he responds. I'm not worried about anything permanent --" That obviously to relieve Rafael of any worries -- "but I want to know what more I need to do to get past this trouble as quickly as possible."

"What kind of damage?"

"System shock. Nerve damage," he said, pointing out some readings on the wall graphs. "A hematoma that I took care of right away but has probably given him a massive headache anyway. I suspect that's what is holding him back, and there's not much I can do about it. I just want to know he really is here."

"H . . . here," Rafael whispered. His dark eyes fluttered opened for a moment, focused on the two of them. "Here. Let me sleep."

Yang grinned brightly and slapped Morgan on the arm as though they had just pulled off a dangerous operation together. And maybe they had. He could see some of the readings pull down into more acceptable ranges. Rafael started to turn his head but froze again as a spike of pain went off the chart, though nothing showed in his face except he paled even more. His eyes moved and focused on Morgan again.

"Neva-" he whispered softly.

"I'll tell her you're doing better."

He blinked. Morgan wished he could read more in the look and the play of lines on the monitors, but many of the red lines slipping downward to yellow, at least. The best he could do was look at Yang who seemed pleased with the change. Yang gave a nod as Rafael slipped off to sleep and Morgan backed out of the room and started toward the hall -
-

"Morgan, can I have a moment?"

He looked back, surprised to find Yang had left his patient. Maybe Yang didn't want to talk about something in front of Rafael, knowing he listened. Morgan stopped and waited, afraid to find out something he wouldn't want to tell Neva. Besides, though he didn't know Rafael well, he still didn't wish him badly.

And neither did Neva, which said very many things.

"You helped, no matter how unintentional." He stopped and looked at Morgan, his face set in worry. "She really did ask?"

"Yes. I think she might even have come herself, but Tali. . . ." He stopped, uncertain what more he should say. He knew more about the family than others did. He was not going to use the knowledge to present any information Neva might not want said.

Yang didn't ask for more. "I want your help."

"My help?"

He gave a nervous look, running his fingers through is dark hair. The man looked harried and that had to be mostly because of Rafael. The station seemed usually calm otherwise.

"I want you to help monitor Rafael and look over the changes taking place in his brain. They're small and subtle, and I don't think this is a real problem in the larger sense, but I'm the only one who has been keeping a watch on him. I want a second opinion, Morgan, and you are the only one with the qualifications."

"I --" He started to protest on many levels: he wasn't a medtech, he was too busy and this wasn't his work. He stopped himself. "I can go over the work if that's what you want."

"Yes, thank you," he said and looked relieved.

"If you sent the information on Rafael off to the IWC, they would send someone qualified -- ah. No, that wouldn't be good, would it? Not for Rafael, at least."

"Not good for him at all, I fear." Yang leaned against the wall as though some huge weight had just been lifted from his shoulders. "I don't want to make Rafael into a guinea pig for some researcher trying to make a name for himself. And I don't want someone taking control of him and telling him what he can and can't do in the name of a science experiment. It wouldn't help him in any real way, and it could certainly be a problem for the rest of us at Xenation."

"How does he control the Displaced?"

"That's the big question. He told me he doesn't control them. They seem to be drawn to him, perhaps because of his link to the station. The link also allows him to call on her and get her to round them up again."

"Contact with the station. Actual contact. I thought it was a metaphorical contact --"

Yang nodded. Morgan stood there, trying to sort this through his mind again. He looked at the wall where Yang stood and saw the change in color flittering through the surface. The change frightened him in some odd way he hadn't expected.

"You're saying the station has some kind of real intelligence at work --"

"I'm not saying anything at all about the station," Yang said with a quick shake of his head. "I'm just reporting what Rafael has explained to me."

"But it is plain that something is going on when he asks for this help."

"The plate on his face is a graft, Morgan. Something is going on underneath the surface. I can't get a clear reading, not from the front or the back of his head, or any other angle. It doesn't seem to be anything dangerous. Intrusive, yes -- but the work seems to be slow, and careful."

"Something is directing the work?"

"I don't know. I can't find any kind of link. But then, I can't find a link to how Rafael deals with the Displaced either. The station does react when he calls but doesn't respond when the rest of us ask for help with the Displaced. I want you to help me figure this out."

"I'll do what I can," Morgan said. The entire idea intrigued him, of course. A scientist who didn't find this interesting wasn't any good in his field, no matter what that field might be. He wished he had more equipment, more people and a subject he could lock up in a room and watch without feeling guilty about it. "I'll want all the medical reports. Do you think we can get him to wear a monitor?"

"I had one on him but it died the moment the Displaced came near him. I don't have enough equipment to just keep throwing away."

"Maybe my guys can come up with something. Was it a power drain?"

"Power drain that dragged every bit of energy out of the components. Nothing would take a charge again."

"Ah. I'll see what we do." He looked back at Yang. "We may have to call in outsiders anyway, you know."

"I know. That's part of why I want you in on this. I want

a second opinion because I am far too involved to see things clearly. My focus is on keeping Rafael alive."

"And is that a problem?"

"It is getting to be more of a problem. You saw the readings. They've been getting progressively worse the last few times he had contact with the Displaced. And the Displaced have been harder to disperse as well."

Morgan hadn't been here long enough to get a feel for the situation, but he didn't doubt Yang's presentation of the facts. They had a problem. They had several of them, all linked to Rafael: keeping him alive, finding out how to deal with the Displaced, and learning if the station really did have a communication's link to him.

Communication's link.

"Ardi gave him a commlink. I'll want to see it."

"I'll bring it over to your office along with the reports," he said and glanced back towards the medunit door again. "I'm not going to send the reports over the lines. I don't want the information getting into the hands of people who might use it for their own gain. I better get back. Thank you."

Morgan gave a nod of farewell, fearing he may have gotten into more than he suspected. Rafael, beyond a doubt, was trouble.

Morgan started for his desk to get to work, but turned and headed for Neva's office instead. She would be fretting and she didn't need that kind of worry on top of everything else.

"Morgan!"

He managed not to curse as Ritter hurried towards him. She looked excited, which might mean something other than bad news on a day filled with one problem after another.

"Some of the lights burnt out in the bay this time," she said, nearly breathless. "This is the chance."

"Chance?" Morgan asked, confused.

"We can put sensors up with the bulbs," she said, looking pleased and hopeful. "I just need you to okay it --"

"Let's go!"

They hurried back to his office after all. Ritter went to get a few of his sensors ready. Then he considered another problem.

"I already talked to Neva and she said if we can get them up without notice, we can do it," he said, looking over one of the devices. "I did that maybe the third day I was here. But we have a problem. This is in Ekhardt's realm --"

"No. He doesn't do the work, after all," Ritter said with a sound of disdain. "We'll go to Felice. She'll get them up."

"Ah. Good. We can trust her?"

"Yes, especially if we let her know this could help Rafael."

"Ah. Are they --?"

"Friends is all. I get the distinct feeling Felice isn't much interested in men."

Morgan felt an odd relief for Neva's sake. "Let's go talk to her, then."

They found Felice in Xenobia, her hands wrapped around a cup of something warm though she didn't sip. She sat in a darkened corner at a small table and stared at the wall across from her with such determination Morgan almost didn't want to disturb her. Ritter didn't have that problem. She crossed to the table and sat down. Felice might have looked relieved for the company and curious when Morgan joined them as well.

"Some of the lights need to be replaced this time," Ritter said. "I figured you were the one to come to for the work."

"Ah. Yeah. I'll get it," she said and sounded weary. "I suppose this needs to be done right now?"

"Soon," Morgan replied. He nodded and Ritter put the small bag on the table. "These are sensors which might help us learn more about how Xenation works. How it communicates, especially with Rafael. However, we want them placed discreetly, because --"

"Because the Norishi Bitches will assume any surveillance is aimed at them," she said and finally took a drink from the cup. Tea of some sort. She looked cold still, reminding him that she had been in that maelstrom with

Rafael. "I shouldn't still be here, you know. I'm starting to get a really bad attitude."

"But you'll stick around a while longer," Ritter said. She looked worried. "We need you, Felice. You can work with the crews and with the bay workers. Otherwise, we're stuck with Ekhardt."

"Someone needs to start thinking about replacing him," she said and looked at Morgan. Admin: that was what she looked at.

He didn't have leave to say anything important. "I think it's obvious that things are already changing where Ekhardt is concerned."

She sipped again and she didn't look any happier. "And what about Rafael? Who is going to make sure he stays alive?"

"Yang --" Ritter began.

"Yang isn't out in the bay where the trouble hits. People have to go and get him which usually means me, you know. I don't want to leave Xenation and find out Rafe died, but I don't want to stay and see him killed, either. He's not going to survive this."

"And he can't survive leaving," Morgan added softly. "So we're trying to find the best way to deal with the problem."

"Are you? Everything keeps looking worse instead of better."

"That's not anything from our side. But maybe if we can get a better handle on Xenation --" He reached over and tapped the bag -- "then we might have a better chance of finding out what is happening with Rafael. Maybe we'll even get a better handle on the Displaced. We need information, Felice, and there aren't a lot of ways we can get it."

She took the bag into her hand and nodded, looking better. "Yeah, you're right. I know this situation is screwed where Rafe is concerned. Damned bad time for me to pick up another stray, you know."

Ritter smirked, but Morgan laughed as Felice grinned.

A pair of Ksa came in, so they left off the other

conversation. Felice put the little bag into her battered tool kit and Morgan didn't think anyone noticed. Ritter left a few minutes later and Morgan had a drink and then left to go see Neva. He didn't dare put this part off any longer, though he almost convinced himself he should stop and see Rafael again first.

Neva sat at her desk on the slightly raised platform in the large room they used for control. Communications links and the vid cams, both inside and outside the station, sent info to an array of monitors on the far wall. The main screen showed the market today. Ardi stood watching the screen with a frown. Morgan saw a lot of security people walking there and wondered if there had been trouble. Probably not. Rafael wasn't there and they were keeping an eye on things.

"Morgan," Neva said, noticing him for the first time. She started to say something and stopped herself. A shame she should couldn't bring herself to ask about Rafael but he didn't pursue the point as he crossed to her. "Is everything all right?"

"Yes, fine," he said, which made her nod and look less worried. "You remember me mentioning the problem with sensors? I think we worked it out. They'll be going into the new lights."

"Excellent." She leaned back in her chair. She glanced at the screens. "Bad time for Rafael to be down with a new ship in and all."

Careful, even here, he realized. He glanced around the room at the dozen people at their posts. Any of them could be working with Ekhardt. He didn't know them well enough to make any guesses.

They didn't speak of Tali, either. That would come later, in private. Maybe the discussion of Rafael would as well. Here, they kept the discussion to matters of business which helped them both, but neither forgot the other troubles.

Too much going on, though. Morgan left with the feeling of things getting worse.

CHAPTER FIFTEEN

Rafael stared for a long time at the gray ceiling spotted with color before he tried to move. He couldn't say how long until he finally decided he did want to survive. For a while, he hadn't been sure; not a new thought, but it had been more powerful this time, echoing through his mind for a long time before he started to feel better and could banish such thoughts back into the shadows again.

He sat up. Alarms went off and Yang arrived at the doorway. He looked tired.

"I need to get up," he said. "I need to move."

Yang had seen him like this often enough to know the truth of what he said. He offered a hand, but Rafael shook his head and pushed his legs over the edge of the bed. He wasn't ready to stand just yet. Just move. Just prove that he could.

His arms twitched. His right leg caught in an agonizing muscle cramp he thought would never go away. He hadn't even noticed that Yang had gotten an injection and pressed it into the leg until he felt the muscle begin to relax.

"Thank you," he said and meant the words sincerely. "That was miserable."

"You strained more muscles than before. What changed, Rafe? Why was this so different?"

He'd been wondering that as he had stared the ceiling. He frowned and thought about not talking to Yang but that seemed unwise. He had never kept anything back from the man yet.

"There's only one thing I can see that was different," he

said. "Tali was there."

"Tali?" Yang asked and clearly didn't understand. "Why would there be more trouble because of her?

"She's Neva's daughter, but more than that, she's *Ashur's* daughter."

"Hell."

"I don't know much about her except that she was a problem," Rafael admitted. He finally dared one foot to the floor and tested to see if his leg would hold him. Then the other. Nothing felt right as he stood with a hand on the bed.

"Rafael?"

"I feel disconnected still," he admitted. "This is lasting longer than usual."

"You took a hard hit this time, Rafael. I sure as hell hope that doesn't happen again anytime soon. Check out the commlink Ardi gave you."

He frowned and pulled the equipment out of his pocket. It would be dead, of course --

But it wasn't.

"Oh, now that's odd," he said, finding something to draw his attention away from how he felt. Yang came to look too, frowning as he saw the power unit light up. "It should have been dead."

"So, why isn't it?"

"I don't know --" he began and then rethought it. "Maybe because I didn't have it turned on during the time with the Displaced. No, that hasn't stopped them from draining things before. Maybe too small? This doesn't have much of a power core and I gave them something far more powerful."

"I'll try that one."

"Try?"

"I want to try another monitor," he said. "I'll try burying a small power core as a backup to something larger. I want to know what is happening. Is that going to be a problem for you?"

"For me? No. I want to know, too, you know. And it's your equipment you're risking. Go to Morgan and Ritter. I think they'll have the best chance of coming up with something that can still get you the data you want."

"Small," he said with a nod. He was plainly already considering what he needed. "Walk across the room."

This was the usual test. Rafe didn't make it far the first time or the second. He did the third and then again the fourth time. He got lucky, because Novi came in with a burnt hand and took Yang's attention for a while. He got himself in order, gave them both a nod, and walked out while Yang dealt with the other person.

"Come back here tonight," Yang said as he headed out the door.

Rafael nodded agreement, thinking the quiet of the place would help. The rest of Xenation seemed loud and harsh today. The headache had begun to ease, but pain pulsed at every shout down the halls and every beep from equipment in offices. He wanted somewhere quiet and he knew he wasn't going to find it anytime soon.

What he did need was to find Ardi. He thought about calling him but he wanted to do this subtly. Time had already passed, after all, so what he had to tell the man wasn't new.

There was nowhere particularly quiet on Xenation. His room, maybe. He could retreat into the back corner of the little closet of a space and pull blankets and pillows over his head until everything eased. He'd done so before, but he wouldn't see Ardi if he went into hiding.

He spotted the man in the main control but he was not going anywhere near that area for fear of running into Neva or Tali. He thought about going out to the bay and maybe the market but as he cleared the Human Enclave, the sounds very nearly put him down to his knees. He went instead to Xenobia, staggering in like he was already half drunk. Buris looked up from the counter and dropped the glass he was cleaning -- too loud as it clinked on the counter -- and quickly crossed to him. Even the man's boots against the flooring sent slivers of pain through his head.

"Sit down. I'll call Yang --"

"Just left him," Rafael mumbled. "I need to sit down.

And quiet. Don't even talk to me, Buris. Just let me have some quiet."

Buris looked worried as he took hold of Rafael and settled him in a corner table away from the door. Quieter here. Rafe took a deep breath and lowered his head into his hands, hoping the pain would ease. The scents of food and drink were not helping. He heard Buris mumbling and suspected he had called Yang anyway. At least he did so quietly.

Midday and not many people around. The whole matter with the Displaced had probably unsettled more than him. He had some idea of what to do with them, even if he didn't know exactly how he did it. The rest had to depend on him and he imagined that worried almost everyone.

The thoughts made his headache double, as though even the words in his head were too loud today. Buris brought him a glass of water and when two bay workers came in, he asked them to hold down the noise for a little bit. Rafe saw the two look at him and nod.

Good people.

He sipped the water and his head started to feel less likely to explode. He relaxed, knowing that this wasn't going to be permanent. Every time he dealt with the Displaced he had a fear he wasn't going to come back from it. He thought Yang felt the same. He never said so aloud.

He still needed to see Ardi. Buris might call him here on some pretext --

And Ekhardt came in.

Rafe knew this was going to turn bad from the minute the swaggering little man appeared in the doorway. He stomped over to a table near Rafael and threw himself into a chair, glaring.

"I want a drink!" he shouted to Buris.

If he had done that even a few minutes earlier, Rafael probably would have passed out from the pain. He did wince, which was unfortunate. Ekhardt didn't miss the reaction, and that meant this encounter would get worse   .
Rafael thought he should get up and leave, but he feared he

wouldn't make it to the door, and he didn't want to show that kind of weakness to Ekhardt.

"I want some music! Crank it up real loud."

"No," Buris said, sitting the drink in front of the man.

"Why the hell not?"

"Because I said so."

"Because of him," Ekhardt said and sounded like a petulant five-year-old. He glared over at Rafael and his voice grew louder with every word. "What's the matter, boy? Work too much for you? Taking on my job more than you can handle --"

Rafael wasn't sure how he did it, but he pushed himself up and took three steps over to the table where Ekhardt sat, startling the man with the sudden move. He grabbed hold of the bastard's arm.

"Shut the fuck up, Ekhardt," he said, his voice deceptively soft given the words. "Just shut up."

"Let go of me."

Ekhardt's voice had grown dangerously soft as well. Rafael could tell they had both been pushed too far and he had the feeling he had just done something Ekhardt wanted. He still didn't let go. Probably some macho gene kicking in. Buris came over to the table and tapped him on the shoulder. He made his fingers release the man's arm. They'd clamped so tightly he probably left bruises.

Ekhardt came up out of his chair as Rafael stepped away. Buris pushed Ekhardt back down.

"Not here," Buris ordered, glaring at both of them.

Rafael bowed his head in apology; Ekhardt did not, and Rafael supposed that was the big difference between the two of them. He knew when to back down and to admit he had been wrong.

Yang arrived before he even stumbled back to his chair. Ardi came a moment later. Someone must have called security when this looked likely to get out of hand. Ekhardt stood, looking Ardi in the face.

"He assaulted me. I want him locked up," Ekhardt said, his voice loud. "He grabbed me --"

"He was about to fall," Buris said. "He grabbed hold of Ekhardt to keep from going down."

Rafael wasn't sure if he should be pleased or appalled that the man lied for him. Ekhardt certainly looked shocked and no one else in the room said anything different. They all knew Ekhardt was on his way out. No one cared any more. The man had pushed everyone too far.

Yang had been running a scan on him. He hissed without words and grabbed something out of his magic bag, shoving it up against Rafael's neck so fast that the pressure snapped his neck to the side.

"What the hell --"

"Shut up and sit still."

The words were harsh and probably meant something dire, so he did what he was told. Yang kept the scanner running in one hand and had a hand on the side of Rafe's neck -- pulse, he thought. The medtech kept shaking his head.

"I'm not dead yet."

"I bet there were a couple minutes there when you wished you were, though," he said, sounding a bit less worried.

"Let's just say it was a bad time for Ekhardt to push me," Rafael replied. His head no longer pounded with each word. "What happened?"

"An incredible spike in blood pressure. I didn't see it coming. I want you back to the medunit. Now. No, don't even think about arguing with me. That was damned dangerous, boy --"

Rafael gave him a sharp, quick glare. Yang had stopped calling him 'boy' after the first couple weeks, and he suspected this was a sign of his worry that he did so now, but the timing was bad. Ekhardt not only heard, but he noted Rafael's reaction. He guessed he had better get used to the term. Only a word, after all.

Yang had noticed the byplay as well and he looked apologetic. Rafael looked over at Ardi, but Ekhardt still watched and there was no way he could get the man's attention without Ekhardt seeing. He wanted to be discreet.

Yang helped him up. This was going to be a totally wasted effort. The annoyance made his head start to pound again before they even got a table away. He stopped and put his hands to a chair and started to tell Yang he was all right . . . and then got a better idea.

"Ardi," he said, hardly any sound at all. "Help."

Yang looked bothered.

"Can I get some help here, Ardi?" Yang asked.

Ardi had been lecturing Ekhardt. He left the man so quickly that Ekhardt looked annoyed. You just couldn't please some people.

Ardi carefully took hold of Rafe's waist and led him away, which did help. By the time they were around the corner from Xenobia, he had gotten some of his wits back again.

"Hold up," he said. "I need to tell you something. During the problem with the Displaced, I saw Ekhardt meet with someone in Xenobia." He looked quickly around but they were alone. "No one local. Small, rat-faced, thin. They were back in the shadows and I didn't see much, but it wasn't a chance meeting."

Ardi looked at him, startled. "You were in the middle of all that trouble and you still noticed Ekhardt? Damn. No one else did."

"Just chance," he said, and finally drew away from Ardi. "But I thought you better know. Any idea who it is?"

"We tagged everyone who came on Xenation from the last ship. Had to be one of them," he said. "You really do look like hell, Rafael --"

"I am taking him back to the medunit. Come on. You can talk there."

"I have some pictures of the people. If you can identify him --"

"Not here," Rafael said. "Ekhardt is going to come out any minute."

Ardi agreed. He took hold of Rafael's arm again. He didn't need the help. Still, he supposed the impression they needed to get him back to medunit kept others from questioning what Ardi was doing. People moved out of the way and no one tried to stop them.

But once there, he quickly helped Rafe sit down and then yanked out his pocket comp. "Keep a watch, Yang. Don't let anyone in for a moment."

Yang frowned. "I should -- hell, all right. It'll help him calm down. If he gets worse, yell."

Ardi looked worried at those last words and almost stopped Yang from leaving. Rafael caught his arm. "I'm not going to fall over dead."

"Ha," Yang mumbled but he did leave the inner room.

"Let's do this quickly," Ardi said. He called up the file and handed the comp over to Rafe. "These are the pictures of people as they came off the ship. Use the spacebar to cycle through them."

"That's him -- it IDs him as Wood. Just about the first person off the ship," he said and handed the pocketcomp back.

"You're sure? You said they were in shadows --"

"I can see pretty well in the dark these days," he said and met Ardi's look of surprise. "Yes, there are changes from the graft. That's him."

Ardi nodded, still looking a little worried. "Are you up for this kind of work, Rafael? Really?"

"Well, considering I may have found something already, I kind of think so," he replied and tried not to get annoyed. "Just leave me to it for a while. Yang will tell you if he thinks I shouldn't be helping. You can trust him even if you don't think you can trust me."

"Sounds like something you're kind of used to saying," Ardi observed.

Rafe lifted his hand and ran a finger over the metal plate at the side of his face. "Yes, I am used to saying it. And yes, I know there is a reason why people worry about trusting me. I haven't done anything that has harmed anyone on this station, Ardi. I *never* have."

He saw the little flicker of movement in the man's eyes

as he considered those words and the reason Rafael had the graft on his face and all the other problems. Ardi had arrived shortly after the accident and Rafe didn't know what he thought, but he had needed to say the words to someone other than Yang. He had been saying nothing for too long. It hadn't helped, and he had the feeling that things were going to change. . . .

The bed picked up on his worry and translated the feelings into a series of beeps and buzzes that drew Yang back before Ardi could even walk away. He sighed and forced calm again. The head of security left the room and Yang waved him to lie back down.

He almost argued but something was not going right and they both knew it. The bed wasn't uncomfortable, at least, and he was used to being here. He let Yang run his tests and he relaxed and napped which he suspected came from an injection or two. He didn't care. He didn't want to go through another of those headaches so he would stay and hope Yang could figure out the problem.

He didn't have anywhere better to go.

CHAPTER SIXTEEN

Tali remained curled up in a ball in the corner of the small bed with the blankets pulled up over her. Suffocating in this place. She had stopped screaming into the pillow, trying to muffle the sound. Afraid.

Fear always made her angry. She had started to hit the woman -- *mother* -- and barely caught herself in time, though she suspected *the woman* would have forgiven her the indiscretion. She wished now she had done it. Hit her. Again and again until the anger went away.

Though it never really did.

"Tali."

Norden's voice drew her out of the ball. She unwound and turned, glaring at him in the doorway where he had pulled aside the ratty blue cloth. No real privacy in this place.

He gave an imperious nod that nearly set her off again until she realized he was acting for the person who passed by the door. Spying on them, but they knew how to play their parts.

"Come in," she said in the timid voice she had practiced for so long.

Norden settled in the dirty white plastic chair near the bed, his hands very properly in his lap, his look concerned. They couldn't be certain they weren't being watched, even with the cloth covering the door. A place like this had far too many secrets. She almost glanced at the walls but she hated the way the pattern would change. She couldn't stand it. She wanted everything to be still and to do what she wanted.

"I was worried about you, Tali."

"Sir?" she said. She still nearly choked on the word, even after months of practice.

"That was quite a show out there," he said, and she did see the smirk this time. He'd pay later. She wouldn't forget how he made fun of her. Maybe he did it on purpose because she did snap out of fear. No matter -- he would still pay. She never forgot people making fun of her.

"I will only be here a couple more days until the ship leaves, if all goes well," he said, leaning back. "At the moment, I'm concerned about you."

Concerned about her part and about doing her job. She wanted to be angry because he doubted her, but she nodded instead. The job outweighed her emotions. As long as she could focus on what needed done, she would do all right.

"I worried my mother," she said softly.

Which, they both knew, was good. They wanted Neva focused on Tali and paying less attention to other things. He nodded and the corner of his mouth nearly curled up in a slight smile. That part had worked far better than they had planned. She had *the woman* off kilter already, and she could keep playing on that over the next day. This was not going to take long. She refused to be stuck on this place for long.

"Are you doing all right here, sir?" she asked, a little more interest in her face.

"Quite all right. I'm staying on the ship mostly, but I've gone to the market, which is every bit as fascinating as I've heard. So are the aliens. I would like to know more about them."

A sign of what she needed to ask *the woman*. She gave a slight nod. This would be easy as long as she kept control. Tali sure as hell did not intend to spend more time here than she absolutely had to, but she wasn't leaving empty-handed, either. *The woman* owed her. She was going to pay.

"I'll let you rest," Norden said and stood, giving a little anxious look towards the door. "I'll be in the market for a while if you need to talk to me."

He left and she sat there, staring at her hands for a few minutes before she could bring herself to lift her eyes and look around again.

The colors in the walls glowed and moved. She reached over and hit it, a hard slap and felt how warm and unnatural the wall was. She hated it all the more.

Get to work on what she needed to do and then leave. She hated this place worse than she hated the hospital --

But she didn't want to think about that place right now and about the dead they'd left behind. Ghosts; her father staring at her like he was real. She wasn't going to dwell on that part. No.

She stood, straightened her clothing and wondered about her bags. She would need them. First, though, she had to go out and play the good daughter for a while.

Morgan was going to be a problem. She might have to find some way to get rid of him. She would have to study what he did here.

And Rafael. She wanted him.

Plans. She could do this, as long as she didn't look at the walls.

CHAPTER SEVENTEEN

When Ardi came to see Morgan, he knew this had to be serious from the look on the man's face. Not a surprise; everything had been serious over the last few hours.

"Do you have time to talk?" Ardi asked softly.

Morgan glanced at a computer simulation and put the program on hold. He wanted to know more about Ritter's latest readings but the research could wait a little longer. The station wasn't going anywhere.

"What do you need?" Morgan asked.

Ardi settled in the chair across from the desk and leaned forward. "You had some new sensors put up with the lights. Damn smart move --"

"Ritter's idea."

"Yeah, she's been desperate for something like that for a long time. Glad to see she finally got her chance because I sure as hell want to know more about this station. But . . . do the sensors pick up anything I could use as well?"

Part of him instantly wanted to say no. Working that closely with security seemed filled with potential problems. Then he rethought his outmoded reaction. Cooperation was important on Xenation, so far from any other help.

"There are problems, aren't there?" Morgan asked.

Which was probably a stupid thing to ask but he didn't think it deserved the guffawing laugh he won from Ardi. Then he laughed as well, which eased the situation. The laughter made him feel more at ease with Ardi. He knew he could trust the man.

"Sorry, sorry," Ardi said, wiping tears from his eyes. "Oh, I needed that. It's been insane here lately. Yes, I would say that there are problems. Problems at just about every turn and I need . . . I would like to access your material in order to keep an eye on . . . people. I don't want to send Rafe back out there too soon. Even so, he can't be everywhere, even when he is patrolling the area." Ardi stopped and pushed his hand through his greying hair. Morgan hadn't considered how intense the man's job must be until now. "I don't want to put any more pressure on Rafe. Yang fears there might be something seriously going wrong with him, though he can't pinpoint the trouble."

"Let me get Ritter," Morgan said. He wanted to ask more about Rafe from a science perspective. Better, he knew, to go to Yang and get the information first hand. "She knows more about the sensors than I do. I don't know how she'll feel about you co-opting some of the info, but she is the one with the equipment to take the readings. I could order her to help you --"

"I don't want that kind of trouble with the science department," Ardi said, which showed he was a very smart man. "If she doesn't want to cooperate, I'll just go with what we have."

Morgan called for Ritter and she came in and listened to the problem. She looked skeptical at first, but a mention of Rafe plainly changed her mind.

"Rafe is really one of us, you know, even if we can't have him doing work in the lab. Many of us still go to him and ask questions, including me."

"No one has mentioned this before," Morgan said, surprised by the revelation.

"You're still new. We didn't mention it to Samplin because he didn't care and we didn't want the news getting back to Neva."

"I am a close personal friend of Neva's," Morgan reminded the woman.

"You are, but you are also a professional. If you tell Neva, it will be for more than just to make some points."

"What kinds of problems do you take to him?" Morgan asked, too curious to let go.

"We go to him any time we get stuck on a process, trying to figure out why you can't trace a to b. Theoretical stuff, mostly, but that's the majority of what we do here. I think if the Ksa didn't give him hands-on stuff to work with, he'd have gone crazy, though."

Morgan knew the Ksa had given Rafe items they'd like to know more about. Morgan, being uncommonly blind, hadn't really thought about why until now. Probably just too much else to think about.

"What do you say, Ritter?" Ardi asked, bringing them back to the original discussion.

"I can rig you up a reading code right on your pocket comp. The fewer people who know about this, the better, though. We don't want word getting out, even among our own, that we're doing more than monitoring station functions."

"Humans do tend to be paranoid," Ardi agreed and handed over the pocket comp. "Be careful with this."

Ritter nodded and left the room. Morgan didn't think this would take long.

"I'm sorry to interrupt your work," Ardi said.

"You're fine. I'm having trouble focusing anyway," he admitted. "This place is too much to take in, you know. I'm still trying to understand things and figure out what fits where."

"And not everything will fit into a nice, neat little compartment," Ardi said.

"So sadly true. That's very hard for a scientist, you know. We try to make everything fit, to be able to take something apart, look at the pieces, fit them together again. I can't even be sure what the pieces are to this station."

"Are you glad you came here?" he said, looking curious.

"Yes, of course. We want places that don't just hand over the answers, you know. We want to *discover* things. But what about you? How did you end up here?"

"They asked for a volunteer. I'd just divorced and

wanted as far away from the old memories as I could get," he admitted, frowning. "But this has turned out to be far more work than I expected."

"Thought life would be easy shepherding a bunch of scientists, right?"

He grinned. "Yes, you are right. I signed on and was on my way before we found out the Ksa had moved in as well and the Norishi were at the door within three days of me showing up."

"And the Click?"

"They arrive later. I still don't know what the hell they're doing here. It's an odd combination of beings, you know."

"I have noticed that part."

"And the oddness makes this all the better for you with all those things to discover . . . but it is hell for me, trying to figure out what they're doing and what they want. I still don't know if the market was a good idea even if we have some control over trading rather than letting everything happen behind closed doors."

"If there were doors to close."

"That's true. But you know, it's amazing how much can go on in secret around here, right out in the open."

Ritter came back with the pocketcomp and explained the work. "I've given you the slimmed down version because you aren't going to want to know every time the station makes a beep in a range we can't hear. Visual cycles 5 seconds each camera and dumps after 24 hours. If there is something you see you want to hold longer, hit the space bar and save any visuals off into their own file. Escape to leave the program."

"That's going to be a great help, Ritter. Thank you," he said and took the comp back.

Ritter looked surprised by the sincerity.

"We all know there are things going on out there," Ritter said with a shrug. "We don't need the kind of trouble Ekhardt is trying to make. Just use this wisely. We don't think the Norishi are on to us but they'd cause trouble if they knew about the sensors, especially now that you really are going to use them for surveillance."

Ardi nodded. He looked vastly relieved.

"We're just scientists, you know," Morgan pointed out. "We like things to be calm and quiet so we can do our work. So we'll cooperate as much as we can, within reason."

Ardi looked at the pocketcomp and left again with barely a muttered goodbye. Busy man these days. Morgan didn't envy him all the work of keeping trouble at bay.

Morgan pulled out his pocketcomp and held it up. "I want the same program, Ritter. And with the extras."

Ritter gave a nod, not at all surprised. "I thought you might. I'll have this back to you within the hour. The program is more complex than what I did for him."

Ritter returned to her work and he *tried* to go back to his, but his mind wouldn't focus on anything. Instead, he started thinking about the Norishi who seemed to be a problem everyone tiptoed around.

The Norishi were, without a doubt, powerful. They were also unfriendly, which meant they weren't here for the company. Were the Ksa here just to be part of the group and because they were friendly?

Too simplistic of a theory and therefore likely far from the truth. It took a lot of work to maintain a presence on Xenation. So what were they really here for? To keep watch on the rest of them?

Then what the hell did the Click want? What brought them?

The entire idea of working here on Xenation suddenly took another of those frightening leaps: overwhelming in complexity, and far too many things to try to understand. He sat back and mentally drew boxes around all the separate sections as he tried to pull everything apart and look at them in individual pieces, rather than as part of a whole.

Of all the questions, though, the one that remained the most pervasive, and probably the one he would never really understand, was wondering what the Click wanted here. What made the odd creatures take to space at all? Morgan was more intrigued by that question then by anything else.

The Click were complete unknowns. He didn't like unknowns . . . or maybe he liked them too well. He wanted to find answers but not have them given to him too easily.

He wanted to talk to a Ksa about them. They seemed the most approachable and they might give him some idea of where the Click had turned up elsewhere, which might lead to what brought them here.

He imagined the Norishi came to Xenation because they didn't trust humans or Ksa and wanted to keep an eye on them. He could imagine the Ksa were here because they were a naturally gregarious people and seemed to like humans, besides being interested in the station itself. Humans were here because curiosity was their strongest trait.

But the Click? It could be any of the reasons he'd attributed to the others. Or he might not understand the Norishi and the Ksa, let alone the Click.

He spent the next hour reading over some reports they had on the Click and their nuisance pets. The reading proved fascinating even though the reports inevitably lead to more questions than answers. Some of the earliest notes were from Rafael. Morgan hadn't thought to check for anything he might have written before the accident changed things. There was another interesting project --

Ritter brought the pocketcomp back and showed him how to access the readings. He thanked her and then finally closed down the main computer where he had been jumping from file-to-file for too long. Morgan headed off to find some Ksa. He had questions. It was time to start asking them.

CHAPTER EIGHTEEN

Run check
Repeat.
Exchange data.
Await Key.

CHAPTER NINETEEN

Rafael left the medunit feeling wary. He could almost feel trouble in the air. Something wrong, he thought. He wanted to tell someone but he feared even Yang would think he'd gone over the top.

Something felt out of kilter. He could feel a shift in Xenation that meant *something*. He sensed a building of power and something ready to be released. This might not be bad, but he'd learned not to trust those feelings from Xenation. Not at all.

"Rafe."

He looked up and gave a belated nod to Ardi, surprised to find him in the hall. "Problems?" he asked.

"You're quick to think so," he said with a frown.

Rafael lifted a hand and then frowned because his arm shook. Ardi looked worried but Rafe shook his head. "I expect trouble everywhere these days. Besides, you really shouldn't be working this late."

"Ah. True. And you are out here because?"

"Because I haven't had anything to eat and I hoped that Xenobia might still have something left."

"Yang doesn't feed you?"

"He's not my keeper."

Ardi's left eyebrow lifted in a little show of disbelief and made Rafe laugh, finally. That felt better and even helped to ease the feeling of impending disaster. Maybe he was starting to impart too much of his own feelings onto the station --

Ardi snapped his fingers in front of Rafael's face, startling him.

"You do need a keeper. If this place was any larger, I'd worry about you wandering off and getting lost, the state you're in. Come on."

"I can find my way to Xenobia."

"I suspect so. But I want to talk to you anyway unless you'd rather not talk over dinner."

"I don't mind." In fact, he felt grateful to have the distraction. Anything to draw him away from the feeling he kept getting.

"I am still worried about you doing this work," Ardi admitted as they started down the curving hall. "If Yang thinks --"

"I need the work, Ardi," he admitted.

"You have other pay --"

"It's not the money. I need the *work*. I need things to keep me occupied, things I can do that are not going to make anyone else nervous. I can observe what's going on, Ardi. It gives me a new reason to track movements, to pick up data and to try and figure out patterns, reasons, and why we and the others are doing what we do. And also who is moving outside that pattern."

"Ah." He glanced at Rafael with a new look of understanding in his face. "I had never considered the work in quite that set of terms. That's an interesting take on the job."

So they talked on the way to Xenobia where he found something quite odd: Morgan sitting with Etinon and Saris. Etinon waved them over. This looked intriguing enough that they both went and took seats.

"Buris -- whatever you have left over from dinner?" Rafael said, looking hopeful as the owner came over.

"I can get you a sandwich," he said and then frowned. "Two. You need to put on weight."

"I just want a bit to eat," he replied before he turned back to the unlikely trio. "What's going on?"

"Do you renenver the very first question to us?" Etinon said. "Norgan just asked as well."

"What are the Click doing here," he replied and looked

at Morgan. "I don't suppose they gave you any better answer than they gave me?"

"I suspect not," Morgan said with a sigh.

"The Click nerely arrive at 'laces," Saris said. He gave an elegant little shrug. "We don't know why. We don't know where they cone fron and how they find us or what they want."

"That's not much help at all," Rafael said with a laugh.

"Sonetines there are no answers," Etinon replied.

Both Morgan and Rafael shook their heads at the same time which won a startled reaction from the Ksa and a laugh from Ardi.

"There are always answers," Morgan said as he leaned forward and Rafael nodded in agreement. "Nothing moves without a purpose and the Click do not go through all the trouble of taking to space and coming to different places for no reason at all. Something draws them here."

"Or *drives* them," Rafael said.

Morgan gave a quick nod of agreement and the conversation verged over into science for a while, surprising and pleasing Rafael who so rarely had a chance for such discussions anymore. The Ksa listened, obviously intrigued and they asked a few questions. They clearly didn't have much of a clue about how humans thought through things, which, in turn, made Rafael suspect that he didn't understand much about the Ksa, either.

A couple Click pets even wandered through and Rafael was able to imitate the sounds well enough to get them to come to the table.

"You can tell a couple of them apart but only because they've gotten into dangerous situations," Rafael explained, patting one of the pets on the head. "This is Daredevil. You can see where he lost some fur coming too close to a torch. There's also some variation in fur tones but they're harder to tell. I can't even be certain they don't change with time."

Morgan nodded. "I read all your reports on them."

Rafael looked at him, shocked again. "My reports."

"Yes, yours. You should add any new observations."

He hadn't thought anyone still read the reports or would be interested in anything more he had to say. Morgan was obviously not going to give him the same kind of trouble that Neva and Samplin had. In fact, Morgan just gave him an unexpected gift.

"I have a few things written up. We can --" But he lost track of what he was saying.

"Rafe?" Ardi said, leaning closer.

He shook his head, trying to hear something --

And then he spoke. He didn't know what he said. The words were nonsense and yet there seemed to have meaning. Something.

Everyone looked at him with open shock. He shook his head. "What the hell was that?"

"You . . . maybe you better tell us," Morgan replied. Even the Ksa looked at him with obvious worry and dismay.

"I don't know." He ran his hand over the metal plate, frowning. "There's something wrong. Really, I think there's something wrong and we need to clear the bay areas --"

Ardi didn't even stop to ask questions. He stood, grabbing his com and putting in a call to clear the areas. People around him began to move. Xenobia would be cleared as well, and even Buris had already begun to shut things down.

"I --" he began, and then winced at a sharp pain through the side of his head. "Damn, I hate when that happens. I could be wrong, you know."

"I don't think so," Etinon replied. "It would ve vest that we take this seriously."

"I think the trouble is outside," Rafe added. "Beyond the station."

Saris nodded and gave a quick signal to Etinon who left at a run as warning alarms began to sound through the area. Buris started herding everyone out of the shop and around the corner to the Human Enclave. Etinon started to turn away, but Rafael snagged his arm, startling him.

"Your pardon, but come with us. I think the danger is too close."

Etinon nodded and stepped into the human sector with the rest of them. He had been there before as part of a regular delegation that sometimes came to see Neva, but Rafe had never invited one of the Ksa in with him before.

And Neva arrived.

"What is going on?" she demanded of Ardi.

"There's trouble coming," he said and glanced at Rafael.

Neva's face went red and her eyes narrowed. This wasn't going to go well. He could see the reaction in her face as she took a step forward. "I don't know what the hell you think -- "

"Something just came through slide," Ardi said. "Picking up on the tracking cams!"

He held up his pocketcomp and shot the picture to the wall beside them. The ship was still too far out and the wall itself distorted some of the view, but they could see the movement of something huge against the stars.

"What the hell is that?" Brody asked as she moved up closer to the wall.

"Nothing I recognize," Neva replied and turned her attention to the view. "It's huge."

"That is Norishi which cones vehind it," Etinon said.

Rafael looked back, startled. He could barely see the shape of another ship, coming off slide and into the same area. Following the first craft?

"The first ship has damage." Ardi handed his comp to someone else and he went closer to the view on the wall. His finger traced a line along the undercarriage and Rafael could clearly see dark marks crossed the surface and something flared bright along the side. This didn't look good.

Rafe was bothered to see the Norishi coming in right behind them. "Can you get any readings on the Norishi ship?" he asked. "Are the weapons hot?"

"Too far out still," Ardi replied. "But at the speed they are closing in on Xenation, I'd say we're only a few seconds down the time line now. They're moving damned fast!"

Rafael nodded. They had already passed the first satellites, which meant they'd be in range of scanners --

Everything whited out.

"Son of a bitch!" Ardi shouted. "I think they just blew --
"

The world spun. Rafael didn't know what happened, but for a moment he saw more than the video cameras could have seen out there in the void. He saw the Norishi ship, maneuvering and firing again --

Blinked. Back in Xenation.

"They destroyed the ship," Rafe whispered. He shook his head and tried to clear the vision still clinging to his mind. "The Norishi destroyed the other craft."

"We couldn't see," Morgan said. Then he frowned and took a step closer as he took hold of Rafe's arm. "But you did, didn't you?"

"I think so." Rafe rubbed a hand over his face. Everything tingled.

"There is no way you could have seen anything." Neva's voice had the sharp-edged snarl he'd gotten so used to hearing, but the tone still cut. "I don't know what game you're playing --"

"Neva, he knew something was coming in before it came off slide," Morgan said, remaining calm as he faced her.

Rafe had prepared for more of a tirade but she closed her mouth and her eyes narrowed in anger. She looked at the wall where the static filled picture showed debris spreading outward.

"Where is the Norishi ship now?" she asked.

Which, in many ways, was a major win for Rafael. He thought her reaction shouldn't matter much to him, but even now it did. He looked to the view and wished the cameras would clear and they could see what was happening out there.

Something took hold of him again and he caught another vision of the long, sleek ship.

"The Norishi ship is coming our way," he said. He had a hand to the wall. The sense of vertigo when he looked out in space had nearly overwhelmed him. "I don't think they've closed down their weapons."

Etinon suddenly grabbed something from his pocket -- long, thin -- and held it up to his mouth as he started to relay the news to his own people. Rafe hadn't seen a Ksa communications device before and he could not even begin to follow what Etinon said in the rush of words.

Then he lowered the stick, though he probably didn't turn the device off. Neither Ardi nor Neva said anything.

"The Ksa organize in case of trouvle. This is how they come, sonetines, the Norishi attacking at a full run. I do not think they would do such a thing. I do not want to think so. Ships that are in dock --"

Neva's eyes went wide and she spun but Ardi was pulling out his commlink and putting the receiver in his ear as he talked. Rafe didn't know if they could get a ship cleared from dock in time and he thought they might be safer staying here. A moving target might be something that worried the Norishi more than one sitting in place.

Even as he thought so, he could hear Ardi saying much the same thing to someone on the commlink. He heard Etinon speaking to his own people and others around him whispering . . . and he heard whispering he feared might only be in his head. *Sequence, install, lock. Await key.*

The opening to the Human Enclave began to close. People shouted and some tried to rush out, but the wall moved to quickly, the ends pulling in on all sides and the opening disappearing. The light inside brightened and a wave of fresh air swept through the hall, as though Xenation tried to comfort them.

"What the hell?" Neva looked at him, her eyes narrowed, more words already at her lips -- but Rafe lifted a hand and for some reason, the action actually stilled her.

"I haven't a clue, you know," he said.

"You are the one with contact with the station. That's what you claim, isn't it? Why did you close the door?"

"I didn't."

"You can open them. Get this open."

"Neva," Ardi said and tapped her shoulder. "Not a good idea. The *Blue Star* reports the Norishi craft still coming on, guns open. I think the station just made us as safe as it can."

She frowned and then looked over at the view on the wall. Others had been handing the pocketcomp around as the view grew clearer. The Norishi ship had already reached the grow domes and the cams were virtually real time as the ship fired a shot, cutting through the roof of one.

"Son of a bitch," Neva whispered. The dome didn't go out on the first shot, but they'd get a second one.

Something darted across the cam. And then another.

"What the hell?" Rafael said, startled. He wasn't the only one. "What was --?"

Then they came back around; Click ships, weaving and dancing in a way that Rafe found frightening to watch. Two Click ships circled around the Norishi craft so quickly, that the larger ship couldn't get a shot at them.

"Damn. What are they doing?" Morgan asked, clearly intrigued despite the dangerous situation.

"Etinon?" Rafe asked.

"I do not know," he said and seemed as enthralled as the others. "The Click do not show such vehavior vefore."

Then he went back to his own commlink, talking with an increasingly frantic sound Rafe had never heard in the Ksa before. That, more than the scene on the wall, worried him about the situation.

"They're trying to herd the ship away," Rafe said, and almost wished he hadn't spoken when he saw Neva glare at him again. However, he went on anyway. "It's how they circle the pets when they are trying to pull them in."

Morgan took a step towards the wall and nodded. "I read that report. You might be right. I don't think it's going to work with the Norishi, though."

Rafe nodded agreement and didn't look at Neva again. He knew he kept looking towards her and hoping for a change that was not going to happen. He counted himself lucky to have most of the others on his side.

"The Norishi are going to fire," Ardi said. "The weapons are heating up --"

"Can the station survive a shot? Will there be damage?"

Morgan asked and looked to Rafe as though he should know.

"Xenation has prepared. Taken extraordinary precautions," he said, waving a hand towards the closed door. "That makes me think it expects this to be serious. I don't know what is going to happen --"

The Click kept moving around the larger ship. The pattern, though, seemed to have changed and one of the round Click ships took a hit, and then another. The craft kept moving. Tougher than they looked.

"I didn't think they'd stand up to an attack like that!" Neva said, shocked.

"Do Click ships have weapons?" Rafe asked and turned again to Etinon.

"None that we know," he admitted. "But we surnise they would not survive so long without sone way of defense."

"They're moving -- no!" Neva shouted.

The Click ships threw themselves at the larger Norishi ship, impacting in an explosive ball of fire that filled the screen and burnt out at least one cam, though Ardi quickly grabbed the pocketcomp and switched to one outside and near the docks on Xenation itself.

The Click ships had disappeared in a field of debris and explosive gas. The Norishi ship still pressed on, but the shell had started to glow, and a heartbeat later the craft came apart in huge chunks, the pieces flying off in all directions as explosions ripped through the interior of the ship.

"We're going to take some hits," Ardi warned. "This could be dangerous."

A piece of ship as large as a human scout ship went up over the cam and hit with a force they heard and felt well within the station. The floor rippled and a crack appeared in the wall beside Rafe. Morgan drew out a scanner and ran the sequence as quickly as he could. Rafe hoped, given how friendly the man had been lately, that he would have a chance to see the readings later. He couldn't carry a pocketcomp or scanner of his own anymore since they were apt to die as soon as he dealt with the Displaced.

Where were the Displaced now? Would they all become

Displaced if Xenation couldn't protect them?

"The ship isn't going to survive out there in dock," Neva said softly. "They don't have the ability to shield against stuff that large!"

"They're going to try and break out and drop down," Ardi reported, tapping at his ear. "If they can get low fast enough --"

"Say to hold!" Etinon spoke quickly to his own link and words came back. He looked at Ardi again. "Hold. Trust us."

Ardi looked at Neva. She nodded though she looked as though she regretted it in the next breath. They all turned back to watch the screen where the debris still moved, too much of it heading their way.

And then the Ksa ship arrived.

"They left dock," Etinon said, waving a hand towards the screen in what seemed a very nervous and un-Ksa-like gesture. "We ready when craft arrive. Hold. We have it."

And they did. Ksa weapons fired, breaking up the larger pieces of debris, while something shield-like swept out from the ship and deflected even most of the smaller pieces outward again. They still felt a few blows elsewhere in Xenation but the human ship at the dock had been saved from any of the dangerous hits.

He didn't envy Neva right now if the Norishi had turned on them, but that brought another question to mind.

"Etinon," he said with a quick bow of his head, "That first ship, the one already in battle with the Norishi, have you seen the type before? Do you know who they might have been?"

Everyone turned. Etinon bowed his head in return and spread his arm in a gesture that looked far too human.

He glanced at the screen and then back again to Rafe. "I cannot say who they had veen."

Rafe bowed his head, accepting the answer. The others turned away, watching the rest of the work the Ksa did outside Xenation. Rafael, however, turned his thoughts to something far more troubling. The Ksa did not often use ambiguous lines. Etinon had said, he feared, exactly what he meant -- not that he didn't know the ship, but that he *could not say* who they were.

A Ksa secret.

Rafe could have pressed the point but this was not the time to look for more trouble. However, Etinon knew they would discuss this at some point soon. The Ksa gave a little bow of his head. They understood each other.

CHAPTER TWENTY

Tali stood back in the shadows and watched the people of the station during the panic. She despised them all and the way they got scared. Stupid people. So many stupid people everywhere.

No Displaced showed up which probably meant something, but she didn't want to think about them. Instead, she watched her mother who plainly didn't know Tali had arrived. She'd followed the rest of the people when the alarms began.

Interesting to watch what happened, really. Most interesting to see how *the woman* didn't trust Rafael and how Rafael backed down before her. Tali wondered how she could use that against both of them. This could be fun, really.

The door opened to the bay and she heard the relief spread through the group. Many of them headed out into the open, but she slid back, staying out of sight of her mother. She nodded to the others who came by, pretending to normality. Unfortunately, one of the people was Morgan and his eyes narrowed, showing distrust he didn't even pretend to hide. She despised him.

"Uncle Morgan," she said with that same practiced smile she gave others. "I didn't get to say hello yet. I was really surprised to find you here!"

"I could say the same thing about you," he replied and didn't seem at all taken with the smile. Damn. He also hadn't been panicked like some of the others. Probably not smart enough to be. "What are you doing here, Tali?"

"The others were worried. I followed --"

"What are you doing on Xenation?"

"I came. . . ." She stopped and took a breath, trying to keep control. She hadn't been prepared to face this test. She'd prepared to deal with her mother who would be easy to manipulate, but not Morgan. "I had nowhere else to go."

"And you ran to your mother." His voice held a hint of ridicule and scorn. She felt anger growing when he didn't accept her answer. "Tali, you didn't run to your mother when you were three. You really think I'll believe you would now?"

"People change, Uncle Morgan," she said, and kept her voice neutral, though she wanted to reach out and slap him. How dare he judge her!

"Yes, sometimes they do," he agreed with a bow of his head.

"Things changed," she said. Others had been passing, and some of them lingered close by. They made it impossible for her to do anything about Morgan since the action would be traced back to this conversation. She wanted this man dead and she couldn't do it. Well, not yet. Maybe later.

That thought cheered her.

"I'm going back to the room. Mom says we'll have dinner tonight and I'll be surprised by the food. It sounds like an adventure. I'll see you later!"

She turned and hurried away and didn't look back, even though she could feel Morgan staring after her. She hated leaving an enemy at her back, but the witnesses worked for her this time. He wouldn't dare move against her, either.

She went back to the dull little room. Thank God she wouldn't be staying here for long. What a horrible place. She couldn't imagine why people even cared. Alien made? So what? Aliens were everywhere these days.

She threw herself down on the bed and stared at the ceiling thinking about two problems: Morgan and Rafael. Morgan was out of her reach for the moment, but her plans for Rafael were still good.

Norden looked her way and she gave him a nod before she moved towards a corner that seemed mostly abandoned and dark. He followed her and in a moment he pulled out a

ShadowCage and wrapped them in darkness and sound shield.

"This is looking more dangerous than I expected," Norden said. Then he grinned, a show of white teeth in the gray dull light within the cage. "I might have to charge people more when we're done."

She liked the idea. More money was always good.

"I think I can see how to get Rafael out of the way," she said with a bright smile. "It's going to be fun, too."

"Good." He didn't ask the particulars, trusting her to know the work. No one else ever trusted her. "I've been walking the market several times since I arrived. People are already getting used to seeing me there. Our people here have the booths set up and ready."

"A shame your guy got kicked out when we needed him."

"Now that I met him, I think he's more of a problem than a help anyway. I may have to do something about him."

"Creatively."

"Oh yes," he said and grinned.

She didn't ask what he would do, either. "I want off of here with the *Shaw*. If the damned Norishi had damaged it, I would have taken one of theirs. I am not staying here."

He gave a little laugh but agreed. "I don't see anything holding us up. Time to get to work, so we can leave on time."

She agreed with a quick nod, anxious to get moving --

And she saw something moving -- white and filmy --

"No!" The sight of a Displaced so close frightened her. And then she grew angry, because she hated being afraid, and anger was power. She yelled and leapt out of the ShadowCage and rushed forward, straight at it.

Someone grabbed her arm and yanked her back. She swung on them and hit some woman. She blocked her next blow and pushed Tali against the wall.

"Stay back! It can hurt you!"

"They're not real!" she snarled and shoved at her, but she wouldn't let her go.

"They are real." She waved a scanner towards Tali, but it was the appearance of her mother that finally settled her. She had to look calm for anything else to work. "Look, you see these readings?"

"Oh." She acted as though she cared, but she kept her eye on the damned thing. Not her father's face this time, at least. "Why is it here?"

"I don't know. They're usually only drawn to power sources and I thought I read something -- probably just a spike in the station, resettling after this mess."

She nodded. From the corner of her eye she could see Norden moving down the hall, the ShadowCage off and a good distance from them already, so probably wouldn't be linked with her. They'd have to be careful.

"Tali?" her mother asked.

"Sorry. I'll be more careful of them from now on," she promised. "This place is scary, mom. I didn't know so much happened here!"

"Anything else, Ritter?" *the woman* asked.

"No, Neva," Ritter said and finally let go of Tali. "Odd stuff, though. I'll keep checking."

Her mother nodded. Ritter, though, still gave Tali a look of mistrust. If there hadn't been so many people around, she would have regretted that look. Later. She might deal with this one later. Now she walked away with her mother while the Displaced lingered back there for a moment and finally drifted to somewhere else.

CHAPTER TWENTY-ONE

More than a day standard had passed since the incident, and chaos continued on the station. The people out at the domes had used the little flyers to come back to Xenation -- dangerous moving past the debris, but safer than staying out in the domes with no protection at all. The little craft ferried the people in and the domes went to fully automatic. They were now cut off from their largest food source, though they had stockpiled supplies anyway. They could hold out for months here, and by then someone would have come by and found the trouble.

If they survived.

Morgan found one incident especially interesting though. The Click and their pets hadn't come out of their area, prompting people to wonder if all the Click had died in that attack that saved the rest of them. The scanners showed some activity in that sector though.

Neva had called for a Tribunal. The Norishi sent word they would be there but they hadn't arrived yet.

Ritter had reported an odd Displaced and power reading and with Tali in the area, which bothered him, though he didn't say so. Maybe he didn't have to since Ritter found Tali's presence in the hall troubling. Morgan realized others didn't need to know Tali's history to mistrust her. The child -- the young woman -- put out an aura of wrongness.

The Norishi had his attention today. They had to answer for what happened. He'd been surprised to learn they had even agreed to the Tribunal, given the circumstances.

"Something is going on with them," Neva had said as

they walked to the meeting. "Something I don't understand. Looks like you showed up at a hell of a bad time, Morgan. But I'm glad you're here. I can trust you."

And she'd looked at him as though hoping for an answer.

"I'll tell you what I think when I get it all sorted out," he said.

They'd entered the larger area with all the others, both humans and Ksa. No Click. No Norishi yet, either. He didn't think they would agree and then not show up.

Rafael came in, late as well, and still looking like hell. Ritter gave him a chair. The Ksa had a good turnout, a well.

Whispers spread around the area, circling, braiding and shifting. No one knew more than he did so Morgan stopped listening. Tali wasn't here. He didn't know if he should make anything of that or not but he felt oddly nervous wondering where she might be.

And Ekhardt. Where was Ekhardt? That might be a far more important question, and he glanced towards Ardi, wondering what he thought of the missing people. Without a doubt, Ardi noted who hadn't arrived. The head of security crossed over to Rafael, leaned down and said something quiet. Rafael gave a short nod. Ardi moved on and Rafael remained where he was.

Morgan shifted on the uncomfortable chair and started thinking about the work he should get back to doing. However, a band of eight Norishi finally crossed to the area before he made up his mind to leave. They did not pause as they arrived and people moved out of the way. Morgan noted how the Ksa moved more slowly than the humans and how they didn't look happy. If they had carried weapons, this might have gone badly.

The Norishi continued straight to the podium. Two took their places and the looks they gave everyone else seemed to say that *they* were not the ones who had done anything wrong. This looked like quite a show but he wasn't sure he wanted a front row seat.

"Thank you for attending," Neva said; neutral words

that didn't draw any serious looks from the group. "I am officially calling this meeting to order. Recorders are running and files will be sent, as always, to the IWC. We are starting with the file recorded by the head of Human Security at the time of the incident. The file has been verified by five witnesses, including Etinon, a Ksa. Please play the video."

Ardi unfolded a screen to the right side of the gathering. Most of the people watched the drama again. Morgan glanced to the screen and then away. He'd watched the vid several times already and he found himself far more interested in watching the Norishi.

He expected them to be as calm and unconcerned as always, but he saw a slight shift in movement and suspected they didn't know about the vid record. How interesting. It meant they weren't paying attention to human surveillance after all.

Norishi hands moved. Signals given? He'd want to see the vid record of this meeting afterwards.

The attack had seemed to take forever, but today the vid went too quickly, the screen going dark and all faces turned back to the Norishi.

"Commander Tican is there anything you can tell us about this incident?"

"No more than you have seen, except I can tell you the ship you saw -- the Norishi Ship -- had been taken by others at a time measured in many earth months." She gave a wave of her long fingers towards the dark screen. "We have had our suspicions of where it went. The Ksa have made it now impossible for us to tell having destroyed all pieces."

Etinon and another Ksa introduced as Sion both looked at the Norishi with such contempt that Morgan half expected a war to break out right then and there.

"You claim the Norishi ship was no longer in Norishi hands," Ardi said.

"That is what I said," Tican answered, glaring, though perhaps only because a man addressed her. They had insinuated the Ksa had a reason to destroy the ship. Morgan thought they were trying very hard to turn this away from their doorstep.

"Can you tell us anything about the other ship, the first craft the Norishi vessel destroyed?" Neva asked.

"A Norishi vessel not in our hands, Station Master Neva."

"As you say." She gave a bow of her head, accepting the Norishi words if not of the truth. Morgan wondered if the Norishi could read the difference in a human. Hard to tell when all they did was glare. Was that purposeful? Did it hide something else?

He pulled his pocketcomp and started a wide range scan, and then narrowed down on where the Norishi sat. The readings were not human. For some reason that took him by surprise. Shells that looked alike, but little more in common. Adaptations to like environments. Others, of course, had made those same sort of readings and he'd studied them, but now he had a chance to study minute changes in living beings as they faced stress.

"Another question, of course, is why the Click moved when they did," Neva said. She looked upset and with reason. They didn't understand the Click. To have them do something so outlandish just added more questions.

"The Click always appear where the Ksa go," Tican said with a dark glance towards that end of the table where Etinon and Sion sat. "You would do well to ask them what it means."

"The Click do tend to arrive where we have gone," Etinon agreed with a rather gracious nod. "We had thought they did the sane with others as well. I guess it nust ve a natter of taste."

Implying, of course, that the Click didn't like the Norishi.

Everyone else watched in dismay. Ardi looked as though he was trying to figure out how to contain the battle when it started.

They discussed the matter for a few more minutes. Neva did not bring up the information about the destroyed human ship and the Norishi craft that had been spotted there.

Norishi offered nothing of any real help. Morgan took readings and more readings and hoped this wasn't a complete waste of time.

The Ksa took the Norishi accusations without any show of rancor, perhaps because the humans plainly didn't believe the Norishi. Unlike the fiasco with Ekhardt, the Ksa did not look even slightly annoyed.

The meeting didn't gain anyone anything, as far as he could tell. They ended the Tribunal nearly three hours later after a discussion about trade in the Market and very little else about the disaster that nearly struck the station.

The station had been worried enough about the attack to try to protect them. He wanted to talk to Rafael about what had happened and now seemed the best time, seeing him walking away with Ritter.

"Rafe?" He jogged the few steps to catch up with them.

Rafael looked at him with what could be either worry or resignation. Maybe both. He appeared pale and a little unsteady, but Yang was nowhere around, so that must have meant he was well enough to be out on his own. Morgan had already noticed that Yang hovered around Rafe if there was any real sign of trouble.

"Do you have a few minutes? I'd like to talk to you," Morgan said. He could have ordered Rafe to stop, but a little politeness didn't seem a bad idea.

"Now is a good time," Rafe agreed. "I'll be heading out to the market in a few minutes."

They went into the Human Enclave and down a hall past where Tali stood, leaning against the wall. Rafe glanced her way and then walked a little faster.

"I know the area is small and everything," Rafe said. "But why does she always seem to show up wherever I'm heading?"

"I was feeling the same way," Morgan said. Rafe gave him a quick, nervous look. "Problem?"

"I forgot you know her. Knew her before she came here."

"Tali was a willful, destructive child who created

problems everywhere she went. She has not started any trouble here."

Rafe said nothing more as they reached Morgan's office. Ritter went to her own station in the outer room. Morgan waved him towards the chair while he took his place behind the desk. Rafe sat down and looked glad to be off his feet.

"You look like hell," Morgan said. "You have since I arrived, but I get the feeling this is not really normal, is it?"

"It's been a rough lately," he admitted. "What do you want to talk about?"

"Tell me how you get the station to make openings in the wall."

"I don't, not anymore."

"But you could still, couldn't you?"

Rafe frowned, his hand brushing against the line of silver beneath his eye. Odd how easily Morgan had gotten used to seeing it. "Things changed after the accident."

"That doesn't answer my question. You could still get the station to open doors, couldn't you?"

"I haven't tried and I'm not going to." He leaned forward, putting his hands on the desk and looked straight into Morgan's face with an intensity he had not seen in Rafael Karim before. "Things *changed*. I suddenly had far more feeling for what Xenation does, which isn't pleasant because I don't understand most of it. There are dark places in this station, Etech Doreet. There are places where none of us should go."

What had brought this on? The intensity was shocking -- and then he thought he knew the answer.

"You think you tapped one of those places and caused the accident? You are a scientist: do you have any logic to go with this belief?"

"I was worried about Ashur coming home. I hated the idea of dealing with him," he said, his voice dropping to nearly a whisper. "Ashur had been my friend. We got along well. What happened between Neva and me --"

"Ashur and Neva had a marriage only in name, you know. They'd been growing apart since Tali was born."

Rafe looked up with a start, his eyes gone wide. "That's exactly what Neva said."

"And it is true," Morgan added. Hell, this wasn't the conversation he wanted to have with Rafael, but maybe they needed to go through the other problem before he could get to anything important. "They stayed together for their careers. They found it easier to get positions as husband and wife, both of them with extensive science and command backgrounds. In fact, that was one of the big draws for them getting this position. But they had fallen out of love a long time ago, Rafael."

Rafael stared at him with what might be distrust, his dark eyes blinking several times. He was paler, as though the emotional turmoil was taking more from him. Someone else should have had this discussion with him long before now. Who? Neva was the only person left who knew the truth.

"There's been a lot of guilt building up around here," Morgan said. He leaned back, frowning. "And all of it misplaced, as far as I can tell."

"Neva thinks I caused the accident."

"Because of your tenuous contact with Xenation before the accident and the plate on your face. Because you could do tricks with doors."

"And because I knew something was about to happen."

"How did you know?"

He leaned back, his eyes half closing. This had to be something he'd thought about often enough in the past, but he still didn't have a quick answer, which told Morgan a great deal already.

"I'd done a lot of computer reads that day because I felt. . . . I'd have to say that there was . . . a feeling. Did you know my grandfather is Keri ibn Karim?"

"A very powerful psi -- the most famous," Morgan said, startled that he hadn't picked that up. "You think this might be psi related?"

"Maybe. I tested as a possible psi, but didn't show any activity. I don't know. I can't describe what I feel, Morgan. I don't think there are human words for what has happened."

He hadn't considered that possibility and it made him uneasy. He looked at the wall beside him and tried to imagine the alien beings that created this place. He could not connection Rafael made with the station.

"How did you connect the first time?"

Rafael suddenly grinned, making him look far younger and even a little dangerous. "I was singing."

And that, beyond a doubt, was not the answer he had expected. "Singing."

"I have a passion for Old Earth Music of the pre-slide era. I used to perform at college in musicals and I had a chance at a career on the circuit -- but I loved science too much to give it up for the stage."

"Really."

"Really," he replied with a brighter grin. The young man -- yes, young -- had facets Morgan really hadn't thought about before. "I could sing anytime, which was enough for me. But science took the kind of dedication which couldn't be shifted to second stage, so to speak."

"You don't sing now."

"No." He sat back. "I don't want to take the chance of hitting the right notes without thinking. I have perfect pitch. I sang a group of sounds that made the connection. I told Samplin and Ritter."

This explained Ritter's obsession with sounds, at least. She hadn't told him how the work had started, but then everyone had gotten used to not mentioning any connection to Rafael.

"You knew about the trouble with the scout ship when it came back, which came from Xenation to you. Was this the first time you had made such a connection?"

"I think so." He touched the plate again, but seemed less troubled. Perhaps talking helped. "It wasn't as strong a link as I have now. There may have been other little touches, but I brushed them off as my own emotions, which they might well have been. I was keyed up as hell, you know. And maybe . . . maybe Xenation picked up my worry about Ashur coming back and tried to stop them from coming in."

"That's not what happened, you know."

Rafael looked angry for the first time. "You weren't here. You aren't me. You don't know --"

"I've read every report leading up to what happened. The station had been doing massive changes for the previous thirty-six hours. Power readings were low everywhere, There had been a slight glitch about ten hours earlier when the *Agro* tried to leave port and Xenation didn't respond as quickly as expected."

"Yes but -- but --"

"You are a damned good scientist, Rafael --"

"I *was* --"

"You *are* a damned good scientist. Why is it you can't look at this sequence, analyze what happened, and come to the same conclusions as the rest of us? The station had overtaxed its own systems and didn't expect the scout ship back. Xenation tried to warn everyone through you."

"Not everyone believes that," he answered, his face gone stone still and cold.

Neva.

"I can't change what Neva thinks any more than you can, but you know you did not set out to kill Ashur and the others, just to keep from having to speak to him about your relationship with Neva."

Rafael said nothing for a moment and then finally looked him in the face. "I think we're done."

"No we aren't."

The words surprised Rafael. Interesting thought; Rafe was probably used to setting his own agenda these days and no one pushed him. Morgan decided he would because he didn't believe Rafael had been responsible for the accident and this might be the best way to prove it.

"What is it you want?" Rafael finally asked. He looked annoyed.

"I want to understand Xenation."

Rafael laughed, already back into a better mood. Good. Maybe they could still work together.

"I think you come the closest to understanding the

station, Rafael. That's pretty obvious -- and yes, I know you don't know much about Xenation at all. I came here to find the answers in whatever way I can. You know things."

"I know the station is changing," he said.

"Changing?" Morgan tried to keep his voice calm, even though he felt a little whisper of cold moving up through him. Stations should not change by their own decisions.

"Xenation reacts differently, even under normal circumstances. The atmosphere cycles, for instance, are not on the same schedule they were when we first arrived. And the gravity has changed."

"To suit you."

"I don't think --" Rafe stopped and frowned. "Earth Standard gravity. Because I'm from earth."

"And the station is linked to you. There's no denying that part," he said.

"True." Rafael's hand touched the plate again.

He wanted to ask specifically about the plate but didn't think this would be a good time. They needed a better rapport first. Oddly, he thought having annoyed Rafe might have helped by forming a more varied and normal relationship between them rather than the ones where everyone whispered around him.

"You get along well with Ardi," Morgan said, which seemed to take Rafael by surprise with the change in direction.

"He wants a job done and there are no strings attached," he replied with a little shrug.

"And he needed you. You get along well with the Ksa and the Click. And I heard even the Norishi made some acknowledgment that you have status."

"I don't trust that part," he said and leaned over the desk, surprising Morgan with the sudden intensity again. "I don't trust it at all, and neither should anyone else, especially at a time when there are far too many things turning up that show they are not to be trusted. The Norishi are up to something. It's out of character for them to acknowledge any male."

"You believe Norishi controlled that ship."

"Yes, but I don't think that's really the bigger issue."

"They were coming for us to destroy --"

"No, I don't think they could have seriously damaged Xenation. In my opinion, the real problem began with the appearance of the other alien ship, the one no one has so far claimed to recognize. I think the Ksa may know something about it and I think the appearance of the craft unsettled them. I hope they'll tell me something about it but so far I haven't heard from any of them."

"Do you think this was a Ksa ship?"

"No. I think this was another alien group."

He sighed. More complications? "And then we have to wonder what they were doing heading for us."

"And wonder why the Norishi didn't want them to reach Xenation. I assume Neva intends to send out a scout to look over the area where the ship was destroyed?"

"Yes. It will go out in a few more hours. There's still too much debris near Xenation, and she doesn't want to risk anyone."

He nodded. "I wish --" But he stopped, though Morgan could easily guess the rest of it. *I wish I could go out there and look.*

"The plan is to grab everything they can and hurry back. We fear more trouble could be coming our way. Or do you know?"

"I haven't felt anything. I'll let you know if I do." He stood. "I'm going to spend some time out in the market today in hopes the Ksa have something to say to me and maybe the Click even come back out. I can't get answers from them but I want to know that they're doing all right."

Morgan nodded. He had wanted answers and Rafe had sidestepped them. They'd have to talk again another time; a calmer time, if there was such a thing on this station. He watched the man leave, giving a wave to some of the others in the science lab. The people he used to work with; he was going to start working at getting Rafe back in here, at least on occasional projects.

He needed to talk to Neva about the situation which was not going to be easy. However, if he could get her to see reason, maybe they could ease some of the pressure from Rafael. He wanted Rafael Karim clearheaded. He wanted this man who had such strange links to everything alien here to be able to deal with what he saw, and not to paint it in colors chosen by Neva. He didn't look forward to the discussion.

CHAPTER TWENTY-TWO

Few people wandered through the market today. Even some of the booths remained closed and Rafe wondered if people had applied to leave. Serving on Xenation was entirely voluntary --

Except for him.

The thought made him angry. Then, in the next contrary thought, he knew he wouldn't have left if he had the choice. If Xenation did listen to him -- he could never be certain -- she probably caught that second feeling and didn't worry about trapping him here.

Or maybe contrary humans drove her crazy, the way she drove him crazy.

He sighed and glanced towards movement at the edge of one of the booths. Ekhardt in a big dark jacket and a cap tried to slip away before Rafe saw him. The man knew he'd been spotted and he took another step before he stopped, straightened his shoulders, and dared Rafe to come on.

If he hadn't already felt like shit, he probably would have gone straight to Ekhardt and antagonized the man enough to get a reaction -- which wouldn't have been difficult even in good times -- and then decked the guy. Instead, he carefully hit the warning button on his commlink, thinking Ekhardt would notice the move and want to get clear before anyone else came to stand with Rafe.

"So, playing a good little watch dog, are you?" Ekhardt asked when Rafe reached the man. His beady eyes narrowed in the fleshy face.

"Just doing my job. Something you never figured out,

which is why I have the position now and you don't," he said with a bit of a smile. He hoped Ardi sent someone quickly. They were both in moods.

Of course Rafe annoyed Ekhardt. Anything Rafe said would anger him so he didn't bother to play polite. Besides, it gave him a little satisfaction to deal with the one person he didn't have to tiptoe around. He didn't know what Ekhardt had expected, but no one stood up to him often enough. Well, today was the day to do it --

And then he saw something startling. Three Click came at a bounding rush through the market towards him. Ekhardt either saw his look or heard the movement and glanced back. The sight plainly unsettled the man and he took the opportunity to dart past Rafe and keep going.

Rafe had always considered the Click harmless and perhaps even a little helpless . . . right until he saw two of their ships take out the Norishi craft. Now he watched the creatures coming at him and wondered why they still hadn't considered things like if it meant the Click might be at war with the Norishi.

Would the Norishi even say so?

As the Click drew closer -- odd behavior, the way they rushed like that -- he gave what he hoped was a credible greeting clap. The three stopped the headlong rush and he wondered if they had been going after Ekhardt. Maybe he shouldn't have interfered. It might have been an interesting confrontation.

The Click greeted him with obvious agitation. They leapt up and down and the chorus of sounds overlapped and rose in ways he had never heard before. Something wrong, he guessed, though this could have as soon been laughter at seeing Ekhardt run.

Felice reached him before anyone else. The few people in the market had all backed away and everyone appeared more nervous at the behavior.

"This is odd," Felice said. She sat down on the floor in front of the Click which seemed to help.

He hadn't thought how towering over them might be

intimidating, so he sat down as well. The Click formed up in a line in front of them, still agitated and moving in odd ways, but quieter, at least. Damn, he wished he had some idea of how to really deal with them, or even a clue of what they wanted. A few more came, and then even some of the pets showed up, though they didn't stay with the Click for long, moving off to get into things. That at least looked normal again, and gave him a little hope.

The Click made a few more noises which might have been the same exasperation that he felt at not being able to communicate. Did they have much the same range of emotions as the rest of them? Except for the Norishi, of course. He never knew what the Norishi really felt and he wasn't taken in by their human-like exterior.

The Click finally moved away and he stood, offering a hand to Felice. She was the only other person on the station who had a good rapport with the Click, mostly through dealing with them on the docks. He'd have to sit down and talk to her about it again soon. They'd exchanged information in the past and anything that helped build up even a little understanding of the furry aliens would help.

"What do you make of that?" Ardi asked, coming up behind him.

"That the Click are odd," Rafe said with a quick, unexpected grin. Having them come out made him feel better. The pets moved around, perhaps a little more frantic than before, but still there. "But they weren't the reason I called you. Ekhardt was in the market and he didn't want to be seen. Wearing a cap and a big jacket. He took off running as soon as the Click appeared."

"Was he?" Ardi asked and glanced around. "I'll look into it. Good work."

"He hasn't been harassing those of us who work the bays," Felice unexpectedly offered. "And that's strange behavior for him. He always makes trouble for us. It's his way of making certain we know he's boss."

Ardi nodded. "He's into something and he's too stupid to do it wisely," he said, though softly. "So he breaks his usual pattern and just draws more attention when he least wants it. Keep your eyes open, both of you. This just feels . . . not good, and we don't need more trouble right now."

Felice gave a quick nod of agreement. Good to have her on their side because she was observant and she had a good position out there in the work yard. He suspected she'd done this kind of thing for Ardi before from the way she accepted the orders so easily.

Ardi headed off to work and Felice turned to go back to work at the bays. Rafael intended to continue to wander the market, but then he saw Tali standing a few feet away watching him. He decided to go with Felice instead.

Avoiding trouble, he told himself. The hair on the back of his neck stood on end as he walked away from her, thinking she was more trouble than Ekhardt. More dangerous. He still didn't like how she always showed up where he was working. If only he could go to Neva and ask her, if only things were not always so much trouble.

CHAPTER TWENTY-THREE

Morgan dressed for dinner with Neva. He had decided to wear something better than his casual work clothing although not too formal. He'd arranged for a quiet table at Xenobia and already paid for one of the better meals. He doubted Neva treated herself very often, if at all. The guilt she harbored affected everything she did, though it rarely came into conflict with her excellent work ethic.

He had also arranged for Tali to be busy somewhere else. This wasn't too difficult, knowing what he did about Tali. He arranged for Reneta Diez to take her in hand for at least an hour, asking questions about her home world and about herself. *Make her think she's important* was his best advice. The ruse might work, and with Neva and him in the back corner of the café, Tali might not find them anyway.

He suspected Neva might even know why they had the secluded corner table and were partly hidden by a screen. She looked a little relieved, in fact, as she sat down and relaxed. She had also dressed for the night and he was probably as amused as she was at the way people watched when the two of them passed. She did look lovely in an old-fashioned blue dress and her hair done up in curls.

They had a wonderful meal. The steamed vegetables were fresh after all. They had small gardens on all of the grow domes and these had come in from the damaged dome where they'd suffered through the attack. The grow dome had not been destroyed, but some of the plants had suffered enough damage that they were picked and shipped into the station for whatever use they could be. Buris also did wonders with synth meats and gravies. He was an excellent cook and they were going to have to exchange recipes.

Morgan almost didn't bring up the subject he'd wanted to breach from the start. He didn't want to ruin what had been a wonderful evening, but he also feared he would not get another chance very soon. They all knew they were heading into trouble.

So, over a real chocolate cake dessert and wine all the way from earth, he finally charged ahead when the discussion had drifted back to work-related material again.

"There is a problem, Neva. There is someone here who is afraid to report things for fear of annoying you."

"We're talking about Rafael," she said, her face going hard as she held the wine glass.

"No. We're talking about me."

"That's ridiculous, Morgan!" Her voice rose and then lowered as she put the glass down, frowning at him. "You can always come to me. You know that!"

"I'd like to think so, Neva . . . but things are odd here. Ritter thinks she's getting closer to finding a link to Xenation, and that could be interesting and dangerous. "

"I trust you can judge what needs to be done and will do your best to keep everything in line, Morgan." She leaned forward, looking very serious. "I wanted you to take this position for a reason. I can trust your judgment. You can always talk to me."

"The Norishi are up to something . . . but you don't need me to tell you so. The question, really, becomes if they're doing something truly bad or if they are just covering themselves because they don't trust us. And then we have to ask how much we trust the Ksa to be saying the truth."

"You don't trust the Ksa?" she asked, looking surprised.

"I *want* to trust them. I'm not certain I can *trust* that feeling. It might be blinding me to other things, you know. It might be blinding all of us."

"True. I've thought so myself. But I think it's important to keep looking at actions. The Ksa have helped from the first day they arrived while the Norishi have created endless problems. And that whole incident with the alien ship keeps me awake at night, Morgan. The craft was *heading here*. I want to know why the Norishi wanted it stopped. I want to know what battle they were fighting before both craft arrived. I've sent off questions, of course, and I hope someone else has seen something, but even if they have, it's going to be a while before word gets back to us. And by then. . . ." She finished with an elegant shrug.

"You feel like something is going to go wrong soon."

"And you don't? Granted, you've only been here for a short while, but you have seen that things are more than a little crazy here right now. "

"True," he agreed. "I've had some interesting conversations with some of the others. Rafael thinks --"

"I don't want to hear what Rafael thinks -- *shit*. You did that on purpose."

He nodded and she had the grace not to start ranting, though she had to clamp her mouth shut over whatever she wanted to say.

"That's the problem, Neva. I'm sorry this trouble exists, but it's there and we need to do something to make things workable. Rafael is in the thick of everything going on here. He does have important observations and we *all* need to listen."

"You trust him."

"I trust him. I don't trust Xenation or the link he has to the station. How can I? We don't know what Xenation is doing or wants, and because the two of them are linked, that means there are times when I will not trust everything he says without having some proof. But that's not the problem we're talking about here, Neva."

"You have a problem with me."

"We all have a problem with you, my friend. We dance around and pretend Rafael doesn't exist when talking with you, which creates an entirely different problem. Even I have mentioned things and let you believe the information came from me or someone on my team when it actually came from

Rafael. We all do it. And that's dangerous because Rafael is working outside the group and what he sees may or may not be right. You won't know if you should trust something because you think it came from us."

Her eyes narrowed, her mouth opened . . . and closed again. Neva was good at her work, and while Rafael was a blind spot for her, he trusted she would see the problem now that he had explained the situation to her. No one else had dared bring up the subject.

"It's been a mistake," she said finally. He'd never heard the tone before; the loss and the regret all rolled up into those few words. "I don't know how this happened, Morgan. I really don't."

"As stupid as this sounds, the truth is that things just happen sometimes. The trouble is dealing with the aftermath."

"I have put so many people in danger because of my relationship with Rafael --" she began, new emotions beginning to rise in her voice. He could hear fear and anger intertwining in each breath. "From start to finish, I have endangered --"

"The only person you have truly endangered is Rafael and that's because he's become a pariah, Neva, and I don't think you did that on purpose."

She had started to stand as rage took hold, but then the emotion disappeared. She dropped into her chair as though she hadn't the strength left to hold herself up. Neva looked at him, blinking several times and he thought something saner started to take over the part of her brain where she had shoved everything dealing with Rafael.

"I don't trust him, Morgan. I don't. He said he would deal with Ashur. And then -- and then --"

"You really don't think he meant anything more than he would speak with Ashur, do you?"

"He knew, though. He knew about the trouble."

"And he tried to prevent the accident from happening. He saved lives. He tried to get the ship to pull back but they didn't. Why haven't you blamed the pilot instead of Rafael?"

She looked at him, saying nothing.

"Ashur was piloting, wasn't he?"

She nodded and swallowed, unable to speak.

"Damn."

Neva picked up the wine glass though she didn't sip. Her hand trembled and the pale wine danced in the light as she stared at it. "Whom should I blame, Morgan?"

"No one. Rafael didn't understand what was happening and Ashur didn't see the trouble at all. No one was to blame, Neva, and you need to accept that truth. And if you can't, I'm going to put in an official request that you be removed from Xenation as commander."

"Why would you do that to me?" she asked. The pain and shock in her face felt like a knife jabbed into him.

"Not *to you* Neva -- *for the* others. Because you've let this blind spot get way out of hand and cause dangerous trouble, and you know it. Rafael is on the outside and we need him in. Hell, he has more contact with the Ksa than he does with us. He's safer with the Ksa."

"No one would hurt him!"

Now *there* was an interesting reaction and not just what she said but also the look of concern that came with those words. She did worry about Rafe somewhere within all that guilt. The words had taken him by surprise. He recovered and met her look. She had returned to the stone stare of a few moments ago, but he knew he had reached past the wall she put up around all things relating to Rafael.

"Others take their cue on how to deal with Rafael from you," he said softly. "You're lucky because Ardi didn't play the game. Ekhardt was another matter and a few people took their sign from him because you didn't treat him as though he did anything wrong."

She said nothing at all this time. The meal, he knew, was over, but at least she hadn't stormed out. She even finished the cake; it would have been a sin to leave it behind in a place where chocolate as so rare. He did not bring up the problem they still had with Tali. That would have been over the top. He needed to get things settled with Rafael and maybe by the time they sorted the first problem out, Tali would already be gone. He couldn't believe she would stick around for long.

Neva stood, finally. He did as well, but she stopped and stared at him. "Would you really have me removed because of Rafael?" she said and sounded hurt.

"No, not for Rafael. However, I would ask for you to be removed if something you did -- anything at all -- put others in danger, and you continued to ignore the problem for personal reasons."

"Yes," she said and nodded. She took a deeper breath. "Yes, you're right."

"I won't mention this again."

She nodded and walked away. He hoped the discussion didn't affect their friendship for long. He found Xenation tough enough without standing on the outside.

Like Rafael.

He hoped -- really hoped -- she did the right thing.

CHAPTER TWENTY-FOUR

Rafael had decided to go back to his room and rest until later in the day when business would pick up again in the market. Ardi was watching Ekhardt and this was likely the best chance to relax before . . . whatever was going to happen finally happened.

He'd had a rare day without people poking him with scanners and looking at him as though he had turned into an alien. If he could avoid Yang and head for his own room, he might. . . .

What he didn't need was to find Tali leaning against the wall to the right of his room. He stopped and shook his head, trying to fight his thoughts past a growing headache and sense of panic. She should not be here.

"Hey, Rafael," she said with the kind of smile that made Rafe think he ought to run if he could move fast enough. "I have a proposal for you."

"I'm not interested."

He backed away. He needed people around. She followed, closing the distance between them and he realized he would not turn his back on her. He could tell Tali meant trouble even before she reached out and grabbed hold of his arm.

"Don't do that." He pulled away but she smiled again, her lips pulled back like some wild thing about to attack. This could not be Ashur and Neva's daughter. It just was not possible.

"Come on, boy." The smile spread and her eyes grew wider, making her face look far more alien than any look a

Ksa had given him. "This is your big chance to see how much alike mother and daughter are."

He yanked free of her and this time reached into the pocket where he'd put his link to Ardi, jabbing it on but not pulling it out. She might not realize what he'd done. "Get away from me, Tali. Just go back to your room and don't bother me again."

"Want to play hard to get, huh, boy?" She came close enough to rub her body against his. "You can have this." She pealed back the front of her shirt, revealing both breasts.

"Don't mess with me, you stupid little child." He let rage start to overcome even his panic. "I am not interested in you. I wouldn't be interested in you if --"

He heard movement close by and turned and felt a swelling of relief to know security had come so quickly --

Saw nothing at first and then a little movement and pain through the side of his head as he fell.

Ardi -- he hoped to hell Ardi --

"You should have gone along with this the easy way, though really, the end would be the same," Tali said. She knelt down in front of Rafe. "Hit him again."

He didn't feel anything at all for a while, and then everything hurt and everyone was so damned loud! He tried to move, but someone had rolled him onto his stomach and secured his hands behind him. Damn, damn -- he wished Ardi would --

He turned his head. Ardi *was* here. So was Tali, Neva and a dozen others. He didn't understand at first, except he had the idea he was in a hellish amount of trouble --

"He grabbed me," Tali cried, a little whimper of a sound that turned his stomach, knowing what the words meant. "He dragged me here. I tried to yell, mommy. I tried to scream, but I was so afraid! He said . . . he said this was payback time. He said awful things!"

"I --" Rafael began, but the single word came out in a slur through his swollen mouth. He couldn't see out of his left eye at all, and he felt as though some wild animal had clawed his face. "I did not --"

"Be quiet." Neva's cool words turned his blood to ice. She moved closer and he could see the tips of her shoes . . . he remembered those shoes. *Comfortable for work*, she had said to him one morning, *though ugly as sin*. "Just don't say a damned thing, Rafael. Ardi, take him down to the cell. I'll be there to deal with this in a minute."

"Neva --" Ardi began, sounding as though he might argue.

"I am in charge of this station. Take him there, now. And get Yang there. I want him to know what I'm saying when I arrive."

"Yes, ma'am. Can you get up, Rafe? Can you move?"

"I didn't --" he said, starting to feel the rush of panic. Locked in a cell? Trapped and trapped, and no way out --

"Don't say anything," Neva ordered. "Nothing, until I get there."

Ardi looked enraged. Rafael didn't have the energy to feel more than numb disbelief. At least they didn't have far to go. He let Ardi take care of him and listened while the man *ordered* Yang down to their makeshift cell, a square room of iron bars and an old-fashioned lock. It wasn't far.

Ardi released his hands. He did not lock the cell closed. Rafael gratefully sat down on the cot and lowered his head into his hands. Damned mess --

"Rafe --"

"Don't ask. I'm not going to say anything before Neva gets here."

"She does not have the right --"

He looked up, squinting through one swollen eye. "I am not going to say anything. There's no reason you need to be in trouble, too. Just wait, Ardi. Just keep quiet and let me have a little peace."

"Yang is on the way."

This wasn't going to go well. He winced when he heard Neva coming into the area and apparently talking to Yang. Neither of them sounded happy.

He didn't know what he would say since nothing would make a bit of difference at this point. He really hadn't thought things could get worse between them, but when she walked in with her face red and her eyes narrowed, he wished . . . almost anything right then. Wished someone had killed him and then wondered if that wasn't the only real answer left. Xenation wouldn't let him do the work himself. Maybe he could push someone else into it. A Norishi might work --

Yang cut between the two of them. The damned scanner came up, moved, and moved again and this time Yang looked worried, which didn't help at all.

"Damn. Someone hit you pretty hard across the back of the head, Rafe. I'm reading a thin skull fracture."

"It wasn't Tali," he said and even looked up at Neva. What did it matter? He could only say the truth, after all. "Someone else was with her."

She frowned. "Morgan is on his way."

Why? That was an odd answer, and he blinked, trying to parse the words. Yang pressed something against his neck and eased some of the more obvious aches. He didn't know what to think -- wait for Morgan? Why?

"Relax just a little, Rafe. If your blood pressure spikes like the last time, I'll have to knock you out and I don't think that's what you want right now."

"I want peace," he said.

Maybe Yang could read more in that line than he had intended because he looked worried. Rafe didn't try to see what Neva thought. He didn't think he could bring his head up again, and he only glanced a little when Morgan and Ritter arrived. Ritter even looked angry, which threw him, and she brought up a scanner -- for a moment Rafe had enough enthusiasm that she wondered why, but he let the thought go with the next breath. It didn't matter.

"Not here," Ritter said. "As far as I can tell, the area is clear and safe to talk. I'm going to head back down the hall and make certain nothing gets close."

Okay, maybe he was interested. Rafe lifted his head, frowning. Whatever Yang had given him was already working on the swelling around his face because he could see more clearly and move his mouth without pain. He started to say something and changed his mind. Let them ask. He would tell them whatever they wanted to know.

"Rafe, are you listening to me?" Morgan asked.

He hadn't been. He looked to Morgan with another frown. Yang sat on the cot beside him and put a hand on his shoulder. Maybe he had been that unsteady.

"I'm listening now," he said. He could pay attention for a little while longer.

"Ritter has been running tests on the various power waves that move through the station. You helped set it up."

He nodded.

"Recently, she's picked up two unusual sources -- or, more likely, the same source in two different places. We suspect someone has a ShadowCage on the station."

"That would explain --" He stopped, glanced at Neva, and then went on. "That would explain why I didn't see anyone before they hit me." He started to put a hand to the back of his head but Yang pulled it away and ran the scanner again.

"Rafe, both times we've had the reading, Tali was in the area," Morgan said.

He didn't dare glance at Neva. He'd let the others work this out. He'd stay here in the cell. At least once everyone left, this would be quiet and once the door was locked he wouldn't have to worry about unwanted visitors waiting for him in quiet halls.

"Neva?" Morgan asked. "What are we going to do?"

"Tali is a problem," Neva said. Her voice remained oddly calm, and Rafe realized this statement came from years of dealing with her daughter. They had seldom spoken of Tali back before everything went bad. When he finally glanced at Neva, she met his stare without the usual hatred, which threw him again. "I knew the moment she showed up on Xenation that there had to be something more to this visit. I fear she wasn't truly released from the hospital and that means trouble back on Terra Nova, too. I am sending back a request for more information, but we'll learn what she wants before I can get any answer."

"We can keep an eye on her," Ardi said. "This station is small. Now that we know --"

He cast a glance at Rafe and then frowned again.

"She has an accomplice," Rafe said softly, both so that he might not draw Neva's ire and because he wanted -- desperately wanted -- quiet. "And they were smart enough to get Tali here and make certain she draws attention. The medtech with her has to be in on it."

"Yeah, but he was with me when you were attacked," Ardi said. "And now that I think about it, he was very persistent about being with me. I'll get people watching him right away."

"But why attack Rafe?" Neva asked. For a moment she almost sounded as though she cared, and he felt his heart give a sudden quick beat. Yang patted his arm; damn the scanner that betrayed emotions he kept from his face.

"It could be two-fold," Ardi said. He looked bothered.

"First, to get to me," Neva offered and gave a quick and almost embarrassed glance to Rafe. "Because this incident would distract me, worry me, anger me: Any and all of these things."

"Right." Ardi looked around at the group as though he measured them all in this business. "But there could be a second reason. What if they were surprised to find Rafael in the job where they expected to find Ekhardt?"

"Oh." Neva leaned against the wall, contemplating that possibility. "That would make some sense, wouldn't it? We know Ekhardt is into things he shouldn't be. We took him out and put in someone who is actually doing the work."

"I need to be back out there," Rafe said. He started to stand but Yang grabbed his arm and held him down. "No, I really need to be out there, Yang. This isn't a time to hold back. We have enough other trouble going on."

"Someone else can do it," Yang replied. "You got hit in the back of the head with something that did damage, Rafe. A metal pole of some sort would be my guess, probably pilfered from the bays and put back again. Someone should run a trace for it. Unless they cleaned it off completely, Rafe's

DNA should show up in a scan. Maybe theirs as well."

Ardi nodded and pulled out his commlink.

"Hold it. Where's my unit?" Rafe asked. He didn't find it in his pocket.

Ardi stopped. "I got your call. I could almost hear voices, but there was a lot of interference, besides the cloth. The inference was probably the ShadowCage. You don't have it now?"

"No."

"If they have it, we don't want to let them know what we're doing."

"I need --" Rafe began.

"You need to go to the medunit where I can do some more damned work before you go out. Give me a few hours, at least. We'll need that long to figure out why we would let you back out at all."

"The Ksa are upset," Neva replied with a lift of an eyebrow.

"Tell them everything is all right. Let one come to see me," Rafe began and fell quiet when she lifted her hand. Damn, they didn't need the Ksa upset over this.

"*The Ksa are upset.* I've already heard so from Etinon. We can use this as a reason to turn you back loose."

"Ah." He almost smiled, but not because of what she said, but because she said the words *to him.*

"Dealing with the Ksa would be something Tali doesn't understand and she can't control," Morgan said with a nod of his own. "Rafe, do you think the Ksa would even play along with this? It might be a way to keep her off guard."

"They might." He felt momentarily dizzy and put a hand to the cot. That might have been from the odd sense of relief, or just as likely, Yang was right and he wasn't ready to go out. "But Tali really isn't the problem."

Neva looked at him, shocked by the words. Then her faced changed and a new worry came in. "She has an ally."

"A *smart* ally who worked hard to get her here." Yang said and caught hold of Rafael's arm and helped him stand. He'd felt better sitting. "I'm taking him up to the medunit and he's going to spend the night there. Maybe longer if this is worse than I think."

"Could someone send Etinon or Saris there to see me?" Rafe asked.

"You need rest!" Yang exclaimed in frustration.

"And I will after I talk to the Ksa. We need to get this set up and going right away. And then I'll rest. Gladly."

Yang gave a reluctant nod of agreement. More than Rafe's future depended on what they did and how well they handled this mess.

"Be careful of the commlinks," Ardi said looking at his with disgust. "I'll get you another one, Rafe, and we'll set up a private band for you, me, Neva and Yang."

"And me," Morgan added. "As long as I'm in this far, keep me in the circle of what is going on. I'll let Ritter know to warn me every time she picks up that power source, too."

"Yes, good idea," Neva agreed. Then she shook her head, looking bleak. "I'm sorry my daughter is causing so much trouble --"

"You are not at fault," Morgan replied. "Sometimes children becomes problems, no matter what the parents do. You knew the problem, Neva, long before you came here."

"Yes," she said with a sigh. "But still --"

"You are working to help us, rather than against us," Yang said while trying to shepherd Rafe towards the door. His legs felt weak. "You could have decided you had to protect her, instead. That never helps, you know."

"I know." She moved aside. "I don't know how this could have happened."

"Sometimes things are just out of everyone's control, Neva," Morgan said.

She looked at Rafe and nodded agreement . . . and perhaps not even about what was happening now. Things out of their control, things they tried to stop. He thought about the scout and how he had tried -- but before he could speak she turned and walked away.

CHAPTER TWENTY-FIVE

Morgan realized his talk with Neva at yesterday's dinner had come at the right time and saved Rafe from considerable trouble. He liked to think Neva would have seen the truth anyway, but she had too much emotion locked up in this mess between Rafe and Tali. Having convinced herself Rafe was guilty of the accident, she might not have looked too hard at this second incident.

However, she had handled everything well and he needed to turn his attention to other problems. And damn, they seemed to have a lot of them suddenly. His mind bounced around between the Norishi, the Click and maybe the Ksa. Tali beyond a doubt. Should they lock her up? He didn't want to be the one to suggest so to Neva, but he would if she so much as twitched in the wrong direction. They knew what she was capable of now. He had feared Rafe was dead when he first arrived.

If they locked her up they lost the bait to draw the others in. They could have grabbed Norden, but there was someone else as well.

This shouldn't have been his problem to worry over. He was Science, not Admin. He decided to go back to his office and work on something interesting for a while. He hoped to immerse himself in some good, solid scientific studies which might help clear his mind of everything else.

The ploy worked until Neva showed up looking harassed and more than a little angry. He waved her towards a chair and shut down the report he'd been reading. She needed his full attention.

"I have a complaint from the Norishi about the Click," she said and surprised him with this new twist. "I don't even know why the hell they brought this to me. No one has any control over the Click."

"And what was their complaint?"

"Click pets have been grabbing things from their supplies."

"Do you think it true?"

She frowned a little. "What if it is? What the hell am I -- ?"

"No, no. That's not what I meant. I'm asking from a scientific point of view because I want to understand the Click."

She sat back in the chair before she continued. "Maybe they are. I asked around the bays and the market and a few pets have been out and spending more time around Norishi areas. The guards even chased them away from the Norishi Enclave, and I don't think the Click have ever tried to go there before."

"So this is new behavior."

"Apparently so."

"And possibly linked to the loss of their ships in the fight with the Norishi ship."

"Oh, I suppose that is possible. Getting payment for the loss, maybe?"

"Probably nothing so simple to define, but that would be my base guess," he said. "We're probably completely wrong, of course, but at least this is a change in behavior we can see. Right after I stepped off the ship to this wonderful paradise I watched Felice give some sort of tool to one of the pets and everyone seemed happy."

"Oh yes," she said with a nod. "That's been something we'd been trying to do for a long time. The pets are fascinated with tools. They tried to pick up discarded, broken ones, but we didn't think that was such a good idea. So we finally got them to take a good one. Sometimes the Click themselves would bring things back out to the market later and trade them. That tool hasn't turned back up yet."

"Do you think it wise to give them human technology?"

"Morgan, chances are they'd walked off with enough to already to build a ship. Things go missing and the pets are the best bet. The wrench was the first controlled gift we'd managed."

"Damn this place is fascinating."

He made her laugh again as she patted his arm. "I know we currently are mired in a damned mess and I don't know how things got so far out of hand. I don't know what good we might be doing here anymore. I want peace, Morgan. I want enough calm that I can look around and see how fascinating this place is again. I don't think that's ever going to happen, not with the history I have here."

"Do you want to go on to another post?" he asked.

She stared at him and blinked several times. The night was late, but they both looked inclined to keep working. "I don't know if I can let go yet. I want . . . I want a closure with Ashur, Morgan. I want an explanation of what and where he is."

In that line, she gave up her belief that Rafe was doing this to torture her. Morgan nodded, thinking about that first time when Ashur had looked into his face. Not dead, he had thought in that moment, but the longer he stayed, the more confused he became on the subject. Were the Displaced nothing more than recreations from Xenation? Were they something more? He realized how hard this must be for Neva to look into that face as well. She had loved him, even if they were no longer as close as they had been when they first married.

Damn mess.

"Do you think there's any chance we'll have an answer about them?" she asked and looked to him as the head of the science department.

"I want to think so. I want other things to calm again so we can focus back on the Displaced. Have they been quieter than usual?"

"They sometimes go for a few weeks without making an appearance. There is no pattern. I don't know if this is good or bad that they haven't shown up lately. "

"I need to work with Rafe, Neva."

She nodded and didn't even flinch this time. "I've been a fool to let the problem between the two of us get so out of hand that it made a problem for everyone else. Thank you for making me face my own stupidity."

He smiled and felt a huge weight of guilt lift. "We better get back to work."

She started to speak but he leaned closer. "ShadowCage. No telling where it might be."

"Ah. True."

He walked out with her and they parted company in the hall. She went towards control and he headed out to the bays, though not for any good reason except he felt the need to walk. The day had been far too tense and he still worried about matters that had nothing much to do with real work.

Was he starting to look at work in too narrow a focus? The entire station should be his project, including humans, Ksa, Click, Norishi and even the Displaced. They all interacted and to tell himself that his work was only to study Xenation was blinding himself to the larger view of this place. He knew it, but sometimes the rest just seemed too much.

As he stepped out into the open bay area, Morgan purposely took note of all the different areas. A pet rushed past heading from the Norishi area and towards the market. He couldn't tell if the creature had anything in hand or not. Felice and some others worked on some parts in the bay with a couple Ksa standing by and pointing out things. Did they work on Ksa equipment? Hadn't he read that sometimes they did? He needed more information.

Ekhardt stood by the work yard with his arms crossed and looking angry. Morgan wondered if that came because no one looked to him for help.

Ardi stood at the entrance to the market and gave a lift of his head in a signal to come on over. Morgan considered ignoring him and then decided otherwise. If Ardi had something to say, he probably needed to hear it.

Ardi looked both ways with a casual glance when he neared and then nodded back to him again. "You talked to Neva, didn't you?"

"Pardon?" he asked, surprised by the question.

"She needed someone who could talk to her. I think it must have been you."

"We talk all the time."

Ardi made a frustrated sound. "You talked about *Rafe*. Look, I'm the head of security and the whole problem with Neva and Rafe has been a major pain in the ass for me. We've had all kinds of trouble we've had to work around because of her reactions. However, she was reasonable today at a time when I expected her to become a raving lunatic. She hasn't been reasonable about Rafe for a long, long time."

"Yes, I talked to her about Rafe and I hope will help in the long run."

"Good. Excellent. I'm waiting for the Ksa. I sent one to get Etinon if he would meet me. I don't like pulling the Ksa into this mess, though. I like human matters to stay in human hands."

"Is anything on Xenation truly only human?" Morgan asked.

Ardi gave a frustrated sigh and looked him fully in the face. "That's the problem with working around so many scientists, you know. You guys cut straight to the truth and don't leave the rest of us with our illusions. I would like to think that some things really do pertain to the humans and not the others, but I'm not blind."

"Sorry. I want to see the wider picture again. That's why I came out here to look around; to reacquaint myself with the whole of Xenation, instead of looking at little pieces in my office. And it is such a fascinating wider picture. I'd really like to sit down and talk to you about everything precisely because you aren't a scientist. I've found that sometimes others have insights the rest of us just look around without noticing."

"Huh. Here comes Etinon. Stick around and help me explain this, will you?"

"I don't know the Ksa nearly as well as you do."

"No one knows them very well except for Rafe."

"And there's the problem again," Morgan said with a sigh.

Ardi said nothing more. He bowed his head when Etinon arrived and Morgan did the same. The Ksa's brows were drawn down and there was such a look of worry in his face that even Morgan couldn't miss the reaction.

"Rafe would like to see you," Ardi said.

Etinon nodded. "We had word that he attacked this young fenale. It is not true."

"No, it isn't," Ardi said softly. Morgan wondered more at the Ksa's unquestioning belief in Rafe, but he didn't try to pursue his questions right now. "But the young woman has an accomplice with equipment which can hide him. We wish to flush him out."

"Flush hin out?"

"Make him think we believe the story so he does something that brings him to light," Morgan offered.

Etinon considered the words. Here, Morgan thought, was where they were going to have a problem. The Ksa were known for their strict honor and this was likely going to touch on areas that humans could not fully understand.

"Rafe asked to speak with you," Morgan said softly.

Etinon gave a nod. Had the Ksa picked up the nod from the humans?

They escorted him into the Human Enclave. Morgan noted how Felice watched and she didn't look happy. Should they take her in on the story? Probably a good idea since she had a link to Ekhardt and a place on the bay where she could watch people better than some of the rest of them. He'd talk to Ardi and Rafe about her later.

Odd how many furtive looks they drew as the three headed down the halls. They did not go to the cell though, at least. He thought that might not have gotten as good a reaction as the medunit. He didn't think taking the Ksa down to the cell and seeing Rafe treated like a criminal would have helped.

"I have to go," Ardi said at the door to the medunit. I don't dare stay out of the market for too long today."

So Morgan escorted Etinon into the set of rooms. Rafe looked like hell. Bruises covered half his face and he appeared both pale and shaking. Morgan heard the Ksa's breath catch a little at the sight. Odd, odd: What drew the Ksa to this man?

Rafe looked up and then bowed his head in greeting. Yang hovered nearby and looked worried enough that Morgan prepared to tell the Ksa he would have to leave and they would handle this later.

"Etinon, thank you for coming," Rafe said softly. "I have a request, if this will not create a problem."

"If such can ve done with honor, I shall see to the natter."

Honor, honor . . . Morgan wanted to start taking notes.

"I have a problem, but we think I am only the tip of the iceberg . . . ah, just the part that shows while the rest remains hidden," he said. "You have heard --"

"Yes, about you and the fenale. This is not true."

Even Rafe appeared surprised by the power of those words. Morgan would want to talk to Rafe -- hell, he really wanted to talk to Etinon, but had more of a fear he would breach that honor system than he'd had before now.

"I want to know who hit me from behind," Rafe said. He put a hand to the back of his head -- or started to. Yang caught the fingers and pulled them away, which annoyed Rafe. "It's not that bad --"

"You have a new, but much smaller, plate, Rafe," Yang said softly. "And this was serious, but Xenation stepped in again and saved you."

"Damn! Well, at least I can hide this one under my hair."

"This is not a mark of disgrace," Etinon said and sounded shocked for the first time. He unexpectedly sat in the chair by the bed so he was face-to-face with Rafael. "This neans the station has found good in you."

"Chances are you never would have regained consciousness if Xenation hadn't stepped in," Yang added.

And a look at the medtech from Rafe . . . a moment when he clearly wondered if that wouldn't have been better. No one said anything.

Etinon reached out and touched a long, oddly shaped finger against the edge of the plate on Rafe's face. Rafe had started to pull back but he stopped himself and held still, his eyes wary. "This is not a sign of dishonor."

Did Etinon know more about what the plate symbolized? Morgan thought Rafe might ask, but maybe he wasn't ready for any answers and a long discussion. Or maybe he just had too much on his mind right now. He shook his head, winced at the movement, and then looked back at Etinon.

"This that we ask your help with is a human problem, you understand. We do not know what Tali and her ally really want, and so we are trying to work a way which will not alert them that we do not trust them," he explained.

"And so they will look you away? This is acceptable?"

"Actually no. What we would like is to say the Ksa protested my being locked up and for that reason I have been set free again. In this way, we do not say we don't believe them, and they cannot question the reason."

Etinon looked at him for a long moment. "This is not just a hunan trouvle, you know," he said. "It is the station. We are here, all of us. Such provlens as affect the hunans, affect us all."

"In some ways, yes. But this might simply be a family matter between the chief magistrate and her daughter."

"You do not think so."

"Someone is working with the daughter and brought her here. That makes this less likely to be simply related to the family. Most people will not take chances for such petty reasons."

Etinon tilted his head to the side. "You wish that we say we wanted your release. The chief nagistrate will agree with this?"

"Yes."

"She knows we do not denand such a thing. That, even

though we velieve you inca'able of such a crine, we would
not interfere in hunan dealings."

"Yes."

"This is a strategic nove to draw the foe out," he said.
"We understand the need of such actions. We will agree and
say we only trust you in the narket. We will also be watchful
of you, Rafael. We know you do this to draw the foe to you.
They did this attack to stop you. They nay try again."

"Yes."

"And that is the reason you go out there, to draw this
danger to yourself. To stop they fron doing worse."

"Yes."

"You are honoravle. We will aid you, because it is with
honor that you do this."

"Thank you," Rafe said. "I will remain here for the night
and then go back at my work tomorrow. If anything happens
that you find troubling, please let us know. It may be that
they'll take this time with me away to do what they are
planning. Ardi is going to try and keep watch, but I think
there must be a reason they wanted me out of the way."

"You have contact with everyone," Etinon said. He
stood and brushed a hand over his tunic. "Shall we go to the
Chief Nagistrate now that I can nake this denand for all to
see?"

"That would be most helpful," Morgan agreed and
realized he would bc thc person to escort the Ksa.

"Take care, Rafael," Etinon said with a bow of his head.
"Take care. There is trouble here."

"Will you tell me the importance of things I do not
understand?" Rafe asked.

Etinon looked back at him with an odd expression.
Morgan had the idea they were maybe talking about
something specific, too. The plate?

"The alien craft," Etinon said after a moment. "The craft
the Norishi attacked cane fron such a far distance we have
only ever seen such three tines in our history and they have
never stayed for contact. That they were coning *here* unsettled
us."

"Why did you not say so before?" Rafael asked, surprised by the admission.

"It was not ny place to say it then," he admitted and still frowned. "And there was a Norishi among us. I did not wish to let her know we recognized such a ship."

"There were no Norishi --" Morgan began. Then he fell silent as a chill went through him.

"Damn," Rafael mumbled. Equipment spiked and alarms went off but he waved Yang back and calmed again. "Norishi among the humans."

"At least one. We think no others," Etinon said and looked worried now. "It is not that you knew this? That you acce'ted her in?"

"No, we have not," Yang replied. His own voice had gone very hard. How had one gotten past him?

"We thought this an agreement vetween the Norishi and hunans." Etinon looked relieved to find it wasn't true. "And not a thing we should ask if such a secret existed and you did not want to say."

"How did you know she was there?" Rafael asked.

"I could scent her suddenly; very worried when the craft cane and when the Norishi attacked."

"I am going to have to do some quiet scans," Yang said. He looked at Etinon and bowed his head. "Thank you. This is news I suspect will save us considerable trouble later."

Etinon nodded and looked relieved as well. "Shall we go and nake this show for your Chief Nagistrate?"

"Yes," Morgan agreed, anxious to get to Neva and maybe slip her word about the spy.

Too much going on.

Morgan was glad he went with Etinon to see Neva. Etinon put on quite a show which he had not expected. However, given how Etinon felt about Rafe, maybe this wasn't much of an act at all. Neva played her part as well and only reluctantly agreed to put Rafe back into the market again. Plainly, no one in the office disbelieved the act.

However Morgan was there for more than the show. A slight movement of Etinon's hand indicated a woman standing over by communications. Morgan had not, for some reason, expected to find the Norishi spy so close to Neva.

He needed to get word to Neva immediately. She, no doubt, trusted her people. She might even say something about the ruse so they didn't worry.

"Neva, would you come with us," Morgan straight out said. "I want to speak to you about how we can handle this matter."

She frowned, then turned her position over to her second and went with them out the door. Morgan already had his commlink up. "Ritter, I need you for a moment to speak about your project. Meet me at Xenobia and we'll have lunch."

"Yes sir."

They spoke about releasing Rafael and what might be done to keep others safe *from* him. The Ksa grew increasingly angry at the words and by the time they reached the opening by Xenobia, he left with hardly even a nod.

"Gods, tell me that was an act," she whispered.

Morgan patted her arm. Ritter arrived and showed she had a working scanner in hand, mostly hidden. "I brought the project. The scans are reading clear around here."

"Good. Come on. Neva, we have an entirely different problem."

"A new one? Another one? Hell." She followed the two into the little café and they took seats in a back corner. They even ordered lunch while Neva fidgeted and looked upset. Everyone would think this had been about the Ksa and Rafe which suited him very well right now.

"When we first saw that attack on the alien ship, Etinon didn't identify it. He did so today. He says the ship was from so far away they have only seen a couple in all their history, and never had direct contact."

"Why didn't he say so then?" she asked, still toying with her fork.

"Because there was a Norishi in the group, and he didn't want to give away anything."

"There wasn't a Norishi. I looked at the entire group --"

She stopped. "Hell. No."

"He identified one just a few minutes ago. She was standing by the communications equipment while we did our little act. Brown hair cut short, tall --"

Ritter looked shocked. She sat silently staring at the two. This had gotten a little more complex than any of them had expected.

"Hell. That can't be true --" But even as she said it, Morgan could see her thoughts running ahead. "Carlee Tanner. She arrived late and was a replacement for someone who decided not to come out. Her files were a bit odd but nothing that really rang bells. Damn, Morgan. She works comp and comm. Not the top person, but there often enough to know much of what we're doing."

"She's a problem we can deal with," Morgan said.

"I need to be rid of her. Or no." Neva bit at her lower lip, contemplating something else. "We need to feed her what we want the Norishi to know."

"Are there such things?" Ritter asked.

"I think there might be, given some of what's going on," she said. She pushed her hand through her hair. "Carlee Tanner has been at her position for over a year. I'm going to make a study of what we've done and what she might have had her hands in. I want to know if she's been here for something specific or just to grab everything she can from us. I'm betting the later. And I want to know about the woman who was supposed to be here. If anything has happened to her --"

This was more than Morgan wanted to deal with right now. "You know, with everything else, I think she's somewhat secondary in the list of troubles. Unless the Norishi act up, she can't be more than a cypher. We can feed her what we want. And I'm starting to think the first thing is to make her think we're at odds with the Ksa."

"No allies." Neva turned to him, worried. "Is that safe? Do we really trust the Ksa?"

"If it turns out you have a Norishi spy, yes -- we trust them. How did she get in past Yang?" he asked, worried for a while new reason.

"He wasn't here when she arrived. There had been an . . . an accident out in one of the domes. Several injuries and one death. I'm liking the Norishi less and less."

"I'm going to talk to Yang. Neva, take a look at the records of any other women in your group. Just because Etinon came across one doesn't mean there aren't others."

She nodded, grim faced.

"I can make you a scanner that looks like a commlink," Ritter began. She'd obviously been thinking while they were talking. Then she shook his head. "No, that might not work if you grabbed the wrong one. I can take a commlink and add a little more to it, though not noticeable. One extra little light which would flash red if a Norishi is nearby, and yellow for a ShadowCage. Just those two. Anything more would take too much space and be noticeable."

"I'll give you access to a few extra commlinks," Neva said. "Fix them. We'll need to pass them out to me, Ardi, Morgan, you and Rafael."

"I'll get back to my station and start working up the specs. This won't take too long," Ritter said.

"I'll have Ardi come by with the equipment," Neva said. "We need to do this quietly, of course. Thank you, Ritter."

She nodded and hurried off, a woman already thinking about the work ahead.

"I want to believe this is all little things that we happened upon at once, but something tells me everything is related," Neva said, leaning closer to him. "Not the part with Tali -- I think whatever she's into, it is outside the rest of this. She just complicates things. I'm sending her back on the ship, Morgan."

"That's probably wise," he agreed. "I'm sorry, Neva."

"Thank you." She bowed her head and finally took a few bites of food. "I don't know where we failed. I really don't. We tried everything when she was a child. I wish Ashur was here. I wish I could talk to him about *our* daughter and feel like I was doing the right thing."

"Do you think Ashur would know what to do with her?"

Neva gave an unexpected little laugh. "No," she said. "No, he was just as lost as I was in all of this. Probably more so."

"You are doing fine, Neva. Don't shake your head. You are doing fine under very trying circumstances. I've known you for a long time. I've known Tali since she was born. You did everything right. Sometimes, unfortunately, that isn't enough."

"We shouldn't have left her behind."

"You could not have brought her here without people to care for her. You knew it. She shouldn't be here now. She's the problem, Neva and not you, not the way you raised her, and not anything you have done. She has been a problem for a long time. You can't fix it. And I am sorry."

"Like I can't fix the problem with Ashur," she said, looking up again. "Both of them beyond my reach . . . and here they are, anyway. I'll need to tell Tali that she's leaving. She won't take it well."

"Do you want me with you?"

She looked at him and smiled. "I don't think so --"

"Neva, she's working with someone else. Someone who tried to kill Rafael. I'll go with you when you talk to her. Or better yet, bring her to dinner. We can make this a social occasion."

"And I can use the unreasoning reaction of the Ksa as an excuse to get her out of here," she said. She looked a little relieved. "Good. Tomorrow, Morgan. Lunch, I think. The *Shaw* is leaving the next day if everything is clear of debris finally. I want her on it."

This sounded like a good plan and a hope to get one piece of trouble away before everything else turned bad. They were, he feared, running out of time.

CHAPTER TWENTY-SIX

Tali sat in her dull, grey room, legs pulled up and chin resting on knees as she tried *not* to see the walls around her. The faint hint of changing colors made her angry. She didn't want things to change unless she said so. She hated not having control.

She waited for Norden who would come for his usual nightly talk, to keep up appearances. He had a device that would play conversations they'd had on the ship which anyone would hear while the two of them talked about real matters. She liked it. She could say anything.

He looked pleased when he finally arrived and she waved him to come in, trying to look worried and afraid about everything that had happened. They could watch all they wanted and she and Norden need only be certain they sat close together, making it harder for people to see their faces.

He wasn't sure the others had a camera in the room. She thought that naive. Of course they watched her.

"You did well, but we have a problem still," he said and frowned. "The aliens are demanding the release of Rafael."

"The damn aliens? Which ones? They don't have a right --"

"The Ksa, of course. The news has spread all over the station and many of the humans are unhappy. Damn, that man must have a head made of stone. Wood doesn't mess around when he hits."

"I wanted him out of the way. I wanted my *mother* busy dealing with him! Now the damn aliens --"

"We're fine, Tali. Don't glare at me. This means we get a second try at him, and if we do this right, we'll create even more trouble. By the time we're done, people are going to blame him for everything that goes wrong."

She felt a little mollified.

"We are coming down to the line. The ship will leave soon. And either we're going to be on it with our cargo or we leave and abandon the plan . . . or we stick it out here longer. I don't like that last idea."

"No. We'll do it now." She felt better knowing the real plan was about to start. "Let's go walk in the market. We need to look things over and make our decisions."

He stood, ready to get to work. Two hundred thousand credits for each of the little pets they brought out. This was going to be easy money. They had it set up with crew on the *Shaw*. All they had to do was get the crates to the loading area and their person there would do the rest.

Some people would pay anything for things they were told they couldn't have.

The two went out to the market. She could sense the edge of trouble here, like a little electric buzz that brushed against her. People looked at her, frowning. Why didn't they believe her story? How could they doubt her? Stupid people.

The Ksa avoided her completely which made her even angrier. She felt the emotion start to well up and she wanted to go kick the hell out of them. They were ruining her plan. What the hell did they want out of this? What did they care about Rafael?

And then something *odd* happened. A group of dark-haired, tall women -- no, they were Norishi -- walked up to her and bowed their heads, so unexpectedly polite she found herself returning the movement, though it half annoyed her.

"Tali, daughter of Neva, welcome to the station. If you require help, come to us. We shall stand by you in times of need."

And then they walked away.

"Well hell," Norden said and looked shocked this time. "We'll have to see how we can use this."

She smiled agreement. Maybe things weren't as bad as she thought. She had powerful allies just like Rafael.

CHAPTER TWENTY-SEVEN

By the time Rafael came back out of the Human Enclave he had an overwhelming sense of impending danger and not as something he'd picked up specifically from the station. He'd heard word about Tali and her new friends the Norishi and about how they walked with her every time she came out. The idea of this new development had frightened him until he caught sight of Tali and the way she kept trying to get away from her Norishi guards. He found himself standing in the shadow of the entrance to the Human Enclave and grinning despite himself.

"Rafe," Felice said quickly crossing to him. "You shouldn't be out here. You really shouldn't."

She took hold of his arm and physically pulled him back away from the entrance. He looked at her, shocked by the behavior.

"Felice --"

"The Norishi are causing trouble, Rafe," she said softly. "They walk around with Tali and they act like the rule the place. We don't what the hell is going on, but we're staying as clear of them as we can. They're even pushing the Ksa and that's going to blow up. You wouldn't be safe if the Norishi decided to turn on you for Tali's sake. I don't know what the hell is happening and why they suddenly think they have control --"

"Oh hell," Rafe said. He even found himself grinning again, which shocked Felice. "I think I might understand. It's cultural: They have the *daughter* of the most important woman as their new ally. They think she gives them the power. And the fact the rest of you are backing away from them has only confirmed that belief."

Felice stared at him, considering the situation before she laughed. "You might be right. Even so, it's still not safe, Rafael. The Ksa are acting odd, the Norishi are pushing, and even the Click seem to have gone a little strange."

"Something is going on." He looked towards the market where only a few people wandered today. "But that's why I have to go out there, Felice."

"Rafe --"

"We need this settled and done well."

She seemed to take more of his meaning from those words. "You shouldn't go alone."

"I can't have a keeper and still deal with the Ksa, which is my prime concern today. You take care. Watch things. There is far too much going on and Tali is up to something that probably isn't even related to the rest of the trouble."

"Just making things worse," Felice said with a quick nod. "I should go with you."

"No."

She finally let go of his arm. "You are an idiot."

"I know."

She snorted and headed back to her work. Rafael stepped outside of the opening and to the right. Ekhardt missed seeing him as he came out of the Human Enclave and spotted Felice. Ekhardt began shouting curses before he got to the bay area where she had already gone back to work. However, a group of Norishi settled the problem. They came across from their own area and stopped by the bay to glare at him. Ekhardt backed off quickly.

So that was some good, at least. Rafe waited until the Norishi had gone wall past and into their area of the market before he headed in the same general direction. He saw Ekhardt slinking away, hurrying to join a couple crewmen from the ship as they went into Xenobia.

Brody looked up when he walked up to her stall and she leaned forward, catching hold of his shoulder.

"What the hell are you doing?" she demanded.

"Just walking around, Brody. Doing my job."

"Looking for more trouble."

"No, I'm not looking for trouble." He leaned forward, glancing down at the shells. "I don't have to *look* for trouble."

"You are right there, my friend."

"You have sold a few. Good."

"Mostly to the Ksa," she said. "They're fascinated. I'm seeing about getting some books cleared on sea life for them."

"I'd like to read a copy, too," he said and hoped he didn't sound too wistful. She frowned and he brushed his hand across the plate, reminding himself as much as her. "I miss the ocean, Brody. I grew up on Earth and I spent a lot of time on beaches collecting shells like these. I miss a lot of things. I manage anyway. You know, I finally make enough creds in this job that I can probably buy one or two of these in a few weeks."

"If you survive that long," she said.

"True."

"If I gave you one now, would you take it and go away for a few days?" she asked, surprising him with the offer. "Just sit in your room until this insanity blows over?"

"I can't, Brody. There are things I have to do."

She sighed and then gave a decisive nod. "Then I'm going to tell you something that is either going to help or get you killed. Someone who came in on the ship has been asking questions about shipments *out* of Xenation. He says he wants to set up a business, but he's no business man."

"We've had those before," he said.

"Oh yes. Come in and make their fortune trading for alien goods. And he's asking some of the same questions, but he never talks about bringing something in for trade, only taking it out. He's not even interested in what the Ksa or Norishi might like. He does ask questions about the Click, though."

"Damn." The observation did bring a new wave of worry. They moved carefully around the Click, mostly because they didn't know enough about them. Someone

interested in them in an odd way made him worry all the
more.

"And here's the next bit," she said. "I've seen the guy
talking to that psych tech who came in with Neva's daughter.
More than once, in fact. And he talks to Ekhardt all the time.
I even saw him and Tali together."

They could have met on the ship, though the addition of
Ekhardt to the mix made Rafe strongly suspected real
trouble. Stupid trouble. And Tali involved moved the worry
up another notch.

"Damn, damn. What's the guy look like?"

"You can't miss him. Thin, sharp face, a thin mustache
that looks like is drawn on, and shaggy dirty, blond hair."

"I have seen him," he said. He tried to remember where
and thought it was probably at Xenobia.

"Don't make me regret this one, Rafe."

He gave an unexpected smile which seemed to worry
her. "You know this is going to be dangerous for me no
matter what I do. But I now have a chance to avoid trouble if
it comes right at me."

She gave a nod of agreement, but he could still see
worry and regret in her eyes. He looked back at the colorful
shells for a moment, thinking which one he might want . . .
and moved away to go do his work.

The interest in the Click worried him far more than
anything else, especially after the Click had attacked the
Norishi ship. And back in the corner of his mind, the vid he
had seen of a Norishi ship attacking and destroying a human
ship seemed to be on a constant replay. What as he missing
there?

The Click were out today. He saw them bounding
through the market, a few pets in amongst them. He couldn't
decide if he liked seeing them out in force or not. He had
been working on his *danger* clap for a while, but he didn't
know if they would understand if he used it and this wasn't
something he could practice on them.

He walked slowly through the area, talking to just about
everyone. The Ksa had come out, too, and he found he had

an escort, even though he didn't want one. He wondered if he should feel like Tali and the Norishi.

He spotted the man Brody had described. Their eyes met for a moment before the man turned and walked in a different direction. Rafe marked the path he took, but did not rush in to follow.

It wasn't until he saw Ekhardt sliding along the shadows where he shouldn't have been that Rafe started to get worried, thinking something might be going on after all.

"Your pardon," he said, turning to the Ksa woman who had been hanging at his left side for the last hour. "I must go somewhere. Thank you for your company."

He bowed his head politely and turned away, catching a glimpse of her worried face. He wasn't certain she would hold back or not -- but he wouldn't be able to get very close to anyone if he had Ksa following him.

He wanted this trouble settled and to get some calm back to the station as soon as possible. The trouble with Tali and her allies might be something they could handle quickly and easily before this got worse.

And he had that gut-wrenching, all-to-human feeling this was going to get far worse. So he went after Ekhardt in hopes of clearing up one problem.

It was probably not wise.

CHAPTER TWENTY-EIGHT

S omewhere between the time Morgan went to bed -- early, because he was so exhausted -- and four hours later when Ritter woke him, all hell had broken loose.

"You need to get to command," Ritter said for the doorway after he'd come from the back room, barely having pulled his pants on. She looked nervously out into the hall. "We've got trouble."

"What *now*?" Morgan demanded while looking for the clean shirt he'd dropped on one of the chairs. Or was it the table?

"Five dead Click, two dead Ksa, and probably a few Norishi. We can't get a number on those. Four dead humans and no one can find Rafael at all."

"What the hell happened?" He stood there with the shirt in hand, unsure what to do. A chill washed over him.

"Some kind of battle happened near the Ksa section of the market. Brody -- do you know Brody?"

"No."

"She works tech part time, but she also has a place in the market. She sells seashells --" Ritter stopped and they both grinned, a moment of trite humor in an otherwise heart-pounding moment. "Anyway, she talked to Rafe earlier. He was out looking for trouble and maybe he found it."

"And dragged everyone else in with him?"

"Maybe so. Or maybe this was just trouble about to happen anyway," Ritter said. "Neva contacted me to see if I'd had any odd readings. Nothing. She asked that I quietly get you."

"This isn't going to stay quiet for long."

"No, it isn't." Ritter leaned against the doorjamb, arms folded across her chest and *trying* to look relaxed. "If there is a war starting up between the Ksa and the Norishi, we're going to be caught in the middle with nowhere to go. The *Shaw* might take us in, but we'd have to abandon the equipment."

"I'm as worried about the Click. They're the complete unknown here. Damn. Not the kind of mess we need."

He had gotten fully dressed, but didn't remember doing so. They quickly moved out into the hall, which was nearly empty. He glanced at his watch and found it almost midway through the night, local time. The night hours were the busiest for the market area since there was nothing else to do here.

They reached the command room and found Neva there with only two techs on duty and both male. Even so, Ritter ran a quick scan and nodded indicating they were safe, at least from Norishi spies and ShadowCages.

"What have you got?" Morgan asked as he pulled a chair over by her desk. Both the techs glanced their way, worried.

"I've got some vid sequences," she said. Her voice sounded steady, but her hand trembled as she keyed up the comp. "Thank God we put in the other cameras," she said softly. "Otherwise, we wouldn't have any clue at all."

He leaned forward and watched. She had lined the vids up from several cameras and ran them through for him. It wasn't a long sequence, the first part showing a few dozen people wandering through the booths. Ksa were there but no Norishi.

Then a rush of people headed out of the market. He could not, unfortunately, see why they ran. Even a switch to another camera only showed the sudden movement which spread in various directions. Soon the Ksa moved out into the darkness at the far edge, grabbed up at least one of their own, and rushed back to their Enclave. Norishi rushed past the humans and into the market, and they moved in a way that told him they were trained soldiers, acting in sync with each other and hands on their weapons. They seemed to have found trouble a little later as the Ksa fought to protect one of their own wounded.

Then the area almost completely cleared, except for Click, who still appeared agitated. He could see bodies, and couldn't tell if they were Ksa, Norishi or Human. He thought he saw dead Click as well.

"Damn."

"I've talked to some of the people," Neva said. "They ran because others ran. Someone said there was a fight between Norishi and Ksa, though that had to have happened afterwards, unless there were Norishi we didn't see. Which is possible, and may be why their own came at a run."

"Son of a bitch. I wish we knew what happened."

"I'm asking. People say the Click started acting oddly. Then the Ksa moved in and apparently tried to grab some humans --"

"And the Norishi found out and rushed in to save us? Why do I find this really doubtful?" He was still watching the screen and saw Click along the edges of the booths. A Norishi went down under a couple of them. She struggled to get away and then did not move at all.

The vid ended.

"What the hell . . ." He stopped and took several deep breaths, feeling his own hands start to tremble and his heartbeat pounding far too hard. "What are we going to do?"

"I've ordered all the humans into the Enclave," she said. "We have guards at the opening which is small enough that we can defend the spot. The Ksa and the Norishi have both backed off to their own areas, but the Click are still out there and extremely agitated. And we can't find Rafe. Brody says he was in the market not long before this mess started and she never saw him leave. She admitted to telling him about trouble she suspected that involved Ekhardt and possibly my daughter."

"And they're here?" He stood, intending to get answers from someone.

"My daughter took refuge on the *Shaw*. We haven't

found Ekhardt yet."

He looked at the vid which had switched to the live view, and cycled between cameras in different areas of the market, the opening to the Human Enclave, the bay, and then towards the Norishi Enclave. Click moved through most of the scenes. He saw movement at the dark opening of the Norishi Enclave, but couldn't make out what was happening.

"We need to shut down the view to all but the cam by the entrance," she said softly, keying things off quickly before he could protest. "Our Norishi spy will be here soon. We don't want her to know even this much."

He agreed. Besides, he could go somewhere else and pull this up on his pocketcomp if he wanted to see more. They needed a plan. They needed to find some way to make certain they were safe here --

He felt a sudden chill as the light in the room dulled and equipment went off line. Neva cursed.

"Displaced," she said. "Of course they are going to turn up now."

"Where?" he asked looking around.

"Must have been passing by," she said, nervously checking the monitors again. The pictures flickered, though he thought he could see movement just outside the Human Enclave. "They usually don't get this close to our main equipment or stay long enough to be a problem. We were lucky."

Equipment came back up with a slight buzz and the flash of a dozen lights and monitors. Some more crew arrived, called in for the emergency. They'd heard about the trouble already. Word would pass quickly in such a small community.

"We're sticking close to home today," Neva announced. She sounded remarkably assured and calm. Damn good at her work, Morgan realized again. The people in the room visibly calmed in her presence. "As soon as we get the power built up, I'm going to punch a message out to the relays and see if we can get a cruiser this way, just to be safe. I suspect, however, that everything will be settled before anything can get here."

She didn't say how the matter would be settled, of course. Morgan had a feeling of doom coming at them. He wanted answers and he stood, ready to go out and find them.

"We need to see where the Displaced have gone," Neva said. "And see if we can find Rafe to get them in hand."

Her eyes flickered a little at those words: Worry that they'd already lost Rafe, and their only chance to control the Displaced, let alone the link he represented to the others. Hell. This just kept looking worse. He gave her one pat on the shoulder and then headed out, not certain what he could do in a mess like this.

"I'm going to look things over," she said and stood. Going with him. Good -- or at least better than her going off alone.

Ardi stood at the entrance to the Human Enclave, staring out at what appeared to be an empty bay. He glanced back at the two as they neared. "Figured you'd both be here soon. This just doesn't look good, Neva. The Norishi are massing at their entrance. I don't know what they intend, but it can't be good. They lost three people, I think. And they didn't take it well."

"What the hell happened? Do you have any idea?"

"No. I watched the vids and *still* missed whatever set it off. Tali took refuge in the ship, by the way. I told them not to let her back out until we give word. None of them are to come out, but I made a big deal about her being the Station Master's daughter and a special case."

"Good," Neva said. "That gets her out of our hair for a while. Is there a chance Rafe is in there, too?"

"No. Or if he is, they're not saying so, which wouldn't make any sense. There's a lot of Displaced activity out in the market. God knows what drew them out to add into the trouble."

"Ksa? Click?"

"No Ksa. A few Click, but they finally left the area as well. What do we do now?"

"Go out and talk to the Ksa," Neva said. Ardi nodded agreement.

"Not the Norishi?" Morgan said, glancing their way. He could see the movement.

"No. I don't trust they'd tell us anything true anyway," she said. Then she shook her head. "We'll end up talking to all of them, eventually, but the Ksa first, because they might have seen what happened. And it looks like the Displaced are gathering near their Enclave. Damn, damn -- we don't have anyone else we can rely on. We need to find out if we have any allies at all."

CHAPTER TWENTY-NINE

Tali and Norden had grabbed two of the pets, shoved them into boxes and hid them, and then paid someone to move them into the proper container and on to the ship. The woman from the ship came back and gave them the sign -- they did not stand too near -- and they went back into the market, snares in hand, hoping to find a couple more. This was easy money.

Things tuned bad almost immediately. Tali didn't even see what happened. Suddenly, though, a line of Click headed through the market, knocking over things, pushing down humans and aliens --

"Get to the ship," Norden said and looked around with frantic worry. "Get to the ship."

"The ship?" she said watching as the other humans ran for the Enclave.

"The ship has our cargo. If we have to pull out, at least we'll have those two. Go!"

She hated to be ordered but she didn't snap back. The Click were acting mad or upset. It couldn't be because they'd grabbed a couple of the damned pets. Hell, she'd have paid them for the creatures if the Click had been smart enough to even know what money was. Stupid animals.

They reached the airlock. The crewman let them inside the first door, but no farther until he had checked with the Captain. A couple of the bay workers had come in too, so at least it didn't look strange for them to have sought the ship during the trouble. She looked out to see Wood start towards them, but change his mind when the Click rushed forward and the Norishi, with blades in hand, leapt into the fray. At least they looked like they were going to get something done.

Captain Stern came to the airlock with security. Tali frowned, worried and annoyed that they didn't just let her in.

"We're going to do a quick scan, just to make certain there is nothing you inadvertently picked up and brought with you. This won't take long."

Tali wanted to protest, but that was probably stupid. It would look like she had something to hide. Instead, she stood still and looked with worry out the door when more Norishi rushed past.

"Oh, I hope this isn't real trouble," she said softly, looking at the Captain. "I hope my mother is safe."

"Your mother? Oh -- you're Neva's daughter, right?" Stern said. Tali didn't like how the woman implied she was an equals with her mother. She gave a quick nod. "Don't worry. We'll keep you safe here."

They'd keep her locked up. They'd try to run her life --

Norden touched her arm. She held back the curse. Not now. Not here.

"How long do you think this will go on?" Norden asked, looking out the door. They hadn't closed the airlock yet, though they kept people on guard. Since they were inside the ship, they could even have real weapons. That was something she had forgotten and the sight of the laser pistol in the guard's hand made her feel better again.

"I don't know," Stern said. "I've never seen or heard of behavior like this before at Xenation. Neva sent out a request for the nearest IWC ship to come help, but I doubt there is any close enough to give us aid if we really need it."

She hadn't thought about not having help. At least she had Norishi friends and they would protect her. She didn't trust the Ksa, though. And the Click -- why would anyone fear them? Just kill the stupid beasts. She wasn't even sure why they bothered to let them on the station.

Stupid people. Tali wondered how long it would take them to get this mess cleaned up.

CHAPTER THIRTY

Rafe had followed Ekhardt straight into trouble. It had probably been a stupid thing to do, but he wanted things to calm so he had willingly taken the chance.

Ekhardt met with the rat-faced guy, Wood. They were in the darker shadows far back from the market. Damn, he didn't want to go so far from possible help, but he also wanted to know what Ekhardt was up to. He couldn't quite hear the voices, though.

Too many things were not right. Ekhardt and his companions might be the only easy thing to fix if they could just get a link to what was going on.

Yang had told Rafe that his eyesight was changing and he could see far better in the dark and shadows than other humans. He decided to put that theory to the test. He moved into the shadows along the edge of the market, keeping to the darkest areas as he headed towards the wall. Spots of light showed in the wall where bacteria moved but the shades were the darker purples and blues and he knew those wouldn't show him unless he stayed against one spot for too long. He kept moving, sliding carefully forward and making as little sound as possible.

"I was in on the deal," Ekhardt said quite clearly, his voice louder than it should have been, even back here. He shifted from foot-to-foot. "I was in on this from the start --"

"But you haven't done a damned thing. Don't try to pull this shit with me. We set up our person in the market, we bought our man on the ship and we've done all the work. "

"Yeah, but you still have me, don't you? I want my full

share, or I'm going to the others --"

Rafe thought Ekhardt was about as stupid a person as he had ever known, at least until Ekhardt pulled the knife from his pocket and showed he was ready to deal with his double-crossing companion. Even rat-faced Wood looked startled.

"I want my share and I want it now."

"I don't have --"

"Then let's go find someone who does," Ekhardt replied, the snarl in his voice growing. "I'm on my way off this damned station. I am not leaving broke. We had a deal, and we're going to go through with it."

Wood nodded and he didn't look happy. He also had a hand in his pocket, which meant a surprise of his own. Rafe stood with his back pressed against the wall, wondering if he should step in or not. He reached in his own pocket, though not for a weapon. He could call Ardi as soon as the two got far enough away that he didn't draw attention --

And then all hell broke loose.

Click.

Click rushed through the market in a mass that knocked over stands, pulled apart cloth and wood . . . and he feared might have done the same with people, though he couldn't clearly see what happened. He heard screams that could have been pain or fear. People began to run including human and Norishi. He saw several Ksa take a stand and try to hold back the Click. They needed help.

Rafe headed in that direction, not caring that Wood and Ekhardt saw him.

"Son of a bitch. I've had enough of him," Ekhardt shouted. Rafe turned and found Ekhardt, his face blazing with anger, heading his way with knife in hand. Wood smiled and Rafe saw him pull something from his pocket.

"Look out!" Rafe shouted, an automatic reaction.

Ekhardt didn't pay attention. He raced on and even took two steps after Rat-face Wood put a knife through his back. His face went white, his eyes wide, and then he fell.

"Well, this is convenient." Wood had drawn the knife

back out though he gave a nervous look to the sounds and battle not far away. "Two problems solved at once."

Rafe knew he didn't have time to even try for his commlink. He took advantage of Wood's moment of distraction at the sound of yelling. His quick move probably saved his life, though Wood still spun and made a quick and dangerous swipe with the knife. The blade cut Rafe from shoulder to mid chest, deep enough that he stumbled back with a gasp and went to his knees.

And the Click arrived. He thought they were both going to die. They swarmed through and grabbed Wood, dragging him off. However, Click only went around him. He saw too many eyes, mouths with sharp teeth, and several limbs that seemed to extend out of the body at will. He tried to crawl away, but they were around him on all sides.

Ksa arrived. He saw them shoving and kicking at the Click, though the closer they got to Rafe, the less trouble they had.

Saris dropped to his knees beside Rafe. "This is not good."

"What the hell is going on?" Rafe asked, gasping as the pain of the cut worked its way through his panic.

"We do not know." He looked at the wound and grimaced. "The Click are killing sone others. We have never seen they do so vefore."

"Can we get to cover?" he asked, keeping an eye on the nearest group of Click who were starting to turn and regroup. He thought he saw a human hand in the midst of them.

Saris gave some quick orders he couldn't follow. The others looked to Rafe and he thought he saw distrust for a brief moment. Saris spoke again and the group bowed almost as one. Four came forward, grabbed Rafe up and carried him away, while the others fell in around them, protecting the group.

He saw dead and he suspected Wood would be counted among them. He had hoped for answers there, but instead they'd only fallen into more trouble.

He thought the Ksa would take him to the Human Enclave. Instead, they turned to the right and raced straight for their own area. He thought to protest and then thought again. More Click were heading into the market and he wanted the hell out of the way and to somewhere they could protect. Taking him to the humans would only put the Ksa in more danger.

They couldn't move fast enough, though it wasn't the Click who came for them this time. The Norishi had arrived and they screamed as they attacked. The Ksa fought them off, forming a line as the others worked to get him inside.

He had never seen such looks of rage in the Norishi and it seemed they turned those looks on him and not the Ksa who protected him. Rafe shivered and didn't do anything to slow the others as they rushed to the doorway ahead.

He felt lightheaded by the time they reached the safety. He had never been beyond the opening and it took him by surprise to find the area within darker. They didn't slow until they brought him to a room filled with pillows and tables. There they laid him down to rest. Etinon arrived at a run, gave a quick and almost half-hearted bow, and knelt by the pillows. He already had bandages in hand.

"This is trouvle, ny friend," he said. He did fast work with the wound and then provided another shirt, which looked human-made and fit well. "This is such that we have never seen vefore with the Click. And the Norishi . . . who knows what has set they off?"

"I am grateful you took the time to rescue me." He bowed his head, trying to get his wits back.

"Rest," Saris said and Etinon gave a nod of agreement. "We watch over the station. Rest while you can."

He didn't argue. What energy he'd had seemed to have fled. He was not going to sleep, not with the memory of the insane Click and the murderous Norishi still so fresh in his mind, but he could close his eyes and try to regain calm --

And everything dimmed. He thought, for a moment, that he might be about to pass out. Then he felt the chill.

"Hell. Displaced."

Etinon gave a quick, worried nod and looked back at the doorway where more of his people appeared. There was much bowing and whispered words along with hand signals that he'd never seen before. The people left. Others came. Etinon dealt with those as well.

A little later someone arrived with a long, thin box and sat it beside Etinon. The woman spoke quickly with several bows. She left again, Etinon saying nothing this time, though he gave the box a troubled glance.

Rafael dared say nothing at all.

Etinon finally looked back at him and Rafe could tell from the narrowing of his eyes that there was something wrong.

"If I am a problem, get me out of here. You do not need to create trouble over me."

Etinon blinked several times and then bowed his head -- a show that might have been apology, acceptance, or something else.

"You, friend, are not a trouvle. Not nuch of one in this larger ness."

"What are we going to do?" he asked.

"The others say everyone has gone to their own 'laces again, exce't some Click. They search, we think. Why were you there, so far fron others?"

"I saw Ekhardt meeting with someone I had been told was a problem," he said. He touched the bandages on his chest. "They were right."

"What vusiness would they have?"

"Black market," he said, shifting a little.

"I have heard this said. What is it?"

"Trading in goods that would not be allowed by law. Sometimes these would be dangerous things and sometimes only things they do not want to pay taxes on."

"Tolls."

"Yes, something like that." He was not in any shape to explain the antiquated monetary system that had followed humans into space and that they clung to even in places where money meant nothing at all. "This can be a very lucrative business, working outside the laws -- but if you are caught, it can mean years in prison."

"For selling things others want vut are not allowed."

He nodded, wondering if this sounded stupid. No matter. This was the kind of thing the Ksa probably needed to know if they kept working with humans. People were bound to do something illegal. But he still couldn't figure out what they might have been doing --

"Hell. Interest in the Click."

"Yes?" Etinon asked. He sat cross-legged by Rafe and looked hopeful. "We try to understand what the hunans are doing, vut you are odd sonetines."

Rafael laughed a hand to his wounded chest. Etinon looked uncertain.

"It's all right. We find ourselves odd, too. Humans are too diverse in thought. We can't always understand what others are doing or why."

"Ah. Ah." This was apparently something the Ksa had not realized. "We look for unity in what you do. We look for 'attern."

"You will find patterns in some places. In the purpose of our work, for instance, especially here where we have gathered mostly scientists. But we are individuals when not at work and we often have our own agendas. Most of the time those activities are harmless things that please us. Sometimes, though, people move into areas that will harm others. They may even take such activities as a replacement for legitimate work."

"Ah." He looked as though he tried to figure out how to encompass this new view of humanity. "This does hel' to ex'lain sone of what we see in hunans."

"I imagine so. But the Click --" He stopped and shook his head, because he thought this might not be something he wanted even the Ksa to consider about humans.

"These others have traded with the Click? It is not easy -_"

"No. I think they took a Click to sell."

There. He had said the words and watched as Etinon

looked at him, eyes blinking though he didn't see surprise or even shock. That worried him about what the Ksa might be doing as well, but he hoped he kept that thought to himself.

"It is hard enough to deal with the Click," Etinon said with a shake of his head. "If the hunans have done sonething --"

"Not the *humans*. Don't think of this in terms of an entire group. I, obviously, do not like it if this is what happened. And this is only a guess on my part."

He nodded but Rafe thought maybe this wasn't the time to lecture him on group-think and humans.

"It is calner now, vut the feel is not good."

Rafe nodded.

"If this is such that they did, we can get the Click vack?" Etinon asked.

"I think so. They can't have taken him any farther than the ship."

"Where the daughter ran when trouvle started."

"Yes, she is probably involved as well," he agreed. He started to fumble for his commlink and then shook his head. "I can't do this over the open lines. They may have one of our commlinks. We don't want to frighten these people into getting rid of the Click rather than being caught with them."

"Getting -- kill?" Etinon said.

"Yes."

"Then careful. Yes. I would not wish such an evil on a Click. And I would not wish the consequences on us."

A few hours before, Rafe wouldn't have thought much about what the Click would do. Now he remembered being on his knees as they swarmed past, and seeing far more of the furry little creature than they'd all come to accept.

The lights dimmed again.

"Yes, yes. And the Displaced. I need to get out there, Etinon," he said. He ran his fingers through his hair and looked at his companion again. "Is there anything you know that might help? I would appreciate any advice."

"Listen to Xenation," he said, which surprised Rafael. "You are the link. We think the station knows nuch."

Rafe didn't think he could trust the station. He found it odd that the Ksa did and he thought to ask questions . . . but no time. He saw one of the Displaced hovering in the hall outside the room and he didn't want to invite it in.

Etinon looked startled. "They do not cone here vefore."

"It's me. I am trouble."

"Not trouvle," Etinon insisted again. He glanced at the door. "You only have interesting con'anions."

That made Rafe laugh again. "Let me see if I can at least remove the Displaced from the current trouble." Rafe stood, determined not to look weak. Then he bowed his head, trying not to wince at the pain from a headache and the cut. "I am grateful for the aid that you have given me."

"You live in honor," Etinon replied, which he had never heard before. The Ksa stood as well and looked at the box that had been placed in the room earlier. He finally reached down and opened the top.

The Ksa drew out a long sword -- only not a sword, because both ends had long blades which were wickedly sharp all along the edges. From tip to tip, it was at least four foot long, with a grooved wood-like handle in the middle. Etinon held the weapon in his hand, twisting it a little right and left as though to get the feel. He seemed pleased and drew a harness from the box, slipping it over his left arm and neck. The blades folded inward, like a Swiss knife, and slid easily into an embroidered pocket.

Etinon looked back at him. "Your own kind do not shield you. I am now your guard."

Those were not the words he expected to hear and the shock left him momentarily speechless. "I don't think --"

"No, you do not, at least at tines when you should carefully consider choices. I know hunans are given to argue at all tines. You cannot argue with I. This is decided."

"But --"

Etinon turned fully to him, left hand resting on the weapon. He stood there, saying nothing, while Rafe, with a growing sense of panic, knew he could not argue the Ksa out of his new found position.

"You don't want to do this. I know you don't," he said.

"This is decided. Is it a dishonor to have a Ksa as a guard?"

"No!" he said, and then regretted the quick answer. He might have been able to talk the Ksa out of this madness if he had been thinking.

Etinon had him right there. He didn't think things through too often these days, living so much on the edge of panic. He had no choice now. The room grew noticeably cooler and the single Displaced hovering back and forth at the door appeared agitated.

"Let's go."

"If I say you should do sonething, you will do it. This is a rule when one has a guard. You do not know the way in which such things are done, so this is the only rule I will ex'ect you to ovey without question. If you do not, it will likely get us voth killed."

He wanted to argue. He didn't have time. They would have to discuss this later.

"I will obey to the best of my ability," he answered.

Etinon bowed his head in agreement. "Let us go vefore natters get worse."

As far as Rafe could tell, 'natters' couldn't get any worse. However, he headed out of the room with Etinon falling in at his back and keeping pace with him. Rafe tried very hard not to think about how he could explain this latest situation with the Ksa to Neva.

CHAPTER THIRTY-ONE

M organ kept watch on his pocket comp, holding the device mostly out of sight and making a quick change to a graph of the fluctuating temps if anyone came near. The vid scenes had not been good. Even the Norishi had retreated from the Click.

The Displaced grew agitated. They swarmed in circles, high up at the ceiling and as they swept downward, the lights went out one after another and the bay grew dark and cold. Two of the vidcams had gone out as well, and he only hoped that meant they were too low on power and not that they'd been destroyed. He wanted those views back. He wanted to know everything he could about what was going on out there. They needed answers.

Ardi came back from the market, moving at a quick pace, but not a run. That, he hoped, meant at least a little good. He arrived, slightly breathless but gave a quick nod, as though to reassure everyone. Morgan glanced back as Neva hurried to his side. He had heard her sending the others away from the opening for their safety and now only the three of them remained.

Morgan didn't feel very safe at all.

"The Click have drawn back, but they're formed a line outside their Enclave. The Displaced aren't focusing on anything in particular this time. And I didn't see Rafe. No other dead that I could find, either. I'd guess he's under cover somewhere."

They both nodded.

"What now?" Morgan asked. "This is way out of my

league."

"We could stay holed up until a ship comes in," Neva said. "We have all our supplies here, and the ship can leave, I think. God knows what Xenation is going to do."

Morgan hadn't even considered the Xenation problem. For all he knew, no other ship could even dock and they were truly trapped. He felt a sudden, odd chill at the thought, realizing for the first time how they were at the mercy of this station and they didn't have a clue what it could, or would, do.

He looked at the walls. He hadn't been looking at the walls lately. He'd been caught up in everything else for too long. The designs changed as he stared. Did they mean something?

"I want to get back to the work I came here for," he said with a sigh.

"You and me both," Neva agreed. She looked out the opening and then frowned. "Some movement down at the Ksa area. Ah. There's Rafe."

She sounded pleased, which showed another big improvement in her attitude. Though she did look a little worried when he finally cleared the market and came on, a Ksa staying at his back the whole way.

"That's not normal," she said with a nod to Morgan. "Something must be wrong."

"No surprise there," Morgan said. He was glad to see that they were making good time, though. "At least things look as though they've calmed down."

Morgan stepped aside, making room for the two as they neared. A group of Displaced had started to swarm nearby, and Rafael looked over his shoulder, shaking his head. He kept coming and in a moment the two had entered the little area.

The Ksa was wearing what looked like a weapon. Etinon, he realized. The man looked far too serious which didn't make things any better. Except damn it was good to see Rafe had survived.

"What's going on?" Neva asked -- actually asked it of

Rafe, which seemed to take him by surprise.

"I an a guard for Rafael," Etinon said before Rafe spoke. "You have no nore say in this than he. If this is a 'rovlem, we will stay in the Ksa Enclave."

Neva's eyes went wide, and a little bit of a smile started to play on her lips. She held it back and looked at Rafe.

"I don't know what's going on, though I have a theory," he admitted. A group of Displaced started to move closer to them. He looked back at them. "But I had better get this part in hand or else we're going to be a month trying to build power back up. I hate the cold."

"They aren't acting like they normally do," Ardi said with a shake of his head. He put a hand on Rafe's shoulder and got a twitch from Etinon. Morgan thought that looked like all kinds of trouble, but Ardi only glanced his way and nodded. Maybe the move had been a test between them.

"Nothing is acting like it should," Rafe said. He put a hand on his chest. Morgan hadn't even noticed the bandages and the bit of blood that showed near his neck. What fight had he been in? Did he have answers to what had happened out there?

"Did you get attacked by the Click?" Morgan asked, somehow shocked that they would do such a thing to Rafe.

"No. This was someone from the ship. I think he's dead. I have an idea of what's going on," he said, glanced at the Displaced and then back again. "I think someone may have grabbed a Click or two, Neva. I think the kidnapped Click may already be on the ship. You need to find out and see if we can get this cleared up."

"Grabbed a Click? Son of a bitch," she said, and plainly didn't doubt the possibility. She stared across at the ship. "Tali headed there instead of coming here."

Rafe said nothing more. Instead, he turned and started away and then stopped again when Etinon followed.

"No," Rafe said. Etinon started to say something. "No, not out with the Displaced. I have a hard enough time with them. They're unstable and they're dangerous and there is *nothing* you could do to protect me from them. You could, however, cause me more trouble if they decided to go for you. Stay here."

Rafael turned and walked away. Etinon took one step to follow him and then stopped. He whispered several things in his own language, which might have been curses or prayers or both. Morgan was doing the same, though silently. The mass of Displaced grew dense and agitated and Morgan wondered if even Rafael could get them in hand today.

Everything was out of sync. He wondered if the Displaced were a problem now because they sensed the trouble. Knew the trouble? How much did they see? How much did they really interact with reality?

Or were they a manifestation of the station? Did Xenation send them out because the station sensed things wrong? Sent out these ghostly shapes of people the humans would understand to some degree?

He was starting to think he hated having come to Xenation, though not because it wasn't fascinating. He feared he would never have any answers. Xenation would drive him crazy before he left this place.

If any of them ever left again.

Rafael moved to the area that was roughly halfway between the Human Enclave and the ship's airlock. The Displaced swept in towards him, so thick that they looked almost solid in spots.

"They aren't going for a power source like they normally would," Ardi said. "I don't know what that means."

"Nothing good," Etinon said.

The others agreed. Morgan felt more akin to the Ksa again and he glanced towards the Norishi Enclave, wondering if one of them were here, if they might find a common cause after all. But the Norishi stayed in their own place and he couldn't say he was sorry.

Neva moved up closer to the opening. She glanced to the left and put a hand on Morgan's arm, her fingers tightening. "The Click are moving."

"Hell!" Ardi began to talk into his commlink. Morgan found himself torn between watching Rafe and watching the

Click. At the rate the Click were moving, it wouldn't be long before they were both in the same place.

Etinon started to step forward and stopped. He muttered something and pulled his own, thin little commlink from his pocket and began to talk in a quick set of words that sounded more than a little panicked. When he put the unit back away he glanced at Ardi with the sort of stare that made Morgan think the two held similar jobs and shared like worries.

"The Ksa are waiting," Etinon said. "We do not wish to antagonize the Click into action so we hold away. Night they only cone to find if Rafe can control the Dis'laced?"

"Yes," Ardi said. A few of his people had gathered in the shadows behind them. He scowled out into the open area. "Let's hope the Norishi hold back as well."

Etinon glanced in that direction and shook his head. "The Norishi are trouvle. They are trouvle in ways that worry us all."

"Will you tell us in what ways?" Neva asked.

He looked at her, eyes narrowed. Then he purposely looked out at Rafael and back at her. "I will consider such a thing."

She glanced at Rafe and Morgan saw a little consternation in her face. Her actions towards him had come back to haunt her and Morgan suspected she was beginning to see the wide range her problem had created. She gave Etinon a very polite nod.

"I hope we can work things out," she said. And then she looked at Rafe as well.

CHAPTER THIRTY-TWO

Rafe stood in the midst of the Displaced as they swept around him, sometimes even touching him which they had never done before. He didn't know why the change and the brush of feathery fingers left him feeling chilled, though not only because they drained warmth. Something had changed and he didn't know what it might be.

He stood still and tried to get the feel of them. Ashur was there and looked worried. He wanted to believe that meant Ashur really was still connected to the world somehow. He wanted to believe he could still bring Ashur and the others back and make everything right again.

That was a secret wish he held, though not founded on anything reasonable except that he could still see them, and they interacted with him sometimes. Rafe suspected that he only needed better control and a better connection to Xenation.

And with that thought, he started to try to reach her, to wake her up and have her come and get --

Then he saw the Click were moving again, which stopped him from doing anything while he tried to figure out what they wanted. He did not want to find himself under attack, but he didn't want to scare them, either.

No way to really communicate. He had a better connection to the Displaced which was a frightening thought. Rafe watched the Click but they had stopped just outside the market and waited.

The lights went dimmer. He had to get moving and deal with what he could. If the Click took offense at this, there wasn't much he could do to stop them.

He closed his eyes, trying to ignore the cold feel of unreal fingers against his skin. "Xenation, are you awake? I need your help here."

Base, key. Unlock. Auto function.

Wait.

He shook his head. Where the hell had that come from? "I need help with the Displaced."

Storage data. Auto function. Unlock.

What the hell? Something in his subconscious was trying to draw his attention. This could not be Xenation since the station was an alien construction. They did not communicate in words.

Except that Xenation did understand him.

Computer codes. He was hearing something that made him think the machine was assimilating data from them.

This wasn't the time to start trying to figure that possibility out and get involved in some new insanity.

"We need some control. We need them away. Or tell me what they want!"

That was something he had never asked before. His head filled with such a sudden influx of data that the pure weight of the information stunned him. He didn't know what anything meant but he had the feeling Xenation was giving him an answer. Hell. He wanted to know --

The area went almost entirely dark. He thought the Displaced were starting to go crazy, too. They swarmed around in frantic haste, sweeping up to the few remaining, but very dull lights and some even heading towards the Human Enclave.

Power.

Power sources. They always went for power sources. They'd known that for a long time. But now . . . with some odd new data in his head, he thought it might be a power conversion of some sort. He needed to look at vids -- old ones and new ones.

He didn't know what brought them out just now, but Ashur hovered there a moment, gave an odd nod and then darted off as though to herd back some figures who were heading toward the Norishi Enclave.

"Xenation we need help!"

The help came slowly and a vortex caught the Displaced and pulled them off and up while Rafael went to his knees, exhausted, his head pounding, and wondering what the hell was going to go wrong next.

The lights were coming back on, though. One here, another there. Xenation had added warmth to the wind, which helped as well. He wanted to rest now --

Etinon crossed to him. He gave the Ksa a weary nod and started to stand but then noted that the Click were moving as well. That brought Etinon over faster, but the Click just leapt and a half dozen landed around Rafe.

"Don't do anything," Rafe said, speaking softly and as steady as he could manage.

"You will drive ne insane," Etinon said, but he kept very still.

Rafe looked into the mass of fur surrounding him. Calm fur this time, though it didn't remove the nightmare of what he'd seen when they came at him and Wood. There was, however, a slight rumble to their sounds and perhaps a little trembling.

One moved forward with more of a little leap than a walk. It clicked several times and very quickly so he couldn't follow the pattern. He lifted his hands and the little guy backed up in haste, as though he expected to be hit.

Etinon made a little growl of a sound. The Click around him started to get antsy and that worried Rafe -- but the same one moved forward again. Rafe dared to clap his hands this time with a slow beat he hoped conveyed a hint of calm.

The ones near him settled. Those by Etinon were still excited though, and he feared they would get out of hand. He didn't want to be here on his knees if that happened, so he started to stand --

His Click got upset. He dropped down to his knees. They calmed.

"Kneel beside me, Etinon," he said softly.

"I cannot kneel and 'rotect --"

"Kneel. It will help them to calm. I don't think they like having us stand over them."

Etinon said something somewhat loud and doubtlessly rude.

"I didn't catch that," Rafe said with a quick grin at the Ksa.

"Just as well," he said and he knelt with a slow, gentle movement from standing to the ground; the movement fascinated Rafe in its own right. The legs did not appear to be quite the same as human ones, and that made him want to know more about the Ksa --

The Click before him made several soft noises. He turned back and did his best to focus. Too much. Too many inputs too quickly together. He needed rest.

"So we kneel," Etinon said. "And what does this gain us?"

"I don't know yet," Rafe said. "I just know that they're calmer if we kneel."

The Click had all settled now that the two of them had knelt. Etinon gave a quick nod, showing he understood. Then his eyes swept over the crowd of Click before he looked back at Rafe.

"I think the entire Click is here."

"All of them?" he asked, startled again. He looked over the group, but couldn't begin to count them. He only saw a wave of fur and little round bodies. He hadn't thought anyone knew how many Click were on the station. He should have thought to ask the Ksa. "If none of them are missing, then I have to be wrong about my guess. So now I don't know what they want."

"No one does," Etinon said and Rafe thought he heard a little bit of frustration there that matched his own. "Vut you have estavlished sone link to they."

"It's not a help."

"Everything hel's," Etinon replied. "We had not seen the kneeling. Their level. It hel's."

A Click came closer again and began to click rapidly.

Anxious. Upset. He could tell that much, but what the hell had set them off? What brought all of them out here --?

Not all.

"Where are the pets?" he asked aloud.

Etinon lifted his head and looked around, turning in almost all directions. "Not one," he said. "This, I think, neans sonething."

Rafe agreed. He turned his attention to the Click and called up a pattern he'd heard them use to bring the pets into line. He'd used the pattern himself to get the attention of a pet on occasion. So he used it now with a quick pattern of claps.

The Click reacted. Several of them jumped up and down, and the feel of agitation grew again, and then died down once more. Several, however, had moved off to the side.

Towards the ship.

"They've veen focused on the craft," Etinon said just as Rafe began thinking it. "It is where they have taken a 'et?"

"Maybe. We need to find out. I'm going to slowly stand. If they get too rowdy, I'll kneel again. But I think they know I've figured this out so we might have better luck this time."

Etinon nodded. "Go slowly. I will follow. Vack to the Hunan Enclave?"

"Yes. I need to get the ship searched, but I don't dare ask for this over open lines."

Rafe slowly stood, feeling a little weak and hoping he didn't fall. Yang wasn't going to be happy when he saw the wound.

The Click shifted slightly. When he moved towards the Human Enclave, they became agitated again. He tried a step towards the ship, and they calmed.

"Etinon, I need you to get the others and meet me at the ship's airlock," he said. Etinon was slowly standing and looking like he was going to protest, but he didn't. He gave a quick bow, stepped back several times, and then turned and hurried across the open area. Rafe thought he could hear his friend cursing again as he moved.

Rafael slowly inched his way closer to the ship, though the Click looked inclined to move faster. He didn't want to get there ahead of the others though. He hoped someone was talking to the people in the ship. He didn't know if the Click would want to go inside or not, but he certainly wasn't going to be the one to make the decision.

Neva and Ardi arrived just a little behind Etinon. The Click made way for them and he thought they must understand much of what was going on.

"Etinon explained," Ardi said. Neva nodded; polite still, he realized. This was a change in their relationship, and he wasn't certain how or when it had happened. The change threw him when he needed his thoughts focused. "Neva talked to the Captain. She's on her way."

"Good. We don't want the Click lose in there," he said. "I don't know what they'd do. But maybe we can find out what we need and pray that no one actually killed a pet, if that's what's going on."

"Oh hell," Neva whispered. She must not have considered that possibility until now. "I should have thought of this. We had someone through here about a year ago trying to catch pets until we stopped him and shipped him off. I never considered someone might get more serious about the work."

"You have been distracted," Ardi said. He inched a little closer to the airlock door. It was starting to buzz and would open in a moment. The Click began to get agitated. Rafe moved to stand closer to the door, and blocked the way when it started open. One Click tried to go up the wall and get past him, but he gently pushed the creature back to the ground. Then he slapped his hands in a quick, sharp pattern that at least got their attention. Neva, he saw, looked impressed that he could have that much control. Rafe just thought it odd they cooperated at all.

"You think we have a Click pet aboard," Captain Stern said. She gave an emphatic shake of her head. "I haven't taken in anything though --"

"Not true," Ardi replied. "I think you just weren't

informed."

"That isn't likely --" the woman replied but Ardi held up a hand. He brought out his pocketcomp and did a quick search. Rafe glanced over to see vid of a container going into the airlock.

"That was about an hour before all hell broke loose."

"Damn," she said softly and her face blanched. "I need to call ship security. We need to get down to the bay and sort through the packages. Are they going to come aboard?"

She gestured towards the Click and clearly looked worried about the possibility.

"I'll try to keep them out. Or, at worst, maybe only take one or two," Rafe said. He wasn't certain how he was going to hold them back, but he had begun to think that the Click were far more reasoning than they suspected, at least in terms of how humans defined such things.

Etinon stood close by, looking passive, but with his hand on the weapon. He saw the way Ardi kept glancing his way and wondered what the head of human security thought about the Ksa guard. Rafe suspected he would find out.

Stern had been talking on the ship comm system. She kept her voice calm and steady, but Rafe could see the rage in her eyes. This incident would cost her rights to port here if Xenation decided to distrust the ship. The station had stopped other craft from stopping here.

He couldn't decide how the station would react. He had no feel for her now, which made him oddly nervous. He even found himself touching the edge of the plate on his face, as though to reassure himself it was still there . . . and that had to be insane. He really didn't want to be tied to the station.

But if he wasn't, what would they know? What would the station do? Some nights, lying awake, he wanted nothing more than to go *home*. But then there were times like this, where he felt he might be doing some good, and he couldn't regret his part in helping.

He had odd connections. The Click listened to him. The Ksa put a guard on him and even the humans were paying attention this time.

Captain Stern turned back to them. Her face had gone pale, but Rafe hoped that only meant she was worried, and not that she had learned anything worse.

"Down to the bay," she said, waving them in. The Click, thankfully, did not try to follow, and Stern got the door closed behind them. Even Rafe gave a sigh of relief.

The woman said nothing as they headed down. He did see frantic movement in one of the halls, and suspected they were trying to track down the woman who had taken in the cargo. Once they reached the bay, though, Rafe felt a real welling of hopelessness. Crates sat everywhere, secured to the walls, floor and ceiling by grav plates.

"Oh damn," Ardi said, looking around. "How the hell are we going to find anything here?"

"I'm getting the cargo master," Captain Stern said. "We have to hope that she's not involved in the incident. She's been with me for years, though, and I've never had any trouble with her."

Neva and Ardi agreed while Rafe tried to look around, guessing at the crates.

"If they have pets in here, we have to believe that they wanted them alive, right?" Rafe asked. "And that they would want to be able to get to them quickly."

A short woman in uniform arrived; obviously the cargo master. She looked grim, but she gave Rafe a quick nod. "Good points. So, someplace accessible. Not the ceiling or high up the walls," she said. She looked up and down and around, her hand beating against her hip. "Still a lot of places. And I think Barker must have gotten the stuff in pretty much by herself. She's not been seen with other crew, though she did. . . ."

She stopped and glanced at Neva.

"She met with my daughter. We suspect she might be involved," Neva said, her own voice calm, though Rafe could hear a little hint of worry and disgust in the words. "And the man traveling with her, Norden, has to be involved as well."

"At least one other," Rafe dared to say. "And he was

involved with Ekhardt. But I think he's dead."

"Let's look at that vid again, Ardi," Neva said. "Maybe we can see the crate and get an idea of what we're looking for."

Ardi brought the vid up. The Cargo Master watched and gave a quick nod. "Yes, that helps. There are not a lot of Max 3 crates here. Okay. Start looking along the edges --"

"What makes a Max 3 different from the rest?" Neva asked.

"Oh. Dark blue line with a red dot at the end," she said, pointing to one nearby. She crossed to it, drew out a scanner, and did a quick check. "No, not that one. It still has my palm print on it. Just point them to me and I'll do the scans."

That sounded like a good idea. Rafe moved to the side of the cargo bay, trying to peek behind other crates to find things that were not too far out of the way. He wondered if they should drag Tali in here -- but it occurred to him that she probably wouldn't know where they put the crate. She'd just cause more trouble. Norden?

He was starting to get worried. They weren't finding anything --

"Here, Rafe!" Ardi shouted.

He turned around, startled to find Etinon at his back. He was not going to get used to that any time soon.

"You are too quiet," he said.

"It is a skill."

"I imagine so," Rafe said, but started him thinking along the lines of what Etinon would normally do with such a skill. He didn't know nearly enough about the Ksa.

The bay felt cold. He hadn't noticed until now and fought not to shiver as he crossed to where the others were dragging a crate out. Maybe the chill came because he feared what they would find and what the Click would do.

"Son of a bitch," Captain Stern said. She looked angry. "Sealed against us. That's illegal, that the Captain and Cargo Master can't inspect a crate. Not a surprise, I suppose, but I think that says what we need to know."

"Get Tali down here," Neva said. She straightened her

shoulders and the look of worry about her daughter disappeared. "Get her down here now. And Norden. I want them both."

Rafe didn't want to be part of this. On the other hand, he didn't want to leave the ship and face the Click, either. He started to step back, and realized he had Etinon at his shoulder. Whatever happened, he was not going to face this alone. He stopped his movement and waited with the others.

Neva started to pace and only stopped at the sight of her daughter dragged into the bay by two burly security officers. Rafe had expected Neva to make some protest.

"Stop fighting them," she said, her voice so harsh that it stilled Tali, the girl's eyes going wide. She did 'poor little girl' act very well when she wanted to, but Rafe remembered her in that hall, setting him up to be killed. He didn't trust her.

Neither did Neva.

"We can't find the other man," the guard said. "He came aboard, but now we can't find him anywhere on the ship."

"He has a ShadowCage," Ardi said. "Damn. Should have thought of that. No matter. We'll track him down."

"What -- what's going on?" Tali asked, her voice trembling. She looked frightened. "Mom? Oh! What is he doing here? Get him away! Get him away!"

She tried to pull as far from Rafe as she could which would have put her closer to the exit if she'd gotten lose.

"Oh, turn off the act," Neva said, and with such anger that the words shocked everyone. "None of us have fallen for it, you know. You were involved in an incident that has caused trouble with the Click --"

"I have never --"

"Shut up."

She looked so shocked Rafe wondered if her mother had ever said those words to her before. Well, probably not in a long, long time. Maybe no one else had used them either. It did do the job for however long the shock might last.

"You were involved. We know it. We knew it, in fact, when you and your companion attacked Rafe. So you can stop the act now. Things are way beyond that kind of childishness."

"Yes, it is," Tali agreed, her face gone hard and her voice little more than a growl of rage. "But whatever you want, you will not get it from me."

The change was so complete that Rafe wasn't the only one who looked at her, a little dismayed. Even her face changed and the way she stood. She looked like someone else entirely, and if it hadn't been for Yang's DNA scan when she came aboard, he would have thought she had been an imposter.

"We need this crate open. I suspect you can do it."

"Maybe I can," she said, glancing at it. "But I won't."

"It's a simple palm scan," the cargo master said. "It won't take much to get it."

The two men from the ship pulled her forward. She fought, and fought dirty but they held on, though obviously this was going to be a difficult job.

"With your 'ernision?" Etinon said to Rafe.

"If you can help, please do," he said with a quick bow of his head.

Etinon bowed in return. He moved around the crate and grabbed Tali with a hand clinching the back of her neck which must have hurt because she yelped and then tried to kick him. He squeezed and she gave a cry of pain this time, but she stopped fighting him and the others.

"Your hand on the scanner," he said.

"No."

He reached with his other hand and yanked her arm out. She still fought, but the security men grabbed hold and in a moment they had the palm pressed securely against the scanner.

The crate began to open. Etinon let go of the girl and she pulled back, snarling.

"There, it's opening. So what? They're just some damned animals."

Rafe looked down into the crate. The pets weren't moving. "Hell. If they're dead. . . ." he whispered and felt the chill take him again.

"They're just damn animals. You can't care more about them than you do about me."

Rafe looked at her. "I couldn't care about you if you were the last human alive in the universe."

He reached down and holding his breath and gently touched the soft fur of the first pet. It trembled.

"Not dead. Damn good thing. But they're scared, I think."

"What should we do?" Neva asked. "Bring in some of the Click? Or try to carry them out?"

"Let me try something," Rafe said, surprised to see that Etinon was already at his back once more.

Neva nodded. Rafe lifted his hands, intending to clap -- but then he stopped. Too loud. He wanted something softer. He leaned closer down into the crate. He could see they had some feeding and water tubes attached the walls, so maybe they would have survived. Maybe not. He didn't care at this point.

He clicked softly and slowly. At first, he got no response, so he tried a slightly different pattern. One pet moved and then the other. He heard Neva make a sound of pleasure, but they were not ready to come out yet. He kept clicking for a while, and then gently reached a hand in. Etinon made a sound of displeasure, but Rafe moved slowly, ready to leap back if anything happened that he didn't trust.

He recognized one of the pets. Daredevil was often friendlier than the rest. That would explain how he could be caught and probably the other two -- no three -- with him, since they sometimes moved in groups. He hoped this didn't affect the little guy too much.

He dared to pat Daredevil. He'd done it before, and the little guy responded this time. He even started to leap up a little and in a moment perched on the edge of the crate. He made soft clicking sounds and finally let Rafe pick him up.

It took longer to get the others out, and they would not allow anyone but Rafe to hold them. That proved awkward, but they perched on his shoulders and two in his arms. He could feel little feet digging into his shirt and skin. Well, what were a few more scratches at this point?

The guards still held Tali a few feet away. "Get her out of here," he said. He could feel the pets getting agitated.

"You can't order --"

"Get her out," Neva said with a wave of her hand. "We'll be taking her off ship, Captain."

"Thank you," Stern said, and sounded very sincere.

Tali began yelling, but the men dragged her out ahead of them. Captain Stern and the Cargo Master followed, obviously to make certain the way was clear of Tali and anyone else.

"We need the people she worked with," Neva said.

"Ekhardt," Rafe said. He shifted slightly, finding it difficult to walk like this. "He's in on it, though I think they tried to cut him out when they found he lost his place in the market. I saw one of them stab him. I don't know if he survived."

"He did. He said the Norishi had stabbed him, and we didn't know any better," Neva replied. "Ardi, gather him up. And the medtech traveling with Tali if he comes to light. Have Ritter look for the ShadowCage."

He nodded and started away, although only after a glance at Etinon. Apparently the Ksa looked sufficient to keep watch over them. Ardi pushed out ahead of the others.

Neva walked with Rafe, which proved disconcerting. He didn't dare glance at her for fear of how he would react. He concentrated on keeping his balance along the path back to the airlock. He hoped to hell this went well when they got there. The pets were getting anxious. Maybe they could scent the air of Xenation ahead.

He stepped out into the still cold and mostly dark bay area. The Click had moved back from the door. Security had hold of Tali to the right and Ardi was talking on his commlink on the left.

He could see a few Norishi coming their way on the left and a few Ksa on the right -- he suspected, since the Ksa were not quite as close, that they came to make certain there was no trouble with the Norishi. Good. However, Rafe focused on the Click.

The Click started to make sounds, though nothing like he had heard before. The pets moved, but it was as though they feared to climb down.

"Move Tali back," he said.

They dragged her away. The Click made a little louder noise but something still didn't sound right. His arms were starting to ache and the little claws began digging in worse in his shoulder.

"Rafael?" Ardi asked.

"I don't know. They're starting to move a bit and I can hear sounds -- but this not quite right. Maybe -- maybe they think I have hold of them. That I'm trying to take them."

"Put them down," Neva said. "Don't let them attack you."

And that threw him again, her concern. He looked at her for a moment, then had to look away. He couldn't deal with the confusion.

"I think if I can kneel this might work. They do better with people who are on their own level."

"I will hel' you," Etinon said. He put a hand under Rafael's elbow, helping him keep his balance. He ached and he wasn't certain he liked being down on the floor when he remembered how the Click had acted during the trouble. They were agitated again.

However, as soon as he was down, the first of the Click immediately bounced forward and one of the pets dropped from his shoulders. The others began to move all at once, such a sudden shift that he saw Etinon start to step forward, but he reached out and tapped him on the knee -- or where the knee should be -- and Etinon stopped.

Click and pets swarmed around each other, and a couple even came up over Rafael, clicking wildly. He smiled. This had the feel of a joyous celebration.

"Big deal," Tali said, still not far enough away. "So the animals got back together --"

"Shut up," Neva replied, her voice barely held in check this time. The Click noticed the tone and quieted. Neva glanced at them and took a deep breath. She sounded calmer when she spoke again. "You have been part of a plan that got others killed --"

"You can't prove --"

"Your palm opened the crate."

"They're just animals. I don't know why --"

"Hell," Rafael said. He looked at the Click and pets and took several breaths to calm himself. Others watched him, waiting. "They aren't *just animals*. I think the pets are children."

"But they don't look like --" Neva began. "Shit. Butterflies."

"It might be," Morgan agreed. He'd moved closer and had a scanner in hand. "It would mean some drastic changes in anatomy, but it might be. Damn, I wish we could communicate more with them."

"I think Rafe might be right," Neva said. She looked both worried and excited. "That would be a great find. We need to go back over our data. Did all the pets arrive with the Click? Etinon, is there anything you can tell us about the Click that might help?"

Rafe glanced to see Etinon looking from one Click to another. "The young of the s'ecies. This night ve. We have had contact with Click in elsewhere, but not so nuch as here. We arrived once to a world where we found the Click already; rare to find such a thing. There were no 'ets at all. This was a dangerous 'lace and we thought they did not vring their con'anions. Later, when we returned, there were 'ets. We had not thought a craft arrived in that time, but sontines their craft go where we do not see. Oddly, by then they had nade the 'lace safer."

Maybe they had chanced on something here. Rafe just hoped that reuniting pets with the Click would settle things. They had trouble enough with their own.

The Norishi still came forward in force, marching -- literally marching -- across the bay.

"Stand," Etinon said with a quick tap on Rafe's shoulder. "Do as I say."

He stood, wondering why he couldn't have a few minutes peace. He couldn't imagine what the Norishi wanted now.

He had not expected the problem to be *him*, but he wasn't terribly surprised by it, either.

"We demand that he be locked away," Tican said, and without any preliminary statements. She waved a hand towards Rafe, her eyes narrowed with anger. "To allow such a creature to walk freely among women after he attacked --"

"Rafael attacked no one," Neva said, her voice uncommonly calm.

"That's not true! Oh how could you say such a thing --" Tali began and cried, immediately playing to the new crowd.

"Shut up," Neva said, and not kindly this time.

"How can you take the side of that man against the girl-child?" Tican demanded, astonished by the show.

"The girl-child *lied*."

"You cannot know. It is a male --"

"What the hell do you know about males at all?" Neva asked.

Not the most diplomatic thing Neva had ever said but it got an interesting reaction. Tican stepped back, her eyes narrowing, though the anger never left her face. Tali started to say something, but fell silent at that look.

"We do not trust the males. Males are unstable and cruel. We do not trust this one. It must be removed from the station."

"Rafe isn't going anywhere," Neva replied and she honestly seemed to be enjoying the exchange. Rafe imagined dealing with the Norishi had been tiresome. However, he hoped he wasn't the fuse that started a war with them.

"So be it." Tican took a step forward her hand reaching toward Rafe.

Etinon stepped forward, putting himself beside Rafe. Something going on here and Rafe knew he wasn't going to like this much at all.

"I stand as guard to Rafael," Etinon said.

Tican looked at him her face coloring, her breath

coming in in a short gasp.

"This changes nothing," she finally said although Etinon had shocked her.

"You are warned."

She snarled something in Norishi and Rafe caught the bare jest of it being about old battles. Etinon replied in her own language which took her by shock. Did they think no one would figure out their words? Or was it just that a *male* dared to say them. Damn, he wished he could figure out why the women had such problems with males because this was plainly going to be a problem for him.

And he needed to figure out what it was Xenation really wanted.

A form x side. Delete. Awaiting key.

"Rafe?" Ardi asked.

He had gone blank again, he supposed. Now he shook his head and looked around. Nothing much had changed except that the Click had started to retreat. He could not see the pets in the mass of them. Neva stared at her daughter.

"We'll hold her in a cell until the next ship comes," she finally said. This was not an easy choice. Tali looked at her in shocked disbelief. "We can't send her off on the *Shaw* without knowing if she has other people aboard who are involved."

"Yes, true," Ardi agreed. He gave a nod to the men who had Tali in hand. Rafe didn't envy them the job. Tali was already starting to protest, and loudly -- and in language that seemed to be taking the Norishi by surprise, too. "I'll locate her companion."

"You cannot mean to lock the girl-child away --" Tican began and looked surprisingly irate. "She is the daughter of the leader --"

"She has done evil," Neva said. Tali stopped long enough to frown, as though such a thing couldn't possibly apply to her. There was a child with a lot of problems. "She is treated like everyone else."

"But --"

"This is a human matter."

Neva had reached the end of her patience with the Norishi. Rafe saw the growing anger and it was best to just vacate the field.

"I'm damned tired," he said aloud. That drew all the attention, which he really didn't want. "I'm going to my room --"

"Med," Ardi said. He lifted a hand. "Yang said either I bring you in or he'd go out and find you."

"I just want rest."

"You'll get it," Ardi promised. "I think between Etinon and me, we can keep everything at bay for a little while."

Etinon looked at Rafe and gave a quick nod. "To Yang," he agreed. "You will not go anywhere else."

"Oh, for the love of God -- when did everyone decide they could run my life?"

"When you no longer took care of it," Etinon replied and sounded far too serious.

"It is not your job --"

"Vut it is," Etinon said. "I an your guard. I an now to see over your life, and nake certain of the care you need."

"Fine." He gave up. Right then he didn't care where they went as long as it was out of this mess. Etinon and Ardi moved to flank him and the three walked away. He could hear the disagreement between Neva and the Norishi still even after they entered the Human Enclave. He glanced back, but she had Morgan and a couple others as her guard.

"Any sign of Tali's other accomplice?" Rafe asked.

"Not yet," Ardi said with a quick, worried look at Etinon. Then he shrugged. "I guess I had better get used to you being around."

Etinon gave a bow of his head in agreement, but said nothing more.

Rafe looked at Etinon and almost asked how long he intended to follow him. He decided this was something he just didn't want to face right now. It was probably, as things went lately, the first real wisdom he'd shown in a long time.

CHAPTER THIRTY-THREE

A s it turned out, Rafe was not the first person to have suggested that the pets might be offspring of the Click. Morgan found the reference in something written by one of the first people to see the Click and pets, but she had not stayed long on the station and her idea had gotten buried in the mass of other information on the Click. Too many things to study, not enough scientific staff -- he could have gotten hundreds more staff in if they could have supported them. The team had always intended to focus on Xenation. They didn't ignore the Click, Ksa or Norishi, but the aliens were secondary to getting some handle on the place where they had come to live.

Dangerous place. Dangerous neighbors.

Morgan went over all the Click reports he could manage to read in the next few hours. Even though they were not the focus of work here, there will still hundreds of files on hand. Some of them seemed contradictory and little had any follow up. He started making an index of incidents and tried to sort them --

"Morgan, you need to rest."

He looked up, surprised to find Neva at the door to his office. He knew he had dismissed the others, said good-bye to them as they left, one-by-one, earlier. Some were going to the wake for one of the people who had died. He hadn't known him. The other three who had died turned out to be passengers from the *Shaw*. Also no one he knew.

Looking at Neva, he suspected hours had passed and he had lost all track of time.

"I'm trying to decide about the pets and the Click," he said, waving towards his computer. His voice sounded gruff and his eyes didn't want to focus on her. "I do think we misjudged the relationship, no matter what it might turn out to be."

"You need rest," Neva repeated. She leaned against the door. "I think we all do. Rafe, last I heard, is sleeping at least."

"Yeah. Rest." He purposely closed down the comp. The information would be there the next time he keyed it on. He needed to back away for a while. "Rafe isn't the first person to suggest the relationship might be parent and child, but the other person was very early on and she didn't stay."

"It is interesting that we focused on the idea of pets for some reason," she said as he came out of the room.

They walked down the hall; empty now, the off hours.

"It was an easy answer," he replied. He glanced at his watch and winced. His team would be back into the office in about three hours. "We needed any kind of easy answer, Neva, and we couldn't make any other judgments, after all. But still -- well, the truth is that there is so much going on here that my people can't possibly really study everything with the focus it needs. You know that, right?"

"Samplin let them go wild. I thought about stepping in, but --"

"No, they did all right. They're all professionals. And really, letting them ferret out some of the things they wanted to study turned out to be a good move. All of them gravitated to something they specialized in and allowed to just go at it without oversight worked well."

"Hadn't thought of that," she said. "Good. I didn't want to think that we'd been wasting time. Are they learning anything?"

"Ritter is really on to something with the wave lengths," he said. "And Veris has some very interesting data on latent chemicals in the atmosphere. They're all doing well. Nothing outstanding but it's all adding to the larger picture."

"Who do you have studying Rafael?" she asked with a

quick, sidelong glance.

He slowed. The hall where they would part was only a few steps away. "Yang, Ardi and me. Yang sends me his reports each night and I send him anything I have from the day, some of it from Ardi. I also look over Ritter's reports to see if anything Rafe does corresponds with Xenation activity."

"And?"

"Too early to make any real conclusions," he replied. She made an amused snort at the typical scientist reply. "No, it really is true. Yes, there are times when he reacts and Xenation is reacting, too. But Neva, he's not the only one. There are times when we all seem more attuned to Xenation, and that means everyone, not just Rafe."

"Ah." She sounded intrigued and stopped at her hall. He almost suggested they go have coffee instead -- but no. They both needed rest. "But Rafe --"

"Rafael has a special link, beyond a doubt. I'm also trying to see how much Xenation is influencing all of us."

She looked worried. "That's something I don't like to think about."

"Sorry. Go get some sleep, Neva. We've handled the Click, but . . . things still feel out of place. Do you feel as though things have settled back to normal?"

"No," she said and sighed. "Hell, no. I think we're in for a lot of trouble. The Ksa are acting oddly. The Displaced were even worse than usual. We haven't even discussed the Norishi and the two ships they attacked. Go get some sleep yourself."

Neva purposely turned away. Morgan watched for a moment and then went on to his own room. He took a quick shower, pulled on a robe and went to sit on the edge of the bed. Sleep, he reminded himself, but his mind refused to slow down. Too much input lately, too much going on.

Morgan threw himself down on the mattress, pulled the blanket up over him and buried his head under the pillow.

He didn't sleep well.

And not nearly for long enough, either.

"Etech Doreet?"

He came awake with a start, his head pounding and dizzy with the sudden rush from deep sleep to wide awake. Someone had a hand on his shoulder. He rolled over and looked into the worried face of Ritter. She was not the only one standing inside his room.

"Wha --" he said, barely able to get that much out.

"Trouble sir. Serious trouble. We don't know what's going on, but the Norishi have gone crazy."

He blinked a few times. "Norishi."

"Yes, sir. They're out in force. They're ordering everyone to obey them and they've wounded at least one Ksa."

"Hell. What is going on *now*?" He could hardly call up any energy for this one.

"We don't know. Ardi wants everyone up in command, though so we're closer to where we can watch out for each other. The ship is sealed closed and The Norishi are between us and it. There's no way out and they look like they intend to come in."

"I'll get dressed. I'll be right there."

"I'll wait for you," Ritter said. She offered a quick smile, but waved the others on. "Better not to be out there alone."

"Damned mess." He rolled off the bed. His legs felt rubbery and even with the news, all he wanted to do was crawl back into bed and sleep. "No idea what set them off?"

"None. I didn't expect this to get worse."

Morgan grunted an answer. He was not completely naked, though he hardly cared at this point. He went into the portable refresh cube they'd set up in the rooms -- worked on the same system as the ships. He wanted a shower -- two minutes was all he allowed himself. Then, not even fully dried, he pulled his clothes on and came back out. Ritter stood alone at the door, the cloth covering pulled slightly back as she looked outside.

"Some sounds down the hall, but quiet now," Ritter said. "Let's get up to command and the labs. We can help keep guard on them. Ardi is short of people."

Morgan didn't want to face more trouble, but Ritter's

worry overlaid his sleep-fogged movements and he soon found himself rushing along the hall. Before long, they could hear shouts not far away, and the distinct cry of Norishi voices. He wished he knew the language.

Ardi's people had taken up spots on the main hall and near the main control room. The labs were off to the left, also protected by the thin line of guards. He didn't see Ardi at all.

"I'll go to the labs," Ritter said. She looked worried as she glanced towards the room. "Any orders?"

"Yes. Copy off all computer files to portable disks, password lock them, and wipe the memories of the machines clean," he said. Ritter looked startled. "Hide the files as best you can."

"Yes. Yes," She and hurried away. Morgan hoped anyone else in the office listened. He was not going to hand over their research to the Norishi if they got in here. Maybe this was petty. After all, the research hadn't really brought anything important to light yet, but he wasn't going to let what they had fall into Norishi hands. He didn't trust them.

He had a link to his own computer via his pocket comp. He stopped and did the work of clearing his own machine from where he was. He locked the pocketcomp to his voice only and a few key words. He saw a couple of the security people glance his way and nod. Maybe he wasn't being so paranoid after all.

The control room appeared to be chaotic. He stopped at the door and glanced around. This was not the place he needed to be. He started to back out, but Neva spotted him and lifted her hand, signaling him to hold there. At least he didn't have to go in. He saw her pause by someone and realized, with a start that was the Norishi spy. There was something he hadn't thought about until now. Damn. One more thing --

But Neva came to him, took his arm, and led him out of the room and down the hall.

"Damn mess," she said, shaking her head. "We called that one right last night."

"What the hell do the Norishi want?"

"Tali and Rafael. They are not going to get either."

"This is crazy. Why would they do this?"

"We don't know," she said. They had reached the entrance to the medunit. Yang was pacing inside and he could see Ardi. Through another door Etinon stood guard and Rafael slept peacefully on a bed, unaware of anything going on. Morgan doubted that would for very long.

"What is the word?" Yang asked, coming to them as they entered the room.

"Not good," Neva reported. "We really don't know what's going on out there, except what we can see by the vidcams. None of it makes any real sense at this point."

"They want Rafe and Tali," Yang said and glanced back at his sleeping patient. "They still think Rafe is in the wrong?"

"I have no idea what they think," Neva answered. She dropped into a chair, plainly as exhausted as Morgan felt.

"Rafe needs rest. He really does," Yang said and gave Neva a worried glance.

"My hope is that we can work this problem out without resorting to having him step in this time."

"I am working with Captain Stern," Ardi said, drawing all their attention. "If things get worse, we're going to try and form up a corridor and get everyone onto the ship. I didn't want to say anything in the control room, given that we have a spy there. It will be a tight fit and we'd have to abandon everything, but it would get sealable doors between us and the Norishi."

Neva had started to say something and changed her mind. "Yes that is a good idea to have an option open." Then she blanched. "We can't take Rafael off station."

Ardi nodded grimly.

Etinon had come to the door and listened. "The Ksa will take Rafael into our care if the hunans feel they nust leave the station," he said. "We will hold here as vest we can."

"We aren't going to jump ship just yet," Ardi said.

"This neans?"

"Leave in a hurry during danger," Ardi said. "It's an old Earth term from the nautical -- the sea-faring days. Sometimes it referred to leaving a ship without permission when in port."

Etinon apparently filed that information away for future use. Morgan wondered what the Ksa thought of their sayings. That last one said a great deal about them, after all. Leave at a time of danger. Abandon duty.

Only it was not true of them as a species.

"If the situation becomes one where we think our presence will make more of a problem than our leaving would, then we might leave," Morgan said, drawing his attention. "If it looks as though the Norishi would kill us all, we would try to go. There is no honor in dying without a good reason. We'll fight back, but we are mostly scientists and not warriors. We will save our information, retreat from the trouble, and come back when it is safer."

"You would cone vack?" Etinon said. "Even if the Norishi is still here?"

"If we thought we could make things safe," Ardi said. "And if we didn't, we might remove the Norishi first."

Etinon started to say something. He stopped. "You think you could renove the Norishi."

"You would be surprised at what humans can do," Neva said and looked up at him. "We are extremely territorial. We believe that once we have settled somewhere, it is ours. It is hardwired -- it allows us to believe we are *home* wherever we settle for a few years. And we *defend* our homes."

"Ah. Ah." He looked from one to the other and then glanced back at Rafe as though he understood him better. When he looked to the others again, he appeared troubled. "The Norishi are dangerous."

"So are we," Neva replied. The words seemed to give her strength and she stood. "I need false information to feed to the Norishi spy. Let's come up with something inventive to tell her."

"We can fake the call of a ship coming in," Ardi suggested. He tapped his commlink. "If she has direct contact with the other Norishi, we might be able to scare them into backing off."

Neva shook her head. "By the time we could hear from a ship, it should be on the sensors. Even if she reports it, the others will be able to see there's nothing there."

"What if Ksa also saw such an inconing craft?" Etinon asked and there might have been a glint of daring in his eyes. "A vattlecruiser of such size and 'ower that we 'rotested the arrival."

"You think we could fool them into believing their own scanners aren't working properly?" Ardi asked. He looked hopeful.

"Of all the peoples here, I would think the Norishi would be the least likely to trust that others are right and they are wrong," Neva added.

"True," Etinon agreed. He looked from one to the other. "We could only do this once."

"If . . . if things got worse and we needed to get to the ship, it might be a way to clear them from this area. Especially if we made it look as though the *Shaw* prepared to leave in a hurry to make room for something large," Ardi said.

"Can the *Shaw* even get free of Xenation?" Neva asked. Then she shook her head. "That doesn't matter, does it? We want the ship to look like she's going, and even if she can't get clear, we're safer onboard than here. The Norishi might try to attack the ship, but at least it has weapons we could use in defense. It might be better, but as a last resort."

"Let's just see if we can get the Norishi to back off without resorting to anything else yet," Ardi said. "Send out a distress signal, Neva. Maybe there really is a ship in the area that can come in. Right now, though, we need to find out what it is that set the Norishi off like this. It can't be the trouble with the Click. They don't care about anyone but themselves. We feared Tali and her companions might have grabbed a Norishi --"

"Hell!" Morgan said, frantic--

"We had Stern check the entire ship. If they had, she's

not there. We think this is something we don't understand at all, Morgan."

"Maybe the behavior of the Click set them into offensive mode," Morgan suggested. "Where is Ekhardt and Norden?"

"They haven't turned up yet," Ardi said. He ran a hand over his face, looking more worried this time. "Norden was on the ship, but he must have gotten out when he saw the trouble heading for the bay. He has a ShadowCage. It wouldn't have been impossible."

Morgan heard a slight buzz and Etinon pulled out his little commlink and began talking quickly to his own people. Morgan wished he understood what was said on both sides. It sounded increasingly troubled. The conversation didn't take long. Etinon shoved the device away and put a hand on his weapon, which was not reassuring. "Saris is nissing. They feared to say thinking ny friend dead fron the Click battle but they can find no sign. He was last seen fighting against the Norishi. Another dead where he fought, but not he."

"I'm going to go back over the vids again," Ardi said. "I'll look at everything I can find and see if we can learn what happened to him."

"Good," Neva said. "Morgan, I need you to do something fancy with your equipment and get ready to do the fake communications transmissions and maybe make our scanners look as though something is coming in. Yang, do what you can for Rafael, because he really might have to be moved quickly and sent off with the Ksa."

Yang nodded and went back into the room. Etinon followed and took up his position as a guard again, but he kept his commlink in hand and sometimes spoke into it.

Morgan left and went back to his office. Ritter sat there alone and they had guards at the door. Ritter would be good help on this project. At least he had something to do as he tried not to listen to the wild cries of the Norishi echoing through the area.

The barbarians were at the gate.

CHAPTER THIRTY-FOUR

Rafael awoke feeling groggy and unhappy. He'd been dreaming about walking on the beach with the sea breeze brushing softly over him and the tangy scent of the ocean in the air. Even as he awoke, he could still hear the faint echo of seagulls . . . a melancholy parting song.

But he awoke to a place he knew better than his own room in Xenation. The equipment beeped quietly and he could see Yang working at his desk in the other room. A slight shift showed Etinon standing by the door, still guarding him. He felt safer for having him there, which was bad. He didn't want to feel like he needed someone to stand over him.

He could tell just by looking at Etinon that something more had happened. When had he gotten so good at reading Ksa body language?

"What's wrong?" he asked, forcing himself to sit up, though he moved slowly. There was no need to rush into the new trouble and the equipment barely beeped louder this time. He'd has worse awakenings.

"Ksa are nissing and Norishi create nore trouvle."

"Damn," he said. Equipment beeped in protest this time as his blood pressure leapt upward.

Yang came in, looked over the boards and shook his head. "You shouldn't have told him."

"Not? He is in need of facts. Trouvle could come for Rafael at any tine. Vest if he is ready, yes?"

"Yes," Rafael answered emphatically. "I need to know. Is there anything else?"

"Quiet for a while. This is not good. The Norishi denand you and Tali."

"Give them Tali," he mumbled. "That would keep them busy for a while."

"They'd just give her back," Yang said.

Rafe grinned and Etinon finally realized they joked, though maybe he wasn't sure where the joke began and where it ended. Rafe wasn't certain himself.

"What do we do?" Rafe asked.

"You get ready to go with the Ksa if you need to," Yang said and looked worried.

"Go with --" His heart began to pound a little harder and he looked around with worry. Things were too neat. "You plan to abandon the station."

"Only if we have to," Yang assured him. "And then we might not go any farther than the ship in dock. However, if we have to clear the station, you can't go with us Rafe. The Ksa say they will do their best to protect you."

He nodded, unable to speak. He hated this station right then; hated it with a force that made his head ache and his heart pound. He didn't want to be left behind --

Sequence began. Awaiting key.

Oh hell, oh hell. He looked around, frantic and afraid he had started something in that moment of despair.

"Rafe?" Yang said, coming close enough to put a hand on his shoulder.

"I may have started something," he admitted. "Calm. I need calm. I don't know what Xenation is picking up and what she will do."

But something was happening. He felt the floor shift slightly beneath his feet. Everyone looked startled and worried.

"Calm," he said. "Nothing is really bad."

And maybe she listened to him again. Maybe she was getting used to his changeable human moods. It seemed as though calm slipped in around them. The lights in the walls even changed to a more soothing light blue and he found himself grinning at his two companions. He'd never had that much control before and the change gave him hope that he might be able to do something more.

"Tell me the situation," he said. Yang shook his head, looking worried. "No, tell me. I do far better with the facts than I do imagining what might be wrong."

"Good point," Yang finally agreed. He sat down on a chair and told him about the Norishi, which was the biggest problem. He also explained about the trick they hoped to play on the Norishi via their little spy.

"If you get them to back off, can you contain them in their area?" he asked. He even glanced at Etinon for that answer.

"We can try," he said with a bow of his head. "We are ready vut we cone farther across the station. They will see. I an not sure the hunans can hold they until we arrive."

"He has a point," Yang said. "But we'll do whatever we have to, I suppose."

"Duty," Etinon said with a nod.

"Yes, but our duty is often to protect others," Rafael told him. Etinon looked a little surprised. "Why do you think we patrol the market? Not just our own people, but all the market?"

"We thought you did so to s'y."

"Partly to study, yes, but not to spy. We would be far less obvious if we were spying," Rafael replied.

"Like the devices in the lights?" Etinon asked.

"Oh yes, like those. They're cameras," Rafe replied. "We have a far wider view of the bay area now. Seeing through them, we know some of the things that have happened."

"Ah. Ah. This is good." Etinon looked very pleased.

"Do you think the Norishi realize about the cameras?"

"No," he said, and his nose wrinkled as he gave a quick smile. "No. The Norishi kee' too nuch to theyselves. They do not look at what others could do, even when others clearly -- veing here with they -- have high technology."

"I wouldn't think others would put up with this kind of attitude for long."

Etinon smiled again. He looked far more relaxed than

Rafe had ever seen him and it occurred to Rafe that the Ksa hadn't known much about humans either, even though they were closer to them than the Norishi.

"The Norishi do not share locations with others vefore," Etinon admitted. "They kee' well away. This 'lace draws they in. They do not want to lose out on what is found."

"That makes sense," Yang said with a nod. He went back to picking up a few things around the room but it had the look of nervous movement. "I still want to know how they slipped one of their own in among out people. She got past *me*. The records show I did the scan, but I didn't."

"Computer control," Rafe replied. He thought about standing and decided resting a while longer wasn't such a bad idea. "They have a link into our system?"

"Morgan says no and Ritter backs him."

Rafe nodded, relieved. "Then just a one-time access to slip her info in. They've had some contact with humans before, so they could have learned a bit about our systems before now."

"You give con'uters away," Etinon said. "You do it for connunications with others."

"True," Yang agreed. "Basic computers, but it wouldn't take much for them to get more data and learn how to make a file or two. When I have time, I'm going to look at her file and compare it to others. And then we'll send the results to the IWC and let them start checking other locations."

"Ah. Yes." Etinon appeared bothered by the idea. "Yes, it is wise to check."

"What happened to the Norishi males?" Rafe asked, looking at his Ksa guard. This wasn't something he had ever dared to ask before, but now seemed like the time to get some information.

"We are uncertain there are any," Etinon said. "They nay have died out eons in the 'ast."

"Then how --" Yang began, but then stopped. He seemed to consider the idea. "Cloning, parthenogenesis. It's possible."

Rafe wondered --

Shouts rang out in the hall nearby. He started to his feet before Etinon signaled him up. The Ksa even grabbed Yang and pulled him back to stand by Rafe, which surprised them both.

"You with Rafael," he said, with a bow of his head. "You stay safe with he."

Yang looked as though he would push past, but Rafe caught his arm. "Don't argue with Etinon, not now," Rafe said. He looked around, trying to see if there was anything he could use to defend himself. "I'd feel better if I had a knife at least."

"Let me get something from my case."

"Quickly," Etinon said. He'd stepped forward into the doorway. "We nay need go quickly. Rafe? You can nove?"

"I'll keep up with you."

"I'll help him," Yang said. Etinon gave a nod of thanks. Rafe realized he was having trouble staying steady, but he suspected that would pass once the adrenalin kicked in again.

The first shouts he heard seemed distorted and he couldn't make out the words. Then he realized they were not human words. Norishi, beyond a doubt and that worried him because he did not want to fall into their hands.

Yang handed him a long, slim-bladed instrument. "That's damned sharp and it will cut deep, Rafe. Be careful with it. And remember the Norishi's anatomy is not quite the same as human. The heart is more in the center and a little lower, behind a thick wall of muscle."

The words plainly shocked Etinon. "That would ve a killing wound."

"Yes, it would. I don't expect Rafe will use it unless he has to. I don't trust the Norishi and I don't want them taking Rafe. We would have to go back in after him. It could get far worse."

Rafe held the weapon, listening to the growing sounds. "If they take --"

"Don't say something stupid," Yang said. He looked bleak and angry. This was not a good situation for a medtech. If Rafe could have found a way to get him out of here, he would have taken it. Yang did not need to be involved in a battle, especially over him --

The sounds changed. He felt himself start to relax even before Etinon did.

"What?" Yang said.

"Ksa," Rafe explained.

Etinon nodded. He brought up his commlink and said a quick rush of words that sounded more than a little worried. There was an answer and then more shouts not far away. A number of Ksa quickly appeared at the doorway, dark and tall against the light outside. One conferred with Etinon, bowed, and left. Four remained, ranged in a row out in the hall.

"The Norishi denanded Rafael and Tali," Etinon said. He frowned as he looked at Rafael.

"Why me?" Rafe asked.

"This is a question we would like to know," Etinon said. "They use the 'retense of your attack on Tali. I think it nore likely they want the link to Xenation."

"Probably," he said with a sigh. Nothing he could do to change the link. "For all the good it would do them since I really have no control. And Tali as a pretense because they think I attacked her so they will take us both away?"

"I think other things," Etinon replied. "Tali, vecause she is the daughter of an in'ortant woman. It is instinctive, I think."

"If Tali had been a son, they wouldn't have looked twice," Yang said with understanding. Rafe nodded as well, since he had thought something like this already. "You can't fight instincts. I can see where taking the daughter of a powerful woman would be an important part of their culture."

"To protect the daughter? Maybe to gain some power over the mother and thus raise their own station?" Rafe asked. He moved to a chair and sat down. The bed looked far more inviting but he feared he would go back to sleep and he wanted to stay awake to make certain the Norishi were not going to try to grab him.

For how long? He couldn't stay awake forever. A while longer, though.

"Maybe something like that," Yang agreed. He looked Rafe over and nodded. "Go take a quick shower and change. I'm going to see if I can get us some food. If this is going to be a long siege, we need to pace ourselves and make certain we're able to face the trouble."

The thought of a long siege, trapped here in the rooms, worried him. He stood -- though slowly -- and limped back to the portable shower unit. Having spent so much time here, he kept clothing in the cupboard inside. The idea of being clean appealed to him. He sat the timer for a full seven minutes -- a luxury he rarely took -- but he figured he was safe enough in here with Yang, Etinon and the other Ksa guarding him.

Relax. Rest while he could. Hope the Norishi came to their senses -- though that last seemed unlikely. How could they have survived so long out in space with others if they behaved this way?

The Norishi didn't spend much time with others, he realized as he washed his hair. This might be the first time they'd shared space with others for any length of time. They hadn't even spent much time at the human stations throughout the human-visited areas.

They had attacked a human ship and the Ksa brought them the information. He hadn't heard anything back from that one but he knew Neva and the others hadn't forgotten. The Norishi later attacked and destroyed the alien ship that had been heading toward Xenation.

Pattern? Reason? He didn't have enough data and he thought about it as he got dressed and came back out. He went straight to the chair and sat down, too worn to do anything else. Etinon gave him a nod and said nothing. Rafe sat back, considering what he knew.

The Norishi were hiding something. The human ship they destroyed must have seen what they were doing. And the alien ship as well? Could they have --?

Compbox.

He looked up with a start. Etinon watched him, worried. "I want to talk to Neva."

"You? Go to Neva?" Yang said, startled.

"Yes. I need to ask her something," he said and stood. He'd been blind before this -- but maybe they all were. "I think the Norishi attack on the human ship and on the alien ship might be related. Etinon, you saw the material --"

"What we could. Codes -- you hunans code too nuch sonetines," he said with a rueful shake of his head. "We dared not try to learn nore for fear it would not work at all. Vetter to give it over to the hunans."

"I wonder if anyone has broken the code yet," Yang said with a frown.

"Hunans do codes that other hunans cannot read?" Etinon asked, startled by the idea.

"We trust no one, especially ourselves," Rafael replied, but didn't want to pursue that one any farther. "I want to know if anyone learned anything more. I think it might help with understanding what's going on."

Etinon nodded which seemed to settle the matter for Yang. He had hoped the man would stay behind, but the medtech tagged along, making Rafael all the more aware of his own condition. He didn't feel as though he was going to fall over dead at any moment, but he did feel weak. His head pounded. He touched the spot at the back of his head where Xenation had placed another piece of shell over his brain and wondered what this one would do.

Maybe . . . maybe he should stop thinking of it as a problem and start considering how interesting this made his life. Hell, as long as he was trapped here, he might as well make the most out of it.

He felt a little better for that thought. Stop fighting the system; go with it and see what interesting things might happen.

Outside in the hall, he found humans and Ksa in far too great a number. Normally that wouldn't have bothered him, but today they watched as he passed as though they expected him to have some sort of answer. He wanted to help, but maybe he -- and they -- expected too much.

What did Xenation know? What did Xenation act upon? Where were the Displaced right now?

Data displacement. Await key.

Hell, he wished he knew what that meant.

He could hear the sound of trouble somewhere off in the bays and hoped the problem didn't get worse. He couldn't imagine what the Norishi thought they would gain.

He found the control room crowded with far too many people, and though he spotted Neva, he couldn't actually get to her. People came and went in vast numbers -- he would have thought there were far more humans on the station, given the crowding here.

Etinon stayed close at his back, which drew attention to him . . . though, to be honest, his being here would have drawn notice anyway. He hadn't been to the command area since the accident, and walking in here now gave him a slight shiver. He moved out of the doorway and to the left, near to the computer banks with rows of lights. The click of keypads almost overcame the sound of talking, all of it filling the small area with a buzz of sound he found reassuring. In a real station, they would have been buried somewhere back in the depths of the construction, safe from damage. Here, they shoved the huge towers into a corner. These computers didn't run the station, though --

Data relay. Post stress remerge. Await key.

"What damned key?" he said aloud and saw Etinon give him an odd glance. He shook his head and tried to focus back on the room.

Neva spotted him, which wasn't a surprise since everyone else kept looking his way. She didn't appear happy as she crossed the room, but he had the feeling it was not about him this time. No one looked happy, and with good reason. Neva frowned and it probably helped with the little Norishi spy -- and yes, she was there, standing near the communications equipment and glancing their way. Yang had showed him the picture to make sure he knew if she showed any interest in him.

He had to do this carefully.

Etinon nudged Yang who looked surprised.

"Stay vehind her. Hold others at a little distance. Not ovvious," Etinon said softly.

Yang nodded. He crossed to someone who had a bandage on his arm and drew the person a little away from all the others. Damn good work. Rafe suspected, from the way Etinon blinked several times, that the ease with which Yang did this surprised him. Humans were far more resourceful than he had likely realized.

"What are you doing here?" Neva demanded, her voice just loud enough to carry. She looked worried, though, and he felt his heart beat harder again.

He leaned in closer and lowered his voice, making certain their spy could not clearly see his face.

"The compbox -- has the code been broken?"

"No," she said, and blinked, a furrow appearing in her forehead. "Might be linked. I don't know if I have anyone who can take it on --"

"Give it to me. I used to be good with codes and at least it will be something I can do during this mess."

She nodded and started to turn away --

He caught her arm. She looked back with a start and he quickly let go --

"Watched," he whispered. "Closer."

The Norishi spy had moved all the way up to where Yang stood which was far too close. He hoped when Neva had started to turn away, she caught sight of the woman and knew the danger.

Neva had taken a step away from him. "I don't care what you think," she said aloud. And people turned to see the confrontation and then turned away in haste. The Norishi had a look of pleasure for a brief moment. "I don't trust you, Rafael. I won't trust you. You and your Ksa guard get the hell out of my sight. Yang, get him out of here. Now."

"I'll go," he said and turned away. Yang and Etinon fell in around him. People got out of the way. He suspected the show had worked well, but the scene had left him feeling odd. He found it hard enough to know what was real and what wasn't some days.

As he was walking away, he heard Neva ask if Morgan was around. She said it louder than usual and he took that as a sign. Outside the room, he turned back towards the medunit, but then took a detour down the hall toward the science room and through to Morgan's office.

"Morgan," he said softly. He and Ritter were going over some files on their pocket comps.

"You shouldn't be up," Morgan said, looking him over. He glanced at Yang. "What are you doing letting him wander around?"

"You try to stop him," Yang said with a snort. "But I think we're heading back for the bed soon, right?"

"Yes." There were people at the door, so he leaned down and put a hand on a table, as though too weak to go on. Not far from the truth, he feared, feeling a little dizzy. The move allowed him to speak quietly. "I think Neva will get you something. Bring it to me as quietly as you can, with little notice."

"You can't really think I'm going to let you have computer time, Rafe. Not the shape you are in," he said aloud. "Go on back and rest. I'll look in on you later, and we'll see. Right now is not a good time for any of us."

"It's me they want," he said, standing up straighter again. "I want to find out all I can. I want to know why."

However, he brushed his hand against the plate on his face, and he thought Morgan probably picked up on the hint.

"We're studying it."

"It's not your life."

"But it is my computers. Go rest."

He had no choice, really. He had to believe if he went back to the medunit, than everything would come to him.

People out in the science section and the hall looked his way with worry and some with harder stares that didn't make him feel very safe at all. He hadn't expected he would feel better for having the Ksa guard at his back, even here in the

Human Enclave.

This was not going to go well.

CHAPTER THIRTY-FIVE

Morgan didn't know what to expect, but he kept close to his office for the next hour. He knew Neva wouldn't take long to get whatever it was to him since, if he read Rafe right, this might be important. He and Ritter kept busy watching computer scans and working on the material for their pretend ship heading in if they needed it. Others were clearing their computers, some for a second time. No one was happy

Things appeared calmer out in the halls. Some of the people had gone back to their rooms to rest so they could take their place as guards later. He had tried to send Ritter off, but she outright refused.

"We need to work on this material as quickly as possible," she pointed out -- the very words Morgan had used a couple hours before. "And it's obvious something is going on with Neva and Rafe. I'm too curious to leave before I find out."

Morgan thought about arguing and then thought Ritter probably had the right idea. Sounds unexpectedly rose and died down as quickly; he didn't even go to find out what the problem might be this time. He didn't think he could live like this for very long.

"Etech Doreet?" someone said, coming to the door. He looked up to see one of the techs from main control. "Neva asked I bring this to you. She said it was the rest of the data on the Norishi that they had in storage there."

He handed over a comp box. Odd. Morgan nodded like he knew what was going on. "How does it look out there?"

"Crazy. I went to the entrance and took a look about half an hour ago. The Norishi were still lined up between us and the ship."

"I wish I knew what they wanted," Ritter said looking up from her own work, which she had slightly angled out of view.

"They want Neva's daughter and Rafael," the messenger replied. His eyes narrowed in a look Morgan didn't like. "I don't want to give them over, but if it comes to the two of them or the rest of us --"

"And you think that would protect the rest of us?" Morgan asked. "You think once the Norishi get what they want, they'll just walk away?"

"I -- hell. No. I'm not that stupid. Just wish there was an easy answer."

"Rafe might not think that such an easy answer. And what would we do the next time the Displaced show up?" Ritter asked.

"Yeah, yeah." He started to turn then shrugged. "Maybe it's just time to leave this place."

"Maybe it is," Morgan agreed. "Give it -- and Rafe -- over to the Norishi and leave. Maybe that's just what they want."

"Yeah," he said. He didn't look happy. "That doesn't sound like such a great idea, either."

The man left. Ritter looked across at Morgan and shook her head. "They're all going to start going crazy soon."

"I know. And the ship out there looks like a quick way out of the trouble. But I'm betting that even if we made it that far, the Norishi wouldn't let the ship get away. We've seen they're good at firing on ships --" He looked at the comp box and saw it had some damage along the side, and suddenly realized what he held. "Shit. I need to get this to Rafe."

Ritter looked at the compbox and plainly didn't understand. Morgan didn't stop to explain. He had a sudden feeling this was a far wider a problem than just the station. They were not the only ones in danger from the Norishi.

Damn mess.

He left the science section which had emptied except for Ritter who headed back to her station. Not many people were in the hall, either, which was good since he wasn't in the mood to talk to any of them. His mind worked on different threads, trying to tie things together.

The Norishi had attacked a human ship. The Norishi attacked an alien ship. The Norishi were acting oddly now. Or maybe not; this might be normal behavior for them. He didn't know and neither did anyone else.

He quickly reached the medunit and stopped in the doorway, only faintly aware of the people there.

"Morgan?" Yang said, coming closer.

Morgan blinked and then shook his head. Yang looked worried.

"Sorry. I was having some thoughts and they took over my brain. This is all tied together, isn't it?" he asked, lifting the compbox and looking at Rafe who sat on the edge of the bed in the next room.

"I don't know yet," Rafe admitted. Morgan crossed the area and handed over the compbox even though he didn't want to let it go. "I'm going to try and work out the code for this one. We don't know why the Norishi destroyed the human ship. I might find an answer."

"Why they destroyed either ship."

"Right." Rafe nodded and looked as though he regretted that simple move. "I get the feeling we're running out of time."

"Who took the Ksa?" Morgan asked. He turned that question to the Ksa guard, uncertain if he would answer.

"We do not know. Where is your Ekhardt and Norden?"

"Did they take the Ksa? Or are they victims, too?" Morgan said, appalled at the idea.

"That is the question. Or one of nany," Etinon answered. "There is not such areas to easily hide on Xenation. Who hides they now?"

"We aren't hiding them," Morgan said and looked at the Ksa.

"Not the Ksa," Etinon replied. "Would we do such a thing and send one to guard you as well?"

"Humans might," Rafe said. "They might send a human in the guise of one job but really he came to spy or to lead others away from a truth."

Etinon looked from Rafe to Morgan and back again. "How do you ever trust each other?"

"It's not easy sometimes," Rafe admitted.

Morgan wasn't certain the Ksa needed to know so much about the humans. But then again, maybe this was a moment of trust. If the Ksa were behind the problems, then they were already in trouble. The Ksa were within the Human Enclave and working with the humans to hold back the Norishi. If the Norishi were not the real problem, they were all screwed.

"I need to work on this," Rafe said. He stood and went to a computer at the side of the room which was normally used for nothing but medical records. The compbox linked into it without a problem.

Morgan started to turn away. Then he stopped and looked back. "Would you mind some help?"

"Mind?" Rafe said looking up. "Good God. I'm not in this for my ego, you know. Get a chair. Help. I don't know what we'll find or if it will make a difference, though. It was just a hunch."

"More than a hunch: you saw a pattern of unusual behavior and you're looking for a key," Morgan said. He grabbed a chair and pulled it over.

"It's *assumed* unusual behavior," Rafe said. "When I was down on my knees facing the Click, I finally realized how much we have been assuming about everyone here. Etinon, do you think this is normal behavior for the Norishi?"

"Who knows what Norishi do in the wideness of stars," he said. "I think, though, this at Xenation is not nornal. To look beyond the walls of Xenation is wise."

Morgan leaned closer to the screen. This was going to be a long night, but it would have been no matter where he sat and at least here he had a puzzle to work on.

CHAPTER THIRTY-SIX

Tali paced the little cell, back and forth, back and forth, rage growing with every step. How *dare* they -- how *could they* do this --

Nowhere to go. She couldn't get out. She looked down the hall past the bars of the portable cage where they'd put her. Bars -- they put her in a cage like an animal, and not even a real cell like she would have on the ship. Bastards --

She hit the bar. It hurt.

She had heard loud noises earlier. People had shouted about the Norishi and had taken off running. They'd left her. She would die here. Her mother abandoned her again! The woman hated her --

Something odd happened in the hall. A guard suddenly fell for no reason. Gas? Poison gas?

She started to back up -- and Norden appeared. ShadowCage.

"You came for me," she said, stunned.

"Of course. We're a team," he said and flashed a smile. It looked fake. He glanced at the lock on the door and then looked around. He found the old-fashioned key not far away. In a moment she stepped out.

"Quickly. Stay at my back. We're moving away from here as fast as possible since we know they can sense the ShadowCage."

She nodded and didn't argue and didn't even demand to know where they were going or what took him so long to get her. That could wait. She moved up close behind him and they started away like they'd practiced. He switched on the device and everything looked odd and distorted, but she had no trouble keeping up with him. They went past guards, past other panicked people, and then headed for the open bay area. She didn't think she really wanted to be here -- but then she saw the Norishi. They treated her better than her mother did. Yes -- time to go where someone appreciated her.

This was going to work out. And her mother would be sorry.

CHAPTER THIRTY-SEVEN

Rafe typed in another sequence just before Morgan's pocketcomp chirped. The man sat back and pulled it up, frowning before the expression turned to worry.

"ShadowCage reading," he said and stood. "Hell. Two of them!"

"Close?" Rafe asked.

"One -- Tali," he replied. He stood and started for the door. Then he stopped. "The other is close."

"Away from the door," Etinon said softly.

Morgan wisely obeyed. Rafe stood and moved so he stood behind Etinon and signaled Morgan back with him. Etinon had his weapon in his right hand and held up the left, signaling for silence. He had it, at least in this room.

Rafe saw light shimmered at the edge of the doorway, slow and careful movement. Etinon had perhaps heard something, because he shifted somewhat --

"It's at the door, just stepping through," Rafe said.

Two things happened. Rafe heard a curse; Ekhardt, without a doubt. And Etinon moved with a kind of speed Rafe had not expected. The sword slashed out and struck against the shell of the ShadowCage, sending out a flash of light that unexpectedly blinded Rafe. He almost panicked but he could hear Etinon still moving and then the sound of running feet.

"Go for him --" Morgan said.

"No. I am the guard. I stay."

"Hell," Morgan said though he didn't argue. Rafe blinked the light spots out of his eyes and looked around. He could see a little blood of the floor.

"Got him," Rafe said. "Good. That might slow him down. Ardi -- it was Ekhardt and he's wounded -- can you get someone to follow the trail?"

Ardi had appeared at the door where he had obviously come at a run after having noted the ShadowCage coming their way. He glanced down, saw the blood, and nodded. "They took Tali," he said, and took off at a run again.

"Damn!" Morgan growled. He ran a hand through his hair, glanced at the computer and then shook his head. "Finish the work, Rafe. I'm going to go see if Neva needs anything."

Rafe started to follow Morgan, suddenly worried for Neva but he stopped before Etinon lifted his arm with the sword still in hand, a bit of blood on the edge of the tip.

"No," Etinon said.

"No," he agreed and went back, sitting in the chair by the computer. He watched Morgan leave, and envied the man right then. Neva would be glad to see him.

He hadn't felt that loss in a long time. It came, he knew, from having unexpectedly finding Neva less antagonistic lately. Not friends, but not the enemies she had made of them for so long.

He should have felt better for the change but instead he found it hurt in new ways. He felt as though he had gone into some new realm of purgatory he hadn't known existed. He didn't know his place again.

Damn stupid thing to be thinking about now. He turned his attention back to the computer and forced himself to focus on the data, trying to find a way through the block. Trying, in essence, to think like someone he had never met and who was in a dangerous situation which would result in the destruction of the ship. The Captain had expected trouble and had locked almost all information away. Maybe he expected capture by the Norishi rather than destruction.

Then Rafe realized something he should have considered before this. The block had been put in place *before* the ship had been attacked. In fact, some time before, if he read the timeline correctly. The Ksa had lined the point up where he would see the destruction, but what the captain didn't want shown was behind a block hastily applied over their normal codes, and some time before that point.

Had they seen something the captain didn't want let out with other info automatically picked up by computers at relays and stations? That might be jumping at conclusions, but given the current situation, he tended to think in odd terms. It would have helped if he'd known what the ship might have been doing. He had managed to drag some basic info out of the box and had a name now. The ship had been a free trader out of Tempest called *Intrepid*. Not a military craft.

Would that have mattered to the Norishi? Maybe they didn't know the difference between civilian and military craft. Maybe it wouldn't have mattered anyway.

The Captain of the *Intrepid* had been a man, which also wouldn't have helped if the Norishi realized it. Crew of fourteen: just a little ship, flittering along the trade lines, picking up what they could and not following any regular route. Nothing outstanding in the manifest.

What did they want to hide?

And from whom?

He sat back and frowned at the computer screen which was frozen in that moment before destruction.

"You need a break, Rafe," Yang said. He stood in the doorway. "Things are quieter out there. Maybe we have time."

"Maybe. But I need --" He stopped and looked up at Yang. "We know the Norishi were involved in this. I don't think the crew expected to be killed. The Captain put a quick block into place because he suspected the Norishi might be able to access the ship's computers and he wanted it kept secret."

"Yes?" Yang said, clearly intrigued. "There have been rumors almost from the start that the Norishi could access our equipment. I'm not sure it is true --"

"Doesn't matter if it is true or not," Rafael replied. He

glanced at the screen again. "All they had to do was *fear* that the Norishi had access. So the captain slammed a block into place to hide something. Probably something they saw. He did this quickly because he realized they had Norishi company. Maybe. . . ."

He leaned over the computer, his shoulders protesting the movement and winning a sharp pain through the side of his head. He winced but waved Yang away when the medtech started to protest.

Back to the security level. He typed in one word.

Norishi.

The block cleared.

"Got it! Get Ardi, Morgan, Neva -- any or all of them."

Etinon looked startled and then pleased. "It is good. Now you will know?"

"We'll know *something*," he said. He started to call up files, but stopped. "I'll wait for the others. I don't want to mess with the files without someone else being here as a witness."

Yang stepped back out to the doorway on the hall. Human guards stood there. Rafe had hardly been aware of them. One took off in a hurry, so he knew that it wouldn't be long before one of the others showed up. Good.

"This probably won't really help us, you know," he said, looking up at Etinon.

"Knowledge is always a gain," the Ksa replied. He looked more relaxed again. "We do not know what the Norishi do elsewhere. It is tied to what they do here."

"Maybe so," he agreed. "I hope so. We could use a little help in this mess. We need something we can use to understand them."

Etinon turned. They could already hear others coming. Morgan arrived first and Ritter with him. Ardi followed and they crowded around the little computer. Rafe felt odd with all of them at his back.

"Neva is keeping an eye on things," Ardi said. "Tali and Ekhardt went off into the market area and we're not going in after them. We're not certain what the Norishi are going to do next. And the Click are starting to move as well. And. . . ."

Rafe looked up at him, frowning. Then he nodded. "Displaced."

"Yes. There are a few gathered out over the market. They are less active than usual. Like they're watching."

Rafe nodded and started to turn back to the computer. Morgan, unexpectedly, put a hand on his shoulder. "Are they watching? Are they aware, Rafe?"

"I don't have enough data," he replied, waving off the question.

"Rafe --"

"I think they are aware," he finally said and looked at Morgan. "I suspect they are out there because Ashur is aware that his daughter is in trouble. Does this surprise you?"

"No, actually, it doesn't. I just wanted to hear it from someone who has had more contact with them than I do. Do you know what they want?"

"I think they want *back*," he said. Then he shrugged. "I don't know if it is possible. I don't know what Xenation has done. Let's look at this information on the comp box and see if we can figure out something with the Norishi before we delve into something else."

Rafe could tell that the man intended to pick the conversation up again. None of the others looked particularly surprised by what Rafe had said, either.

Rafe did his best to focus on the work at hand. Etinon, he noted, moved from the door to stand behind him and watch, still guarding. Ritter kept at the door with her device on and guarded. No one else would slip in. For a little while, they could be open about what they found.

"I worked on two assumptions," Rafe said, his hand hovering over the enter key. "First was that the *Intrepid* had trouble with Norishi which we know since we have seen the last little vid where they were destroyed. I worked back from that to where the block is in place. There is a lot of frantic activity; several quick jumps, for instance, but nothing in the computers about why. Two days, Earth Time, earlier, though, the Captain had put a quick block in place. A very quick one and only over data for a 24 hours period. My second assumption was that he wanted something that would be easy to remove, later. So I tried *Norishi* as the keyword."

"Son of a bitch," Ardi said. "If I were any stupider, you could metal plate me and use me as a lamp post."

Etinon made a little coughing sound of Ksa laughter, barely suppressed.

"I have set the data to where the block starts. This was put in to cover a specific amount of data. We'll do a fast scan from there through the first time. The comp box has four main cams and computer feed in the bottom screen. I haven't looked at anything yet. I don't know what we'll find."

"Let's see." Morgan sounded worried and Rafe understood. What they were about to see might be far worse than the trouble on the station. However, Etinon was right: knowledge is always gain.

Rafe hit the keys and started the data flowing to the computer. The images came up clear and fast with data at the bottom, four screens at the top, all showing outward views.

"Looks like they just came off of slide," Yang said. He'd spent time on ships. "We'll need that data clip at the bottom right to give us the location."

Rafe made a quick grab of it, shunting the information off into another file. They'd look in a few minutes. There was nothing they could tell from the vid itself. The stars looked like normal stars, with nothing exceptional to draw his attention. The ship had begun maneuvering, probably turning towards the next slide point. Everything looked so normal Rafe almost found himself relaxing as though he didn't know that something would happen.

"There," Ardi said, leaning closer. "Run back. Something just showed up on the right screen."

Rafe could see a blur of movement where there shouldn't be any. He ran the data back, slowed and tried again.

A ship arrived; the same sort of alien ship that had been heading in for Xenation when the Norishi attacked. And that meant --

"There they are," Morgan said softly. The Norishi craft appeared on the screen. They watched the Norishi destroy the ship and by then the Captain must have known they'd seen something dangerous. They ran for their slide point and left the system.

The Norishi must have followed them and the *Intrepid* didn't have the Click to save them.

"Etinon, what did we see?" Rafe said, looking back at the only alien in the room. He stood at Rafe's left shoulder, a hand on his weapon and Rafe thought that might be a reaction to what he witnessed and not to his worry about protecting the human in his charge.

"They hunt the old ones, I think," Etinon said. He frowned and leaned closer. "Go vack, 'lease. Freeze on a clear shot of the Norishi craft. I wish to know which one."

Rafe carefully ran the vid back. The battle took place far off from the *Intrepid*, but they had got clear shots. Perhaps battle was not the word that he should use. He thought the other ship did nothing at all in defense.

Etinon looked at the screen for a long moment. "It looks like the sane craft as cane here."

"Destroyed this one and then hunted down another?" Ardi said. "What are those other ships? What can you tell us about them?"

"Not enough," Etinon replied and sounded apologetic. "We know little, the Ksa, avout these veings. Not where they cone from, what they look like, what they want. Nothing, really, exce't the look of their craft."

"So," Rafe said, looking up, "As far as you know, the Norishi might even have a good reason to destroy them."

"Yes," he said, but plainly didn't believe so.

"We really don't have anything that will help us except we know two things have been tied together," Rafe said.

"And another thought," Ardi said, leaning closer and staring at the screen. "They destroyed the *Intrepid* because the ship witnessed the attack. I think they might be trying to destroy us for the same reason."

"That may be true," Morgan said. "And that makes me

think that the Norishi couldn't possibly have a good reason for doing what they did. Etinon, we need more information. We really do."

The Ksa looked from Rafe to Morgan and finally gave a quick nod. "I will s'eak to others," he said. "I will ask that they nake notes in hunan and give they to you. What we have is very old, though. Legends and nyths of our old days. Not history. Not knowledge."

"There are often hidden secrets in myths," Rafe said. He stared at the screen again. "We need to find out where the *Intrepid* first saw the alien ship destroyed."

"Give me the data," Morgan said. "I shouldn't have any trouble with the coordinates. We know where the Ksa found the ship and that begs a new questions, Etinon. Did you just happen upon it?"

"They were on a slide 'ath we often take," he said with a shrug that made Rafe think it was the truth. "Quite near the vorder vetween hunan and Ksa s'ace. We have trade 'osts along there --"

He stopped and looked back at the screen, his eyes narrowed.

"Etinon?" Rafe asked.

"If this ha'en in Ksa s'ace, the Norishi destroyed the hunan ship so we would not know they were where they should not ve."

"Where they were and what they were doing," Ardi said with a nod. Etinon mimicked the move and didn't look any happier.

"I'm going to find out where they were," Morgan said.

"And I am going to look this over a bit more," Rafe added, leaning forward. "Would any of you like copies?"

"No," Ardi said. "If something happens, the Norishi will not expect Neva to have given you anything important, but the rest of us will not have that protection."

Rafe nodded though he would rather have had some of the others hold on to the material and look it over. At least this still gave him something to do, though. Something that might be potentially helpful.

"We have information," Morgan said with a slight frown. "Let's see if we can use it. I'll see if I can talk to Neva without our spy learning anything."

Morgan, Ritter and Ardi left. Yang stood at the edge of the door until Rafe looked up. "If there is trouble, I'll treat the injured elsewhere and we'll say it is specifically because no one should be around you."

"I could go to my room," Rafe suggested.

"No. Stay here where the others can come without being too obvious, and where you are closer to the control stations. Everyone is staying close, you know. It doesn't look odd, especially since you spend so much time here already."

"You can trust me, you know."

"No, I can't," Yang replied. Etinon looked shocked by the words. "I cannot trust you to take care of yourself. And I can't trust others -- except Etinon, Morgan and Ardi -- to keep watch over you. They may not be enough if the Norishi come in for you."

"If they come for me -- if they really come in fighting -- then I need to go with them."

"No," Etinon said. He should have realized that Etinon would object. He looked back at his guard, ready to argue the situation, but Etinon leaned down and looked him straight in the face, startling him. "No. You will not go with the Norishi. They do not hold honor with 'risoners."

"You know this?" Rafael asked.

"They kill all 'risoners they take, unless they high ranking fenales of the race. They want you vecause of the link to the station. That would save you for a while. Or they nay have decided that a nale linked to the station is sonething they nust destroy. *You will not go with they.*"

"I need to talk to Neva and make certain no one surrenders," Yang said. He hurried away.

"That's something we needed to know. Humans will sometimes surrender if they think that continuing a battle will lead to inevitable destruction or that it might harm others."

"It is so?" he said. "Then good that they know this is not

an answer."

"Yes," Rafe replied. "Let's see if we can figure out anything else in this information."

Etinon moved closer. Rafe waved him towards the chair where Morgan and sat and worked.

"It is not proper for a guard to sit."

"There are things going on which are far more important than you guarding me, Etinon. It's not that I don't appreciate your work but we need your help to save others. That's more important."

"You do not understand your own in'ortance."

"Then explain it to me . . . but it had better be good to make my life worth risking the lives of others rather than help me find answers."

Etinon blinked several times. Then he looked at the chair. He finally took hold of it and pulled it over. He sat down, stood, moved the chair again, and sat down once more.

"None can get 'ast ne to reach you," he said with a nod. "Let us see what we can learn."

CHAPTER THIRTY-EIGHT

Morgan went straight to the control room to talk to Neva. She looked at him when he arrived and shook her head, but the look had as much disgust as worry at this point.

"She went willingly, the little fool," she said with a snarl. "And they headed straight back out to the market. I don't know what she expects now."

"I'm more interested in what *they* expect now that they have her."

"Oh, yes. I expect they think she'll be able to win them some sort of deal in this mess. Or else they took her because she knows things. But . . . ."

"But they would have killed her easier than taking her," Morgan said.

"Yes. Yes, you're right. Despite everything, I don't wish her ill."

"Of course not!" Morgan replied, shocked that maybe she thought they would expect her to turn on Tali.

She took a deeper breath. "Too much going on," she admitted. "Just too much."

He took her by the arm and led her aside. The others would think they had a personal conversation, but Neva knew better before he even started talking.

"Norishi attacked another of the alien ships and destroyed it. That's what we found on the comp box."

"Damn."

"We suspect they destroyed the *Intrepid* because they saw. It may be what they're trying to do with the rest of us."

"Well, this just keeps getting better," she said with a sigh. Three people began arguing across the room, their voices rising though Morgan couldn't tell what the disagreement was about. "I need to get back to work."

Morgan stuck around and he took the call from Yang. The news wasn't good and he hoped he kept the dismay from his face. The others might only think they discussed Rafe, and they probably expected bad news on that level anyway.

He glanced over at their spy. Did she need to know they had learned something very dangerous about her people? No. The less she knew, the better.

He couldn't get to Neva so he went out to Ardi instead. He found the head of security out by the 'front lines' in a spot where his people had taken up defensive positions near Xenobia and in clear site of the Norishi who stood between the ship and the opening to the Human Enclave.

"You shouldn't be out here," Ardi said. He looked and sounded exhausted.

"From the looks of things, neither should you."

"Just on my last rounds and then at least five hours sleep or at least until the next round of madness."

"Well, I have something that's going to make things worse. Etinon says the Norishi kill all prisoners unless they are high ranking females."

"Shit." He looked annoyed and suddenly seemed less tired. "I'll start spreading the word. You are just a fount of good news, you know."

"I'm just the messenger," Morgan replied. He moved back into the main area. He was tired, too. Time to rest.

This was going to get worse soon. They all knew it.

CHAPTER THIRTY-NINE

They huddled by a stall in the market. Tali was uncomfortable and cold, and Ekhardt kept whimpering.

"You make one more sound and I'm going to kill you." Tali leaned close over his pale face and stared into his bloodshot, wild eyes. "One more sound. I don't need you."

Norden said nothing when Ekhardt gave him a quick glance, plainly hoping for support. Then Ekhardt went still, his mouth clamped shut. Hell, it wasn't even much of a cut there, on his shoulder and the other on his back. They hardly bled at all. What a baby. Why the hell was she stuck with him?

What did she need either of them for?

She looked back at both of her companions. They were hiding. They were weak and useless and she didn't need to be with them, did she? Norden kept looking at his computer and going over things and wasn't even talking to her about what she wanted. Ekhardt needed to be dead.

She didn't need them.

Norden had Ekhardt's ShadowCage. They'd turned it off so they could have one to run later, when the first one ran low on power. The thought of being stuck here with the two of them that long was unacceptable. They were waiting to be caught. She hated them for being so weak.

The shell made everything around them look odd and distorted, but she had seen Ksa move past, speaking that horrible alien language she didn't understand. They probably talked about her -- about what they would do if they caught her. She didn't trust any of them.

The Norishi treated her like she deserved, though.

A glance at the two men, and then a decision. She stood and walked out of the ShadowCage.

"Son of a bitch. You stupid child!" Norden shouted.

She turned back and kicked, even though she couldn't quite see him. She hit something. Probably Ekhardt and that was good enough.

"I don't need you."

She turned and walked away. When she looked back, Ekhardt lay on the floor, trying to move. Norden had abandoned him. Served him right for being stupid and nearly getting caught. He couldn't even deal with Rafael. She hoped he bled to death before anyone got to him.

She glanced up. Displaced moved above her. She hadn't realized it, inside the ShadowCage. She turned to go back to the covering but Norden hadn't told her where he was going. Bastard. He left her out here with them!

She hurried to the Norishi.

And they, wise women, headed to her. She hurried a little more, and came, nearly breathless, into their group.

"Neva's daughter," one of the women said. She had a bit of a sneer that annoyed Tali, but she nodded. "You came from nowhere."

"We were hiding, some men and me. But I left them --"

"Wise to leave the men."

She nodded.

"Come with us."

It was an order and she almost bristled. The woman wasn't her mother, after all. Tali looked back and saw Displaced and Click, so she decided maybe going wasn't such a bad idea.

"You will stay with us now," the woman said. "You will tell us things we need to know."

Another order. She started to pull away from the woman's hold, but she wouldn't let go. He hands felt strange and the stares were not right. They shouldn't take hold of her. It wasn't right and she yanked again and almost got free, but several more of the Norishi surrounded her.

"No. You will come with us. You will tell us what we need to know."

"You have no right to tell me what to do."

Their stares were wrong. Alien. And they wouldn't let go of her. She had expected better of them.

CHAPTER FORTY

Rafe tried to sleep. Exhausted, he stretched out on the bed he knew too well with the monitors reading every spike in his thoughts as he tried to will his body to relax. He didn't think it would be too difficult. He was right in one way. He slipped off into sleep without hardly any trouble.

Unfortunately, this was not to a good sleep. He seemed to be drowning in colors and sounds with everything so strong his senses couldn't take them in and his brain couldn't decipher anything. The senses tried to invade, to suffocate and destroy --

He awoke with a start. Etinon sat on a chair by the bed, watching him. Yang had come to the door. He suspected alarms had gone off.

"Bad dream," he mumbled and rolled over. Back to sleep. Escape the nightmares and the real world for a while --

The nightmare returned as strongly the second time and he was fully sitting up and gasping before he came completely awake. Etinon had a hand on his arm, an odd connection that startled him. Yang came into the room this time, shaking his head.

"This can't be good."

"Nothing lately has been good. You haven't noticed?" Rafe asked. He didn't try to sleep down again.

"I can give you something to make you sleep, but --"

"But then I might not be awake when I need to be," he said with a shake of his head. "Not a good idea, Yang. Something is happening. Something more, I think. I don't want to be unconscious and helpless. Besides, I'm the link to Xenation. You might need me for whatever little help I can be."

"Yes, true." Yang watched the screen over the bed and shook his head. "It's not good, Rafe. You need -- I don't know what, exactly, but something different."

"I wish I knew what Xenation wanted."

Await Key.

He almost snarled at the thoughts in his head, but that already translated into trouble on the screens, so he calmed instead. He wanted to sleep but suspected he wasn't going to get much more.

Morgan arrived at the door only a moment later. From the look on his face, this wasn't going to make things any better.

"I thought you should know that we're reading a huge flux in the station. There's more change than there has ever been before and most of it very close to where we are. The dome cams show something growing pretty much on top of us."

He knew where. He knew the color, feel, shape of it and had felt it there in his dreams as it happened. Even now, he could feel Xenation moving.

Morgan put a hand on his shoulder. "Rafe, look at me."

He realized he'd slipped away for a little bit. Slipped far away, in fact, traveling along the corridors of the station in places he had never walked. The realization probably should have frightened him. He knew, though, what was happening.

"Rafe!"

"Sorry, sorry," he said and pulled himself fully back to here and now. "Something --"

Await Key.

That wasn't just his mind playing games. The words meant something and now he had to wonder what that key might be. However, he looked back at Morgan again and gave a quick nod. No reason for the others worrying. Especially Yang, who had a habit of doing drastic things when he thought Rafe might be in danger.

"I'm okay. Well, in a relative sort of way," he said, which won a moment of amusement from Morgan, at least. "There is something going on with the Station. I felt the change. It's not the boxes growing this time. There are domes and spikes."

"Damn," Morgan said, startled. "You're right. And I assume you have not looked at the vid of this yet."

"He has not," Etinon said. He looked startled as well.

"I am linked," Rafe said, and the thought didn't bother him as much as it used to. "We all know I am, but something has changed. I don't know what, but I'm closer to Xenation this time. It wants some key and I sure as hell don't know what that means or what I would do even if we found it. I think some of the changes might have come from me. I've started feeling trapped here. Maybe I was making more room."

"Ah," Etinon said and nodded as though this made sense. "That is so. And if true, this is not all vad, though trou'ling if you cannot rest."

"I was thinking the same thing," Yang added. "Rafe, you are already running on the edge of collapse. Too much has happened lately."

"I know. I can't change anything, though." Rafe leaned back on the bed relaxing as best he could. "I have the feeling things are going to break soon."

"Vreak?" Etinon asked.

"Change. Things that are building up will finally come to the point where they must be resolved in one way or another."

Etinon gave a quick, solemn nod of agreement. His companion was picking up a lot of human terms and would likely understand a great deal more about humans just from such things. That might be good. He thought that the Ksa and humans would work well together, but the Ksa needed to know about human eccentricities. It might not hurt for the humans to know more about the Ksa, but humans were used to dealing with people from different cultures within their own species and they were better able to adapt to situations with aliens. The Ksa, as far as he could tell, seemed to have a settled into a single set of rules. Or did only certain groups settle together, and those with other rules would be elsewhere?

Something to discuss in the future. He had to deal with Xenation. Then he heard shouts of anger which meant more trouble. He started to stand but Etinon pushed him back down again.

"Ksa arrive," he said. "We will know the answers without you throwing us into the danger too soon."

Rafe had to consider his actions in light of having a guard now and the realization changed how he would move. He was not going to put Etinon into unnecessary danger. Odd way to think, he supposed. His decision would probably have appalled the Ksa but thinking this way would keep him from doing something daring and likely stupid.

Rafe sat back and waited. He could see movement in the hall and heard sounds that chilled him, but he remained still, even while Etinon drew his weapon and waited. Things went quieter, finally, and a handful of Ksa appeared at the door. They spoke quickly to Etinon in a flurry of words, bows, and such exaggerated politeness that Rafe knew something serious had gone wrong.

They backed away, though not far. He thought he now had *guards*, rather than a single guard. He worried the humans might do something that would create friction and they'd have even more trouble. They couldn't be happy with having Ksa standing armed in their halls.

A true and total mess.

"Etinon?" he finally asked.

"Norishi tried to get here. They were 'ushed vack out. I know little nore," he said.

Yang left with medical supplies in hand and Morgan met him outside the door. Yang wasn't gone for long and came back with Ardi at his side. The Ksa did nothing to even slow them as they entered.

"Things aren't as bad as I feared," Yang said. Ardi nodded agreement although he looked frayed. "A few injures, but nothing serious. We think there was at least one dead Norishi, but they took her away with them so we can't be certain."

"This natters to you?" Etinon asked.

"It matters if they say we killed her and that creates problems with the relationship between the Norishi and the humans later. Right now, though? No, I can't say that I care too much except that I hate to see anything die needlessly."

Etinon gave a bow of his head, a true show of politeness. Yang had said something that struck a chord with the Ksa. That he didn't want to see things killed or that it didn't matter right now?

"We have other problems," Ardi said, which didn't surprise anyone. He leaned against the wall, plainly exhausted. "There are far more Norishi on Xenation than we thought. That doubtlessly comes from dressing alike and from the fact we haven't had good security cams up where we could really watch their area. The *Shaw* is sealed and they won't be getting in there from the inside. We don't know if they will dare try cutting in from the outside -- or just destroying the ship where it is -- but that's not something we have much control over. I think they won't because they're going to worry about Xenation's reaction. Neva has asked if the *Shaw* wants to try to cut and run and they've voted to stay in case we need, and can, get to them."

"The ship can try to leave?" Yang asked.

"We've suggested they try. We don't know if Xenation will let them go, though." Ardi looked at Rafe but he only shrugged. "That's what I thought. And one more problem. They have Tali and they are using her as a shield so we're having trouble getting to them. She marched right up to them and let them take her. We don't want to put the girl in danger, no matter how misguided she may be."

"Tali is bound to be a problem no matter what happens," Rafe said with a shake of his head. "How the hell did Neva and Ashur ever end up with a daughter like her?"

"Not something I really want to ask," Ardi said though he apparently felt the same way. "And one last problem:

Both the Click and the Displaced are out in mass."

Rafe felt something he hadn't thought about before, and he wondered if it was his imagination or --

"I think the Click and Xenation are all connected in some way," he said. "I can't really tell you how, exactly, but I think -- I don't know. Maybe I'm just going crazy."

"Well yes, that too," Ardi said and looked far too serious which made Rafe laugh. Etinon clearly didn't understand. He didn't even consider stopping to explain this time. "But you have been right about other odd things. This is something we should probably take under consideration."

"When we have time," Rafe said.

"Yes, of course. Like that's going to happen soon."

Etinon stepped up to the door and took the place to guard again. He looked back at the others. "I think now all is in the hands of the Norishi. We wait."

Rafe wondered if he should tell the Ksa that humans were not good at waiting. He suspected it was something Etinon would soon learn.

CHAPTER FORTY-ONE

Morgan wanted peace. He wanted to return to his work but he didn't dare load the info back into the main computers. Instead, he found himself stuck working with the limited power of the pocketcomp and it wasn't linked to much more than the vid cams. He watched them constantly. Obsessively. He needed to let go. This could continue for a long time. He didn't dare burn out.

Treat this like a research project where he went into a new place with little in supplies. He'd loved the two of those assignments he had gone on despite the wilderness conditions. He remembered, amused now, how he had even loved the idea of not being tied to a big computer system, so he had to rely on his own observations without double-checking every fact with other authorities.

Yes. Maybe this time he needed to study the situation himself and not base everything on what Rafe, Neva or his predecessor in this unfortunate position had written. Treat this like a whole new project.

Morgan began typing down lists of observations and divided them between human, Ksa, Norishi and Click. After a couple minutes he added a list for the Displaced as well, and then another side list for the other aliens, the older race he knew nothing about. He wanted to discuss them with Etinon when this calmed down.

The humans and Ksa intersected on many levels. They seemed to have common goals and beliefs, though he temporized that with a note to ask why the Ksa put a guard on Rafe when the humans had not. This wasn't because Ardi didn't like him or anything having to do with Neva. Maybe this came as a part of the 'group' thought in the humans and that they were all watching over Rafe in their own ways.

This did, however, still point to other, deeper questions. Why did the Ksa protect Rafe? What was he to them? Or did they do this merely because he was their friend and they thought that the humans were not doing the job? They were even right on some levels. Rafe had gone into dangerous situations where he should never have been alone.

Every time Morgan turned around on Xenation he found more questions but rarely any answers. He suspected this would drive him crazy before he left.

Morgan went back to work on his notes, which filled the time. More than that, he found them rather entertaining. A text message turned up; a quick note from Neva. Xenation was going through even more changes. They could see them again on the vids. He watched for a while, trying to figure out --

Ritter appeared at the door. "I caught a signal!"

He looked up, startled and wondering what the hell Ritter was talking about. The woman came right into the office and pushed her pocketcomp across the desk while pointing to a couple graphs on the small screen.

"It's because of all the changes out there," she said, waving a hand towards the walls. She looked exceedingly excited. "I was able to keep narrowing down the bands and I caught the edge of one of the signals!"

"From Xenation," he finally said and found himself growing excited as well.

"Yes, Xenation," Ritter replied with a little laugh. She ran her hands through her hair. The woman didn't look like she'd slept much lately and she certainly wasn't going to any time soon. "The changes have stopped but I think I am very close. The next time, I think I can echo it."

"I don't know if that's wise --"

"Just in our comp system," she said, tapping the pocket comp. "Just so I can get a closer look at the signal and see how closely human equipment can mimic what Xenation does."

"Yes. Good." He looked up and grinned. "Glad to see someone finally making progress around here."

"I really want to be able to analyze the links to Rafe," she admitted and looked almost embarrassed for a moment. Then she stood straighter. "Maybe find a way to break the links so we know we can trust him and so he can have his freedom back. If we have to leave the station, he'd have to remain. I don't like that idea."

"Neither do I. This is good Ritter. Memorize all of it you can in case you need to wipe the data."

"Hell." She looked at the comp, worried now. "This has taken me years . . . but you're right. I don't want the Norishi to get hold of this."

Ritter picked the comp back up, staring at graphs and numbers as she walked away.

"Good work, Ritter."

She gave one distracted nod and went back out into the main work area. A few of the others had come in as well and Ritter appeared to be getting them all interested in her work. Good. Spread the knowledge out. Then he thought of something else. He stepped to the doorway, drawing attention.

"Don't speak of this beyond our group," he said. "We have to be careful of the Norishi learning anything they might use. I'm not worried about the Ksa or the Click for that matter."

He looked at the couple women but that was just paranoia. Once they knew they had one Norishi infiltrator, they'd checked everyone else -- male and female -- and made certain there were no others.

"We have people out there with ShadowCages," Ritter added. "It may be some of our own people we need to worry about as much as the Norishi. They could be anywhere, listening. We can track when the ShadowCage, but we might not be able to get to any of you before you have said something important."

Now there was a good point. "Keep at the work. I'll

discuss this with Neva as soon as I have a chance."

Ritter went back to her desk with her pocketcomp, her mind obviously on other things, reminding Morgan that they could still do work outside of this mess. The trouble would pass, and with Ritter narrowing in on a connection with Xenation things were going to be really interesting soon.

Ardi arrived a few minutes later and gave a quick nod. "We need the ship," he said quietly and then disappeared again.

So he started that ploy in motion. Morgan went over the files one last time and then turned on his main computer. Having the main machine come up virtually empty still startled him. He ran the data through the system, though, checking out current links into the communications station in control. Things looked good.

He bounced a message out to the grow dome which was closest to in line with the usual human jump points, and back again, garbled but distinct enough to make it apparent something was out there, lurking along the edges, and considering coming in.

And, at Morgan's suggestion, they used Brody's voice. A woman's voice (and one the Norishi wouldn't have heard much), because he suspected that might draw the Norishi in a little quicker to the deception and make them believe the ruse was true.

He sent the first message which was hardly more than a note that they'd arrived and awaited more data. In a few minutes Neva would send off coded data packets which was something she told him they had only done when a true military ship had been coming in rather than the usual traders. He waited, watching the info to go out. Then he had to wait because even messages punched through with high power would take a while to get back and forth from the outer edges of the system. Timing would be very important.

Morgan tried to do other work but instead he thought about all the trouble that had made this insanity necessary, and how this really wasn't going to be much help, except to worry the Norishi and perhaps keep them in line for a while.

Maybe something big and dangerous would arrive soon. They had, after all, really requested the help.

He finally sent a very short affirmative on getting the data and to await reply. They would play this for a little while. *Something* would even show up, a bleep or two, on the human sensors. The Ksa would put in their protest. They'd play the game for a little while, at least.

Stupid games.

Before long, word spread through the Human Enclave. Not a lot of people knew the truth and he felt badly, though maybe the humans would feel less anxious and that might help. The Norishi would pick up on the human reaction, which should also help their situation.

A little later, Morgan went out into the hall, past people milling around. He noted fewer and hoped some might have gone to their rooms. He didn't know if that was good or not, really. They might need them --

This wasn't a very big area. They would never be far away. And rest is wise.

The control room looked far too busy after the quiet halls. Even Ardi stood there, and they all looked so upset that the sight unsettled Morgan again. He had just begun to think things were starting to calm. He didn't need more trouble.

"Ardi tried to get Tali away from the Norishi," Neva said. He winced because looking around he could tell things were not going well. "Two Norishi are dead and one of our people, but we couldn't get her out. They pulled her back into the mass of them and there was no way we were going to fight our way through."

"I never thought Tali would --" Morgan stopped himself and shook his head.

"You didn't think she would do something this stupid," Neva said with a touch on his arm. She looked worried about him, and he realized she had finally gotten beyond her guilty feelings about Tali. "I've been thinking the same thing. I don't know what we're going to do. They have her out there in the midst of them, and its plain they think she's going to be some sort of shield to use against us."

"And it will work," Morgan said. "We won't purposely risk her life -- but that would be true of anyone they held. Any sign of Ekhardt or Norden?"

"Ekhardt is out in the market, wounded. We saw him on the vids for a little while. We couldn't get out there to help him even if we wanted to. The ShadowCage is still out there, so that will be Norden," she said. "Norden might have gone back for Ekhardt, though I don't know why he would."

"Information would be my guess," Morgan said. "Ekhardt at least knows this place."

"True."

Morgan looked up and saw their spy coming closer. Time to use that to help them. He put a hand on Neva's arm and squeezed a little. They had to do this carefully still.

"The ship, it isn't too far out, right?" he asked, just a little bit louder than he had spoken before.

"Not too far, but we can't tell if it will come straight in. This kind of ship tends to be stealthy. I think they won't take long, given what we've reported to them."

"Good. Having that many troops arrive will certainly get things in line. And they're used to this kind of trouble."

"Exactly."

The woman moved off in some haste. Morgan managed not to smile, but he did give a nod to Ardi and then towards the woman who appeared to be heading out of the room. Ardi spoke with another woman and she went out as well. Not too obvious, good.

"She'll report now, apparently," Neva said. She shook her head. "I don't need more pressure, you know. I would love to kick her out on her ass, but I'm stuck for a while so we can play this out. Maybe that's good. I keep fixating on her and that takes my mind off of other things."

"Here's something else that might help. Ritter has very nearly narrowed down a bandwidth that Xenation uses."

She looked at him, blinked a couple times, and then laughed. "God, I love living with scientists," she said, slapping him on the arm. "Nothing ever really stops you from working. I needed the reminder that there are still things we're here for."

"I felt pretty much the same way when she brought me the news," he said with a bright smile. "We'll get through this, Neva. We aren't alone."

Which was his way of reminding her that they still had allies even without their fake ship. The Ksa were on their side and he thought that between them they could hold the Norishi back and maybe, if necessary, push them off the station. They also had Rafael, who was a powerful link to the station, if they could find a way to use him.

The Norishi spy soon returned to the room. Best to move on. He gave Neva a last pat on the arm and she turned back to her own work. He went out and looked at the front line, trying to get an idea of what was going on there.

Nothing looked good there. In fact, the sight of the Norishi lining up and plainly meaning to come at them got him to back up even before Ardi started his way.

"This is a mess," Ardi said with a shake of his head. He didn't look all that tired at the moment but Morgan thought that might be adrenaline pushing him.

"They heard about the incoming ship and started moving?" Morgan asked and worried they'd pushed the wrong way.

"No. They were already on the move before they heard." Ardi glanced back at the Norishi and shook his head. "We caught the blip of info passed, so we know she sent the information. They are more agitated, but I think they would have been anyway. There's no way we're going to get to the *Shaw*. And the crew of the *Shaw* have to wonder what the hell is going on since they can't read the other ship."

"Captain Stern is smart enough to catch on."

"Yes. True." He looked back, startled by sudden movement along the Norishi line. They did not, however, move any closer and he gave a sigh of relief. "There is something unsettling about seeing them all lined up like that. It makes them appear less human, I think."

Morgan didn't think the line would make a difference,

but when he glanced back out at Norishi, he felt a chill. There was something just in the way they stood and moved. They swayed now and then, in a sinewy motion that seemed to echo up and down the lines, like a long, dark snake. They dressed alike, they wore their hair alike and even though there were differences in height and faces, they looked unnaturally similar. Necks, which had always seemed a little too long to Morgan, twisted and turned in ways that were not human-normal. In small numbers, you didn't notice such things. Now, in a group of a couple hundred all moving together, they struck him as being . . . wrong.

And that made him want to retreat even faster into the shadowy entrance of the Human Enclave.

"This is going to be a problem," he said softly. "Our people are going to be unsettled before we get to a battle."

"Unless the Norishi hold off long enough for people to get used to this," Ardi said. He turned and looked, as though to force himself to watch.

"Do you think you can get used to it?"

"I sure as hell hope so. The only thing that might save us, if it goes that far, is that they can't stay in a line if they try to get into the Human Enclave again. We can deal with them, I think, if we don't have to fight them out here."

"I don't want them in there. They look --" He stopped and looked at Ardi and back out to the group again. "Ah. They look like people used to fighting as a group and in a line. So far, they've only done raids and we've held those off. If they are used to fighting as a group and in formation, we might be able to use that to help us."

"Excellent point. I hope it doesn't go that far. "

Morgan agreed but he said nothing. Norishi glanced their way; first one, then another and then a dozen. He thought they looked half wild. He had expected civilized people and for the Norishi to be more like the Ksa. Now that he knew they weren't, he wondered if he should trust the Ksa as well.

There was a dark, insidious thought that could, if he let it go too far, either save his life or put him in more danger.

The Ksa were helping the humans. Not to trust them could well put him outside their protection when he most needed it.

Trust. Don't link the Ksa and the Norishi. They were not the same. The Norishi had never been friendly, and now he suspected he saw more of their true colors. He forced himself to stand by Ardi and analyze what he saw. The movements seemed to be linked. He could hear words, a rush of sounds that rose and fell in some pattern. For a moment, he even found himself fascinated by something so totally alien . . . and that helped.

Something triggered them into this behavior. He reached for his pocketcomp but then realized he didn't want the Norishi to see him make any notes or do any readings.

"I'm going to take some readings," he told Ardi. "Behind you, in the archway where they won't see me. There is definitely something going on here, and if I can find some link, maybe we can disrupt the behavior pattern. I just don't want them to realize I'm studying them."

"Conner! Come here!"

Conner was a tall, short-haired woman who moved up beside the two. The Norishi watched her. She was like a beacon to them.

"Etech Doreet needs to do some readings without the Norishi noticing," Ardi explained softly. "So you stand here and talk to me for a little bit while he stands behind us and gets the data."

"I'll do this as quickly as I can," Morgan said, already pulling out the pocketcomp as he stepped backwards into their shadows.

"Take your time," Conner said without looking at him. She had a Tempest accent. "I'll keep the bitches entertained for a little while. Shall I sing and dance?"

"Not yet," Ardi replied. "We're reserving that for a time of true need. It's too dangerous a weapon to let loose this early."

They both laughed as did some other people nearby. Did the Norishi laugh? The Ksa did in their own way, but he hadn't heard of anything like that from these aliens. Did they understand laugher? He doubted it and from the way they looked at the humans he suspected the laugher annoyed them more.

Morgan turned the scanner towards the Norishi and spread the collection net out past the humans, filtering them out. He didn't have much power in the device and he might have to go get something better from Yang. He turned on the full spectrum and knew sorting through this was going to keep him busy for a while. He thought he saw a couple interesting spikes in some of the readings though, but he wasn't fast enough to catch what they were.

Interesting things.

The comp indicated repetition in many of the readings after a couple minutes.

"Thanks. Got it." He shoved the comp into his pocket. "I can't be certain, but I think there are some readings far off the scale from what we've had before. We'll see if we can use them."

"Good." Ardi said and then muttered a little curse. "There's Tali. What a stupid little fool she is. Sorry. I know you've known her a long time --"

"I've known her long enough not to be surprised that she did something this stupid." Morgan could see Tali and she didn't look happy, probably because her new friends were not paying her enough attention. Ardi gave him a curious glance, and he supposed what he knew might help. "Tali has been under care for most of her life. There has always been a disconnect between her and anything outside of what she thought was important.   She had been hospitalized and we think Norden got her out specifically to come here."

"That, at least, makes this more understandable," Conner said. "This isn't wanton 'I'm getting back at my mother' behavior. Not good, still, but at least it isn't the actions of someone purposely trying to cause this trouble."

The sounds from the Norishi grew suddenly louder, the movements a bit more intense.

"Looks like they're working themselves up into a frenzy," Ardi warned and waved Morgan away. "You better get back, Morgan."

"Ksa coming," Conner said looking towards the market.

At least thirty Ksa headed their way and Morgan feared they were about to throw themselves into the fray against the Norishi; or worse, a sudden thought came, that they would join with the Norishi and attack.

His skin went clammy at the mere thought. Morgan fought to get control as the Ksa moved up and took their places in the line with the humans, helping to fortify the defense between them and the Norishi. Ardi thanked them and took his place there as well.

Maybe the Ksa were only here to protect Rafael.

There was no reason to mistrust the Ksa. He had to get the idea out of his head. Morgan looked across the open area and knew they couldn't reach the ship to get away. He had the feeling of being trapped in a little cage, ready to be slaughtered if the enemy came through.

The feeling of panic was not normal for him. In fact, this was so atypical that he suddenly wanted back to his office and look at those readings.

"I think --" he began, then stopped when the others looked at him and rethought some of his ideas. "I think there's more going on here than we can see. Something is setting us off, Ardi. Chemicals, maybe. The same things that are getting the Norishi riled up."

"This just keeps looking worse," he said with a shake of his head. "Find a way around it, friend."

"We don't have a lot to work with here," he reminded them. "But even finding that this exists might help. A thing named loses its power. If others know they're being affected and manipulated by an outside force, they'll work against it."

"I'll start spreading the word."

"I might not be right, you know."

"Doesn't matter," Connor replied and stared out at the Norishi. "Just thinking it might be true will help."

They were probably right but Morgan wanted something

more concrete. He headed to his office, hoping he might find something that could help.

Better than watching the Norishi and doing nothing at all.

CHAPTER FORTY-TWO

When Etinon said he would only rest if Rafe did, Rafael finally stretched out on the bed and forced himself into sleep. Etinon slept on the floor beside the bed while two more Ksa guards stood at the door.

However, sleep itself didn't help. Rafe awoke several times, certain he had heard something. Finally exhaustion drew him fully into complete sleep. He wanted to slip into total darkness, away from all thought, but it didn't happen. Instead, he found himself in a place of colors and sounds where everything melded together and nothing made sense. Even in his dreams, the place annoyed him.

So he started sorting things out. He was a scientist, even still. He wanted to understand what he faced.

Odd things, strange things. He felt disjointed; with a thought he looked at the control center, the bay and then outside looking back at the station. Then. . . .

Places he knew could not be real. Dark places with chanting as figures moved to a primal beat. Then elsewhere - - then many places at once, all of them coming at him in such a surge he could not find his way out again. Drowning in the sounds, buried in the colors --

He came awake shouting something. He didn't know what he had been saying, but Etinon had gotten instantly to his feet and had a hand on his sword. He looked more startled than worried.

"Damn," he said. "Sorry."

He rolled over and went back to sleep. For a while he pushed the nightmare away, but it came back eventually, slipping in around his sleepy thoughts and drew him back into sounds and colors until he thought he almost understood. The process intrigued and maddened him at the same time, and he came awake again speaking more words and still not certain what he said.

This time Etinon already sat on a chair by the bed, watching him. The Ksa at the door looked in, gave a nod to Etinon, and went back to guarding. He could see Yang moving around in the other room.

"I've slept as much as I'm going to for a while," Rafe said and sat up.

"I think this is so," Etinon agreed.

Good. If his guard had told him to go back to sleep again, they might have argued and he would no doubt regret doing so later. He ran a hand over the back of his neck and grimaced.

"Shower," he said, nodding towards the cubicle at the back of the room. "No way in or out for anyone else. I'm going to go get cleaned up."

He did not mention taking care of 'nature' which made him wonder about human and Ksa hygiene, morals, etiquette --

"Shower, yes. And I after you."

That said something, he supposed. Rafe slipped off the bed and stood unsteadily while Yang came to the door, frowning.

"You didn't sleep well."

"I doubt very many people are sleeping well right now," he replied and Yang agreed with a quick nod and went back to his own work. Good. That helped as well.

Rafe headed towards the cubicle, expecting someone to come along and stop him because a shower sounded like a wonderful, great idea and lately things had not gone so well for him. Rafe didn't take a full breath until he had the door closed and locked. Oh, Yang could get it open easily enough, but he thought they might leave him alone for at least a few minutes.

Rafe didn't waste time. He paused at the mirror to note

bruises and cuts; he looked like he'd been beat against the wall a few times. And he felt like it.

He stripped and stepped into the small cubicle, pulled the inner door closed, and dialed the water on for something almost too hot. The shower helped, right until he closed his eyes for a moment and suddenly felt the return of that nightmare. Sucked down into color and sound --

An alarm went off and he pulled himself back from a near fall. The door to the outer room opened.

"I'm okay!"

The door closed again.

He didn't close his eyes after that and started worrying about ever resting again. He could feel his blood pressure start to go up and forced himself calm again. It was only a dream, after all. It wouldn't kill him. Just a damned nightmare.

He could make himself believe that for a while.

When he came out, Etinon nodded and headed straight into the cubicle. Since Yang didn't stop him, he didn't worry about the Ksa adding anything to the reclamation system that couldn't be filtered out. Two Ksa guards stood inside the room and they looked worried enough that Rafael gave them his best behavior. He bowed properly and then settled on the bed and waited for his companion to come back out.

Etinon didn't take long. When he came out, the two guards bowed and quickly left, though one went only as far as the next door that lead to the hall.

"And now?" Rafe asked.

"Work," Etinon said with a nod towards the computer.

Work appealed to him and he went straight to it. He only stopped for Yang to do a quick check with the scanner.

"Well, not really worse," Yang admitted, waving him back to the chair by the computer. "Just different again. You didn't sleep well. Your brainwaves were all over the place. We might have to really put you under, Rafe. Otherwise, I don't know if we'll be able to trust you."

He had started to protest but stopped, because what Yang said made sense. Sleep deprivation could do odd things to a person and he might not even trust himself at that stage.

"We'll see how today goes," Yang said. He looked at his readings and frowned. "If things look calm tonight -- well, we'll see."

Rafe nodded and stopped thinking about the problem. He and Etinon went back to the computer, working their way through the comp box files almost frame-by-frame. He only drew himself away when Morgan showed up. The man looked as though he hadn't slept much lately, either. It made Rafe tired to look at Morgan, and that didn't help his own state of mind.

"I've come up with some interesting things," he said, settling on the bed. He looked like he wanted to just stretch out and sleep rather than relate anything, which made Rafe feel badly for having wasted sleep since it hadn't done him much good. "Etinon, have you been around the Norishi when they prepared for battle before?"

"Not in contact," he said. "Only from craft to craft amid the stars."

"Audio contact? Video?" Morgan asked.

"Audio only. We kee' our secrets," he said and tapped the pocket where he kept his own commlink.

Now there was an interesting comment and one Rafe wanted to ask about, but he refrained. He saw Morgan shake his head, plainly thinking much the same thing. He wondered if Etinon knew the kind of tidbit he had just thrown out to two scientists who had come here specifically to learn about anything alien.

"In the audio contact, did they seem to be making odd sounds?" Morgan finally asked.

"Yes."

"They're doing the same now," Morgan said. "And there's something else. I've done a quick scan and I found they are putting out a pheromone that is creating a level of anxiety in themselves and in the humans. I think they use it to create battle-ready status for themselves."

"Well damn," Rafael said and leaned back. "That would almost make me interested in studying them."

"This is what?" Etinon asked.

"A chemical reaction in the body," Morgan explained. "And it can be picked up by the others around them, so they all get caught up in a single emotion. It isn't affecting the humans the same way as the Norishi, though. The Norishi are also chanting and working themselves into a frenzy."

"Frenzy?"

"A state beyond rational thought. I'm going to work with Yang to see if we can come up with a quick chemical mixture we can use to counteract the pheromone. If we can get something airborne, we might unsettle the Norishi. And it might help our own people who are starting to feel anxious and overly paranoid because of the pheromone. I'm not certain if it affects the Ksa at all."

Etinon went to the doorway and talked to another Ksa. Rafe caught only a couple of the words and not enough to follow anything of what he said. Etinon came back and gave a bow to Morgan.

"They had noticed a change in scent, vut it had not caused they any trouvle and they had not considered this had to do with the change in vehavior. Hunans notice these things."

"We'll see if we can do anything about it," Morgan replied. He sounded worn again. "But I have other things to report as well. We tracked the site of the battle, Etinon. It appears to have been right on the edge the area where humans and Ksa form a boundary. The last stop the ship made before being destroyed was a small colony called Wayland."

"I know this 'lace," he said and frowned. "The Norishi were where they should not have veen. This could ve that which worried they nore than even destroying the craft of the Old Ones. They know we will not allow such transgresses."

"But you let the humans travel there," Morgan said.

"Hunans and Ksa have not had a war that lasted generations."

Morgan clearly wanted to ask questions; he looked at Rafe as though hoping for some kind of answer from him.

He didn't think now was the time to discuss something outside their current war and he did not want to upset the Ksa who stood by them.

"I have come across one other item of interest." Morgan sat forward and Rafe had the feeling they were about to learn something far more fascinating than anything they'd talked about so far. "It has nothing to do with the problem at hand. I did test analysis of the vid of the Old Ones ship to see if I could learn anything about the makeup of the craft. The computer came up with an interesting corollary between the material of that ship and another set we've seen here at Xenation."

"Norishi?" Rafe asked.

"No. Click."

Even Etinon looked startled by that news.

"The ship designs are not the same but there are trace elements common to both that are not common to the rest of us. I tested against Xenation itself as well, but the station was built completely with local materials. There may be other things hidden back in the recesses of the station that match up, though. I would like to think there is a connection, and that's why the Old Ones were coming here. It is possible the other ship was heading here as well, since it was within the jump point lanes . . . if they even use jump points."

"It might be a coincidence that the Click and the Old Ones have these elements in common," Rafe said. Then he shook his head as he reconsidered the facts. "It's unlikely, though, considering the size of the galaxy. So there is probably a link between them. That's just odd."

"The ones least like the rest of us." Morgan said. "The ones we are least likely to understand, too."

Rafe touched the plate on the side of his head which seemed to startle Morgan, as though he had stopped seeing it. "Xenation isn't often talking to me at all, you know. I think sometimes I might be hearing words, but those might be my imagination. I do get images. Odd things. More intense than before, but not what we need. We're going to have to figure this out on our own."

"Yes --" Morgan stopped even before Etinon lifted his hand for silence. Rafael's guard moved quickly to the doorway and stood there. The other Ksa moved closer as well. And a moment later two more Ksa arrived. One had a cut on his arm.

The battle had started.

CHAPTER FORTY-THREE

R afe could hear the battle coming before he caught any glimpse of the struggle. Humans and Ksa fought a swarm of Norishi; bodies fall on both side. The scent of blood almost overpowered him. Xenation seemed caught in the emotions and images swam over him so quickly he couldn't sort them out. He needed to be focused.

The Norishi pressed forward, swinging both bladed and blunt-ended weapons. They were not deterred by so many of their own falling. Those were dragged back out of the way.

Then a Norishi looked through the doorway at Rafe and he knew he was in trouble. The woman let out a banshee scream that was immediately echoed by those around her and spread backwards through the line; the crew of a pack of predators who had found their prey.

They pressed forward, more frantic in their movements, attacking with such ferocity that they no longer looked even remotely human. Coming, he knew, for him.

Etinon moved in front of him as Rafe found the weapon he'd gotten from Yang and prepared to fight. Others moved into the fray as well, but nothing slowed the Norishi now and the narrow halls were packed with them, making it harder for Ksa or humans to attack.

Rafe looked at the wall and considered doing something he had not done in a long time. He could open a door and go through and close it again. He could come out somewhere else, but could he take Etinon, Morgan and Yang with him? He wouldn't leave them here to fight this battle to protect him while he got away.

He wasn't certain how many Norishi died, but there was always another wall of them behind, pressing in closer by sheer numbers. He feared to know how many humans and Ksa died. He feared he was going to see Etinon and Yang fall and when Etinon took a bad cut across the shoulder and chest, he reached out to steady him with one hand, trying to wield his own weapon with the other.

Something hit him hard on the shoulder, his arm going numb and the weapon dropping. He slugged a Norishi as hard as he could in the stomach. Etinon swung, blocking one blow and another but he was obviously weakening from his own wound. He looked frantic.

Someone grabbed Rafe by the arm and yanked him towards the mass of Norishi who yelled with joy. This was not the sound he wanted to hear as they dragged him past another Ksa who tried to grab him back.

More Norishi caught hold of him; long, thin-fingered hands grabbed at his shoulders, hair and arms as they dragged him back into their midst. The air filled with the cries of triumph. For a moment he saw back behind them. Etinon was still trying to get to him, despite his own wounds. His Ksa guard looked at Rafe with true panic and worry.

They kill male prisoners.

But they had come for him for a reason. If they had wanted him dead, he would have been killed by now.

The Norishi were already starting to retreat. He fought because he didn't want to go with the group. They'd gone crazed -- even more so than they had been before. Their touch felt strange, the scents wrong and overpowering. More Norishi caught hold of him until he felt as though he was being held by a swarm of insects rather than anything even remotely humanoid. The sounds they made had no words he could tell, just noises that changed in pitch. Did they mean something? He wanted to understand, to know what would happen --

They got him into the bay area. Humans and Ksa followed, but the battle, thankfully, had died down. He saw

Tali, held by more Norishi, though they didn't have to fight her into going with them. Foolish, stupid child. He thought he could see some of the worry in her eyes now as the Norishi acted oddly.

He saw hope for a moment. The Click massed at the edge of the market in lines that looked far more formidable than he would have expected. The Norishi backed away in haste, hurrying faster towards their own Enclave. Displaced hovered high above the lights, so far off that they were not even affecting the power supplies yet. He caught a glimpse of them, but they weren't coming closer. He could have wished for them right now.

Xenation? Are you paying attention?

The Norishi retreated, dragging him and an increasingly recalcitrant Tali along. Were they going to take him onto one of their ships and leave? He wouldn't survive if they took him away from Xenation and he knew that wasn't something that would concern them.

"I don't want to go with you!" Tali said, her voice sounding strident and annoyed. "Let me go. "

She plainly believed they would. No connection with the real world, he realized. For a brief moment, concentrating on Tali had helped him slip beyond his own troubles but the feeling didn't last.

They turned towards the Norishi Enclave. He didn't think he really wanted to be there, but better than the ship. The others were going to come after him. However, they would be on the offensive, rather than protecting him, which might help.

They were going through the opening into the Norishi Enclave.

Into hell.

The light and the scents changed the moment they stepped into the new area, overwhelming him with something so alien he felt ill. He even heard a cry of dismay from Tali. This was not right. This was not something remotely *human*.

He saw symbols painted on to the walls, things that

curled and flowed, and often ended in a hand holding what looked like a knife. Not a good sign.

They moved quickly through the curving halls and past an opening where he heard chanting and caught a glimpse of Norishi, most on their hands and knees, naked, and moving around a statue of some sort. He only glimpsed the nightmarish scene before one of the captors struck him across the face, howled, and dragged him on.

Not . . . not civilized.

Perhaps not even *tame*.

He felt ill. His skin turned damp and clammy and Rafe thought he would pass out. Almost wished he would, for a little peace. He wanted away from here in any way he could escape.

They stopped at a little room. Cages sat against the wall. He saw a Ksa in one, though he could not clearly see a face. Another held what looked like a dead Click. They shoved Tali into a cage. She screamed and cursed until one of the Norishi reached into the cage and grabbed her by the hair, slamming her head against the bars.

Tali bit her.

They dragged Rafe into a dark corner and there he saw a square box that held a portable power supply. They had ones like it to keep the equipment going in the Human Enclave. This one sat beside a long table, and it wasn't until they had dropped him onto the flat surface that he saw the clamps.

He fought but they soon had his arms and legs held so tightly in place that they almost immediately went numb.

A Norishi leaned over him. She was not like the others: Taller, darker, and her eyes an unnatural grey that seemed to glow in the faint light. She reached toward the power supply and came up with a long, thin wand.

She shoved it down onto his face, along the edge of the plate.

Agony. . . .

CHAPTER FORTY-FOUR

The Norishi dragged Rafe away while the others fought to stop them. Morgan and several people desperately tried to get him back, but the Norishi turned insanely wild. Once they reached the Norishi Enclave, there was no hope. They dared not go rushing in.

The humans and Ksa made a slow retreat, keeping the injured safe as they moved towards the Human Enclave. A band of Norishi was never far away, but they didn't attack this time. He saw how they sometimes glanced to the Click with worry. He hoped the Click remained on their side. They needed help.

He was one of the last to return to the safety of the Human Enclave. Not really safe at all as they knew now. The Norishi had fought their way in once and he feared they could do so again.

Neva met him at the entrance and looked more frantic than he had expected.

"You hurt your arm," she said. She put a hand on his shoulder and he could feel her trembling. "Let's get to Yang."

He almost said he could do with just a quick medpad, but going back to Yang was their small spot of privacy. She only paused to look back at the others, including their spy. The Norishi woman did not look pleased but she didn't look worried, either.

"The rest of you get back to your work. I want a message out to the ship and tell them we need them as soon as possible. Prepare to retreat back into the halls or to take up arms and fight with Ardi if need be. I want not only the

Norishi watched, but the Click, Displaced and Ksa as well."

People went straight to work. Neva turned away, patted Morgan on the arm again, and started down the hall. He almost had to race to keep up with her and the frantic look on her face did more to bring the situation home to him than the battle had. They were in trouble.

The Norishi had Rafe. The Norishi did not trust males.

Rafe had a connection to Xenation and the Displaced.

The full scope of the problem again coalesced for him as they reached the medunit. Two people left as they entered, both with bandaged arms. They nodded grimly. Inside were the signs of others who had come for care. He saw one body covered with a cloth. He suspected there might be more.

A Ksa stood at the inner door. Yang was on the other side and worked on Etinon, checking bandages on his shoulder and neck. Blood -- a light color, odd -- covered the front of his tunic, and he could see more bandages at the Ksa guard's side.

Etinon looked up at them. Morgan had not expected to see that kind of bleakness in the Ksa's face.

Etinon blinked and looked at Neva and bowed his head once. "Why do you think Rafe lead others to their deaths? Why do you think he is at fault for the Dis'laced?"

She lifted her head and looked at him. "Because I was a fool. Because I was blind. Because I needed someone else to blame so that I didn't take the responsibility myself."

"And you were responsible?" he asked, surprised.

"No. It was an accident. Sometimes bad things just happen."

He nodded. "Hunans do not always act logically."

"Humans rarely act logically under extreme stress," Yang added. That won a worried look from Ksa who no doubt realized he was in the Enclave with a lot of stressed humans.

"As far as we can tell, Rafe is not dead. I think if they had wanted him dead, they would have done it here rather than dragging him back with them," Morgan offered.

Etinon nodded but said nothing. He didn't need to. They all knew that still didn't mean anything good for Rafael.

He wondered about Tali as well, but he didn't say anything about her.

"It is hard to see the reasons," Etinon admitted. "It is hard to nake the connections."

"We have to figure out how to get him back. And Tali. The Displaced are very upset," Neva said. "And I don't know which one might be upsetting them. They've been odd since Tali arrived but their connection to Rafe is enough to cause trouble."

"The Displaced are getting harder for Rafe to control," Yang said with a worried glance at Neva as though he expected her to still explode at the conversation. "If we don't even have him, they're going to be very dangerous."

"We need more contact with our phantom ship," she said softly. "We need the Norishi to worry about what's heading here and focus on the problem. We can't rush in and try to grab Rafe back. People would die and we might not make it far enough to get him. We have to do this wisely."

Etinon appeared determined as he stood, despite Yang's obvious disapproval. Morgan could tell they would not be able to hold him back for long. He noticed that even the Ksa at the door looked worried.

Ksa honor might be at stake since Etinon lost the person he had guarded. Or was this something more? He still didn't know why the Ksa decided to guard Rafael. What made Rafael so important? Why did they make that contact with him when they had mostly avoided the rest of the humans until now?

The answer was obvious, of course: Rafe's connection with Xenation. Even if Rafael hadn't been human, everyone here would still be trying to get him back. That was probably something the Ksa didn't realize. Later, perhaps, they'd talk about Ksa honor and human honor, and what each meant.

"I'm going to my office. I have some work to do with Ritter," Morgan said. Neva nodded, knowing what he went to do and getting more 'messages' passed between the station and a ship that didn't exist. "Keep me informed about what's going on."

"Rafael --" Etinon began.

"We'll go after him," Morgan assured the man. "But we will do so wisely. Rushing in now is what they would expect. We have to believe if they wanted him dead, they would have killed him here in this room rather than dragging him away. We have time -- not much -- but some time."

Etinon blinked several times and then sat down on the bed. "Yes. Do this wisely."

"Yang, if you can come up with anything that might disrupt them -- something to counter the pheromone -- that could be a real help when we go in after Rafe."

"I was working on it. I might have something, but it will be crude. It'll be like hitting with a brick rather than anything subtle --"

"Hitting them with a brick is exactly what we need," Neva said, pausing at the doorway. Oh yes, she looked like she might want a brick or two right now.

"Yes. True. I'll see what I can come up with, but we won't have any way to know if this works before the first use. So don't depend on it."

Morgan left and went back to his office hurrying through the empty halls. People had cleaned up some of the signs of the battle though not enough to erase the nightmare from his mind. He needed peace and he wasn't going to find it soon.

Ritter was the only one in the room. Most of the others stood the line at the entrance to the Human Enclave.

"Run another sequence from the ship," Morgan said. "Keep them up until I tell you otherwise. We need the distraction now."

Ritter nodded, grim-faced, and went back to her computer. "I have a timeline worked out. I can handle this as long as no one looks in on me. I thought about moving to my own quarters, but I have roommates and they could inadvertently give us away."

Morgan nodded. "Do the best you can, Ritter. Keep at this until Neva tells you to stop."

"Neva?" She looked up, surprised. Worried. "What

about you?"

"I'm going with Ardi and the others when we try for Rafe. There's no telling what might happen. You have the work you need to do."

Ritter had looked as though she would argue. Then she looked back at the computer and frowned again. "Damn."

"We need you to do this, Ritter. You know enough about how to make everything *sound* right so that I won't worry if I leave the work in your hands. And you won't let the knowledge of what you've done fall into the Norishi hands, either."

"No, I won't," she said. "And it's not like anything is safe here. I can stay and protect the home front. You shouldn't go, though --"

"I need to go. I have the ability to observe things that might help, then and later."

"Ah. Yes." Ritter nodded and though she looked grim, she turned back to her own work and didn't say anything more.

And now Morgan had to wait and to maybe come up with a plan.

To do something to get Rafe back again before they lost him.

CHAPTER FORTY-FIVE

The Norishi had shoved Tali into a tiny cage at the back of the room, put aside and forgotten. How dare they do this to her! How dare --

She huddled into a ball, gasping for breath between bouts of pounding on the bars. They weren't metal, and they made no sounds at all. She screamed in rage a few times but they hit her. She shut up finally and tried to think of a way to get back at them.

And then they would start in on that stupid bastard again. Rafael screamed and not from anger. He said things that weren't even words, though they seemed to mean something to the Norishi. If she hadn't been so angry, maybe she could have figured it out.

He yelled and yelled and sometimes strange things happened in the room and lights changed.

Make it stop!

She knew she was in trouble. Norden wasn't going to come for her and who the hell cared what happened to Rafe? They'd leave her here to die. They hated her.

She realized someone else sat in a cage beside her but he was only a Ksa and no help.

She would die here. She'd never thought about dying before, not in any real sense. Heaven? Hell? The idea caught in her heart and made it pound too hard. She threw herself into the corner of the cage and gasped again and made pathetic sounds, whimpering like a baby. She couldn't stop.

The Norishi left and the lights went out. She started to scream. They couldn't leave her here! They couldn't leave her to die!

"Ve still," someone said, his voice sharp.

The Ksa. She didn't have to listen, so she yelled and cursed and eventually she ran out of breath.

"Vetter," the Ksa said. He shifted and gave a gasp. Pain - - good, she thought. Served him right. "Rafael, friend, are you still with us?"

"S-Saris?"

"This is so."

"I should not be in their hands, Saris. They want something from Xenation."

"Yes, they do. I do not know what they want, vut it is in'ortant we get you away." Saris moved again.

She didn't hear a sound of pain this time. Was that good? They planned to get away. She needed them to be strong. "Get me out of here!" she ordered, anger growing again. "They have no right to keep me here!"

"Shall we take the girl-child?" Saris asked. Asked, as though . . . as though they might not.

Her breath caught in thoughts of heaven and hell again. Of things she'd done and things the Norishi might do to her, like they did to Rafael.

"Rafael?" Saris asked. "Take her or not?"

"It depends . . . depends on if she is helpful or not."

The words enraged her. She felt the anger grow and come up through her like fire. How dare -- But she said nothing this time. She held her hands in fists and even bowed her head, forcing gasps of air instead of screams of rage.

She kept quiet. She could survive this.

And she could get even later.

CHAPTER FORTY-SIX

Wen the lighting in the walls of Xenation started to do odd things, Morgan finally went back to the medunit where he and Yang worked on the mist they'd fire at the Norishi in hopes of getting them confused. No one said what they all knew: That the changes in the station were linked to Rafe and that this could not be good.

They had too few delivery systems for the mist, but some of the women came back with perfume atomizers. That was going to help. Yang took them and cleaned them out to avoid any contamination. Morgan saw regretful looks since perfume was a true luxury out here.

Etinon had called in many Ksa and made it apparent they would go after Rafael even if humans did not join them. Morgan thought Ardi looked like he might be going a little crazy trying to work with them. Neva appeared worried; truly worried for the first time.

"Time to go," Ardi said. Ksa nodded. Morgan moved up by Ardi who started to say something probably stupid like he couldn't go along. Ardi changed his mind. When Neva came to join them, though, Ardi shook his head and would likely have ordered guards to hold her back if necessary.

"Only as far as the opening to the Human Enclave," she said. "Just that far to see you off."

Ardi agreed, glancing over the humans and Ksa before he turned and started away. Morgan kept up with him, Neva at his side. They didn't have far to go to the opening. He could see Norishi out in the bay area and they appeared more crazed than before.

"I don't know how well we'll do together, the humans and the Ksa," Ardi said, looking first to Morgan and then to the others. Etinon was with them which didn't surprise Morgan. "We don't fight the same. Remember that. Watch out for each other."

Morgan nodded and glanced at Neva. She stared out at the bay but not at the Norishi this time. Instead, she looked up to where several of the Displaced moved back and forth and around in obvious agitation of their own.

She turned to him, her face pale. "I could lose all of you now," she whispered.

And he knew what she meant. Neva could lose everyone she knew and loved, from Tali to Ashur . . . to Rafe.

He put a hand on her arm but said nothing at all.

"We have a limited amount of the mist," Ardi added, lifting a small atomizer he held. "We're going to hold off using this until we are within the Norishi Enclave where it won't disperse far. That's unless you hear me yell 'mist' in which case, start firing. It probably means we are about to retreat, so be prepared."

They formed two lines, the first line to hit the Norishi and scatter them, the second line push on to the Norishi Enclave.

This was not going to be that easy. The Norishi knew they were coming.

Morgan didn't have time to worry. He moved in the first line with the others, Ardi to his right and Felice to his left. She looked formidable enough to break through on her own. He thought that might be a good thing, to have some of the women in the lead.

They had a long ways to go across the bay. The Norishi just stood there as though they didn't understand . . . as though they thought the humans and Ksa would never dare attack.

This reaction made no sense unless the Norishi had evolved as the top predators on their own world. Did nothing normally attack them? But they had fought the Ksa, though perhaps only in ships. Maybe face-to-face battles were something new to them. No -- they knew about lines, about working themselves up to battle. Perhaps they only fought internecine wars with their own kind; savage and ruthless, but both sides following the same style of engagement.

Maybe, since no one had tried to get Tali back from them earlier, they thought she was safe to take. And Rafael was only a man. Stupid things to be thinking about now, he supposed, but this was part of his work and his passion. He filed the thoughts away for future study.

The Norishi started to form their line far too late which won a fierce grin from him. He didn't normally like the feeling of superiority in games of strength, but their mistake gave him power right now. They needed an edge.

The Ksa leapt forward and took on the Norishi, forcing a break in the gathering line. He saw a Ksa go down and a Norishi yowled in victory, but another Ksa moved in quickly and took her on.

He still didn't think they were going to get through. More Norishi poured from their Enclave, screaming in anger. The Click began moving in as well. He leapt aside in shock when one rushed at him and he heard others give a cry of surprise --

And then shouts of appreciation from both humans and Ksa as the Click attacked the Norishi, some bearing them down under a mass of fur. He saw blood, and heard the cries of pain which sent a new shiver through him.

"Morgan! Go with the Ksa!" Ardi shouted.

The Ksa had already broken through to the entrance of the Norishi Enclave. Etinon moved beside him, an arm around his chest where blood showed, though the wound didn't slow him. They had their break and the Ksa were obviously heading in, with or without a human.

He thought, for a brief moment, just to let them go, but he moved on anyway. He wasn't certain if that came from the feeling that a human should go to rescue of another human or if he didn't want the Ksa to think they were cowards. Perhaps he just wanted to see inside the forbidden area of the Norishi Enclave.

The moment they crossed into the area he felt a strange, almost overpowering sense of *wrongness* wash over him. Even the Ksa slowed this time.

"Strange," Etinon whispered, moving to walk beside him. "Too strange. You have the device?"

"Yes," he said, forcing his voice to remain calm.

"Good. They arrive."

Norishi rushed them, but these not in uniform. Some wore nothing at all except for paint or tattoos. They did not look much like humans this time, despite the similarity of shape.

Morgan pulled out the atomizer and sprayed. Nothing --

But that was only because his mind raced and he had no sense of time. The Norishi took two breaths before they reacted. The ones in front looked stunned. Some went to their knees. The others, farther back in the line began to scream in rage.

He sprayed the next group when they came close. He didn't know how they were going to find Rafe in here, except he knew the Norishi Enclave was not any larger than the human one since they could read that much information with scans of Xenation. It seemed, however, to be a warren of little cubbyholes.

And then he realized the Displaced moved with them. He felt a chill and saw the white movement along the ceiling. A swirl moved to the right down another hall. He looked for a moment, wondering --

Ashur appeared before him -- hovered there for a moment -- and then headed down the side hall as well.

"The Displaced are leading us!"

The Ksa moved with him along as wall. Morgan became aware of fighting behind them though he didn't look back. He'd worry about getting out when they had Rafe. And Tali, if she was there. And if she wasn't? Would they go looking for her? Or was that to whom Ashur led them now? They'd already committed to going this way. They'd get whomever they found and decide afterwards where to go next.

They fought hard, pushing through one group of Norishi and then another and Ksa were not going to turn back. He was out of spray in the atomizer, and the Click had not come this far. It was just the he and the Ksa now. He hoped this daring confrontation counted for something.

CHAPTER FORTY-SEVEN

Rafe heard a yell, and another, and then the screams of enraged Norishi. The sounds came closer and he pulled at the metal constraints that held him in place, wanting out before they reached him again. He knew the movement wouldn't work and the generator sent small shocks through him each time he yanked against the metal. He didn't stop. He knew they would arrive soon and from the sounds of rage, he knew he didn't want to be in their hands.

"Rafael, ve still!" Saris ordered.

He held for a moment until something moved in front of his sight, barely glimpsed there in the dark. He cried out in dismay and tried to pull free --

And something else. Whitish, filmy -- cold.

Displaced had found him. He didn't know why and he didn't know what insanity made him think this was good, but their presence gave him unexpected hope, even though they were acting oddly distracted as they hovered near the ceiling.

Ashur swept down towards him. Rafe could clearly see his friend as he hovered there for a moment, then he moved down to the Norishi power generator. Rafe didn't realize until that moment what they intended to do. Ashur and the others threw themselves at the power supply, draining away the charge.

This wasn't like when they came after human power sources, though. Rafe could see that the work affected Ashur oddly and his body rippled with colors when he drew back. He went in again. Others followed.

"No! Don't --"

They weren't listening to him. He wasn't certain if they ever really had. He tried to reach Xenation but that made his head pound with new pain until he feared he would pass out.

He saw something else that might give him more hope even than the displaced: People were fighting in the hall. He saw Ksa -- very many of them -- and Etinon in the group. He spotted Morgan and wondered what the hell he was doing here. This was insane --

Light flashed from the power source and he felt the bands on his arms and legs lessen, which proved a new agony as blood rushed back into hands and feet. What good would it do to get free if he couldn't get away? People were fighting to get here. He had to --

Rafe yanked his arms upwards. The straps gave way on his right arm and then the left. He couldn't sit up, but he could turn better to see the battle. The Norishi fell away from the door, but the fierce battle continued. He wanted to go help. Instead, he sat up, got his legs free and swung them over the edge of the table; more agony as he fought to keep control.

The Displaced moved back to the ceiling. They seemed unsettled, and glittered with odd colors. He prayed they hadn't been done themselves any lasting harm. Then they swept out of the room and down at the Norishi, which drew startled cries.

Why were they helping him? Why the Ksa? He didn't understand.

"Go --" Saris shouted. He hadn't realized how loud the battle had become. "Go out with the Ksa, get away --"

"Not without you," he said. He wouldn't leave anyone behind for the Norishi.

And Tali? Saris first. Rafe struggled to his feet and stumbled over to the cage. He had trouble moving his hands, the fingers tingling. He blinked a few times and finally saw the indentation at the top of the cage. He shoved his finger in and hoped this was the lock.

The cage door popped open. Saris all but fell out and

got slowly to his feet. He looked battered, but he caught hold of the cage and stayed there, nodding to Rafe. "I will help get you out."

Rafe looked at Tali's cage. She stared back like a rabid little animal pressed up against the bars, glaring at him with wide eyes and a snarl on her lips. He felt truly tempted to leave her there but he wouldn't do that to Neva. He just couldn't.

So he let her out as well. She cursed as she stood and even took a swing at him, as though he were the enemy. Saris looked as though he might shove her back in and he might not have argued too much. Maybe he could have convinced himself it wasn't his choice, and be able to face Neva --

If any of them got out of here. He could see people dying at the doorway -- Norishi and Ksa, and the sight made him ill. They were not going to get back out --

Etinon pushed his way through the battle and straight to him. Morgan was at his back. They were both bleeding from cuts and Morgan leaned against the wall a ways inside, gasping.

"Good that we found you again, Rafe," Etinon said, a hand on Rafe's shoulder. "Ah, Saris, glad to see you as well, friend."

"Get me out of here!" Tali demanded shoving her way forward to stand between Rafe and Saris. Rafe had started to reach for her but he drew his hand back and shook his head.

Etinon looked her way and what she saw in his face stopped any tirade she might have thought to start.

"You are not ny child," Etinon said, leaning down to look her in the face. She started to back away, but Saris put a hand on her shoulder, holding her there. She went white. "You are not even ny s'ecies. I have no reason to take you out of here. If you cause trou'le, I will nake certain you cause none else."

Her mouth shut. She yanked herself away from Saris, started to move towards Rafe and then wisely changed her mind. She stood alone by the cages. And she stood there very quietly.

They weren't going to get out, though, so it hardly mattered if she finally behaved. The battle grew worse at the doorway and Morgan moved closer to them, nodding grimly. Rafe needed to sit down -- but not on the table where they'd held him. He shuddered when he looked there, and leaned against the wall instead --

The wall brightened, surprising the others.

"I'm an idiot," Rafe said, pushing away from the wall. Etinon and Saris both turned his way, concerned. "I know what to do, but we have to move quickly if I can get this to work."

"Do?" Etinon said, a little hope in his face.

"Open a new door." He crossed to the end of the room and laid his hands on the wall which again brightened beneath his touch. Xenation knew him; the walls did not brighten where the others leaned.

A long time ago he had been working in the new Human Enclave, setting up offices and singing scales as we worked. It had been a kind of voice practice he played at sometimes, shifting the scales randomly to see what he could achieve.

And a door had opened. He thought it chance the first time and since he had been doing random scales, it took him some time to get the same combination again. He had worked hard to refine the set; however, after the accident with the scout ship, he had stopped opening doors. He feared the link with Xenation more than the others would ever realize.

Now he bowed his head, called back the sequence that had never really gone far from his thoughts, and sang.

"What the fuck --" Tali said, and then shut up. "Oh no. No. You're not taking me in there --"

The door had started to open. He brought the opening about half as wide as a normal door, hoping to be able to close the space faster.

"Get through," he said. "Quickly!"

Morgan obeyed, dragging Tali along with him. She fought. Rafe couldn't imagine why, but he shoved her through. Saris followed, but Etinon stayed at Rafe's back.

"Go through --" Rafe said, waving him towards the door. The Norishi had noticed and were trying to force their way into the little room.

"No," Etinon said and looked him right in the face. "You go first."

"Get the rest of the Ksa to leave the battle and come through, then!"

"No. Norishi will cone in too. We go, and you seal the door and give the rest of the Ksa and the hunans elsewhere a chance to vreak off vattle and get away. They will stay there, 'rotecting us, until we are clear."

Rafe wanted to argue. He wanted the Ksa to come to safety with them -- but he knew it would be dangerous anyway. They dared not turn their backs on the Norishi, and he wasn't certain how fast he could get the door closed on the other side.

"Damn." He squeezed through. Etinon came a heartbeat later. The Norishi screamed on the other side, and seemed to have gone so crazy the Ksa had little trouble fighting them back. That gave him hope. A few more of the Ksa who had been inside the room came through with them.

He sang and sealed the door closed.

Quiet. Such silence he thought, for a moment, they were truly somewhere else. There could not be a battle just beyond the wall.

"It is good," Etinon said, his voice soft.

Rafe brushed his hand against the wall and brought up a little light and then a little more because he couldn't actually see the shape of the room yet. This place proved to be larger than any area outside of the bay. The room was long and wide, so he couldn't see the scope of it yet.

"We need to go towards the Human Enclave," he said and waved his hand to the right. He feared he couldn't walk very far. Everything hurt. "I don't want to open a door too soon and find ourselves back in Norishi territory."

"Good idea," Morgan said. He had tight hold of Tali who still glared. They'd just saved her life. What the hell did she want?

She didn't know what she wanted. She'd never made a connection with them or with anyone else and probably not even fully with herself. It made her trouble for everyone.

"Can someone hold her?" Morgan asked, dragging Tali forward by the arm. "Otherwise, we'll be hunting her down in here and I'd be real tempted to not bother. I don't want to do that to Neva."

Odd how they both felt that way. Saris stepped forward and caught hold of Tali by the arm. She tried to pull away.

"Do not." His hand tightened.

She must have seen something in his face because she finally went still. Morgan nodded and drew out his commlink. "Ardi? Can you hear us?"

"Faint. . . ." The words disappeared and came back. "Door? Where --"

"Rafe opened a door. We're going to try to reach Human Enclave and open another."

"Can't. . . ."

"We're going! Pull back! We're out!"

Static.

"He will have heard from the Ksa," Etinon said. "They'll know where we go. Rafe?"

Rafe nodded. He took a step forward and then stopped again, with a hand to the wall.

"Odd --" he said and shook his head. Things were dancing in his head. "Odd --"

And Xenation began to scream at him.

CHAPTER FORTY-EIGHT

Morgan leapt forward as Rafe went down to his knees, his head bowed to the floor, injuries having caught up with him. He wasn't the only one who moved to catch hold of him. They needed Rafe if they were ever going to get out of here. They needed --

Lights flashed and the others looked around, startled. Afraid.

The walls and floor moved with a sudden, sharp undulation that nearly put them all to their knees. Lights brightened and dimmed and the designs in the wall moved in ways that made them painful to watch.

Displaced seeped through the solid walls with agitated movements of white and blue that swirled in around them. Some seemed to be less real than they had been before while others looked almost solid.

Frantic.

"Rafe?" Morgan asked, putting a hand on Rafe's shoulder. He didn't respond. "Rafael?"

"Something wrong," Rafe whispered. He shook his head and finally looked up. It was hard to see his face in the changing light. "Something interfering with Xenation. Trying to talk. Trying to understand. Sounds, symbols --"

He grimaced and the station reacted with a violent wrench that nearly put Morgan down. "Something is trying to talk to Xenation? The Norishi?"

"No. Human? Human words? Not talking, but she heard? Trying to find again? Confused."

"Oh hell." Morgan's finger's tightened. "Ritter found the

right bandwidth!"

"It neans?" Etinon asked. He had a hand to his side again and looked as pale and almost as unsteady as Rafe.

"One of my people has been trying to match the frequencies Xenation puts out. I think she must have managed. The system isn't linked into anything in the station itself, but Xenation must have still picked up what she did." He held tighter to Rafe who had begun to tremble. Morgan fumbled for his commlink with his other hand. "Hell, hell. Too much going on. Should have thought this through --"

"Make him stop!" Tali screamed. She pushed Etinon aside and he went down to his knees with a grunt of pain. Morgan reached for Tali as she attacked Rafe and caught hold of a wild animal. She screamed and kicked and hit until Saris finally grabbed her and dragged her back. Etinon and Morgan reached Rafe at the same time. He was down, his eyes closed, his face bleeding, but then it had been ever since they got him away from the Norishi. Morgan couldn't tell if he was conscious or not.

"Damn!" Morgan glared at Tali. The Ksa had her tied up and gagged. Morgan took several breaths to bring his temper back into line and gave a bow to the Ksa guards. "Thank you."

Saris nodded and crossed to the three of them. The light flickered brightly again and made the shadows move oddly. Displaced hung near the ceiling, not quite as distinct as he was used to seeing them. Morgan feared these random changes would destroy them.

And Rafe.

He still had the comm in hand. He pulled it up. "Ardi! Neva!" Static at first and then faint sounds. He heard distant voices, but the comm wasn't getting much of a signal. "Damn." He stared down the length of the room. "I have to head for the Human Enclave. I need to contact the others --"

"We all go." Etinon started to grab up Rafe, but he plainly didn't have the strength.

"Follow when you can," Morgan said as he stepped away. "I need to reach the others as quickly as possible. They may not know this is the computer link, if it really is the problem. I need to get Ritter to shut down; she isn't locked into the system, but obviously Xenation is monitoring more than we suspected!"

He turned and started to jog away only to find Saris moving with him.

"We go," Saris said. "Go. No tine."

Morgan didn't argue. He didn't think having Saris along would help until he thought about things he might run into. He didn't know what lay ahead in the dark. They might even find themselves back in Norishi territory.

Morgan followed the edge of the wall, the commlink in his hand, watching for a stronger link while the connection wavered from bad to worse. The walls glowed with lambent, chilling colors moving from dark reds to a strange black that almost glowed and hurt to look at. He stared at his feet and kept moving.

He felt the floor start to buckle and reached to brace himself against the wall but it moved as well. In the next breath Morgan tumbled across an area that seemed to have lost all sense of up, down, left or right. He hit hard against the walls and bounced.

Something caught hold of him. Saris had snared his right arm and held on through more of the bounces and turns. The movement slowed. Stopped. Then the changes came on again, though not as rough. Morgan had no idea where they were. He had lost all sense of direction, and when he lifted the commlink he somehow still held, the device didn't show any better -- or worse -- reading than before.

He and Saris sat where they were, quiet for a moment as the light flared around them. The floor rumbled and moved, though not with the same intensity as before.

"Are you all right?" Morgan finally asked.

"Well enough," Saris answered and bowed his head. "And you?"

"Bruised, but nothing worse," Morgan said. His arm bled from an earlier wound and he thought another might be bleeding on his back as well, but neither cut was serious. He cautiously got to his feet and offered a hand to Saris who took it and stood slowly, as though testing his ability to stay there.

Saris had blood on the side of his face and blinked in a way that made Morgan think he had trouble seeing. He didn't know if he should ask. He didn't know what he should do, in fact -- and it occurred to him, suddenly, that he didn't know nearly enough about Ksa protocol. Probably a stupid thing to worry about right now, but he did anyway.

"I must ask for your forbearance in this," Morgan said as they started walking. Saris gave him an odd side-ways glance. "I don't know the rules for dealing with the Ksa the way that Rafe does. I don't even know as much as some of the others on Xenation."

"This is a little thing to worry avout now," Saris said with a bow of his head. "Vut appreciated. We are strict anong our own, vut learning to ve nore acce'ting to other ways now that we deal with the hunans. You are fascinating. Vut alas, with no sense of direction. This way."

Ksa humor? He found himself grinning, despite the situation, and followed the person who had thrown himself into this danger to be with him. And why?

"May I ask questions?"

"Certainly. Hunans always ask questions. We do not always answer."

"Fair enough. And you know, this means you can ask me questions as well. That's only fair."

He saw Saris give him an odd look again. He wished he had some idea what his Ksa companion thought just then. Not that it mattered in the trouble at hand but it helped him to think about something else. He had no control over Xenation.

He glanced down at the commlink and found the bar a full green.

Morgan jabbed at the button. "Hello! Ardi! Neva! Can you hear me?"

"Morgan!" Neva shouted back. Saris looked pleased. "We have problems -- we think the Norishi have tapped the computers -- everything going wild --"

"Not the Norishi. Xenation. Ritter -- I think Ritter found the frequency!"

"Hell. What do we do?"

"Shut down everything. Get Ritter to clear out what she did."

". . . you?" she said. They were already losing the connection.

"We have Rafe and Tali out of Norishi hands. Rafe opened a door before the computer and Xenation interfaced. Bad for him and the station."

"Hell --"

"Get everything shut down! Restart in safe mode."

He heard nothing but static and the reading slipped over to red again. He lowered the commlink and looked at Saris. "I don't know how long this will take."

"Then we should rest here," Saris said. He leaned against the wall and then slid down, sitting on the floor with a wince of pain.

Morgan glanced back the way they had come, hoping -- but no. Even as he looked, another wall slid into place, changing the pattern and blocking off the path where they had been on only moments before. No going back to the others.

He looked at Saris and slid down beside him.

"This is a hell of a mess," Morgan said. "I don't know how we'll get out of here."

"Rafael will cone for us."

Morgan looked at him, head tilted. "You have a lot of faith in a human."

"Is there a reason I should not have such faith?" Saris asked. "Do you not share it?"

"Actually, yes I do. Rafe won't abandon us."

"And that is what I velieve as well. This has nothing to do with s'ecies, but with individual." The flashing lights suddenly slowed and settled into a soft glow and the floor stopped moving. "Ah. Is vetter."

"Better," Morgan agreed. "So, let's talk about culture,

shall we?"

"Ah yes," Saris said and looked pleased. "This is a good suvject."

Morgan laughed. He had the feeling he'd found someone also looking for answers everywhere. Maybe they would trade a few.

CHAPTER FORTY-NINE

From one breath to the next, everything went calm, quiet and still. Frighteningly so for Rafe who felt as though he had suddenly gone deaf; an odd deafness in the brain as well as the ears.

He heard the sounds of relief from others and realized someone was holding him, shoulders pinned to the floor. Etinon finally released him and sat back on his heels. Rafe didn't know what had happened, but he ached in every inch of his body. He turned over and stared at the distant ceiling and the faint Displaced. He tasted coppery blood in his mouth.

He was really tired of this.

"Easy friend," Etinon said when Rafe started to sit up. "Easy. All is quiet."

"Calm," he agreed and took a deeper breath. He blinked again. "It's all changed. The room."

"Yes."

Lights brightened along the wall with a soft, calm color that allowed him to see a little more. They had four other Ksa with them. Tali sat, bound and gagged, at their feet. She glared, of course, and kicked when he looked her way. He didn't bother with her.

"Morgan? Saris?" he asked because he remembered they went on to do something.

"Went to try and contact your 'eople," Etinon said. "To get sonething to quit. A 'roblen with frequencies?"

"Ritter," Rafe said and finally sat up. "Ritter finally made the connection. Not quite what we expected."

Etinon put a hand to the back of Rafe's shoulder. He couldn't have stayed sitting without the help. He felt as though the room moved and it wasn't Xenation's work this time, either. He'd had a hellish few days.

Rafe watched a few Displaced still lingering near the ceiling, almost out of sight. They appeared to be far less frantic now. Good. He did worry for Morgan and Saris. He thought he knew what direction they had gone, and maybe . . . maybe he could find them, if he could open the doors to get there. That would also be the way they wanted to go, towards the Human Enclave and what safety they could find.

And if the Norishi came for him again? He shivered at the thought and made a silent vow to himself that he would not survive to go back into their hands, no matter how Xenation tried to control him. The thought didn't bother him too much. Probably shock, still. He felt drained and unable to focus on any emotion at all. However, when he looked around, he did find a cause that would get him moving. He had to help the other Ksa.

"We need to get out of here," he said. He looked at the closest wall and frowned. "I don't want to take us back into Norishi territory. We are lucky that no door opened for them during that mess. Any idea of where we should go? I've lost all sense of where I am."

Etinon nodded and gave a wave to the area straight ahead. "That way to the hunans and the Ksa. Vut I fear there are nany walls vetween us. Nany trouvles."

Rafe sighed agreement and started to stand. Etinon reached to help him but another Ksa slipped in and did the work instead, reminding Rafe that his companion had already been wounded.

The best thing to do would be to get Etinon and the others to safety. He walked ahead until he reached the wall and laid his hands on the surface, but he could tell something felt wrong.

"Problem," he said softly. "I can't feel the station like I normally do. She's pulled back, I think."

"You cannot nake another door?" Etinon asked with a

long-fingered hand waving to the wall. He didn't look as worried as he probably should be.

"I don't know. I'll try. This may take longer. I think I might have to get her attention focused back on me."

"Ah." He stopped and frowned a little. "Why she?"

"Why female? We often think in genders, but just as a convention. For some reason, we tend to think of objects as female. That's probably bad." He gave a little laugh, feeling odd. Maybe having Xenation so far away made him feel free.

He didn't want her back. He would have just walked away. Maybe he could leave --

And then he looked at the wall before them. She might realize they were trapped here and let them out. She might. . .
.

He laid both his hands on the wall again and bowed his head. "Xenation, we need your help."

Odd. He thought in basic, but the words were not in the human language. He heard several Ksa hiss in unison. He looked back at them, surprised by the sound from people who normally held their emotions in place.

"What just happened?" he asked and in basic this time.

"I do not know," Etinon replied. He leaned against the wall this time, looking drained. "Say again."

"I was talking to Xenation," Rafe said and waved a hand towards the wall. "I need her attention. And I know the words weren't in basic. I knew it when I spoke, but I have no idea what the language was."

"S'eak to her again?" Etinon asked.

He looked at the wall and tried to focus, which wasn't easy. He really didn't want to drag her back to him. But he did want the others safe and that outweighed the hope he might be free of the tie. He needed to get her attention back.

"Xenation. We need your help. We're trapped. I need to get the others out of here."

Not English again. Etinon's eyes went wide which was not the kind of reaction he expected to see in a Ksa.

"I seem to have made a connection with the Station," Rafe decided. "At least in words. I don't know how. I'm thinking in one language -- at least I believe I am -- and speaking in another, but only when I direct the words specifically to Xenation."

"That is good. Still. . . ."

"Tell me what's wrong."

"You s'eak an old language. One not heard in eons, though written in our history. It is called the Ancient Tongue; the words of the ones who came vefore."

"Before what?"

"Vefore anything we know. Sone say the ancients took us to our worlds, Ksa, Norishi, Hunan and even Click."

He was not nearly as shocked or upset as he should be, and perhaps fascinated that he might have made a connection to something so old. Something to study. "Fruit from the same tree."

"This neans?"

"It's a quote from someone on Earth. He said it when the human-like aliens turned up on other worlds. We are all fruit from the same tree, only the seeds were scattered on different grounds."

"Wise. Yes, it is good. You understand then."

Rafe started to say that this wasn't something all humans believed but he decided not to pursue that kind of discussion. He didn't think any of them were up to a discussion of philosophy just now. However, something else occurred to him.

"Did you know this station was connected to your Ancients?" he asked.

"No," he said with a shake of his head and a look around, as though he reconsidered everything he had seen before now. "Sone few had claimed it so, though they were . . . fringe? Not of the whole. We ignored. Thought it a wonder enough to draw us here with hunans and even the old enemy, the Norishi."

"Old enemy."

"Yes. Long war with they, vut long ago, too. We avoid, nostly. S'ace is large. But they cone here and we stay. Quiet enough until now."

"The ships the Norishi destroyed, were they ancient?"

"We have feared it night ve so," he admitted. He looked at the others. Rafe wondered if any of them understood basic. He suspected most of them did. "We have not seen such craft, you know. Only old carvings in caverns of the ancestors, on a world long lost to us. We have only drawings of such."

"Your home world -- you lost it?" he said, intrigued probably beyond politeness.

Etinon frowned and Rafe started to lift his hand in apology, but Etinon shrugged. "We lost the world in a very old war."

"With the Norishi."

He nodded without even a pause this time. The news did not settle Rafe's worries any. "A war, nore than ten generations ago. We had gone, new to the stars. We are a different 'eople now. We do not know that they are, but we do not fight the old war. Our craft are our worlds. We have little of the world on which we grew. Vut knowledge of the Ancients stayed with us. And now . . . there is you. And it seens this station is connected to our nyths. Shall we die now, with this knowledge?"

"Not if I can reach Xenation. I must be calm."

Etinon nodded and said something softly to the others, and then stood close by, silent. The area had gone quiet, except Tali made some noise and fell silent in the next breath. Rafe didn't look to see what they did.

He leaned his hands against the wall and forced calm, calm, quiet. He could feel her, out there still, confused. *I am here. I need your help.* But she feared all things human, even him. Influx. Data corruption. *It will not happen again. A mistake.*

He didn't think that she -- whatever she was, really -- understood. But he drew her closer, finally.

"I think I can do it. Get the others ready," he said softly.

Etinon moved away. He heard soft whispers. Rafe leaned forward and sang the sequence of notes as a door opened a little, and then a little more the next time which was enough. They went into a new long and narrow room.

Etinon lead him forward and nodded after they had gone quite a ways.

"We are near the hunan area," he said. He frowned when the light began to change and the floor moved a little, but Rafe wished it to stop, and it did. "I think we need to get the others out, yes? Then find our friends?"

"Yes," he agreed. "Here?"

Etinon looked at the wall and nodded. He had his hand on a weapon again.

Rafe put his hand to the wall it brightened immediately, but it seemed to Rafe that there was something frantic in the light and the sensations. He could feel Xenation start to pull away again, but he called her back and spoke aloud again.

"We need a way out," he said softly. "We need the others to get clear. If you do not want us to go out here, show me a better place."

Calm for a moment. The light finally settled in the wall and he sang a door open.

Trouble. Outside he found Norishi, humans and Ksa fighting. This was not the kind of trouble he wanted to walk out into, but the battle was not right on top of them. In fact - - he realized this might help because they were almost entirely behind the Ksa and human lines.

"Out, along the edge of the wall and into the Human Enclave!" Rafe ordered. Etinon agreed with a quick nod and relayed the information to the others.

They got them out, one group and then the next with Tali in hand. She, at least, finally didn't fight anyone. The Norishi didn't notice until the third set had started just out of the door, and by then it was too late for the enemy to get through to them.

"Go," Rafe said, waving his hand towards the group when they stopped. "Etinon -- go with --"

"No. I know what you will do. Close the door. We will go for Norgan and Saris."

"If I close this door it could trap you if I am unconscious."

Etinon looked at Rafe from head to foot and back again,

but still gave a nod for him to continue. Rafe sang the door closed and moved away with Etinon at his side. Xenation whispered to him, curious, wondering perhaps why he didn't escape. He didn't know if she understood about honor.

Etinon did. They turned to the other wall, and he started to open another door. He hoped they found the two soon.

CHAPTER FIFTY

T ali looked frantically from side-to-side as the aliens carried her across the open area. They had not quite reached the safety of the Human Enclave before the battle rushed in on them again. She saw the Norishi trying to reach for her. She saw them with their wild faces and their inhuman stares --

Then humans surrounded her group, protecting them. A few steps later they reached the archway into the Human Enclave. She didn't like the way the humans took her from the Ksa and handed her off, like a bag of grain shuttled from one to another. They didn't untie her. They just passed her back and back and finally someone sat her down and untied her legs and then her wrists while someone else undid the gag.

"You're safe now --" the woman said.

She stood up and hit her, right in the face and hard enough that the woman went down and didn't get back up. She kicked the next person who came close enough. How dare they! How dare they treat her this way! How dare --

An entire group began to close in around her. She yelled and cursed. How dare they --

But the people bore her down and held her there while she yelled until she ran out of breath. Her mother stood there staring at her as though she was some kind of animal they'd dragged in. And beside her was the medtech.

She tried to fight again but he leaned down and put an injector against her neck. She felt the cold touch and then the coldness swept through her body, loosening her hold on her muscles, forcing her to relax. She glared. She could do that still.

"You can let her go," Yang said. He stepped back and gave her a look of sadness, as though there was something wrong with her. She hated him. Hated them all. She tried to curse, but even her mouth wouldn't work now. "We'll have to keep her sedated, Neva. I'm sorry --but the brainwave readings are an indication of true psychosis."

"She shouldn't have been let out," her mother said. There was something sad and pitying in *the woman's* stare. "I'd kept track, you know. I studied every new technique I could, even from here. I would have heard something. Norden used her. He got her out of the facility and lead her along, bringing her here because they knew she would take my attention."

Yang looked nodded. "I think so. I'm sorry."

"You bastards. You evil, bastards," Tali said. Her voice slurred from the drugs. "You'll lie about anything to cover up. You always hated me. You did this to me -- you made me --"

Neva had started to pale. Good. She hated the bitch --

And then something moved, a film of white that slipped down from the ceiling and she found herself looking into the ghostly face of her father. He looked sad. He reached towards her.

She screamed. She screamed and screamed, and even after he pulled away, she screamed. Even after Yang gave her something, she screamed even if only she could hear the sound in her head.

CHAPTER FIFTY-ONE

E verything remained calm, giving Morgan hope things were going better beyond the little area where he and Saris sat. He checked the commlink, but the line remained dead. He wondered if that was his equipment or if everything was still down on the human side.

Patience. He needed patience.

"The Norishi took ny connunications device, alas," Saris said. He'd been sitting with his eyes closed, and Morgan hadn't been certain he was even still awake. His Ksa companion looked battered.

"That's all right," Morgan said and forced himself to lean back again. "I'm just anxious. I want to know what's going on out there."

Saris nodded. Was that something he had picked up from the humans? Was the nod something they shared? He wanted to understand the Ksa now more than he ever had before. But he looked away from his companion and around the room where they were stranded instead. That intrigued him enough that he stood, finally, and crossed to the wall across from him. He was surprised to find Saris do the same.

"You can rest. I just want to see this."

"I cannot rest," he said. He brushed a hand across his face and grimaced. "It is vetter to nake use of the tine given to us. This is an odd room, yes?"

"Yes," Morgan agreed. He reached out and brushed his hand across a small ball-like protrusion, and then leapt back when it lighted. So had Saris. It made Morgan laugh, though the Ksa looked uncertain of the reaction.

"My apologies," Morgan said and bowed his head again. "Sometimes being startled amuses us, as long as there is no real danger."

"Ah." Saris nodded and let his hand brush against another ball which created a different light, but didn't seem to do anything else. "We do not trust that which cannot ve ex'lained."

"And we tend to believe everything can be explained, eventually. So we spend a lot of time working at finding the answers."

"Is that not . . . frustrating?"

"Only if you believe you cannot find the answers," Morgan said. He looked around the room and back at Saris again. "There are limitations, of course. I am unlikely to find many answers to the secrets here on Xenation. However, I know that everything I learn will help lead someone else to learn more. I become part of the answer, even if I do not ever live to see the whole."

Saris looked at him, eyes gone wide, blinking several times. That had to be a look of shock. "We had not seen the larger 'attern."

"The pattern? The way in which humans work together?"

"Yes." He looked intrigued this time and leaned against the wall. "We thought you had no links at all."

"We are linked in many ways, and separated by other things," he said. He pulled out the commlink -- habit -- and looked at it again. Still dead. "I hope Rafe can get to us. I really don't like to rely on someone else for rescue, especially someone who has had so much trouble already. I do think Rafe will do his best to get us free, though."

"I do not understand," Saris admitted. He looked straight into Morgan's face. "How can you have such faith in other hunans? There is no 'attern to what any of you will do. There is no connection."

"We form connections through friendship, companionship and common cause. Sometimes it is enough just to be human to form a connection to another human, especially in times of danger."

"Ah. Vut not at other tines."

"Not usually. And there are those, as you have seen, who do not make any of the basic connections and are a problem for the rest of us, like Ekhardt, Tali and her companions. They will always look to their own gain, even at the cost of others. There have always been humans who follow such paths."

"And you do not try to create a 'attern, to 'ull everyone in so that there is a whole?"

"In small groups we sometimes do. People join together for like causes, and common interests. However, larger groups can be dangerous. Humans who willingly submit their identity to the larger whole are very easy to manipulate. There are those who will create such groups for their own gain and then use the group to hurt and destroy anyone who has not joined. You would have found such an association impossible to work with because the Ksa could never be one of them."

"Vy veing diverse you are able to accept nore into your associations."

"Yes, exactly. We do have some specialized groups. Our military is one which others come most often into contact with. In the old days, the military would have been very aggressive, and sometimes they still are. However, now days the training teaches them to deal with groups that are outside what they might have been raised to believe is normal. They had to adjust because we have spread to so many worlds, and changed in so many ways, that it produced conflict when there shouldn't have been any. And now, because of that training, they were able to deal with aliens without it causing even more trouble. There are a few pockets of the military that remain more aggressive than the others, though. Those could be a real problem. And unfortunately, an incident like this could bring such a group to Xenation. We don't want them here."

Saris still looked uncertain. "You do not trust they?"

"No, I don't. Neither does Neva -- or at least she hasn't

in the past. She may have changed her mind. Humans are apt to do that as they gather more information. It is also, sometimes, a measure of age and adjustment to the life they lead. We sometimes become more settled and accept things we rejected when we were younger."

"They nove into a different 'attern."

"Yes." Morgan looked around the area and shook his head. At the least the company was good, though he still glanced at his commlink and wished for contact. "They're busy out there," he said. "Trouble everywhere. Oh, and Ardi is someone who used to be in the military and that's why he's good at security work."

"He left the nilitary 'attern to take another, vut related, yes?"

"Yes."

"Hunans are intricate."

"Ksa are not?"

"We . . . we have nade our 'atterns. We did this to hold on to what we were when we went to the stars and so when craft neets craft, there are no nisunderstandings. We are the 'eople of the stars, and it is in'ortant we hold these ties."

"What do you do when you go home?"

"Hone?" Saris said, as though he didn't understand the word.

"When you go to your home world. The place where you species began."

"We have not had a hone world for nore than ten generations. Hunans had never veen there, so we thought you knew."

Morgan found himself intrigued -- and a little worried. "There are a lot of places humans have never been. We assumed you just didn't want outsiders on your home world. However, you started somewhere, though."

"Yes. We had a world," Saris said. He leaned his head back. "Ksti, the lost 'lace. We had a war with the Norishi and now the world is gone."

Morgan couldn't speak for a moment at the implications of what Saris said. He'd seen Norishi ships and knew they were dangerous. He had never considered them in war, though. Confrontations here and there, but not worse.

He thought Saris looked surprised by how much this news had affected him, as though such a tale couldn't be of any real interest to humans . . . who were outside the pattern.

"But you live here in peace with the Norishi," Morgan finally said. "Or at least you did."

"Not 'eace. Only quiet. Vut when they noved against hunans, we stand with you vecause they are old enenies, even generations later. They do not change. The Ksa, for all our rituals and 'atterns -- we change. They see neither 'ast nor future. They have only now."

That made them, somehow, more frightening.

CHAPTER FIFTY-TWO

Rafe stumbled as he moved beside Etinon, feeling as though he had gone being merely exhausted and aching. He refused to rest until he found Morgan and Saris, though he had more trouble getting doors to open and Etinon had to keep him heading in the right direction.

"They would go to the hunan area. Norgan wanted to contact hunans. Saris would lead he this way."

Rafe nodded. He didn't doubt Etinon knew the proper direction. However, his voice was going, and Rafe feared that soon he wouldn't be able to open any doors at all.

He felt along the wall trying to locate a place to open. The wall rippled and he tried to sing one section open, but it didn't budge. Was it his voice? Was it something more? Xenation felt distant again and he feared he wasn't strong enough to make the connection.

"I'm sorry," he said, looking at Etinon. "I don't think --"

Movement. Displaced appeared up along the ceiling and then down the wall. They hovered at one point, began to show agitation as they spread out, and then went back to the same point. Rafael moved in that direction and they calmed and pulled back again.

"Showing you sonething," Etinon said which was what Rafe had been thinking.

He was able to open a door here and they entered a huge room and better lighted than any he had ever seen before. They both stepped inside, Etinon at his side and with a hand on his weapon.

The door sealed behind him. He had *not* done it and he

turned back in shock.

"Rest," Etinon said. "This is not a location to rush, I think."

He nodded agreement, looking out into the well-lit room. New patterns covered the walls. And he could see seven halls, though each section only seemed to go a few feet before it ended in a wall. He took a step forward and stopped again, feeling unsettled. This was not like any other place in Xenation.

And he felt closer to the station, as well. Was that because of where they were? Was it because of what had happened? Was it not real?

"Rest," Etinon said again and took hold of him, pushing Rafe against the wall. He hadn't realized he had started heading for the halls again. "Rest and let ne rest with you."

"Ah." That won through, where care for himself would not. He thought Etinon might have realized it would, and for a moment he distrusted being manipulated. The feeling passed. He leaned against the wall and even closed his eyes, but only for a little while. Etinon didn't argue when he pushed away the next time.

The walls glowed with soft yellows and pale blues, the occasional patterns darker and more fluid than those in the outer areas. He thought he saw words this time. He wondered if his closer link to Xenation allowed him to see more. A shame that it didn't really help.

"Any suggestions on where to go now?" he asked. "Which way will take us to the Human Enclave?"

"One of those three," Etinon said, waving to the right three halls. He frowned. "I can't ve certain, ny friend." He pulled out a commlink but he had no luck with it and shoved the device away again with a shake of his head.

Rafe started towards the one on the farthest right, then shook his head and stopped again. He looked up.

"Maybe." He looked back at Etinon and gave a slight shrug. Even that movement ached. "Maybe the Displaced can help us again. I fear to go wandering off and not have the energy left to get us back out again. I don't want anything else to go wrong."

Etinon nodded. "Ask of they. The Dis'laced led us to you."

He looked up again which made him dizzy so he put his hand on the wall. "I need help," he said. "I need to know the way to Morgan and Saris."

That produced some agitation and movement, and finally the Displaced began to move down the middle of the three halls. He couldn't say the choice really meant anything, but he followed anyway. At least he didn't have to make the decision and right now that was enough for him.

Stupid, probably. Likely not sane. However, they began to move, which seemed wiser than standing still. He opened the door at the end of the hall -- and there he found something unexpected.

Click everywhere; not only on the floor, but on the walls, a few traversing the ceiling. Some of the pets, too, though they were gathered back in a corner with four of the older Click. Protection from intruding humans?

"This is odd," Etinon whispered. His hand started to go for the weapon and pulled back.

Click had stopped moving. Some came down from the walls and quite a few gathered around Rafe and his companion, herding them out into the hall. He looked back to see a Click attach himself to the area by the door. He could hear the creature hum.

The door closed.

What the hell was going on?

CHAPTER FIFTY-THREE

They had been earnestly discussing, God help them, courtship rites among humans and Ksa. Morgan wasn't even certain how they drifted into such a strange topic and one he normally would have approached only after a long study on native taboos --

But it had been a good discussion. An interesting one which had passed the time. After a while, Morgan had even stopped looking at his commlink so often.

"We do not --" Saris stopped and frowned. Maybe they had moved into territory they shouldn't discuss. "I -- voices," he said, with a tilt of his head.

Morgan heard them as well. Human? Ksa? The room began to grow brighter, and a wall started to move to their left. They both stood, worried.

Before the door had fully opened, a band of Click rushed into the room, startling both Morgan and Saris. They both backed up as the creatures raced around the room, first ten and then twenty or more. Morgan couldn't keep track of them as they climbed up walls and swarmed across the ceiling. Displaced began to move with them, white filaments flowing along the ceiling.

"This is odd," Morgan finally said. "This is --"

"Morgan! Saris!"

Rafe pushed his way into the small room with Etinon. They looked like they had gone through hell and he wondered how Rafael even stayed to his feet. From the way Etinon hovered nearby, he suspected the Ksa guard wondered the same thing.

"What is going on?" Morgan asked with a quick, nervous glance as a group of Click suddenly surged up the wall.

"I have no clue," Rafe replied. He started to sway and put a hand on the wall. Click moved in around him, and he looked bothered. "They're opening doors, Morgan. They're . . . I get the feeling they really are more closely aligned with this station than we ever considered."

"What now?" Saris asked, his own hand to the wall as well.

"We go. We go wherever the Click want to take us."

Going with the Click was an odd, frightening experience. Morgan wanted to understand what was going on, but only because if he understood, it wouldn't be quite so . . . so alien. He hadn't really believed Rafe about the Click and the doors until they opened one right in front of him.

"Damn," he said and looked at Rafe.

"I know. I have no idea what it means. I think, though -- I think they are --" He stopped his eyes going wide. "Hell. *Key.*"

"Key?" Morgan asked. Rafe sounded breathless and when Morgan moved to help keep him to his feet, some of the Click made quick tapping sounds, and the entire group slowed down.

"Xenation. Awaiting Key."

"What the hell are you talking about?"

"I thought --" Rafe stopped and looked at him, frowning this time. "There are times when I can hear things from Xenation. I thought it wasn't real, to be honest because what I heard was in Basic. Why would Xenation use basic?"

"Because she's been learning the language to be able to talk to you, I suspect," he said.

"You think so?"

"Yes, I really do." They moved into another corridor and more Click joined them. "Hell, Rafe, you should have talked to someone --"

"I'm tired of talking to people about the things in my head," he replied, and sounded, for the first time, more than a little put out. "You know, none of this was my idea. But

I'm stuck with it. Stuck here. And really -- I'm just tired of it all."

"Yes, I understand. But --"

"But, yes." He sighed, glanced at the walls, and shook his head. "Xenation kept saying things like *Sequence Run. End. Await Key.*"

"Yes?"

"I suspect the Click gave me the key."

Etinon made a quick, odd sound that won laugher from Saris. It must have been a show of surprise, shock, or annoyance. Probably all three from the look on his face.

"What the Click gave you in the Ksa market."

"Yes. I started getting the 'await key' messages only after it came into my hands. Hell. Yes, I'm an idiot, Morgan. You don't have to say it."

"I wouldn't. I didn't think it. Even if you had told me, I would have said that you were 'hearing' things that were trying to help you make sense of what was going on, and probably had nothing at all to do with reality."

"Reality and I are only passing acquaintances these days."

Morgan laughed. Click made sounds but none appear as agitated now, so he began to think this might be working out well. They went around another corner, and Morgan slowed despite himself. Walls curved away, halls opened up -- and he thought he say something very strange far down one.

"Is that one of the ancient's ships?" Morgan asked aloud. He got out his pocketcomp and began to point it in that direction, hoping to pick up some information. "I want --"

The Click didn't slow and wouldn't let them stop. They kept moving past walls that were almost transparent and where they could see things they couldn't quite make out.

Morgan tried to get at least a little glimpse of everything they passed, moving the pocketcomp from side-to-side as it downloaded video and other data as well. He worried, though, that he would have to dump this if they ran the risk of falling into the Norishi hands again.

Damn, stupid situation. This was starting to annoy him.

That probably said something about his mindset and sanity when he wasn't as upset about his life being in danger as he was when he wasn't allowed to collect data on something interesting.

Maybe he ought to be amused.

Rafe stopped -- just stopped and put both hands to the semi-opaque wall beside them and leaned forward. Morgan feared he had been about to collapse and Etinon must have thought the same thing. They both reached for him --

"No!" He pulled free of both and leaned closer to the wall, even while the Click tried to get them moving again.

Morgan looked through the wall and his heart gave a quick, hard beat as his mouth went dry. Human ship, a scout. Damaged: he could see the breaks in the hull through the rippling glass. He knew this had to be the ship Ashur had been piloting.

Along the far wall he could see huge tubes, lit from within, and what he thought might be people within them, though he thought some of them might be damaged as well. The shapes were right, though and given the Scout ship in the same area, he had to believe in the link. He saw panels that looked as though some sort of computer lined the area below the tubes, with graphs moving across the glassy surface. He wanted to know that those lines meant, but he could hardly see anything clearly. Brighter light -- yellows and oranges -- moved everywhere, quick and slow; no Click were beyond the wall.

"Oh hell," Morgan whispered. "Oh hell, hell --"

He didn't know what to say. He couldn't draw the entire scene in and understand any of it. His mind went back to the video of the accident and minute and a half where static filled most of the view. In that moment the ship and everything aboard her -- everyone aboard her -- had disappeared. They had all assumed Xenation had destroyed it to avoid worse damage.

What had really happened?

"Not dead. Not really dead," Etinon whispered. He sounded shocked as well. "This . . . We nust go, ny friends.

We nust not distress the Click."

The Click leading them through this area had grown agitated, circling around, some climbing up the walls and even the glass. Rafe looked around, his eyes half wild -- but Etinon took hold of him and started him moving. Rafe started to look back, but Morgan moved in the way so that he couldn't see.

"This is for later, Rafe. We cannot deal with it now."

Rafe said nothing. He moved forward and didn't look towards any other walls they passed, his head bowed, his breathing ragged.

Morgan remained silent as well. He wanted to believe they were going to find their way out of this mess. He wanted to believe the Displaced were not dead, but the situation created an entirely different set of problems. What would he tell Neva?

More complications. They didn't need more complications.

He dared not think it might be hope as well.

CHAPTER FIFTY-FOUR

T ali sat in the chair in the medunit and yanked at the bonds that kept her wrists down and her ankles secured. She wanted to hit people. She wanted to kick. They didn't have the right to hold her here like some animal.

"It's too dangerous to keep her drugged for long," Yang said from the doorway. They had her in a little room in the medunit, secured to the bed.

Tali looked up to see him talking to someone just beyond the door. She couldn't see who it was and didn't care. The shadows moved oddly and the walls drifted in colors. It wasn't right and she hated it all. She yanked at the bonds again, and this time an alarm went off. Yang looked back at her.

"You shouldn't do that. You'll hurt yourself."

She hated that stupid, fucking, condescending tone people always used with her, as though she was some kind of mental case that couldn't understand anything unless they spoke quietly and softly. The words enraged her.

"Let me out of this. You don't have the right --"

Her mother appeared at the doorway. She shook her head with a sad, resigned look.

"Cut that motherly love crap," Tali said. She yanked again, winning another alarm. "Don't pretend like you give a damn about me. If you did, you wouldn't have me locked up here like a prisoner."

"You're too dangerous to let loose," she replied. There was no emotion in her voice. The look of loss, fear and worry had disappeared and that left Tali feeling oddly afraid this time. Nothing there she could manipulate? Nothing she could reach? No ties left? "You are too dangerous to yourself and hellishly too dangerous for anyone around you."

Rage grew like something alive within her, clawing to get free. She yanked and yanked until she saw Yang go to get the damn hypo again.

"How can you treat me like this? How can you keep me a prisoner --"

"We can't trust you, Tali, and you know it. I can see it in your face," Neva said. What Tali saw in her mother's face was something different. Acceptance? What did that mean? "People have told me for years that there was nothing I could do to change you. Your father tried to tell it to me, but I ignored his words --"

"You're lying. He never said that. He wanted you to suffer! He wanted you to pay -- to pay for everything --"

"Your father and I had a good life together, Tali. But we had stopped being a real, married couple a long time ago. Being married was a convenience and a way to get jobs like the one here. This might not have been a good idea in the end, but we came, and whatever happened afterwards has no more to do with you than anything else had for a long time. I wish there was a cure for you Tali. I really do."

"My friends will come for me," Tali said. She leaned forward and looked into her mother's hawkish face. "They'll come for me and you'll pay for doing this."

"You have no friends. They won't come for you because no one needs you, Tali. You served one purpose. You were here to distract me while they did other things. It worked. It will not work again. If the Norishi asked for you right now, I'd give you back. You are not important."

The words stunned her. She fell silent, trying to find her own answer-- trying to find the rage, but everything had slipped away, even without the hypo.

Her mother lied . . . that was all. She lied. They would come for her. *Someone* would come for her.

But she doubted and that made her angry. She started to

shout and didn't know what she said, but Yang moved in and put the hypo to her neck. The drug took her will away and melted her anger. She wanted the rage back. It was all she had.

"I'll start making arrangements to ship her back to the hospital," her mother said.

And she walked away.

CHAPTER FIFTY-FIVE

Rafe stumbled as they went through yet another door. Morgan caught his arm, but he went to his knees anyway, trembling with exhaustion, pain and emotions. Etinon moved to stand at his back, and Morgan knelt beside him. Click moved all around but they seemed less frantic now.

The wall closed behind them. He wanted to go back and free of the Displaced -- or was that a stupid thing to think? What was happening with them? He had to think this through. He wanted answers. He wanted --

His head pounded. He thought Morgan said something but he couldn't make sense of the words. He wanted rest so he bowed his head and stayed that way until they made him move again.

"We have to go," Morgan said a little later. The pounding had eased back to a dull throb that swept through his entire body with each heartbeat. Morgan had hold of Rafe beneath the elbow and got him up, but that wasn't going to keep him to his feet. Etinon slipped in beside him and caught Rafe around the waist.

"You shouldn't --"

"Vetter to kee' you noving, friend," Etinon said. "Vetter we go and let the Click quiet. We do not wish to nake trouvle here since they have given us aid. I see the vay veyond the door. We are almost out, and then we shall go to the Ksa Enclave. We will find safety there. The Norishi will not dare to cone for us."

Rafe really didn't care where they went, as long as he

could rest for a while. However, he found himself watching the Click as they moved in around him. Strange, strange creatures. Clicks and pets. So much had happened lately and so much they didn't understand. He'd been so fascinated by the Ksa that he hadn't looked much beyond them, even to the Norishi.

They were nearly to the opening out to the bay, but to the right he saw something so inexplicable that it did make him stop and stare. A pile of . . . *things* nearly reached the high ceiling. Ksa things, human things. Maybe some Norishi as well. Click and pets moved over the small mountain, picking up items and sometimes taking them down and away. He stared. So did the others and the Click didn't even try to get them to move.

Morgan had his pocketcomp back up and pointed at the pile of items. The Click took items off to the right, into an area he couldn't see. Rafe kept very still and watched, but finally turned to Morgan.

"What the hell is this? Treasure? Study? Loot?"

"I wish we had some way to figure it out," Morgan replied. He looked around. "There's something going on."

The Click had grown agitated again and he almost felt as though he was catching their emotions. Something happening. Something --

"Damn." Rafe bowed his head and closed his eyes, and there in his mind's eye he saw the problem. Xenation had been trying to tell him for some time but he'd been too overwhelmed with everything else to listen.

"Rafael?" Morgan said.

"There's a ship coming in. Another ship of the Ancient Ones. The Click want us back with our own, I think."

Etinon hurried Rafe away from the view of the strange treasure and started out the opening even before Morgan was ready to move. Saris jogged ahead, unsteady himself, but going to get help from the Ksa. Rafe didn't want more Ksa to take on the work of protecting him but he really had no choice. They moved quickly once they were in the bay but still a long, long ways from the Ksa Enclave and even farther from the human area.

"Are they coming in?" Morgan asked. "Are the Norishi going to try and destroy them again?"

He had not considered the larger picture and the trouble with the Norishi. More trouble. There would always be trouble. He tried to get a feel for what was going on but his head ached and the visions he saw made no sense this time. He didn't know if the confusion came from him or from Xenation. He hoped it was him because he didn't want to think the station still reeled from contact with the human computers.

Bad timing for that connection though he understood how it happened. He knew Ritter was trying to find the frequency. Xenation had been more active than usual, so she'd had more chances. And, he realized now, Xenation had been the one to make the bigger mistake. Xenation had sensed something akin to herself and tried to contact, which Ritter never would have done from her end.

The Click went with them to the edge of the Ksa area. Then they turned and rushed back so quickly it made Rafael nervous just to watch them.

"I sure as hell wished I knew what that was all about," Morgan whispered. He still held the pocketcomp tight in his hand.

"Stay here or on to Hunan Enclave?" Etinon asked. He looked past the abandoned market as more Ksa moved in around them, a comforting sense of protection.

"Which do you suggest?" Rafe asked.

"Hunan," Etinon said. "Hunans have a knack for naking things ha'en. It is the 'lace to ve when there is trouvle."

"Except that we sometimes make the trouble ourselves," Morgan pointed out.

"You . . . invite it in. Vetter not to wait for trouvle to take you unawares."

They started moving and Rafe almost protested. He wanted rest. Maybe if he could reach Yang, he would have it. That gave him, finally, a real goal.

And if the Norishi came for him again?

He would not go with them. He had expected, despite everything, that they would be more human-like. He had not expected what he saw within their Enclave, and even thinking about it now made him shudder. He would have nightmares.

The market had seen too many battles in the last few days. He looked around in dismay at ruined booths and items strewn everywhere. Brody's stand had been completely knocked down, and he could even see a scattering of the precious shells. He wanted to stop and pick them up. He even slowed for a moment, but the others were not going to let him tarry here, especially when they could see the Norishi starting to gather near their own location.

"I am damned tired of the Norishi," Rafe said. He tried to judge the distance to the Human Enclave and whether or not they would make it before the Norishi caught up with them. "I need another knife. I'm not going to stand passively by let the Norishi try to take me."

"We will halt they," Etinon said. He looked at Rafe as they paused a moment. Rafe wasn't the only one suffering from the last few days and Etinon looked almost as ready to collapse as he felt.

"I had been judging the Norishi by human standards, and thinking all the rest of you would behave in the same way, as well," Rafe said. He stared at the line of Norishi, still too far away to see clearly.

"Hunans are new to such encounters," Saris said. He looked miserable but he kept with them for some reason. Morgan stayed closed to Saris and nodded in a way that made Rafe think the two of them had discussed such things. "You are not used to judging outside your own kind."

"We need to learn and quickly," Morgan replied. "We want to survive this place."

The Norishi started towards them but Ksa and humans got in the way. Rafe tried to keep moving but it finally took Morgan and another Ksa to get him safely past Xenobia and into the archway of the human area.

"Good you all made it back," Neva said, breathless as

she rushed out to meet them. She put a hand on Morgan's arm. Rafe bowed his head, afraid to meet her look and see the return of her antagonism. "They've gone crazy again, though. We saw many of them trying for their ship, but it looked like Xenation wouldn't let them in."

"Ah," Rafe said. He closed his eyes for a moment. "Another ancient ship coming in. I think the station doesn't want them to attack it."

"Are we safe?" she said, worried.

He shrugged and winced at the movement, wishing he had a better answer for her. "I don't know. I can't tell if Xenation knows the difference between the groups. But the Click -- the Click have a very close relationship with the station. They can open doors, Neva. They can go places. And I think they know the difference between us and the others. I think . . . I think that will help."

"Another thought -- maybe we need to stop pretending we have our own ship out there," Morgan said. "We don't want any confusion. And I think the ancient ship might be a far better deterrent than anything we can pretend to have."

"They destroyed such ships before," Neva pointed out.

"Yes, but now Xenation won't let them go. I am betting if the ships have any crews aboard, they're stuck in dock. Probably the *Shaw* as well. Let's pull back," Morgan said. "Let's let the Click take care of this."

"The Click," she said and looked in that direction. She finally shrugged as well. "Yes, maybe so. Ardi, I think it time we remove our spy, too, don't you think?"

He nodded, though he looked to Rafe and Etinon. "Is this a good idea?"

Etinon was the one who gave a bow of his head. "I think it is so, yes. This Norishi nay have created links within your systen that you do not want her to use now."

Ardi hurried through the small crowd that had gathered. Rafe watched him go and spotted Yang. It was a relief. He knew he would have peace soon, at least for a little while.

Then he heard a shout from the Norishi and knew they planned to attack. The sound made him almost ill with the memory of what had happened once they took him. He hadn't come to this station looking for a war. He hadn't come here looking for anything that had happened to him.

"You don't look well, Rafe," Yang said, a hand resting gently on his arm.

"I'm tired of this."

"I know," Yang said. He saw how Neva gave him a very odd look. Did she think he sought all this trouble? Apparently so.

"Yang?" Neva asked.

He held up a scanner that Rafe hadn't seen. "He needs rest."

"Not yet," Rafe said though he hated to say the words. Yang looked uncertain. "Not yet. They're going to attack, no matter what I do. I'd rather be here and helping."

The Norishi began to move forward. Not a straight line attack, but something that snaked and curved as they swayed back and forth. They came forward while twisting their necks and bodies, and chanting something that sounded harsh and guttural. The humans began to form up as well. A few of them had atomizers but Rafe didn't think they would be enough to do more than slow a few of the warriors.

The Click rushed past. He hadn't dared to hope they would help and he had purposely not looked back to see if they were there. The Norishi saw the Click and their movement stopped almost at once and silence descended over the bay as though everyone held their breath.

The Norishi backed up: one step, another. They plainly didn't want to retreat. The Click formed lines as well, and Rafe felt as though the humans and Ksa were all but forgotten. The others around Rafe started to back away and he went with them as far as the archway again.

Something going on. He could feel Xenation --

"Rafe --"

He held up a hand. Yang had been reaching for him and frowned. He held the scanner up. "Rafe --"

"She's trying to tell me something," he said. And then he felt himself slip into the other language this time. "What is it you want us to do? How can we stop the Click and the Norishi from doing battle?"

Something odd. Faint, a little uncertain. It didn't feel like the usual contact with Xenation. In fact --

"Damn," he whispered softly. He blinked, looking at Morgan and then turning to Etinon. "Ancients. They have contact with the station and with *me*. We . . . we have a problem. They want --" He couldn't figure out what the station wanted, let alone what brought the others here. Were they talking to each other? Were they only talking to him? Was he --?

His head ached. Everything swirled. He thought he was going to pass out and he blinked several times and finally focused on Yang, grabbing the man's arm. "Keep me conscious."

"Rafe --" He looked panicked as he glanced at the scanner. "This isn't good --"

"Nothing is going to get better if you don't have me to keep contact with the others. Keep me conscious!"

Yang shook his head but just then the Click began to make loud pounding sounds and Rafe looked up to see the Norishi forming into lines again. They were not going to be stopped this time. He had to do something because he could feel Xenation and the Ancients unsettled by the events. He had to find an answer from them.

"Yang!" he said and shook the man. The world started to go black around him. "No! Keep me here!"

Something pressed against his neck, cold seeping through his body. His breath caught and then the power of the drug rushed through his veins. He felt the muscles in his arms twitch but he could breathe again, too.

"Careful, careful," Yang said. He had something else in hand. "Just do what you need to do."

Clarity came with a new sort of pain, like something slamming away all the weaknesses, and not doing so with any kindness. He thought he was going to be ill, but he breathed slowly, blinked and blinked and saw the line of Click and Norishi had not moved much yet. They were going to engage soon, though.

He had to stop them. Why? Ah. The Ancients wanted the Click safe.

"Need to get the Click back," he said.

"How the hell do we do that?" Neva demanded. She sounded frantic. "And what happens if we do? What happens if we don't?"

"If we don't, I think the Ancients come in and take care of the trouble and I'm not entirely certain they know the difference between human, Ksa and Norishi."

"Too much alike," Morgan said. "No one can control the Click. We'll never get them --"

"I know a few commands. I think --" He stopped. Something in his head. Something, not words. He smiled and probably looked insane. "This beat. Clap it. Stamp your feet. Do something to make this sound."

Clap, clap, clap-clap-clap, clap.

It took them a few times before they got the beat and the exact timing right. The Click paid no attention at first, though. He tried to clap louder. Then Neva called for others to join them and the Ksa brought their own people at a run.

He saw, finally, that some of the Click moved slightly towards them, confused. He moved closer, even though Yang and Neva both protested before they realized he'd made some progress.

"What the hell. If we are going to fight the Norishi, we might as well do it out here," Neva finally said. Rafe feared his insanity might be spreading to the others but maybe it was needed. They had to do *something*. He could feel the give and take between Xenation and the Ancients. The Station could only provide facts and Rafe feared those might be damning, considering what Tali and her people had done to the Click. He didn't know if the Click really knew the difference between the three races, either. That pile of 'treasure' had items from all three of them, tossed together.

So he moved forward, clapping his hands. Hoping for something that would draw the attention of the Click because he feared no one would survive otherwise. He couldn't say why, and it might only have been his paranoia, but he had the feeling that Xenation, still shaken from contact with human computers, and the Ancients worried about the Click, were not going to be happy here if this battle continued.

He clapped harder. His hands hurt.

The Click began to respond in more numbers. He saw a few start to back up and he almost thought they might be confused, wondering why the humans didn't want them to fight the enemy.

While the Click might be cooperating, the Norishi were not. He heard new shouts as Click started to back away, and when the first of the women moved towards the Click with weapon raised, he shouted and charged in.

Too far away, but his shout and movement startled the woman. Morgan had come with him as well as Neva. He hadn't expected her. They spearheaded an onslaught of humans and Ksa that startled the Norishi. A few had the atomizers and sprayed the mist, unsettling some. However, the Click had stopped retreating once they'd stopped clapping.

He needed help.

"Xenation," he all but shouted. He wasn't even certain what he wanted to ask for this time. "We need this to stop!"

Not in Basic again. Neva looked at him and took a step away. Her look still drove a knife into his heart and at a time when he needed control. If he lost his hold now, they were all going to lose -- human, Ksa and Norishi. He turned away from her, tried to block the feeling out, and concentrated again on the trouble.

"I need help!" He didn't care what language he spoke, as long as he reached someone -- some*thing*. "Help --"

The Displaced arrived in a stream of white that felt icy cold as they passed close overhead. They swept down on the Norishi, who tried to hold their line for a moment and then began to break, some retreating in haste, and a few falling. He thought they might be dead and that scared him in a new way. He had always known the Displaced were dangerous --

And he feared some of the Displaced had not survived, either.

The Norishi screamed as they retreated. He thought them more wild animals than anything akin to human. Wolves in sheep's clothing. They should never have been let close to civilization. They didn't understand the rules.

They were starting to back down and go to their dark little Enclave. They were going to be a problem still in the future, but for now he wanted them away.

Neva came up beside him. Ardi came as well, their Norishi spy still in hand. He'd forgotten about her.

"Time for you to go back to your own," Neva said, looking at the woman. The Norishi's eyes went wide -- such a human reaction that it chilled him. He wanted them to be animals. He didn't want to be fooled again.

Rafe didn't think his legs would hold him much longer. He looked away from the Norishi spy and glanced around, making certain the Click had retreated and the Norishi were still moving away. They were not. They had plainly seen that their spy had been brought out, and they didn't look happy.

"Ardi just shove her off in that direction," Neva said. "If she doesn't go back to them, we'll deal with her in our own way."

"No. Hand her over to the Click," Rafe said.

His words frightened her this time. Good --

No, *bad.* Norishi, it appeared, went insane when they were scared. She screamed, yanked free of Ardi and leapt straight at Neva. Instinct to attack the dominant female? He didn't know. He just saw her pulling something from her belt. He thought it might be a blade of some sort.

Rafe moved out of instinct all his own as he shoved Neva down and blocked the swing from the woman. The little knife cut deep into his arm with a sting that spread upward and to his heart in a couple breaths. The wound wasn't bad but the world began swirling and he barely saw Ardi grab and disarm the Norishi. Yang knelt at Rafe's side. When had he gone to his knees? What the hell -- couldn't breathe. Couldn't --

Slipping away. Didn't think he would come back this time. . . .

And there, in that moment of gray when he felt the world slipping and he let go of being human, something else moved closer to him. *Reset. Await Key. Control link. Awaiting orders.*

He felt the whole of Xenation: The walls, the depth, the knowledge. He knew the Ancients outside and the aliens inside, though those aliens were them. He could see everything and he almost understood.

Too late. Damn too late --

And then he started breathing again. Yang had hold of Rafe, shaking him as though to call him back to life. Rafe focused on the man's frantic face as Yang said something, but Rafe couldn't understand the words. All he could hear was a loud ringing, and lights danced oddly before his eyes. He wasn't dead. Survived.

"Rafe!"

"Here," he said, gasping still. "What the hell --"

"Poison. Damn strong poison. I think she always meant to take out Neva but you got in the way."

He felt horribly ill and he feared that was going to stay with him for a while yet. Yang had a hand on his shoulder, holding him, and while he searched frantically through his box of medications.

"I will hold hin" Etinon said. He sounded worried, too.

"Better," Rafe said. Alive, at least. He didn't know if he could move yet and decided not to try, though he did turn his head to find the Norishi spy. Ardi had her down with his knee to her back and her arms pulled so he could tie her. She looked like an animal again, growling and withering. It helped, really, making her what he wanted her to be. Not human.

Yang shoved something against his chest, right over his heart. He still looked frantic.

"We have a problem," Ardi warned.

"More trouble?" Neva said. She sounded shaken. Rafe couldn't see where she stood behind him.

"More trouble. The damned Norishi are forming up again. We need to retreat. I think they saw what happened to Rafe. They know what the poison will do."

"Hell!" Yang said and looked frantic again. "I don't have the medicines I need if I have to care for more people --"

"Let's get back," Ardi said. He grabbed the Norishi woman up by the shoulder and then looked at Rafe. "What do we do with her?"

"Send her back to her own," he said. He didn't want to think of anything else, and he didn't know why it should be his problem anyway. "The rest of you get back. I need -- Ardi, I need something from my room. In the drawer at the desk. An alien device -- long, cylinder --"

"I know this," Saris said. "Soneone show me his roon."

Saris and Ritter left. He trusted they would both be quick. Good.

"You can't think we'll leave you here to face this," Ardi said. Others nodded. "You can't even stand."

"I can. I will. The rest of you should get back. I'm not sure what will happen." He started to get to his feet and failed. Yang shook his head and tried to hold him down. "No. Look -- I have, at the moment at least, a better link with Xenation. I think -- I think I can get her to help."

"You need to let go of the link," Yang said. He held up a scanner. The readers were fluctuating in a way that Rafe found fascinating, because he could see a pattern there in the way his thoughts scattered; how it was human now and then Xenation, and maybe Ancients. He watched for a moment and then blinked. Had Yang been talking? He needed to pay better attention.

"Come on, Rafe," Ardi said. He had shoved the Norishi off towards her people. Rafe hadn't noticed. "We need to get you --"

"No," he said. And he did stand this time. Steady. Yang looked surprised. "No, we need -- we can't work with the Norishi. We can't live here with them on the docks and always a danger. If we don't do something, the Ancients are going to come in and clear the station of everyone but the

Click. And they won't do it by letting us go to our ships and leave."

"Rafe?" Neva whispered, sounding frightened.

He glanced her way, but she made him feel uncertain and he didn't need more emotions. He looked to Morgan instead. "Experiments. And when an experiment goes bad --"

"You make notes and discard it. Oh shit," Morgan said. He looked worried. "What do we do?"

"I need the key."

"It is on the way," Etinon said. "What do we do?"

The Norishi began to move and the Click lined up yet again to stop them. Rafe moved over to the wall and he hit it.

The sound reverberated through the station. He had known it would. Ardi, moving up beside him, hit the wall as well and it did nothing.

"I am in touch with Xenation," Rafe said. The pounding made his head hurt, but he did it again, and this time with the pattern that worked to call the Click back. And yes, they did listen this time, moving back with such haste that they startled everyone, including the Norishi. The spy had almost reached her people. She looked back at Rafe and screamed -- rage, anger, fear -- but no words.

The others took it up.

"Oh hell," Neva sad. "Rafe, this isn't helping."

"I need the key." He leaned against the wall, lost for a moment, trying to parse human, Ancient and Xenation thoughts in his head.

"He's far too close to having a stroke. I'm going to put him under --" Yang said.

"No. Etinon, stop him."

He heard Etinon whisper something beneath his breath -- a curse or a prayer -- but he moved between Yang and Rafe. Everyone looked shocked.

"We nust do sonething," Etinon said. "We will not survive, otherwise, none of us. I trust Rafe."

The Norishi grew louder and started to move forward.

"Rafe --"

"The rest of you get back," he said. "I just need the key -

-"

"Here," Ritter said and shoved the device into his hands.

The tube began to glow bright blue the moment he touched the smooth surface, which hadn't happened before. He took the change as a good sign because God knew they needed one. With one hand to the wall -- because he would have fallen otherwise -- he moved forward to the glowing, colorful section only a few feet away. The Norishi were moving towards him, their voices loud, screaming --

No time. He saw the pattern in the wall -- the ones that humans could not see -- in the middle of the moving colors. Without so much as a prayer for help, he shoved the key up against the pattern.

The device sunk several inches into the wall.

And he had access to *everything*.

He grabbed at the key with both hands. If he let go, he would lose his connection. Pain like fire burnt through him and Rafe couldn't breathe again, but he could see . . . see it all. The station, huge, ready to move at his orders. Knew the Click had some control. Saw the Displaced, and almost understood --

But the human part of the brain realized the Norishi were within yards of reaching him. He had to do something.

"Back!" A wave of one hand brought a wind that nearly dragged his friends off along with the Norishi.

He brought the wind to an end as quickly as it had started. The humans and Ksa scrambled back to the Human Enclave, but he had only enraged the Norishi who were preparing to move on him again.

"Rafael, this isn't helping," Neva said. "You need to get back so we can retreat --"

"No. Stay back."

"Rafe!" she sounded frantic.

He looked at her and smiled. "One more trick."

The Norishi were closer to their Enclave and preparing for another attack. All the others were nearly to the Human Enclave, including the Click. Now was the time to do something drastic.

With a wave of his hand, he brought a wall straight down from the ceiling, sealing off the entire Norishi part of the bay. Locked out. They had no access to the other areas at all.

He felt as though the power to move the wall had come from him, instead of the station. He wanted to rest. But he still had to hold on. Just a moment longer. Were the humans talking to him? He couldn't tell while he listened to Xenation and the Ancients.

Waiting for a verdict.

"Rafe, let go," Yang ordered. Etinon still wouldn't let the medtech near, though.

"The Ancients," he said with a shake of his head. He really couldn't see what was going on. His sight blurred, and his thoughts bounced but grew calmer. Quieter. Retreating again.

"Whatever is out there, it seems to be pulling away," Morgan said, looking at his pocketcomp. "He did it. I think he really did it."

"Rafe, tell Etinon to stand down," Yang said. "Or else we're going to have to take him down to save you."

Rafe blinked, trying to pull his attention back to here again. The Ancients were going but he felt discord, distrust -- something like that from them still. Xenation was still alive in his hand. He looked down at the key --

"Rafe, for God's sake let go!" Neva said and sounded both worried and annoyed.

If he held on to the key, he could let go of everything else. He might become part of the system. He might become a Displaced. Or he might just die.

None of those possibilities frightened him.

"Etinon, unless you want to see him dead --" Yang said waving the scanner frantically in front of the Ksa.

Etinon turned, grabbed him by the arm and jerked him away from the key. He shouted something in that moment of agony when he lost his hold on the station. He saw the key disappear, sucked into the wall and gone. He wanted it back. He wanted to go with it.

Yang pressed something against the back of his neck.

"Son of a bitch," he mumbled. "I was -- I was --"

"You were dying."

"Yes."

"We're not going to let you go," Yang said. Rafe realized his legs had given way. Etinon held him up. "We aren't letting you go."

And which was worse? That the humans wouldn't let him go or that Xenation wouldn't?

The world slipped away. . . .

CHAPTER FIFTY-SIX

New sequence initiated.
Key activated.
Language protocol installed, translation updated.

Prepare for phase two.

Begin interface recalibration.

Start run.

Await orders.

CHAPTER FIFTY-SEVEN

Morgan had gone with Neva to the newly docked
IWC cruiser as they escorted Tali off of Xenation.
She had a military guard and the chief medtech on
the *Firestar* had spent a lot of time with Yang, checking all the
files and learning what he needed to do to keep her passive
and safe.

"Take care of her," Neva had said at the last moment.
She'd looked at Tali. "I'm sorry for what you are, Tali. I'm
sorry your life is this way. But this isn't my fault. It's not even
your fault. It's just who you are. I hope the doctors can keep
you happy."

Tali had looked up and nodded and for a moment
Morgan thought she might even understand. The guards
took her into the ship. Neva did not follow, though she
might have. This was a door through which she did not want
to pass.

"Thank you for coming here with me," Neva said as she
turned away. "Damn, that's hard, but it's harder still to think
of her loose and hurting others."

"I know. You've done the best for her and for those
others. Come on. Xenobia is open. We can sit down and
have dinner and not have to worry about anything else for a
while."

"What are the Norishi doing?" she said with a glance
towards Rafe's wall, as though she didn't trust the calm.

They weren't coming through again, but he knew that
wasn't what she meant. The Norishi ships still patrolled
outside the bay area, swinging back and forth until the Click

chased them off again.

"I don't think they're going to show themselves with both human fighters and Click ships out there," he said. "Ah, and there's Ardi with the rest of the prisoners. Let's celebrate. We have every reason to, Neva."

She finally gave a tentative nod and waited while Ardi handed off Norden and Ekhardt to the guards. Both men looked worried. They were facing some serious charges.

He finally got her into Xenobia. Ardi and even Ritter came along. A few others joined the table and Buris brought them a huge meal of food he'd actually begged off the cruiser. They had a feast, and they were all in a better mood for it.

He hadn't noticed Rafe sitting back in the corner at first. He hadn't realized Yang had let him out again, but he sat there with Etinon at his side. He looked better. Morgan almost waved them over but then he glanced at Neva and thought it might not be wise. She still had the open wound of letting her daughter go. Dragging Rafe over would not help Neva and wouldn't help him, either.

They talked and laughed but Neva finally said she had to go back to Control and finish reports before the cruiser left. As soon as she stood, Morgan did as well and crossed over to Rafe.

"You look like hell still," he said, finally close enough to see the bruises and cuts.

"I have looked like hell from the day you arrived. How could you tell the difference?" He nodded to the chair and as Morgan sat, Rafe picked up a glass of beer and sipped, his eyes closing for a moment. Etinon nodded to Morgan. There had been fewer Ksa and Click out since the incident, but at least both had stayed calm. They all needed calm.

Rafe sipped again.

"So, do you drink to ease the pain?" Morgan asked.

Rafe's eyes narrowed and he blinked. "Of course."

Morgan nodded.

But Rafe looked past him, and his face unexpectedly turned bleak again. "No one ever asks what pain."

Morgan turned to where Rafe looked and watched as Neva left.

THE END

About the Author:

Hello!

I am an eclectic and prolific author whose has published in a number of genres, including Young Adult Mystery, Urban Fantasy, Epic Fantasy, Science Fiction and numerous works on writing. While I started on the outer edges of traditional publication with sales to small press and magazines publishers, I have since moved most of my work to the Indie world and I am madly in love with the new world of publishing and the direct contact with readers.

I live in Nebraska with my husband, my cats and a small but entirely useless dog.

I also own Forward Motion for Writers and the ezine, Vision: A Resource for Writers.

Connect with Zette:

Web Site: http://lazette.net
Twitter: http://twitter.com/lazetteg
Facebook: http://www.facebook.com/lazette.gifford
Joyously Prolific Blog: http://zette.blogspot.com/

Preview: Ada Nish Pura
Part 1 -- Betrayal

Chapter 1

Marcus tapped his fingers across the touch screen controls, righting the pole-ward drift of his fighter as he headed for the curve of the horizon. He glanced at the two massive starships orbiting almost side-by-side above the world. The smaller *Moonwind* had unexpectedly dropped in system within hours of the larger *Augusta's* arrival -- a rare occasion to have two such well-known craft in the same system. The *Moonwind* had deployed a long, tubular shuttle full of partygoers and ranking crew who were already heading for the *Augusta*. A dozen single-man fighters danced around the two ships' perimeters, sunlight illuminating one after another in bursts of silver light. He could trace their movement, having flown those patterns dozens of times. All routine.

His own fighter followed a different path towards the planet's equator and heading for the dark side of Kailani. Pretty name; he had learned the word meant "the sea and the sky" in an old Earth language. When the *Augusta* came within visual range of the planet he understood the aptness of the name. The colony gave the term *backwater* a whole new meaning. It didn't just refer to the world's lack of technology, though with a few commsats in orbit Marcus wouldn't have needed to take this recon swing. The name came for another reason: he had never seen so much water in one place, the blue broken by occasional white clouds and distant specks of small islands.

Two inconspicuous moons hung above the horizon, gravity linking them in a stable orbit. They cast an odd, grayish-green light back from the sun.

The recon work was a waste of time. The Inner Worlds Council fleet had fought the enemy off two systems away, and the *Augusta* headed here as a protective measure to keep this mineral-rich colony safe while others did the mop-up work elsewhere. The war seemed to be coming to a slow and laborious end and the fighting had become sporadic. Recon flights, and not dogfights, would become more common. Marcus wasn't certain if that was good or not.

As he crossed the twilight line into night, Marcus couldn't even see the distant glow of planet-bound cities since there was nothing larger than villages on the islands. Contact with the *Augusta* disappeared over the horizon, leaving Marcus with a long silent orbit and nothing to watch except the red and green indicators on the boards. They were only little distraction while he battled boredom and fatigue. The infrared scanner finally found a sizable warm spot, but computer analysis read the area as a huge algae patch in the sea, the natural oxygen builders for this water world.

By the time he completed the slow, five orbit sweep of this world the crews of both ships would have had their party and he'd be lucky to get the mess crew to warm some coffee for him.

And it was his own fault. He knew Captain Harris hated him. He shouldn't have been so cocky in their last meeting. He feared a long time would pass before Harris let him fly patterns with the others. He foresaw his future as a series of increasingly boring recon flights unless he somehow won a transfer to another ship. Or he might leave the service entirely, since his option would come up soon.

Could he tie himself forever to some world and never travel the stars again?

Marcus shivered at the thought and fixated on the work at hand. One bit of land poked out from the southern pole into the wide ocean. Somewhere on the peninsula, the IWC center had a small landing port and an observation station. It sent a monotonous automated beep as he passed overhead. The locals mistrusted the IWC, which made officials nervous with the rebels so close.

Not his problem. He needed to scan and report back to

the ship. With one orbit almost completed, he swept the fighter toward the slate-blue horizon while watching the edge of a gigantic storm swirling in a chaotic mass near the dawn's edge. The sheer magnitude of the weather system, and the readings his scanners gave on the winds, almost pulled him out of his bad mood. At a better time, he would have been tempted to slip down to the edge of the storm and ride out some of the bands. Few of his fellow pilots enjoyed atmosphere flying but to Marcus the storm presented a real challenge.

Unfortunately, he dared not do anything except what was by-the-book or else he would chance making things worse between him and the Captain. He took the expected readings from the storm and let his imagination play with the idea of flying into the heart of the weather system.

He rounded the curve of the planet, his vidcam catching the first rays of sunlight as the window polarized. Islands dotted the world below like pebbles thrown into a pond. The ships --

Something wrong.

Something *very* wrong: Fighters out of position, debris, hot spots -- *the signs of battle.* His hands automatically keyed on his weapons, a series of familiar movements and beeps accompanied by the flash of amber lights on the right side of his board. He twisted in his seat, frantic as he searched for the rebel ship which must be somewhere nearby. Tracking went live and overlaid the bubble dome above him with a glowing green grid of lines.

He still couldn't find the enemy.

His equipment picked up signs of massive damage to the *Augusta's* starboard bay. He couldn't get a naked-eye visual from here but with a touch of the controls the vidcam zoomed in on twisted and melted metal -- already cooled -- and debris hugging close to the larger ship. His computer located a few pieces of the *Moonwind's* shuttle, flung far outward from the ship . . . and the computer gave a ninety-five percent possibility of more pieces imbedded in the damaged bay.

The shuttle had exploded *inside* the *Augusta.*

He could find no rebel craft.

His fingers moved by rote, keying the vidcam's range back just as the *Moonwind* fired weapons straight into the *Augusta.*

"No, no, no!" Was that his voice?

The stream of luminous neutrons punched straight through the unprotected shell of the larger ship. In a timeless moment of mind-numbing fear and loss, Marcus watched as brutal explosions ripped through the interior, throwing off pieces of the hull plating and scattering debris out the far side. No one would survive!

"Marcus! Get your ass out of --"

O'Dell's voice, there and as quickly cut off. His comp tracked her fighter as two *Moonwind* craft drew down on her, weapons firing. O'Dell's fighter exploded under their combined attack, a smaller loss almost lost in the glow of the larger one.

His body obeyed her orders. Hands trembling, he reached for the controls and tried to dive out of the path of the *Moonwind* fighters.

They followed, but he maneuvered into a tight swing against gravity, proving himself a better pilot. Marcus flew under the belly of the first fighter before the enemy weapons could track. He fired so close he could see the metal burn before the fighter exploded.

One for O'Dell. It didn't ease the cold, icy feeling of shock taking hold of him. His hands kept moving. Well-trained. How many could he take? Not enough -- not enough revenge for everyone gone --

Hands moved, eyes focused . . . but his mind skittered between rage and emptiness at the loss he couldn't accept or comprehend. Movement honed by years of training and battles became instinctive. He caught the second fighter by surprise, sweeping past and firing, the bubble top bursting and the pilot dead before the rest exploded. He moved on to another craft, fighting his way towards his ship to . . . to do *something.*

Someone shouted his name, dragging him back to the reality of his impossible situation. Whoever had called hadn't survived for long: the comp no longer tracked any undamaged *Augusta* craft in his range. He fired and destroyed another enemy fighter but the rest of *Moonwind's* crew didn't have anyone left to target but him. Two came at Marcus from the side, the first clipping his engine and the second damaging the booster. The combined assault sent his craft tumbling and he banged his arm against the side of the cockpit with enough force that he heard the bone snap before he felt the pain. A moment later, his suit registered the break and shot a painkiller into the arm, and dimmed the pain to an ache. The blocker would only hold for a few hours.

Lights flashed red with warnings of system failure across the board. Power surged as the computer failed to shunt the overload away from the dead boards. He could taste the bitter hint of burnt electronics. Marcus tried to jab at the weapon controls, but pain shot from his right wrist to the shoulder, leaving him too breathless to even curse. He worked the board with his left hand, gliding fingers over the buttons and indentations, powering down what he could of the fighter's controls. His weakened communications system caught part of the broadcast the *Moonwind* put out, warning of rebels nearby, as though they hadn't been the ones to destroy the *Augusta*.

Damn. Marcus focused on the board and the flashing a warning of low power, the charge seeping away with each blink of the light. He couldn't tell if the power pack had a full link to his engines, and he couldn't run a diagnostic. Didn't have time; The *Moonwind's* fighters came for him.

If -- *if he still had power* -- he could make a quick dive into the gravity well, skim along the top of the clouds, and then head into the night side beyond the storm. There he could try to reach some settlement and --

Hell. It wouldn't work. *Backwater world.* They didn't have commsats for a reason, which included a long, bad history with the Inner Worlds Council and a dislike of technology.

He had read the story with passing interest; old history, nothing he thought he would have to worry about. Now he recalled how the majority of the original population had been lab-adapted to live and work in the mineral-rich expanse of blue oceans. A few generations later, the natives had thrown out the company which still controlled them and turned their backs on the technology used to create them. They didn't have much in technology at all. Going to the natives would not help.

He had to reach the Inner Worlds Council's single Kailani outpost on the little strip of land near the southern pole. They had equipment to punch a message out beyond the system. His vidcam held proof of treachery which would get the *Moonwind* hunted through every quarter of the Inner Worlds and the Fringe, if need be.

Survival required him to take action. Reaching the outpost wouldn't provide long-term safety but it was a goal. The outpost, on the far side of a world without commsats, would have no idea what had really happened. They'd know what the *Moonwind* told them -- what the ship already broadcasted and what its tech crew created for vids.

Damn them.

He marked trajectory by dead reckoning and fired the engines, moving when the other craft least expected as they closed in. Marcus felt his breath catch at the sight of stark white pinpricks of stars scattered across the dark sky. He knew reaching the IWC outpost was no real safety and he would probably never fly the stars again.

His sight blurred in mourning at the thought. How strange to be sad for this when he had lost everything else.

The *Augusta* came into view as the fighter made the turn. He half lifted his left hand in a final salute, even to that bastard Captain Harris who had unwittingly saved his life by being so damned prissy and sending Marcus on the recon mission out of spite.

The planet -- *Kailani* -- came into view. He put his left hand on the board and tried to lift the right to the other controls, but changed his mind as pain lanced through his arm and shoulder. He could see the slight glow of friction as his fighter traced a path along the upper edge of the thermosphere. No time left. Marcus fired the right thruster and aimed pole-ward. The damaged fighter bucked and tried to roll out of his control, but he judged the effect and fired the booster to compensate. The *Moonwind* fighters came swarming in as soon as they saw him lunge downward towards the world. He hoped he had no trouble finding the peninsula of land sitting uncomfortably near the southern ice cap. He didn't want to crash into the uninviting wilderness of white. Would going there prove better than crashing into the endless expanse of ocean covering the rest of the world?

A circumpolar route was the shorter route to the IWC outpost, nearly half a world away. As his good hand began to manipulate the sluggish controls, three *Moonwind* fighters swept around to cut him off. He cursed and curved toward the longer route, cutting across the equator and sweeping over the top of massive outriders from the storm. The huge clouds with bubbling cotton-tops spread out on his starboard side, obscuring his view.

The craft jumped and squealed with a sudden hit from the enemy craft. He could hear a hiss of air escaping behind his seat. Marcus tried to head towards the south, but the *Moonwind's* fighters cut him off, herding him north into the wide expanse of ocean.

Damned Kailani technophobes with no communication's system! He needed to get over the horizon and close enough to send a message, even if he didn't have power to send vid as well. He needed to warn them.

A fighter swept towards him, a sudden dark spot coming out of the sun. Marcus skipped out of range with a thruster burst and the mostly-dead craft obeyed his swiftly-keyed commands. If this had been a one-on-one battle he would have had a chance, even now.

He didn't try to count the number of enemy fighters pursuing him. Two more sweeps by the group won a hit to the port thruster. The fighter spun, his injured arm sending needles of pain through his body. He could hear metal tear --

And his fighter slipped into the thick bank of clouds.

Hope.

Marcus held his breath, fighting the sluggish ship controls and firing his remaining thruster. The booster was gone as well. He held his breath and spun into the very heart of the storm, seeking a place to hide. The winds, chaotic and powerful, drew him northward into a maelstrom of hail and sleet. Lightning flashed so near he could feel the tingle as more of the board went dead. He couldn't see through the dark clouds, and thunder shook the ship, deafening him. *Hope, hopelessness*: the two emotions balanced on a single sputtering thruster engine keeping him in the air.

One of the fighters tore through the clouds above, firing at random. They must have lost him in the flash of lightning which had created natural electronic chaff to upset sensors. The shots missed. Marcus breathed again.

He thought more lightning filled the air until the light slipped along the right side of his craft and he saw the outline of another fighter coming at him, weapons blazing. The permaglass bubble cracked, but held. He heard the engine explode and the board went irrevocably dead and all the lights gone. Marcus leaned back, drawing his hand away from the controls. The wind bounced the fighter, tilting the craft at an uncomfortable angle and sending a shock of pain through his broken arm. He watched as the right foil tore off and fell.

That couldn't be right. He should have felt the pressure of the forward thrust die and the craft should have gone straight down with the foil. Instead, he continued to move forward.

Marcus stripped off the harness so he could see behind the cockpit. No power for alarms to ring or safety hooks to stop him. He fought away the sharp pain through his arm.

Worth it. The single starboard thruster still fired. The other, the already dead one, had taken the hit, exploded and fell.

Hope again? Dare he?

Lightning flashed and he felt the prickling once more, like a touch of life returned. He focused his attention back to the controls, his left hand moving over the keys. The board didn't light, but the craft slowly responded when he keyed in a turn. He grinned and unexpectedly remembered Lt. Lisle's last words to him as he climbed into the craft, heading off for a useless recon flight.

"The Captain's a fool to take you out of the fighter wing. You could fly a dead ship through a black hole, Marcus."

This was as close as he would ever get to finding out if Lisle had been right. The controls took finesse. He wanted to head south, but he'd lost all sense of direction and he wasn't certain he could get the fighter to respond anyway. Marcus closed his eyes and tried to envision the clouds from above. The system had been moving south to north, spreading over the equator and across open ocean. But then ninety-six percent of the world consisted of ocean, though some a shallow covering over submerged landmasses. *Shallow* might be a relative term, he supposed. Marcus had no doubt he could drown in any part of the watery expanse.

The fighter squealed and shuddered at every attempt to turn. Something else tore free, and the craft lost more stability. The fighter would not survive much longer. He wouldn't reach the IWC post in this craft, but if he survived at least he might find other transport.

Marcus pointed the nose downward and hoped to find land.

The closer he came to the planet's surface, the harder the winds buffeted him. He kept the craft moving at a right angle to the winds, trying to reach the edge of the storm. Getting out of the weather system seemed the best way to survive, though he wondered where the *Moonwind* fighters had gone and how long they would take to track him.

The nose dipped downward and he had a hell of a time leveling off before he went straight into the ocean. He hoped to see land, but instead he saw only the rush of water around him, confounding sea and storm. He thought he saw occasional spikes of rock and feared he might plow right into one, but he had very little control now.

The damaged permaglass bubble began to crack in a

spider web design, obscuring more of the view. Marcus reached out and pushed his hand over the board's controls and fired the thruster -- fired hard and long as he prayed to reach the storm's edge.

The engine shrieked in protest a moment before it exploded. Even the explosion propelled him forward a few heartbeats longer. For a moment he saw the edge of the storm through the fractured bubble; a low dark line of clouds with the brighter sky beyond and a rolling expanse of turbulent ocean . . . without a single island in sight.

The fighter plunged into the sea.

Oh hell!

His neck snapped backward, leaving his sight blurred and his head pounding. The permaglass bubble shattered, sending shards everywhere. He felt a sting against his face.

Then he felt the slap of cold wind and icy water.

The storm raged overhead as waves rushed over the broken permaglass and into the interior. The water level reached above his knees and then to his waist. He grabbed the harness, knowing the little craft wouldn't stay afloat long, but unwilling to let go.

Cold. Even with his flight suit kicking up the temp to compensate, he still felt the frigid water rushing around him while thunder roared and the wind shrieked as though it became something alive.

Marcus knew he wouldn't survive. He should have thrown himself at the *Augusta* and gone out like a little star impacting against the dead ship rather than die alone in some alien sea. He should have died with the rest of his people.

Remember, your flight suit will float if you go down on this damned wet world. As soon as the suit senses the water pressure around you, it will inflate. The suit will seal off damaged areas. Unless it's totally in shreds, the suit will keep you buoyant until help arrives. Your beacon will come on automatically in one half hour unless you turn it off to avoid detection by the enemy.

Had Spraug or Lisle given the lecture as they came in system? He wanted to remember. Why hadn't he been paying better attention? Why couldn't he remember how they looked, standing there in the crew's lounge, preparing the pilots, all of them there conspicuous in the silver and red jackets and black suits rather than the white uniforms of the IWC soldiers. Oh yes, they'd always made a show of being different --

All dead.

The next wave filled the interior with water up to the boards. He started to release the harness but at the last moment remembered to grab the vidchit from the box on the control board. He shoved the chit into his jacket pocket and sealed it closed, giving himself a reason to survive as he threw himself out into the sea.

Water everywhere as the storm and waves crashed over him, and he could no longer tell where storm ended and ocean began. However, the suit ballooned and he bounced along in this hellish maelstrom. He found a rock spire and grabbed hold with his good arm. The surface felt slick, but solid. He jabbed the beacon off. No one to come for him, anyway.

He stared up into the gray-on-gray sky while the rain and waves washed over him. He would likely drown anyway.

He hadn't gone far, but when he looked back he saw the fighter's wing rise, dip, and disappear.

Alone.

Thank you for reading Xenation: Draw the Line. I hope you enjoyed the book!

You can contact me at zette@lazette.net

www.aconspiracyofauthors.com

www.ingramcontent.com/pod-product-compliance
Lightning Source LLC
Chambersburg PA
CBHW051436260626
47162CB00001B/115